HE REACHED UP AND CAPTURED A STRAND OF HER HAIR.

"You smell so good," Augustus said. Out of nowhere, previous words dripped like poison into Charity's mind: *Augustus's primary duty to his country is to produce an heir.*

One had to admit that he was certainly trying his best, Charity thought resentfully, and for the first time ever, she felt resistance to him stiffen her body. She wanted him to say that he loved her, that he would have run away with her as Franz had run away with Lydia.

I would run away with you, Augustus, she thought. *I would do anything for you.*

"Kiss me," he commanded.

After a brief hesitation, she rested her lips lightly on top of his. He let go his hold on her hair and pulled her down so that she was lying on top of him. The familiar sweet dizziness of desire began to seep into Charity's blood. Their kiss deepened.

She lifted her head and whispered, "Would you kiss Lydia like this?"

"Never," he replied, rolling her over so that he was on top, and began to kiss her again . . .

♫

RAVES FOR JOAN WOLF'S *SOMEDAY SOON*

"Four stars! . . . A subtle sense of humor and a bit of suspenseful 'whodunit' blend for an enjoyable read."
—*Romantic Times*

"Wolf always gives you an exciting story to sink your teeth into and SOMEDAY SOON is another winner. . . . A real honey complete with jealousies abounding all over the place, someone trying to kill the new Earl, and a breathtaking romance all rolled into one thing after another for an adventure to keep you glued to the pages. How it all turns out is a feast you won't forget!"
—*Belles and Beaux of Romance*

"An engaging Regency romance starring two exhilarating lead characters . . . a captivating pair . . . a pleasant historical romance that will satisfy Wolf's fans."
—BookBrowser.com

"An engrossing, poignant novel that combines vivid characters, clever plot twists, and strong emotions. Wolf has a unique style that appeals to her audience on many levels."
—*Rendezvous*

Royal Bride

By Joan Wolf

The Deception
The Guardian
The Arrangement
The Gamble
The Pretenders
Golden Girl
Someday Soon

JOAN WOLF

Royal Bride

WARNER BOOKS

A Time Warner Company

WARNER BOOKS EDITION

Copyright © 2001 by Joan Wolf
All rights reserved. No part of this book may be reproduced in any form or
by any electronic or mechanical means, including information storage and
retrieval systems, without permission in writing from the publisher, except
by a reviewer who may quote brief passages in a review.

Cover design by Rachel McClain
Cover illustration by Franco Accornero
Hand lettering by David Gatti

Warner Books, Inc.
1271 Avenue of the Americas
New York, NY 10020

ISBN: 0-7394-1646-6

 A Time Warner Company

Printed in the United States of America

Another book for Joe

Part One

LONDON
1815

1

The direction on the letter read: Her Highness, the Princess Mariana, Dowager Countess of Beaufort. The elderly princess accepted the missive from a deferential footman, moved toward the daylight of an open window, and unfolded it carefully. A familiar strong, upright script, written in German, leaped out to greet her.

Hotel d'Aramis
Brussels
25 June 1815

My Dear Aunt,

By now, of course, you in England have learned of the Allies' great victory at Waterloo. It was a horrendous battle, and far too many men died, but I believe we have finally seen the last of the Ogre whose greed nearly gobbled up the entire of Europe.

As you know, before Napoleon's escape I was at the

Congress of Vienna where Britain, Austria, Russia, Prussia, and France were meeting to divide up among them the countries that had been conquered by Napoleon. My concern at the Congress was to get the Great Powers to recognize the continued independence of our beloved Jura. In this we were successful. The Final Act of the Congress of Vienna does declare Jura to be a free and independent state.

Austria signed the Final Act, but only after the Austrian minister, Prince Metternich, had worked strenuously to get the other nations to declare that Jura would now be part of the Austrian Empire.

Austria concerns me. If you look at a map, you will see that Jura is now totally surrounded by the empire. I have no doubt that both Emperor Francis I and Prince Metternich will do everything in their power to bring Jura under the sway of the Habsburg empire. In order to strengthen our own position I feel that it is imperative for us to have the protection of one of the other Great Powers.

I discussed our situation with the British foreign secretary, Lord Castlereagh, while we were both in Vienna for the Congress, and he expressed an interest in making a treaty with Jura in which Britain will support Jura in return for the right of the British navy to use our port of Seista.

The reason I am writing to you is that I wish to make a British marriage in order to bolster this treaty. Unfortunately, I understand that Princess Charlotte is to marry the Prince of Coburg, and as there are no other British royal princesses available at the moment, the girl will have to come from a noble family that has strong ties to the government.

I write to you as the person most likely to help me in

this matter. For the next few weeks you may reach me at the above address. I know, Dear Aunt, that you will fail neither me nor your country.

Your Nephew,
Augustus Josef Charles

P.S.—Do not say anything about this to my mother!

The Princess Mariana read the letter through again, more slowly this time, her brow furrowed in thought. She was seventy-two years of age and had lived in England since she was nineteen, but she never forgot that she had been born a princess of Jura, and her first allegiance was to the country of her birth.

What Augustus had proposed made excellent sense, she thought approvingly. She had always known that the boy was physically brave; it was a great relief to discover that he could also think like a statesman.

She took the letter and, using her cane, walked slowly to one of the red silk-covered sofas that furnished the Chinese Drawing Room of the Beauforts' London town house. Carefully she lowered herself onto a silk cushion and smoothed the letter in her lap. She was deep in thought when a familiar voice said commandingly, "Grandmama! Have you fallen into a trance?"

The princess looked toward the small figure approaching her across the red-and-blue Persian carpet. Her younger granddaughter was attired in a simple white muslin dress with one blue ribbon around her waist and another tying back her long brown hair. Her cheeks were flushed with healthy color and her large golden-brown eyes sparkled with curiosity.

"I am perfectly fine, Charity," the princess replied in German to the only member of her English-born family who had bothered to learn the language of her birth. Then she frowned. "What is that you have got on your dress?"

Charity looked at the yellowish smudge on her skirt and said unconcernedly, "I took Hero for a walk and he must have slobbered on me."

The princess sighed. "You had better change before your mother sees you. You know how she feels about that dog of yours."

Charity made a face. Then she noticed the pages resting on her grandmother's lap and she gave a little skip. "Is that a letter? Who is it from? Is it from Augustus, perhaps?"

"It is indeed from Augustus," the princess returned, her fingers caressing the paper she had just been reading.

"Oh, good." Unbidden, Charity came to seat herself next to her grandmother. "What did he say? Did he tell you about the battle? I read in the Dispatches that he and the men from Jura were especially commended by Wellington for bravery. Did he tell you what he did?"

The princess looked into her granddaughter's eager face and said repressively, "He did no such thing. Augustus is far too modest to boast of his own exploits, Charity."

Charity looked disappointed. "What *did* he say then?"

The princess looked once more at the pages in her lap. "He is worried that Austria will try to pressure Jura into joining the empire."

"They can't do that!" Charity cried. "Even though Napoleon occupied Jura, Augustus never gave up! His father may have spent the war years here in England, but Augustus stayed in Jura to fight the French from the mountains. And he fought at Waterloo! Austria has no grounds for annexing Jura. Even the Congress of Vienna saw that!"

"Let us hope that you are right, my dear," the princess replied. She began to fold up the letter.

"Aren't you going to read it to me?" Charity asked in surprise.

"It is very short and you have already heard the gist of it," the princess replied.

"Grandmama!"

"Never mind, Charity. Tell me, is your mother in the house?"

Charity shook her head. "She and Lydia went to pay a call upon the Marchioness of Langton in Grosvenor Square. They have not yet returned."

The princess stiffened. "Good heavens. Does this mean that Lydia is going to accept Langton?"

Charity sighed and slid down on her back. "It looks that way. Mama says that since there aren't any dukes available on the marriage mart this season, Langton is the best catch, even if he is only a marquis."

"Sit up, Charity," the princess ordered. Then, when her granddaughter had obeyed, she said, "Why

Joan Wolf

are you looking so glum? I should think that you would be delighted to see your sister marry and move away. You and she rub against each other all the time."

Charity made a face. "I know, but once Lydia marries, Mama will turn her attention to me. I will have to make my come out and go to boring parties and boring dances and boring old Almacks and Mama will want to find me a husband."

"You are seventeen years old, my dear," the princess said. "It is time you were thinking of a husband."

Charity scowled. "I don't want a husband. A husband would only be a nuisance. I wish Mama would just leave me alone. I don't know why she insisted on dragging me to London. It is summer. I want to be at home in the country."

"You can't remain a child forever, my dear," the princess replied absently, still staring at the letter in her lap.

"What are you thinking, Grandmama?" Charity asked curiously.

The princess's lips tightened, deepening the lines in the fine skin around the sides of her mouth. "I am thinking, my dear, that there may indeed be someone on the marriage mart of a higher degree than either a marquis or a duke. When they return from their call, I must have a little chat with your mother and Lydia."

Three women, representing three generations of the Debritt family, sat in the Countess of Beaufort's newly decorated Chinese Drawing Room and discussed the Prince of Jura's marriage proposition.

Speaking in faintly accented English, Princess Mariana said, "I think Augustus has made a very clever and statesmanlike proposal. He has been the prince since the death of his father two years ago, and clearly it is his duty to marry. His wife will be a Crowned Princess." Here she looked directly at her elder granddaughter. "There are few positions in all of Europe that are higher."

Lydia was seated across the table from her grandmother in a Chinese-style Chippendale chair. "Read me the letter again," she said.

The princess complied, translating her great-nephew's letter into English as she read. When she had concluded, Lydia and her mother looked at each other across the black lacquered Chinese table that divided them. "Your grandmother is right," the countess murmured. "Jura may not be a very large or very important country, but it is always something to be a Crowned Princess."

"Jura is not small," the princess snapped in annoyance. "And Austria certainly thinks we are important."

The countess ignored her mother-in-law and continued to address her daughter. "Italy is just across the Adriatic from Jura, Lydia. You could visit Rome and Venice easily. And now that the Bourbons have been restored, Paris will once more be a great cultural and fashion center. As a visiting Royal Princess, you could virtually rule the salons there. There would be no need for you to spend all your time in Jura." Her lips tightened in disapproval. "Caterina certainly didn't."

The princess said, "I do not think that Augustus is looking for a wife to follow his mother's example, Sophia. He will want a wife who cares more for Jura than Caterina ever did."

Lydia looked thoughtful as she gazed at the slender, elegant hands that lay loosely clasped in her figured French muslin lap. Slowly she raised her beautiful long-lashed green eyes and fixed them on her grandmother. "What does Augustus look like, Grandmama? Have you ever met him?"

"I met him only once, when he was ten years of age and he visited here with his father. He was a nice-looking boy and I am certain he has grown into a nice-looking man." The princess looked down her still-impressive nose. "The Adamovs have always been a good-looking family. My nephew, the late prince, was a handsome man, and Augustus's mother certainly qualifies as a beauty."

At this last accolade, the countess stiffened. Princess Caterina was probably the only woman in London who was even prouder and vainer than Lady Beaufort.

The princess saw her daughter-in-law's reaction and went on: "You won't have to worry about Caterina. Now that Ivan is dead, she will most certainly return to her family in Venice. She lived in Venice most of the time even when he was alive, anyway."

Lydia, whose upright spine had never once touched the bamboo-style back of her chair, inclined her swanlike neck in a gesture that was infinitely graceful. "It is an interesting proposition," she conceded.

"Your son will be the Prince of Jura," her mother said. "Think of that, Lydia."

"I am thinking of it, Mama." The faintest trace of irritation showed in her throaty voice. She turned back to the princess. "What is the Prince's residence like, Grandmama?"

"The Pfalz is beautiful," Mariana replied promptly. "It was designed by the same architects who built Schönnbrun for the Empress Maria Theresa. It is smaller than Schönnbrun, of course, but it is far more impressive—and tasteful—than the Regent's Pavilion at Brighton."

"If only Jura was a little more important," Lydia fretted.

The princess lifted her Adamov nose. "If you do not wish to marry Augustus, Lydia, you have only to say so. I would never wish to push you into a marriage you do not like. I have several other girls in mind who I am certain would be interested in becoming the Princess of Jura if you decide to decline the honor."

"What other girls?" Lydia demanded.

"Lady Mary Bolton," the princess replied promptly.

Lydia's eyes narrowed. The angelically fair Lady Mary was her only serious rival for the crown of beauty of the season.

The princess and Lady Beaufort prudently allowed time for the image of Lady Mary wearing the crown of Jura to settle in Lydia's brain. Then the countess said to her mother-in-law, "Have you spoken to Beaufort about this matter?"

"Not yet," the princess replied. "I thought I would make the offer to Lydia first. You can be certain that Henry will have ideas of his own about whom Augustus should marry."

Lydia gave her grandmother a suspicious look. "Don't you think Papa would want me to marry Augustus?"

"One never knows," the princess said delicately. "Henry is such a political creature. He takes his position as secretary of the treasury very seriously. And you must admit, Lydia, that politics has never been one of your interests."

"I doubt that it's an interest of Lady Mary Bolton's either," Lydia shot back.

The princess gave a very European shrug.

A slight frown creased Lydia's brow. "What if I married Augustus and Austria annexed Jura anyway. What would happen to me then?"

"Nothing would happen to you, Lydia," her grandmother assured her. "Austria has no wish to replace the Adamovs as the ruling family of Jura; it just wishes to make Jura part of its empire."

"But why?" Lydia asked.

"Because," the princess replied in a tone of voice she might have employed to speak to a child, "Austria would like to have complete access to Seista, which is one of the premier ports on the Adriatic."

"Why doesn't Augustus want to let Austria use Seista?" Lydia asked. "After all, he is willing to allow Britain to use it."

"Britain does not desire to impinge upon Jura's independence," the princess said shortly.

Lydia looked puzzled but before she could ask another question the countess said, "Well, Lydia. What do you think? Are you interested in becoming a Royal Princess or not?"

"You may tell Papa that I am ready to accept Augustus's offer," Lydia said grandly.

The princess said to her daughter-in-law, "What about Langton? Charity said that Lydia was on the verge of accepting him."

"A marquis is one thing, but a reigning prince is something else," Lady Beaufort said dismissively. "Langton will have to look elsewhere for a wife."

Lydia laughed.

At least she will make Augustus a beautiful wife, the princess thought with resignation. *He could do much worse than Lydia. And Beaufort has Castlereagh's ear. He will be able to arrange this treaty, of that I am certain.*

"I shall talk to Beaufort tonight," Lady Sophia said.

"Remember," the princess cautioned. "Not a word of this should reach Caterina until Augustus arrives."

The countess shuddered. "I see Caterina as little as I possibly can, ma'am. You don't have to worry about my giving away the secret."

"Why doesn't Augustus want his mother to know about his plan?" Lydia asked.

"Caterina has been plotting for years to marry him to one of her Venetian cousins," the princess said.

"She will be sure to make a scene when she learns he is looking elsewhere."

Lady Beaufort turned to her daughter. "Are you quite certain you wish to do this, Lydia? Once your father begins the political negotiations, your marriage will become a state matter and it will be impossible for you to back out."

"I have never found Langton to be particularly attractive," Lydia said coolly. "I rather think I will like Augustus better."

"I am sure you will," her grandmother said. "I have always found Langton to be a bore."

"He is, rather," returned the girl who had been perfectly prepared to marry him for his title. "And, as Mama said, it is far better to be a princess than a mere marchioness." She gave her grandmother her most enchanting smile. "Why, as the wife of the ruling prince, I believe I would even go in to dinner before you, Grandmama."

"So you would, Lydia," the princess replied evenly.

The countess rubbed her hands together, a gesture that the princess found deplorably bourgeois. "Very well," she said. "Tonight I will talk to Beaufort."

2

Charity entered the back door of Beaufort House and smiled at the young freckle-faced footman whom she met in the hallway. "Good morning, John. What a glorious day."

The footman smiled back. "Did you have a pleasant ride, Lady Charity?"

"Yes, I did. I'm starving, though. Is breakfast set out in the dining room?"

"Yes, my lady. His lordship is already there."

"Oh good," Charity said, and, pulling off her leather riding gloves, she went along to join her father.

The long, narrow dining room of Beaufort House had not been designed by Robert Adam, but it was decorated in the neoclassical style so favored by the great man. In contrast to the vividness of the Chinese Drawing Room, the dining room was cool in shades of cream, pale green, and gold. The ceiling was patterned with octagons enclosing colored circles of green and gold, and the long mahogany table was surrounded by Chippendale chairs upholstered in pale green silk. An immense gilt mirror hung on the wall facing the mahogany sideboard, and a portrait of one of Charity's ancestors wearing a wig occupied the space over the marble fireplace.

The Earl of Beaufort was sipping coffee and reading the newspaper when Charity came in. "Good morning, Papa," she said. "You are up early today."

The earl looked over his spectacles at his daughter, who was wearing an old brown riding habit and polished but obviously worn boots. A black velvet ribbon was tied around her long brown hair, which hung halfway down her back in a braid. "Ah, Charity," he said. "Have you been out riding?"

"Yes." She moved to the sideboard to survey the array of heavy silver serving dishes set out upon it. "I went for a nice long gallop in the park."

Lord Beaufort regarded his younger daughter's back as she filled her plate. "Wasn't your brother with you?"

"No. He was supposed to come but he got foxed last night and couldn't get out of bed this morning."

The earl frowned and his voice took on a sharper edge. "You didn't go alone, I hope? London is not the same as the country. It is not safe for young girls to go out alone in London."

She carried her plate to the table, where she took the seat at her father's left hand. "No, Papa," she said soothingly. "I did not go alone. I took a groom."

"That's all right then," he said and went back to his paper.

Comfortable silence reigned in the dining room as the earl continued to read and Charity worked her way through the food on her plate. When she had finished the last of the poached eggs, she refilled her teacup and regarded her father over its rim.

"Papa," she said, "what is going on with Lydia?"

He didn't look up from his paper. "Your mother has said nothing to you?"

Charity let out her breath in a puff of exasperation. "Please, Papa. Mama never tells me anything. She thinks I am a simpleton."

At that, the earl folded his paper and put it down next to his plate. He looked at her over the top of his spectacles and said mildly, "Stay just the way you are, my dear. If you ever turn into a fashion plate like Lydia, I shall disown you."

Charity chuckled. "Small chance of that ever happening, Papa."

He smiled faintly and nodded.

Charity swallowed some tea, then put down her cup with a definitive clink. "You haven't answered my question. What is the mystery about Lydia? Is she going to marry Langton?"

The earl removed his spectacles, folded them, and put them in the pocket of his blue morning coat. "I suppose there is no harm in your knowing now," he said slowly. "The arrangements are almost completed." He raised his eyebrows slightly and said, "Your sister is going to marry the Prince of Jura."

Charity's mouth dropped open.

Ignoring her expression, he went on; "Jura and Britain are on the brink of signing a treaty that would give our navy access to the port of Seista. In return for this privilege, Britain will guarantee to support Jura's right to be a free and independent nation."

Charity shut her mouth. "What does such a treaty have to do with Lydia?" she demanded.

"You will be able to answer that question for yourself if you think about it, my dear," the earl replied. "Treaties between nations are often cemented by marriages."

"They are cemented by marriages between royal families," Charity said. "Lydia is not royalty. Why should *she* marry Augustus? Why not Princess Charlotte?"

The earl pointed to his folded paper. "The Prince of Coburg is to marry Princess Charlotte, and that is not an arrangement Augustus wishes to disturb. Lydia's blood may not be royal, but it is certainly good enough to merit marriage with royalty. Her grandfather on her mother's side is an English duke, and her grandmother on her father's side is a Royal Princess of Jura."

"Grandmama," Charity said hollowly.

He nodded gravely. "Add it all up, and Lydia is the obvious choice."

Charity's eyes had turned more gold than brown, the way they did when her emotions were stirred. She said passionately, "Lydia doesn't care about Jura, Papa! She can't even speak German. All she cares about is looking beautiful and impressing people. She will make a terrible wife for Augustus."

"I doubt that Augustus is looking for a soul mate,

my dear," the earl said drily. "This marriage is a matter of state, not of personal preference."

Charity stuck her lower lip out. With her long hair, flushed cheeks, and serviceable riding habit, she looked more like fourteen than seventeen. "Will Lydia go to Jura to live?"

"Of course. If she is to be Jura's princess, and Augustus's wife, then she must reside there."

"Poor Jura," Charity muttered.

"The treaty and the marriage are a statesmanlike solution to the very difficult situation in which Jura finds itself," the earl returned briskly. "I applaud Augustus for his astuteness. Both our countries will gain from this marriage. England will get a port on the Adriatic, and Jura will get a Great Power to guarantee its independence. What could be better?"

Charity scowled but had no reply.

The following week saw more letters pass between London and Brussels, and then came the news that everyone had been waiting for. Augustus wrote that he was coming to England to sign the treaty and meet his bride. He recommended that the Debritts prepare to make the journey to Jura for the wedding.

Lydia was furious when she learned that he expected them to be married in Jura, not England. She and her mother had already planned the triumphant ceremony in St. George's, the beautiful church that was only a few doors away from Beaufort House on Hanover Square.

"I want to be married in London, Papa."

The earl, who had not yet finished reading aloud Augustus's letter, looked up at his elder daughter. "Augustus clearly expects the marriage to take place in Jura," he replied.

"I don't know anybody in Jura," Lydia said. "It is cruel to expect me to marry a stranger in the midst of strangers."

"Were you listening to this letter at all?" the earl asked impatiently. "Your entire family will be accompanying you—your mother, your father, your grandmother, your brother, your sister—we will all be going to Jura for the wedding."

The earl, his wife, and his elder daughter were gathered in the library of Beaufort House. Usually the only other member of the family to use this room besides the earl was Charity, and the elegant duo of the countess and Lydia looked strangely out of place in the dark-paneled, book-lined, leather-smelling chamber.

"Mama," Lydia said now, turning to her mother, who sat beside her on the old velvet sofa facing the chestnut wood fireplace. "You know how we have planned this wedding. Tell Papa that I must be married in London."

The countess's cold green eyes regarded her husband, who was standing in front of the chimneypiece. "Is it really necessary for them to be married in Jura, Henry?"

"Yes, it is," the earl replied firmly. "Jura suffered under French occupation for years, and the wedding of their prince will be a symbol to its people that a new day has truly dawned for the country."

just like his father," Princess Caterina
...e stuffed the letter back in her reticule
...r seems to think that Augustus has be-
...ery statesmanlike fashion," Charity vol-
...wisely.

...ncess looked forbiddingly into Charity's
... was so close that Charity could see how
...er skin still was. "Augustus is not a good
...e announced.

...rity dropped her eyes and went back to saying
...ng.

...e princess turned away and crossed the room to
...d in front of the large window that looked out
...on the street. The red velvet draperies framed her
...gure in dramatic fashion. Charity was certain that
she had considered this effect before she moved.

Princess Caterina looked around the elegant
drawing room of Beaufort House. "Why does this
room look like this?" she demanded.

"It is Chinese," Charity explained. "Mama had it
redone recently."

"I do not like it."

Charity found this outrageous rudeness exces-
sively funny. She bit her lip to steady it and said, "I
am s-sorry you do not care for it."

The princess's wandering gaze came to rest on
Charity herself, who was wearing a blue day dress
she had owned since she was fifteen. "How old are
you now?" she demanded.

"I am seventeen," Charity replied politely.

"Seventeen!" The princess's eyes rested on the front
of Charity's old blue frock. "You have no bosoms?"

"A wedding in England will symbolize a new day
just as much as a wedding in Jura will," Lydia said
stubbornly.

The earl looked at his wife for help. "Will you explain it to her, Sophia?"

"Are we to understand that the wedding in Jura
will be a state occasion?" the countess replied.

Beaufort held out the letter in his hand. "Of course
it will be a state occasion. They will be married in
the cathedral in Julia, the streets will be lined with
cheering people, and the whole country will celebrate." He turned his eyes to his daughter, whose
beautiful mouth was looking distinctly sulky. "I can
assure you, Lydia, that it will be a far bigger produc-
tion than anything you and your mother could possibly stage here in England."

For one of the few times in their marriage, Lady
Beaufort agreed with her husband. "Your father is
right, Lydia. You are not marrying a member of mi-
nor royalty. You are marrying a head of state. I am
afraid that it must be Jura."

The image of herself in a magnificent wedding
gown, waving to adoring crowds of admiring peas-
ants, was working its magic on Lydia. She said, "If
the wedding is to be in Jura, I will need a different
wedding dress, Mama. The one we chose might be
suitable for London, but it is not grand enough for a
state marriage."

Out of long practice, the earl's face remained immobile and he said nothing.

"You are absolutely right, my love," the countess
said. "We should go to Fanchon's immediately."

As the ladies appeared to be on the point of rising from the sofa, the earl said hastily, "Augustus also writes that he should be in London within the week, and he is bringing his cousin Franz with him."

"Franz?" The countess subsided back onto the sofa, a puzzled frown upon her face. "Who is Franz?"

"My cousin Marko's son. He and Augustus have always been good friends."

"Well, it is not my affair how many young men Augustus brings with him, Henry," the countess said briskly. "They will be Caterina's problem, not mine." She got to her feet. "Come along, Lydia. We have to cancel the wedding dress that we ordered and choose something grander."

Lady Beaufort's belief that she would not be called upon to house her prospective son-in-law was put to the test several days later, when the Princess Caterina paid a very unusual visit to Beaufort House. Charity was in the Chinese Drawing Room retrieving a book she had left behind the previous night, when the butler escorted the princess into the room and said that he would inform Lady Beaufort of her arrival.

As Evans melted away, the princess regarded Charity speculatively. Augustus's mother had the dark gold hair of so many Venetian beauties, as well as the voluptuous figure. She would be fifty on her next birthday, but she looked ten years younger.

"So," she said in a voice that, after a decade in England as a re[...]heavy Italian [...]

Charity [...] red-and-blue [...] happy to see [...] hope you are we[...]

The magnificen[...] pleased with this ar[...] marry your sister," she [...]

Charity had spent more[...] rina than any other membe[...] had always found the princess[...] be amusing—a sentiment she wa[...] herself. "I am sorry you are not p[...] she replied, now gravely.

The princess opened her reticule an[...] sheet of paper. "I hear from him this morn[...] is coming to England to sign a treaty and ta[...] back to Jura for a wedding." She waved the [...] dangerously close to Charity's nose.

Charity made an indistinct murmur and steppe[...] back out of the reach of the snapping missive. The princess followed her. "This morning I hear! Did he consult me? Did he ask the advice of his mama who has only his interests in her heart? Did he do these things?"

Charity, who knew the answer to these questions, prudently did not reply.

"He did not." The princess glared at Charity as if the Prince's slight of his mother had been her fault. "He did not!"

Charity clicked her tongue and shook her head.

Charity could feel herself slowly turning scarlet.

"Perhaps it is the dress. You must have at least a little something under there."

Charity held her book in front of her chest and said chokingly, "A little something."

The princess glanced with complacence at her own magnificent breast and said pityingly, "Perhaps it does not matter to Englishmen that their women have no bosoms."

The library door opened and a crisp voice said, "Princess. How kind of you to call on us."

For one of the few times in her life, Charity was glad to see her mother.

The princess held her position by the window. "Why do you dress this child so dreadfully?" she demanded.

Lady Beaufort glanced at her daughter. "Surely you have a more suitable dress than that, Charity?"

"I did not expect to be meeting company, Mama," Charity replied with dignity.

Lady Beaufort dismissed her daughter from her thoughts. "Won't you sit and take some refreshment, Caterina?" she asked.

The princess did not relinquish her dramatic pose in front of the window. She said, "I have a letter here from Augustus telling me he is coming to London to marry your daughter and to stay with me. I have come to tell you that he cannot stay with me. I am having my house painted."

Charity glanced at her mother's face and coughed to hide an irrepressible giggle.

The princess swept on. "It is too late to write to

Augustus, but when he arrives I will explain to him that he must stay here with you."

Laughter was bubbling like a witch's cauldron inside Charity, and she struggled not to let it escape.

"You can't possibly be having every room in your house painted," Lady Beaufort snapped.

"The whole house, it is"—the princess gestured grandly with one hand—"upside down. I cannot have Augustus. Since he is to marry your daughter, he can stay here."

Charity realized that this was the way the princess was punishing her son for making a marriage of which she disapproved.

Charity's mother answered in a glacial tone, "I shall be more than happy to offer hospitality to my future son-in-law."

The princess looked around the room. "Poor Augustus," she said. "But perhaps you have another room where he can sit."

"There is nothing wrong with this room," Lady Beaufort replied furiously.

Princess Caterina finally stepped away from the window and came back across the room. She stopped to peer ostentatiously at the black lacquered table with a painted Chinese design that stood in front of the red silk sofa. "So strange," she murmured. She continued on her way to the door, where she turned and announced, "Now I go."

Charity curtseyed. "Good-bye, Your Highness." She hoped the princess would put the quiver in her voice down to the exertions of her curtsey.

The princess swept out into the hall and Charity

could hear her demanding that someone open the front door for her. The countess marched to the drawing room door, shut it, and turned to her daughter. "What a dreadful woman. I hope to God Augustus is not like his mother."

"She told me that he was just like his father," Charity said, her suppressed amusement now bubbling in her voice.

"It isn't funny, Charity," the countess snapped. "It is extremely irritating, this way you have of finding things funny that aren't in the least comical."

Charity looked down at her chest. "She told me I didn't have any bosoms."

Lady Beaufort glared. "What has that got to do with anything?" She looked around her drawing room. "Caterina has no appreciation for what is elegant. She is always falling out of her own dresses. Pay no attention to her."

"Yes, Mama," Charity said.

"I don't care about your bosom, but I wish you were taller." Lady Beaufort moved to the lacquered table the princess had scrutinized, looked it over carefully, then announced, "There is nothing wrong with this table."

"It is a very nice table, Mama," Charity agreed. "Perhaps Princess Caterina just does not appreciate Chinese decoration."

"I don't believe for one minute that she is having her house painted," the countess said, turning away from her maligned table. "She is just too lazy to bestir herself to entertain her son. Her only son. Her only child! The woman is an unnatural mother."

"I think it will be fun having Augustus stay here with us," Charity offered.

Lady Beaufort did not bother to dignify that comment with an answer. Instead she said, "Caterina was right about one thing, Charity. Your clothes are dreadful."

Since Charity wore the clothes that her mother had provided for her, she thought this was an unfair remark.

"We shall have to get you new clothes for our trip to Jura," the countess went on. "You will be one of your sister's bridesmaids, of course." She frowned. "It is a pity you are so short. I suppose there is nothing I can do about it, however."

"You could try stretching me on the rack," Charity said.

"Don't be an idiot, Charity," Lady Beaufort snapped. "It is impossible to have a serious conversation with you. You always make these ridiculous remarks."

"Sorry, Mama." They were the two words Charity uttered most frequently to her mother.

"Now I have to think about entertaining Augustus as well as getting ready for a wedding! I would like to choke Caterina."

Charity, who was thrilled that Augustus would be staying in the same house, was prudent enough not to say so.

3

His Royal Highness, Augustus Josef Charles, Prince of Jura, shifted restlessly in his seat in a vain attempt to get more comfortable.

"Don't look so miserable, Gus," his cousin said with amusement. "We should be in London in a few more hours."

The Prince looked out the coach window at the hedged fields of green and gold that stretched away into the distance. "I hate being cooped up in a carriage." His voice, speaking German with a Jurian accent, was deep and pleasant. "There is not enough room for my legs."

Franz laughed. "If your legs were a normal length, like mine, you wouldn't have such a problem."

Augustus sighed and leaned his blond head against the hard cushion of the seat. "I am absolutely terrified of meeting this girl, Franz. What on earth am I going to talk to her about?"

Franz said, amusement still audible in his voice, "What does one talk to any woman about?"

"I have no idea," the Prince replied frankly. "I have had little opportunity during the last ten years to spend much time in the company of well-bred young women."

In fact, since the age of seventeen, when his father had abdicated the throne to one of Napoleon's marshals and gone into exile in Britain, the Prince had lived in the mountains of Jura, directing an ongoing guerrilla war against the occupying French. He had spent most of his adult life in the company of men, and all of his thoughts and energy had been focused on the effort to free his country.

"Don't worry about having to talk to her," Franz advised. "You're a prince and you're about to make her a princess. That's all she cares about."

Augustus frowned. "I have to talk to her about something, Franz. What do *you* talk to women about?"

Franz's mother was the daughter of an Austrian count, and he had spent most of the war years in Vienna. Consequently, his experience of the world was considerably broader than that of his cousin. "Tell her how beautiful she is," he recommended. "All women like to hear that."

"But what if she isn't beautiful?"

"Tell her she is, and she'll believe you."

The unmistakable sound of galloping hooves came clearly through the open carriage windows. Then a shot rang out and a gruff voice shouted in English, "Halt or next time I'll shoot to kill!"

"Good God," the Prince said in mild surprise. "I didn't think this sort of thing happened in England."

"Neither did I," his cousin drawled in return.

As they spoke, both men were reaching inside their coats to extract pistols. The Prince also grabbed the pistol that was reposing in the carriage pocket.

The coach came to an abrupt stop.

"Come out with yer hands up," the same voice shouted. "If you cooperate you won't get hurt."

"There are three of them," the Prince said. "You take the one on the left and I'll take the other two."

Franz nodded.

"Now," the Prince said, and, one after the other, the young men threw themselves out the door of the coach and landed in a roll on the hard surface of the highway, their pistols already firing.

In less than half a minute, the three highwaymen were shot out of their saddles and their horses had galloped away in panic. Except for the dirt on their clothes, the Prince and his cousin were unharmed.

One of the men the Prince had shot was sitting up, his hand on his shoulder, cursing furiously, and the other was lying on his stomach groaning. Franz was standing over the third man, his pistol pointed directly between the prostrate highwayman's terrified eyes. The Prince glanced at his cousin's set face and glittering blue eyes and said crisply and authoritatively, "No, Franz. Leave him be."

For a moment the Prince was afraid his cousin had not heard him, but then the manic light died away from his eyes and he slowly lowered his pistol. The man on the ground heaved a shuddering sigh of relief.

"Collect their guns," the Prince said, in the same crisp voice as before.

As Franz picked up the weapons that had been scattered when the men fell, the Prince regarded the fallen highwaymen. The one who had been lying on his stomach had managed to roll over and sit up, his hands clutching his lower leg. Franz had wounded his man in the arm.

"You are fortunate," the Prince informed them in his excellent English. "If my cousin and I were not such good shots, you might all be dead."

"Just our luck," the man who was sitting on the roadway holding his shoulder muttered disgustedly. "Our first attempt and instead of stoppin' some rich old gent, we get two marksmen."

The Prince looked at the gypsy-dark face of the man who had spoken. "You are plying your trade rather close to London, aren't you?"

The man laughed harshly, then winced and tightened his hold on his shoulder. He was sweating profusely. "Beggars can't be choosers, my lord," he said sarcastically.

The Prince ran his eyes over the other two men, both of whom looked stoically back. There was something resigned and oddly brave about them that he found curious. "Why do you call yourselves beggars? You look able to work."

The man with the wound in his forearm said bitterly, "We wuz good enough to fight Boney, but now that he's gone we ain't good for nothin' else."

Once more the Prince's gaze went from one face to the next. Then he lowered his pistol. "You were in the British army?"

"Aye," said the man who looked like a gypsy.

"Fought in the Peninsula with the duke, we did," said another, a distinct note of pride in his voice.

The Prince frowned. "Have you no pensions?"

Franz said in German, "For God's sake, Gus, are you going to stand here chatting forever? Get into the carriage and let us be on our way."

"Get in first," the Prince returned. "I'll follow you."

Franz looked at the guns that he had collected. "What shall we do with these?"

"We'd better take them. These fools will only get into more trouble if we leave them behind."

The Prince waited until his cousin was inside the coach before he put his own pistol back inside his coat. When he withdrew his hand it contained six gold coins, which he tossed to the men. "Get a doctor to see to your wounds." He turned, stepped lithely into the hired carriage, and closed the door behind him. The coachman cracked his whip and the horses leaped forward. The three would-be robbers looked at each other in amazement, then scrambled as best they could to collect the coins.

Several hours later, the Prince's hired coach was rolling down George Street in the direction of Hanover Square. This particular square of houses had been built during the reign of the first George, and the present Earl of Beaufort's grandfather had been among the first to purchase a home there. The Prince had stayed in Beaufort House once seventeen years ago, when he had visited England with his father, but he had little memory of London except for that he had thought it to be very dirty.

The architect had designed George Street to broaden as it neared Hanover Square, affording a panoramic view of the square's unique architecture to those who approached it from this direction. In honor of the dynasty for whom it had been named, the majority of the houses that fronted the square had been built in what the architect had conceived to be a German style. Their unifying feature was the connection of the windows into long vertical strips by means of aprons of rusticated stone. Whether or not this detail was German might be a matter for argument, but there could be no doubt that it was extremely attractive. A small gated park nestled in the square's center.

"Charming," Franz murmured as he regarded this vista from the vantage point of the coach's window.

"Yes," the Prince replied in an abstracted tone.

The carriage proceeded along the street on the west side of the square and stopped at No. 12. The Prince alighted and stood upon the pavement, staring at the front door that was less than ten feet away, feeling absurdly nervous.

Damn Mama, he thought. His first stop in London had been to his mother's house, where he had been informed by a very embarrassed butler that the princess was not at home and that her son was to make his home at Beaufort House while he was in London. *Thanks to her, I am going to be trapped under the same roof with this girl for weeks.*

"Courage," Franz murmured in his ear.

Before he could reply, the door of No. 12 opened and a dignified-looking servant was bowing and welcoming him to Beaufort House. The Prince walked forward into the front hall, Franz behind him.

The servant took their hats and their gloves. "His lordship and the princess are awaiting you in the library, Your Highness," the man said with profound reverence. "If you will follow me?"

The hallway they went down was narrow, with a black-and-white marble floor and a variety of landscape paintings hung upon the walls. They passed a graceful wooden staircase and stopped in front of the next room. From the doorway the servant announced, "His Royal Highness, Prince Augustus."

A small, elderly woman in a black silk dress rose from her chair and curtseyed. "Augustus," she said. "How glad I am to see you."

The Prince noticed the cane propped beside his great-aunt's chair, and crossed the floor to take her hands into his own. "Aunt Mariana," he said with a warm smile. "How splendid to meet you again."

She reached up to hug him and he bent from his superior height to return her embrace. When finally she released him, he gestured to his cousin to approach and said, "You know Franz, Aunt, don't you?"

"Of course I know Franz," she replied, enveloping her other great-nephew in a hug that was less awkward, as the disparity in height between them was not so large.

While his great-aunt and his cousin were embracing, the Prince turned to the man who was standing quietly behind the princess. "Lord Beaufort?" he said courteously.

The earl bowed. "Your Royal Highness. It is a great pleasure to meet you again."

Princess Mariana invited them all to be seated. The Prince and Franz she directed to the old velvet sofa, and she and the earl took the two chairs on either side of it. The Prince scarcely had time to glance around the book-lined room before the library door opened again and the same servant who had shown them in arrived carrying a tray with glasses and a bottle of sherry, which the earl poured and served to everyone, including his mother.

"How was your journey, Prince?" Lord Beaufort asked after he had resumed his seat.

The Prince took a sip of his sherry, which was very good. "Uneventful until an hour or so ago." And he proceeded to relate the tale of the attempted robbery, ending with an apology for the dirt stains on his clothing.

"What a dreadful thing!" the princess cried. "You might have been killed, Augustus!"

"There was small chance of that, ma'am," Franz murmured in amusement.

"The economy simply cannot absorb all of the ex-soldiers who have been thrown on it now that the war is over," the earl said worriedly. "The change from a war economy to a peace economy is one of the most difficult things we are going to have to deal with in the coming years."

This was a topic the Prince found interesting, and he and the earl discussed it intently for a few minutes while the other two sat and listened. Then Lord Beaufort said, "I have an appointment for you to meet with Castlereagh tomorrow morning, Prince. We have had a tentative agreement between our nations drawn up for your perusal and approval."

The Prince nodded. "Excellent."

The princess said uneasily, "Augustus, have you informed your father's advisors of this projected marriage? They are still here in London, you know. They came back as soon as they heard of Napoleon's escape."

The Prince's posture was relaxed, with one rather dusty booted foot crossed over the other, but his fingers tightened on the stem of his sherry glass as he said calmly, "I have not written to them, no. I thought I would wait until I could speak to them in person."

"Your mother told them," the princess said.

The Prince sighed. Then he lifted an eyebrow and said ruefully, "I waited as long as I decently could to inform her about it. I asked her to say nothing to my father's ministers until I arrived in London, but I had no real hope that she would honor my request."

The princess looked from her son to her great-nephew, then back again to her son. "I didn't tell you this, Henry, but Count Hindenburg and Marshal

Rupnik came to visit me yesterday. They were seriously upset that Augustus had made marriage plans without consulting them."

The Prince said quickly, "Did you say anything to them about the treaty, Aunt?"

She shook her elegantly coiffed white head. "No. They appeared to know nothing about your plan to give the British navy access to Seista, so I said nothing."

The Prince's fingers relaxed on the glass. "Good. It will be better if they hear such news from me personally."

Franz said, "If they are upset about a marriage with England, they are going to have heart failure when you tell them about the treaty, Gus."

The Prince said mildly, "I hope to be able to convince them that this is the best course for Jura. If they don't agree, that will be a shame."

Princess Mariana leaned forward in a posture of urgency. "Augustus, it will not be wise to make enemies of Hindenberg and Rupnik. They were your father's advisors for many years, and they have friends all over Europe. If you replace Georg Hindenberg as chief minister, or Rupnik as marshal, you will only cause a great deal of trouble for yourself."

"I understand that, Aunt," the Prince replied in the same mild voice as before, "and I have every intention of keeping my father's men in their old positions."

The princess looked relieved.

Beaufort said, "When will you tell them about the treaty, Prince?"

"I will meet with them tomorrow afternoon, after I have spoken to Castlereagh."

Franz said lightly, "That should prove to be an interesting interview."

The princess picked up her cane. "Well, Augustus, I think it is about time that you met your bride."

The Prince felt his stomach sink, but he leaned forward to put his glass on the rosewood table in front of the sofa and said courteously, "I should be delighted."

"The ladies are waiting upstairs," Beaufort said. The princess and the three men rose to their feet.

Augustus was silent as he climbed the graceful oak staircase to the second floor. He followed his future father-in-law into a drawing room at the top of the stairs and beheld with amazement the slender black-haired girl who curtseyed and looked up at him out of extraordinary green eyes.

He took her hand and lifted her from her curtsey. "I am delighted to meet you, Lady Lydia," he said.

She gave him a dazzling smile and he blinked. She was the most beautiful girl he had ever seen in his life.

"Your Royal Highness, may I present my mother, Lady Beaufort," she was saying in an attractive, throaty voice, and the Prince turned to the woman standing beside her and looked into an older version of Lydia's face.

"How do you do, Lady Beaufort," he said pleasantly. "It is so kind of you to offer my cousin and me a roof over our heads, since it seems my mother is unable to."

"It is my pleasure, Your Royal Highness," the countess replied. She indicated the young man beside her. "May I present my son, Lord Stepfield."

The tall young man, black-haired like his sister, bowed. "Your Royal Highness."

The Prince held out his hand to his future brother-in-law and the two men shook. Lord Stepfield looked very much like Lydia. The Prince then introduced his cousin to the Beaufort family.

"Won't you sit?" Lady Beaufort said, gesturing to the chair that was placed beside Lydia's.

The four men and three women took seats in the circle of gilt Louis XIV chairs that had been arranged in front of the marble fireplace. The Prince waited for someone else to start the conversation, as he had no idea what he was supposed to say. Lady Beaufort turned to him and asked him about his journey.

"It was very pleasant, ma'am," he replied.

"Except for the last part," Franz put in.

The Prince looked at his cousin questioningly. Should he tell the ladies about the attempted holdup?

Franz's blue eyes were dancing. "Shall I tell the tale or do you want to?" he asked.

"You tell it," the Prince replied promptly.

As Franz described what had happened, somehow managing to make it all sound engagingly comical, the Prince sat quietly and observed Lydia and her mother, who were gazing at his cousin with utter fascination.

Franz is being charming, he thought with amusement, and moved his eyes to his cousin, trying to see him as would someone who was meeting him for the first time.

Franz wore his silken blond hair longer than was currently fashionable, one lock dangling with careless artistry over his forehead. His brilliant blue eyes were full of laughter as he gestured with one hand to demonstrate how dirty they had become from rolling on the ground. Franz was almost too beautiful for a man, but the Prince knew the ruthlessness that lurked behind his cousin's perfect face, and he never made the mistake of underestimating him.

The Prince was perfectly prepared to let Franz carry the burden of the conversation, but after his cousin had finished the story of the attempted holdup, Lady Beaufort turned his way and said, "I understand that you wish to be married in Jura, Prince."

The Prince was not entirely successful in hiding his surprise. It had never once crossed his mind that he would be married anywhere else. "Yes," he said.

Franz shot him an exasperated look. "The Prince is a hero in Jura, and his marriage will be a cause of great rejoicing for our people." He smiled engagingly at Lydia. "They think Gus is a god, and you will be his goddess, Lady Lydia."

The Prince tried to swallow his disgust at this fatuous comment, but Lydia looked enchanted.

The next hour dragged slowly by. The Prince, who was not accustomed to drawing-room chit-chat, answered all questions that were put to him about

Jura, but contributed little to the banter that went back and forth between the ladies and Franz.

This is normal life, he told himself as he listened to Franz recounting an amusing story about the Emperor Francis. *Living in a cave with a group of desperate men is not normal life. I am going to have to learn to adjust.*

Princess Mariana said, "Before we let you go upstairs to rest and change for dinner, Augustus, I want you to meet my younger granddaughter." She stood up.

A frown marred the countess's white forehead. "You haven't sent for Charity, have you, Princess?"

"I have," the princess returned firmly. "She may not yet be officially *out,* but she must be introduced to Augustus."

There was a step in the doorway and the Prince rose, preparing himself to meet yet another black-haired, green-eyed Debritt. Everyone else in the room stood when he did.

The child who crossed the floor to stand next to Princess Mariana had long golden-brown hair tied back with a pale yellow ribbon, and her eyes were golden-brown as well. They were very large eyes, and they focused on him with total attention.

"Augustus, this is my granddaughter Charity," the princess said, and the child spread her primrose muslin skirts and curtseyed.

"I am pleased to meet you, Lady Charity," the Prince said.

The brown eyes scanned him from the top of his blond hair, which was worn longer than the current

English style, to the tips of his dusty boots. "You look just like I thought you would," she said with satisfaction. "I was terrified that you would be short and fat and perhaps even have a squint."

"*Charity,*" her mother reprimanded. "Show some manners."

For the first time since he had entered Beaufort House the Prince laughed. "I am glad I have not disappointed you."

"So am I," she returned with absolute seriousness. Then eagerly, "Tell me, were you able to get the Lipizzaners back from Hungary?"

"It was one of the first things we did after Napoleon's defeat," he assured her.

Lydia said in a chilly tone, "I am afraid I do not understand. What are Lipizzaners?"

The Prince turned to his prospective bride. "Jura is famous for its Lipizzaner horses, Lady Lydia. We have been breeding them for hundreds of years. The Lipizza stud is where the Austrian Court buys its horses for the Spanish Riding School in Vienna. Naturally, we did not wish Napoleon to get his hands on our horses, so before the invasion we moved the stallions and mares to a farm in Hungary." His eyes returned to Charity. "We have since recovered them, however."

She smiled. With her wide forehead and small pointed chin, he thought she looked rather like a kitten. "I am so glad," she said.

Franz said, "We shall be delighted to show you the horses when you come to Jura, Lady Charity." Then he turned to Lydia. "But you will have to go to

Vienna if you wish to see what the Lipizzaners can truly do. The Spanish Riding School is the most famous in the world."

"Why is it called Spanish if it is in Vienna?" Lydia asked in puzzlement.

"The Lipizzaner horses are originally of Spanish stock," Franz explained. "Jura started its breeding program at Lipizza with Spanish stallions in the sixteenth century. By the middle of the seventeenth century, nobles from all over Europe were vying with each other to buy the best Lipizzaners from our stables."

The immense gilt-framed mirror that hung over the white marble fireplace reflected the circle of people standing in front of it. The Prince made no move to retake his seat. He was desperately hoping for an end to this gathering.

Charity said sadly, "I wish we had a riding school in England, but we don't."

Lady Beaufort said graciously, "I am sure the Lipizzaner horse is splendid, but I myself think the English thoroughbred to be the most beautiful animal in the world."

"The thoroughbred is certainly a magnificent animal," Franz said with a charming smile.

The Prince glanced hopefully toward the doorway. To his profound relief, he heard Lord Beaufort say to his wife, "My lady, I think it is time you showed these two young men to their rooms. They have been traveling for quite some time and must be fatigued."

The Prince wasn't fatigued from the traveling, but

he was becoming very tired from the seemingly endless conversation.

"Certainly," Lady Beaufort replied. She turned to her royal guest and announced grandly, "I will conduct you upstairs myself, Prince."

"Thank you, ma'am." The Prince gratefully followed the countess out of the room and up the stairs to the privacy of an extremely elegant bedchamber.

4

The drawing room of the London town house leased by Count Georg Hindenberg near St. James's Park was filled with heavy oak furniture that looked as if it had been standing in the exact same place for the last two hundred years. The green velvet drawing room drapes looked equally ancient, and there were worn spots on the carpet. None of these signs of decrepitude affected the dignity of the Chief Minister of Jura in the least, however. He was a man in his late fifties, with hair in which the gray mixed indistinguishably with the blond. His square, powerful face looked both intelligent and ruthless as he sat upon a carved Jacobean chair and regarded his prince, who had been given the only upholstered chair in the room.

The third man present, Jan Rupnik, Marshal of Jura, sat in another Jacobean chair, a tight look on his gaunt, severely featured face. Unlike Hindenberg, who was dressed in a cutaway black jacket whose conservative military styling proclaimed to those in the know that it had been tailored by Stulz, Rupnik wore the uniform of the Marshal of Jura: skin-tight white breeches, high black boots, a coat of dark green cloth with a multitude of gold braid, gold facings, and gold buttons. A red silk sash encircled his still-slim waist. Whether he had worn the uniform as a sign of deference to Jura's new ruler, or as a reminder of his own elevated position, was an open question.

The Prince had just finished telling his father's ministers about the treaty he expected to sign with Great Britain.

Angry color had flushed into the chief minister's face as he listened to the Prince talk. "You did not think it worth your while to consult with us before you went ahead and negotiated this treaty?" he demanded as soon as the Prince fell silent.

"I felt I had to move quickly, Count," Augustus replied quietly. "There was no opportunity to conduct a time-consuming correspondence on this matter."

Rupnik said, "With all due respect, Your Royal Highness, you have no diplomatic experience. Count Hindenberg has conducted foreign policy for Jura for the last twenty years. He may have been able to offer you valuable advice on this matter."

"I have not signed the treaty yet," the Prince said pleasantly. "Do you have any such advice for me, Hindenberg?"

"Don't sign the treaty," Count Hindenberg said.

"You will outrage Austria if you do such a thing. The emperor and Metternich will take the opening of Seista to the English as a direct threat."

The Prince lifted an eyebrow. "Surely Austria does not fear an English invasion? That would be ridiculous."

"Of course Austria doesn't fear an English invasion," Hindenberg snapped. "But Metternich already does not like the idea of an independent Jura on the borders of Austria's empire. He will like even less the idea of Jura as an English ally."

The Prince lifted a second eyebrow. "Do you know, I am rather of the opinion that whatever is bad for Metternich is quite probably good for Jura."

Even though it was morning, candles had been lit, as the room's single window afforded little natural light. The sconces on the wall caught the gold in the marshal's uniform and made it glitter. Rupnik said abruptly, "This isn't a game of chess, Your Royal Highness. Alienating Austria is a very serious matter."

The Prince looked from one grim face to the other. *Their minds are closed,* he thought. It was what he had expected, but still he felt a pang of disappointment. It would have been so much easier to have his father's ministers support him. He attempted to explain his thinking, even though clearly it was going to fall on deaf ears.

"I have no wish to alienate Austria," he told the marshal. "However, I have even less desire to become a small cog in the vastness of the Austrian Empire, which is what I am afraid will happen if we must stand alone. And that is why I am negotiating this treaty with Great Britain."

Rupnik fingered the gold braid on his jacket, as if to remind the Prince of his vast military experience. "We were allies with Austria in the late war against Napoleon," he said. "Jurian troops fought alongside Austrian troops at Austerlitz—while you were still a schoolboy, Prince. In the world of today, it is no longer feasible, or even sensible, to look upon Austria as Jura's enemy."

"I do not regard Austria as an enemy, unless it poses a threat to Jura's independence," the Prince replied. Slowly and rhythmically he tapped his right index finger on his chair arm and the expression in his gray eyes hardened. "I have explained to you that Jura's independence is the principle that I wish to see directing all our foreign policy. Before I offer you the post of chief minister, such as you held under my father, I must ask you, Count Hindenberg, if you feel that this is a policy you can uphold."

Relief, like the lifting of a floodgate, surged through Hindenberg. This tall, whip-thin Prince was a complete stranger to him, and he had feared the loss of his position. He bowed his head. "Your Royal Highness, you are the ruler of Jura. It is for you to lead and me to follow."

The Prince smiled at the older man, a particularly engaging smile that was enhanced by the deep cleft in his chin.

He will be wildly popular at home, the chief minister thought sourly. Already the Prince was something of a legend to his countrymen, the unseen mas-termind behind Jura's surprisingly effective guerrilla campaign against the occupying French. Once he ap-peared in public, so tall and young and good-looking, he would be adored.

"I am glad you feel you can support me, Count Hindenberg," the Prince said. "I know you were a good friend to my father, and I am sure that you will be as good a friend to me."

Count Hindenberg bowed his head.

The harsh voice of Marshal Rupnik interrupted. "What of me, Your Royal Highness? Am I to keep my post as well?"

"Do you *wish* to keep the post?" the Prince asked.

Rupnik's hard features became even harder. "Yes," he barked. "I do."

"Then I will be happy to have you stay on," the Prince said. "It will be a comfort to me to know that I have such staunch allies at my side."

"He has allowed us to keep our posts, but how much influence are we likely to have on him?" Hin-denberg said to his companion as they sat drinking brandy in the chief minister's drawing room after the Prince had left.

Rupnik stretched his long, booted legs in front of him and regarded them grimly. He swallowed some of his brandy and said, "This alliance with England is disastrous. Augustus has no understanding of the realities of modern politics. He fought like a tiger at Vienna to keep Jura's independence when he should have recognized the treaty negotiations as a perfect opportunity to become part of the Austrian Empire while still maintaining a portion of our own sovereignty. That is where our future lies."

"We must write immediately to Marko in Vienna and tell him what Augustus is planning," Hindenberg said. "Perhaps he will be able to persuade his nephew where we have failed."

Rupnik stood and went to the corner table where the brandy bottle was placed. He filled his glass and then returned to his seat. "I am surprised that Franz has not tried to change Augustus's mind about this treaty with England," he said. "I always thought that he shared his father's opinion that Jura's future lies with Austria."

Hindenberg shrugged. "Franz has always been one to look out for his own interests first."

"True. Perhaps he thinks his best interest at present is to stay friends with Augustus," Rupnik said.

"Perhaps it will be in the best interest of us all to stay friends with Augustus for the moment," Hindenberg said. "Remember, he is a hero in Jura. He led the resistance against the French and then, at Waterloo, he led what was left of our army to a great victory."

Rupnik scowled and drained his brandy glass. "*I* should have been the one to lead the army at Waterloo," he growled.

"It was not the best of times for you to have come down with a fever," Hindenberg said.

"Damn youngster got lucky," Rupnik muttered.

"He has led a charmed life thus far," the chief

minister agreed. "But remember, even Napoleon had his Waterloo."

The misty light of a warm July morning was bathing the Earl of Beaufort's stable with a pale grayish glow when the Prince arrived in the stable-yard and looked around for Charity. A moment later he saw her come out of the stable, accompanied by a short bowlegged man who was dressed like a groom.

She smiled when she saw him. "You are on time, Prince. How splendid."

He crossed the stableyard to join her. "I am always on time," he said.

"This is Jenkins, Your Royal Highness," she said, turning to the groom. "He is a particular friend of mine and he has saddled Silver Charm for you this morning."

As she spoke, another groom came out of the stable leading a striking tall gray thoroughbred, who danced on the cobblestones of the yard as if he was about to explode.

"Lady Charity assured me you were an excellent rider, Your Highness," Jenkins said a little nervously. "Silver Charm can be a handful."

"So it seems," the Prince said imperturbably. "I think I can manage him, however." He walked to the horse's side, took the reins from the groom, put his foot in the stirrup, and was up before the animal quite realized what was happening. Once Silver Charm felt the weight on him, he snorted, tossed his head, and began to back up.

Long legs closed around his sides and a quiet, authoritative voice said, *"Whoa."*

Silver Charm, whose sensitive mouth had not been pulled on, halted. His ears flicked back and the Prince patted his shoulder and said, "Good boy."

"See, Jenkins," Charity said. "I told you he could ride."

The Prince wondered why this small cousin he had only known for a week should be so certain of his equestrian ability.

Another groom now led a glossy black mare into the yard, and the Prince watched as Charity mounted. She swung into the saddle as easily as he, threw one leg over the sidesaddle horn, and settled her dove gray skirts. Then she picked up her reins and looked at the Prince. "Shall we go?"

"Lead the way," he returned with a faint smile, and allowed Silver Charm to follow the little mare through the narrow alley that led from the stableyard to the side street on which the entrance to the stable was located. At the top of the side street they turned onto Oxford Street and headed in the direction of Hyde Park.

London was starting to come awake. Carts filled with vegetables from the countryside were rumbling along on their way to the market at Covent Garden. The first time the Prince saw one of these high-piled carts approaching, he tightened his legs, deepened his seat, and prepared to deal with a protest from Silver Charm. Much to his surprise, all the gray thoroughbred did was snort once and sidle closer to his companion.

"His behavior is improving," Charity said. "The first few times I took him out, I thought he would kill me."

She said this in a perfectly matter-of-fact fashion, and the Prince turned his head to look at the girl riding at his side.

She was dressed correctly in a gray jacket with a matching skirt. The small foot that rested in the single stirrup of the sidesaddle wore a polished black boot. Her other foot was hidden by her skirt. Defying convention, she wore no hat, and the Prince regarded with pleasure the shining brown hair, which had been pulled behind her small ears and fastened tidily at the nape of her neck.

She was a lovely child, he thought. "Thank you for inviting me to accompany you this morning, Lady Charity."

She shot him a mischievous smile. "I thought you might like the chance to get outdoors for a while."

"You were right," he replied fervently, thinking of the hours and hours he had spent in drawing rooms and government offices this last week.

She fell silent as they continued down Oxford Street, and he concentrated on keeping Silver Charm down to a walk. It was a bit of a project, as the thoroughbred was clearly itching to go.

"He always does this when you first take him out," Charity informed him as Silver Charm gave an impatient buck and shook his head. "He'll be better on the way back after he's had a good gallop."

"Whose horse is he?" the Prince asked.

"He belongs to my brother, but I usually exercise

him in the morning," she replied. They passed a footman walking two small dogs, and Silver Charm bucked again. Charity frowned. "Harry really should send him down to the country. He needs to be out all day, not cooped up in a small London stable."

"What does your brother do with him?" the Prince inquired, thinking that he really would have preferred a less turbulent mount for a walk through the London streets.

"He rides him."

He shot her a glance of mixed impatience and amusement. "Yes, I guessed that. I mean, is he training him for anything?"

She shook her head. "He bought him because he was big and handsome and Harry thought he would make an impressive-looking hack. He's not really a park horse, though."

"Perhaps he would make a good hunter," the Prince suggested. "I understand the English are mad about hunting."

Once again Charity shook her head. "He won't jump. That's why Harry was able to buy him at a price he could afford. His previous owner got tired of being dumped at fences."

"That could become rather tiresome," the Prince agreed with amusement.

At last they reached the park, and as they passed through the gates, Silver Charm's ears shot up and the Prince felt as if he had a bundle of dynamite under him just waiting to explode.

"The bridle path is usually empty at this hour," Charity said. "You can let him gallop."

The Prince lifted his hands and Silver Charm bolted forward. The Prince stood in his stirrups and let the horse go. It was the first time he had ever ridden an English thoroughbred, and the speed was exhilarating. The wind whipped tears into his eyes and the emotion he felt through the reins from Silver Charm was that of sheer joy. He laughed out loud, dizzy with delight at the pounding speed.

They galloped flat out for over a mile before he felt Silver Charm starting to slacken his breakneck pace. A mile later, he was able to slow the horse to a trot, then to a walk, and finally to give him the reins so he could stretch and catch his breath. For the first time, he looked around for Charity.

He heard the sound of hoofbeats before she came into his sight. Her black mare was galloping smoothly along, stretched forward into the bridle and under the easy control of her rider, who, the Prince noticed, had an excellent seat. When she saw him ahead of her, she slowed the mare to a canter, then to a trot. As she came up beside him, the little black slowed again into a walk. Charity turned to him and said, "How did you like Silver Charm?"

"He was marvelous," the Prince replied with enthusiasm. "I felt as if I were flying."

She smiled at him. "I thought you might enjoy him."

The Prince smiled back, then leaned forward to pat Silver Charm's sweaty neck. "You actually exercise this animal?"

She nodded. "He needs to run, and you can only gallop in the park very early in the morning. Harry is usually out too late at night to get up at five-thirty, so I ride Silver Charm for him."

He regarded the small, perfectly poised figure next to him. "He's too strong for you, Lady Charity. You could get hurt."

"He's too strong for anybody," she replied matter-of-factly. "When you think of it, any horse is too strong for any rider. I always think it's a miracle that they allow us to ride them at all."

He had never thought about it quite that way. He looked at her elegant little mare, at the muscles rippling under the sleek, shining coat, and thought that Charity was right. That refined little mare weighed close to a thousand pounds, and Charity could no more control her if she decided to rebel than she could Silver Charm.

"That is true," he replied slowly.

They walked for a while in companionable silence as the early-morning mist began to lift and blue sky peeked out. The trees on either side of the path were heavy with summer foliage and the air was filled with the songs of birds and the rustling sound of squirrels jumping from branch to branch. They were in the middle of London, the Prince thought, but at the moment it seemed as if the city had simply disappeared.

"This is delightful," he said. "Thank you so much for inviting me to accompany you. I wish you had done it sooner."

"I wanted to," she returned, "but there never seemed to be an opportunity."

Thinking about it, he realized that the only time he

had seen her all week had been at dinner, which was one of the few occasions when she joined the older members of her family. Last night had been the first evening that Lady Beaufort hadn't had a social engagement to drag him to, and Charity had also been allowed to join the family party in the drawing room for an hour before being sent up to bed. She had sat beside him while Lydia played the pianoforte, and that was when she had asked if he wanted to ride with her.

He looked at her profile and said kindly, "You are not yet 'out,' I take it."

She threw him a glance, then returned her gaze to between her mare's pointed black ears. "No, praise be. But Mama has threatened to turn her attention to me as soon as she gets Lydia off her hands." Her voice sounded distinctly mournful.

He smiled. "You aren't looking forward to your entrance upon the social scene?"

Charity shuddered. "God, no. Mama says she will find me a husband, but I don't want a husband."

"You are a little young for a husband now, perhaps," he agreed. "But in a few years you will feel differently."

"No I won't," Charity said. Her profile took on a look of amazing stubbornness. "I like my life the way it is now. I don't want it cluttered up with another person. A husband would only get in my way."

This was a point of view with which he could sympathize. "What is it that you do that is so interesting that a husband would disrupt it?"

"I ride my horses. I read books. I learn different languages."

He was surprised. "Languages?"

"Yes," she replied in German. "I learned to speak German from Grandmama and French from my governess. And Princess Caterina taught me to speak Italian."

The Prince stared. "My mother taught you to speak Italian?"

"Yes." She flicked him a glance. "You speak Italian, don't you, Prince?"

He nodded slowly, still trying to imagine his selfish mother taking the trouble to teach Italian to this child.

He said in English, "You are coming to Jura with us, are you not?"

"Yes. Mama says I am to be in the wedding party." She gave him a radiant smile. "Grandmama has told me so much about Jura. I can't wait to see it."

"What do you wish to see?" he asked curiously.

"Everything!" she replied extravagantly. "I am sorry that we are going by ship. I would love to travel through the mountains."

"The mountains of Jura are very beautiful," he agreed.

"And I want to see your horses."

He sighed. "Unfortunately, there has been no opportunity to train our horses for many years. I am afraid you will have to go to the Spanish Riding School in Vienna to see the Lipizzaner in his full glory."

They walked for a time in comfortable silence, while the birds sang more loudly and the sky became more blue. The Prince felt more relaxed than he had since arriving in England, and he patted Silver Charm's neck with his gloved hand.

The child beside him said, "How do you think the Austrian emperor is going to react when he hears about the Treaty of London?"

He turned to her in surprise, then answered mildly, "I don't think he'll like it, but I don't think there is anything he can do about it."

She nodded, her face solemn. "That's what I think too."

They were approaching the park gate and he picked up his reins, ready to deal with Silver Charm on the city streets.

"Did the French do much damage to Jura?" Charity asked. "Will you have a lot of rebuilding to do?"

"There was some damage, of course," he replied. They started up Oxford Street, but evidently Silver Charm had burned off his excess energy, because he walked quietly beside the little black mare, head down, ears relaxed. "They stole artwork from the royal palace and the homes of Jurian noblemen." His mouth tightened. "Napoleon's marshal even removed and had sent back to France the door of our cathedral. It was a beautiful Romanesque creation decorated with animals and doves."

Charity's eyes flashed with indignation, and the Prince thought, *It is too bad that the beautiful Lydia doesn't have the same interest in Jura as this delightful child.*

At the stable they left their horses to the tender care of Lord Beaufort's grooms and returned to the house. As they walked side by side, the Prince courteously bent his head to listen to his companion, the top of whose head did not reach his shoulder. The dining room was empty when they walked in, but places were laid at the table and the sideboard held several covered silver dishes.

As the Prince picked up a plate and lifted the cover of one of the dishes, the butler came in and said with distress, "Your Royal Highness, I did not know you would be breakfasting so early. We have only put out food for Lady Charity."

The Prince looked at the dish in front of him. It was brimming with poached eggs. "My goodness," he said to Charity. "You must have quite an appetite."

She laughed, a youthful, joyous sound that made him smile. "There is plenty of food, Prince. Evans is just upset because of the limited selection."

The Prince raised an eyebrow. "I can assure you, Evans, that I will breakfast quite amply on Lady Charity's choices. Please don't bother to bring more food."

"I expect the Prince would like the newspaper, though, Evans," Charity said.

They filled their plates and sat down, choosing chairs that were opposite each other at the table. The butler returned with a newspaper, which the Prince laid next to his plate, politely prepared to continue his conversation with Charity.

She took a sip of her chocolate and said, "Would you mind letting me have part of that paper, Prince?"

"Not at all," he replied with alacrity. "Which part do you want?"

He divided the paper between them, and a comfortable silence fell as they both worked their way through plates of ham and eggs. When Charity had finished eating and reading, she stood up and excused herself, saying she was expected upstairs.

"Will you be riding tomorrow, Lady Charity?" he inquired.

"Yes. I always ride in the early morning."

"Would you mind if I joined you again?"

She smiled. "Do you want to ride Silver Charm again?"

He smiled back. "Yes."

"Five-thirty in the stables," she said, and then curtseyed and twirled around and flew out of the room.

The Prince went back to reading his paper.

5

At two o'clock that afternoon, Lydia came into the upstairs drawing room of Beaufort House, dressed to pay a call on Lady Northfield, one of the few members of elite English society who was still in London. It had been a great disappointment to both Lydia and her mother that Lydia's engagement had occurred during the summer, when the members of the *ton* were at their country estates or in Brighton with the Regent. That she was not able to parade her conquest around the ballrooms of the great had been a bitter pill for Lydia to swallow.

She expected to find Augustus waiting for her in the drawing room, but it was Franz, not the Prince, who was sitting with her mother. He rose when she came in, and Lady Beaufort looked at her daughter from her seat upon a gold Chippendale sofa. Lydia immediately divined from her mother's face that something good had happened.

"You won't believe this, Lydia," her mother said with not-quite-suppressed glee, "but we have just received a note from the Prince Regent. He wants to have a reception in honor of your engagement! At the Royal Pavilion in Brighton!"

"Oh, Mama," Lydia said. She clasped her hands in front of her heart. This dramatic pose was reflected back to her by the immense gilt mirror that hung between the two front windows. "Oh, Mama."

Lady Beaufort's tone of voice turned from glee to indignation. "Your father received the invitation from the Regent this morning, and he has only just now seen fit to tell me about it."

Franz said in the light, amused voice that Lydia found fascinating, "If you will sit down, Lady Lydia, then I may resume my seat as well."

Lydia went to sit next to her mother. "When is the reception to be?" she asked breathlessly.

"The Regent wishes to hold it in three days' time." Lady Beaufort's indignation flared even brighter. "According to your father, the Regent spoke to the Prince about holding such a reception when they met last week, and the Prince told him it must be held quickly, as he was anxious to leave for Jura."

Lydia's magnificent green eyes widened in horror. "Do you mean to tell me that the Prince knew about the Regent's reception and never told me?"

Lady Beaufort folded her lips. "Apparently that is the case."

As far as Lydia was concerned, this was just another example of the Prince's total lack of solicitude for her feelings. "Really, Mama," she said furiously,

"I do think the Prince could have shown more consideration. As it is, I don't even have time to order a new dress."

For the second time since Lydia had come in, Franz spoke. "I am quite sure that Gus did not mean to be inconsiderate, Lady Lydia. It is just that he has had so little experience of ladies. I can assure you that it never once occurred to him that you might wish to have a new dress made for such an occasion."

"Nevertheless, he should have told me," Lydia snapped.

Franz regarded her with amusement lurking in the depths of his very blue eyes. Lydia felt a little warmth creep into her cheeks. She was never quite sure how to read this cousin of the Prince's. Sometimes she thought Franz admired her, and sometimes she thought he was laughing at her. She felt off-balance with him, and this was not a feeling she had ever before experienced with a man.

On the other hand, she had never before met a man who was fully as beautiful as she was herself.

"Where *is* the Prince?" she asked now, scanning the room as if she expected him to materialize before her.

Franz said, "He received an urgent summons from his mother just fifteen minutes ago, Lady Lydia. He asked me to offer you his most abject apologies and hoped you would accept my escort in his stead."

This was a situation that had happened far too often to suit Lydia. It was not that she objected to the company of Franz. Quite the opposite; she actually found him a much more entertaining companion than the Prince. What she objected to was taking second place to the Prince's other interests, such as a series of boring government meetings and, now, his mother. Lydia was not a young woman who was accustomed to taking second place to anybody or anything. Every young man she had known previously had been her slave.

She turned to her mother and asked, "Do we have to call upon Lady Northfield today, Mama? We hardly have enough time as it is to prepare for Brighton."

Franz said gently, "Lord Northfield is an important figure in the Trade Commission, Lady Lydia. I don't think it would be wise to snub his wife."

"Bother the Trade Commission," Lydia said sulkily.

"I couldn't agree with you more," Franz said, and that intriguing amusement was back in his eyes and his voice. "But I am sure that Gus would want you to go."

Bother Gus. She had enough presence of mind not to say these words out loud, however. Instead she gave Franz her most dazzling smile and said, "Very well, my lord. I will be happy to accept your escort to call upon Lady Northfield."

The admiration to which Lydia was accustomed flickered for a moment in Franz's brilliant eyes. "You honor me," he said. And smiled back.

Recognition flickered between them, the recognition of two people who had traded all their lives on the power of their extraordinary looks. Lydia laughed, a sound of genuine amusement, and Franz's smile turned into a rueful grin.

Lady Beaufort said impatiently, "Then for heaven's sake, let us go. The sooner we are in Lady Northfield's drawing room, the sooner we can leave it."

As the three of them moved across the cream-and-gold rug toward the drawing room door, Lydia said curiously, "I wonder what Princess Caterina wanted."

"I have no idea," Franz replied. "But I am sure that Gus will tell us all about it when he returns."

The Prince sat in his mother's drawing room, listening patiently to the stream of excited Italian that she was directing at him. The gist of her complaint, he gathered, was that her cousin, an unmarried Venetian noblewoman who had been her companion in England for the last nine years, had not been invited to attend the Regent's reception, and the princess was insulted.

"I am certain that the matter can be rectified, Mama," the prince replied in the fluent Italian that he had learned as a child. "I will send a note to the Regent that we wish to include Cousin Maria in our party. He will not object."

"She should have been invited in the first place," Princess Caterina said grandly. "That fat Regent has no manners."

"I am sure it was just an oversight, Mama."

"Hah!" replied the princess, her hazel eyes flashing.

"Was that all you wished to see me about?" the Prince inquired, knowing that it was not.

The princess smoothed the silk of her wine-colored afternoon dress, then lifted her chin. It was still quite firm, that white-skinned chin, and it was made even more attractive by the dimple that was placed exactly in the middle of the jawline.

The princess had always been proud of her dimple. The painting of her done by the great Venetian painter Canaletto, in one of his few portraits, was already famous as *Girl with a Dimple*. On the princess, the dimple looked charming and feminine. On her son, it somehow served to call attention to the essential sternness of the jaw.

"I have heard from Marko," she said now, referring to her husband's brother, the father of Franz. "He has many connections at the Austrian Court and he writes to me that the emperor will view an alliance between Jura and England with great disfavor. Marko says that your father would never have made such a treaty."

The Prince, who was dressed in the correct attire for paying an afternoon call—a coat of blue superfine, skin-tight fawn-colored pantaloons, and polished Hessian boots—frowned. "I don't agree with Marko. Papa prized Jura's independence as highly as I do. I think he would have approved of this treaty."

The sofa upon which the princess sat was upholstered in a dark green brocade. She made a gorgeous picture, with her deep wine-colored gown, her white skin, and her still-gold hair. Her son regarded her out of steady gray eyes and waited for her reply.

"I have received also a letter from my father," she said. "He writes to tell me that all of Venice is outraged that the Allies have given the Austrian emperor the crown of Lombardy-Venetia." She gestured and the diamond rings on her fingers flashed. "He says we do not want those big-nosed Austrians in Venice. Or in Jura either."

"No," the Prince replied a little grimly. "We do not."

The princess leaned her voluptuous torso in the direction of her son, who was sitting in a chair at right angles to her sofa. "At first I was not happy that you were to marry an English girl, Augustus. You know that I have always wanted you to marry your cousin Angela. But I have changed my mind. Now I will bless your union." And she opened her arms.

The Prince left his chair, sat beside her on the sofa, and submitted to a smothering, fragrant embrace. When finally she released him, he returned to his chair and said, "Thank you, Mama. It makes me very happy that you approve of my marriage and the treaty."

Princess Caterina smiled. "I am sorry that my house is being painted and I could not accommodate you, Augustus."

As far as he could see, there was absolutely no sign of any painting being done in the house. "That is all right, Mama," he said.

"You are a good boy."

His lips quirked. "Thank you, Mama."

A faint line appeared between her perfectly plucked brows. "One other thing before you go, Augustus. Hindenberg and Rupnik have been to see me, and they agree with Marko that this treaty is no good."

"I realize that."

She lifted one bejeweled hand in warning. "Be careful of those two, Augustus. I have never liked Rupnik. He has eyes like a snake."

The Prince gave his mother a mystified look. "I never noticed anything wrong with Rupnik's eyes."

"They are small and black—just like a snake's. Never trust anyone with small eyes, Augustus."

He smiled. "I will remember that advice, Mama."

She said abruptly, "Your father was very proud that you stayed in Jura and fought against the French."

The Prince's eyes dropped to the tip of his well-polished boots. "My only regret is that I was not able to see him before he died," he said.

Her voice took on a note of indignation. "It was such a shock to me. One moment he was sitting and talking to me, and the next he was lying on the floor, dead."

"At least he did not suffer, Mama."

"*I* was the one who suffered, Augustus. I was the one left all alone in a foreign land. I never wanted to come to England. It was your father's idea. So ridiculous—just because an aunt of his was married to an English lord. I thought we should go to Venice, but your father insisted that we must be out of the way of Napoleon."

"Papa was looking to the future," the Prince said. "Did you know that directly after Austerlitz, he transferred most of the family's wealth into English banks? Because he did that, we are in a much better position to rebuild than are many of the other smaller states."

"Your father's funeral was very plain," the princess said.

There was a fractional pause as her son adjusted to this abrupt change in topic. Then he replied, "I understood that the Prince Regent himself attended."

"That fat prince came, yes. But who is he, Augustus? His family comes from some little German state called Hanover. All the princes of Italy would have attended if your father had died in Jura."

"I am certain that Papa would have liked to see Jura again before he died, Mama." The Prince's voice was quiet.

In contrast, her own became louder. "Another thing, Augustus. That coronation of yours. You did it too quickly. There was hardly anybody there!"

"I did write and ask you to come, Mama."

She touched her hand to her throat. "You expected me to travel halfway across Europe for a ceremony in front of only a few hundred people?"

He had explained to her in several letters that it had not been feasible, in a recently liberated Jura, to stage a lavish coronation. He said now, "The wedding will be as grand as we can make it, Mama."

She brightened. "That is good."

* * *

When the Prince alighted from his carriage in front of Beaufort House, his attention was drawn by the sight of a girl and a very large dog playing in the small gated park that lay in the center of the square. As he watched, the girl threw a stick and the dog chased after it enthusiastically. The Prince smiled and said to the footman who had opened the front door for him, "I am going to join Lady Charity for a few moments."

The footman bowed and the Prince crossed the street, opened the wrought iron gate, and entered the little park. Hero immediately lumbered up and pushed his immense head under the Prince's hand to be petted. The Prince obliged.

"This animal is almost twice your size," he said to Charity as she came up beside him. "You should have one of those little lap dogs for a pet, not this massive Newfoundland."

Charity looked horrified. "I can't abide those pampered yippy little things. They're not dogs; they're . . . spoiled babies."

The Prince grinned and put out his hand for the stick she had been throwing. She gave it to him and he tossed it to the far end of the park, much farther than she had. They watched in companionable silence as the great furry brown mass that was Hero went charging after it. He brought the stick straight back to the Prince, who threw it again.

As Hero galloped off, Charity said, "I feel I should warn you that you are in Lydia's black books, Prince."

He looked down at her in surprise. "Why?"

Charity shook her head in mock disbelief. Their early-morning rides had made them quite comfortable with each other, and she was able to say ominously, "You didn't tell her about the Regent's reception."

Hero returned, plopped down in front of them, and dropped his stick at the Prince's feet. The Prince said to Charity, "The Regent said he would send an invitation."

"The invitation came today." She crossed her arms over the front of her pale pink muslin dress. "However, Lydia has discovered that you knew about the reception days ago."

"Yes." He gave her a puzzled look. "Was I supposed to tell your sister before the invitation came?"

Charity gave a greatly exaggerated sigh. "Prince, you are hopeless. Now there is not enough time for Lydia to have a new dress made."

He bent, picked up the stick, and threw it again. Hero arose and went after it, tail wagging. "I suppose I am hopeless." He did not sound at all dismayed by this probability. "I never gave a single thought to dresses."

Charity waved her hand in perfect imitation of a gesture that the Prince had seen Lydia make and said, in perfect imitation of her sister's voice, "In civilized society, costume is of great importance. You must remember that you are not living in a cave any longer, Prince."

He ran impatient fingers through his long blond hair. The look in his gray eyes was rueful. "That is true. The niceties of civilized society are not something I have been concerned with for quite some time."

"Don't worry about it," Charity advised in her own voice. "Lydia can wear one of the dozens of new dresses she has had made to take to Jura."

The Prince said, "The Regent has graciously put a ship of the Royal Navy at our disposal. I hope there will be enough room on board for all your sister's dresses."

Charity laughed. As Hero returned, she took the stick from him, patted his head, and said, "That's enough. It's warm and I don't want him to get overheated."

Neither of them made a move toward the gate, and the Prince said to Charity, "You were included in the Regent's invitation. I hope you have something to wear."

Charity looked up at him in surprise. The afternoon sun brought out the gold strands in her hair, and, looking into her large eyes, the Prince thought that if the size of one's eyes was the test of trustworthiness, as his mother seemed to believe, then Charity must be the most trustworthy person that he knew.

"How did you know I was included in the invitation?" she demanded.

He smiled. "I know because I asked the Regent to include you."

She tilted her head in puzzled inquiry. "Why?"

"I wanted to make sure that there would be at least one lady present whom I could talk to," he replied.

Her face lit like a candle as she smiled up at him with unreserved pleasure.

Hero saw a squirrel and chased after it.

The Prince sighed. "I suppose I must be brave and face your sister's anger."

"She won't *yell* at you or anything, Prince," Charity said reassuringly. "She'll just be disapproving." Her face took on a gloomy look. "She's good at that."

He laughed and turned toward the park gate. "Tomorrow morning?" he asked over his shoulder.

She nodded in vigorous agreement and knelt to pet her dog.

6

The Earl of Beaufort and his family arrived in Brighton in the afternoon of the day of the Regent's reception. They had been invited to stay at the Royal Pavilion itself, and Charity was the only family member unimpressed by this honor. She gloomily foresaw hours of sitting in the company of her mother and sister, which almost made her wish that the Regent hadn't included her in his invitation.

On the other hand, Augustus had gone out of his way to make certain of her attendance, and she did not want to disappoint him. So, with heroic stoicism, she resigned herself to long stretches of what she knew would be unrelieved boredom.

Charity did not get along with her mother and her sister. When she was younger she had often been bewildered by this fact. To her mind, the things she did were perfectly rational. She truly did not understand why her mother kept throwing up her hands and pronouncing her to be "impossible."

As she had grown older, however, it had become clearer to her that she and the other two females in the family inhabited different planes of existence. If something interested them, it was certain to bore her; and if it interested her, it was certain to bore them. Being a practical sort of girl, Charity had decided that the best way to deal with this conflict was to keep as far away from her mother and sister as she possibly could. This was a solution that seemed to please them as well.

The important people in Charity's life had been her father and her grandmother. Listening to the princess's stories of life in Jura had been one of the delights of Charity's childhood; her young imagination had been spellbound by the images her grandmother wove of this faraway country with its towering mountains and magnificent horses.

For his part, her father had recognized and nurtured his younger daughter's curious mind. He had made certain that she always had a well-educated governess to teach her, and he had opened his library to her, with virtually no restrictions. Her mother would have fainted if she had known about some of the books Charity was reading on those long winter afternoons curled up in front of the fire in her father's library while he worked at his desk.

There was one other person who had made an indelible impression upon Charity's young life, and this was the Prince. Over and over Princess Mariana would tell her granddaughter stories about Augustus, of how at the age of seventeen he had refused to flee from the French, choosing instead to hide in the mountains with a band of companions and carry on the war from there. Augustus was braver than a lion, the princess would say. Augustus was honorable. Augustus was loyal. Augustus was a brilliant tactician. Augustus was perfect.

Not unnaturally, over the years the Prince had become the impossible standard by which Charity judged other men. *Augustus would never do that,* she would think when someone (her brother usually) did something she disapproved of. *Augustus would not get sent down from school for a stupid prank. Augustus would not get so drunk at night that he couldn't get up in the morning. Augustus was fighting for his country,* she would think. *Augustus was a hero.*

She had both longed and dreaded to meet him. What she had blurted out so rudely when first she saw him had been the simple truth: She had been terribly afraid that his fleshly reality would disappoint her. But to see him standing there in her mother's drawing room, so tall and slim, with a firm mouth and clear gray eyes that looked directly into hers . . . the relief had been enormous.

She would do anything for him, which is how one July afternoon she came to be alighting from her father's carriage in front of the entrance to the Prince Regent's famous Pavilion in the English seaside town of Brighton.

As she stood waiting for her mother and sister, she stared in wonderment at the edifice before her. For a moment she thought that the carriage must have taken a wrong turn and driven into some strange eastern kingdom, so gorgeous and fantastical was the building. A succession of domes and minarets, placed at every angle of the structure, formed the astonishing roofline, and in front of each of the wings was an open arcade composed of arches, separated by octagonal columns and ornamented by trelliswork.

Charity stared at the great onion-shaped dome that formed the central part of the roof and whispered to her father, "Is it Russian?"

"Russian or Indian or Chinese or some such thing," he replied. "The Regent's architectural preferences are deuced odd."

"Whatever it is, it's amazing," Charity said, her eyes still glued to the dome.

Her mother said, "Straighten your hat, Charity." Without moving her eyes, Charity lifted her hands to her straw bonnet and settled it more firmly on her head.

Their arrival evidently had been noticed by the Pavilion staff, for the front door opened and a row of lackeys came parading out, moving toward the carriage to carry in the baggage. One of the servants invited the guests to come with him, and Charity, her father, mother, sister, brother, and grandmother all passed through the door of the Pavilion into an octagonal vestibule, which had a Chinese lantern suspended from the center of a tentlike roof. The Debritts followed the footmen through the palace until they arrived at a large circular salon, where they were requested to wait for the Regent.

The salon had a huge domed ceiling painted to represent a cloud-speckled sky, and Charity's gaze moved slowly from the ceiling to circle the rest of the room.

"It looks as if the Regent likes Chinese things as much as you do, Mama," she said as she regarded the wallpaper panels, which featured a delicate Chinese design of infinitely fragile-looking trees on a pale gold background.

Lydia stared at the curved and backless Chinese sofa, which stood as an island in the midst of an immense expanse of polished wood floor. "There is no place to sit," she complained, looking around the huge room, whose chief furniture was a series of Chinese tables and cabinets set against the walls.

"This is a reception room, Lydia," Princess Mariana said. "That means it is a room in which one receives people. It is not a room in which one sits to entertain them."

"The Regent could receive an army in here," Charity said, looking at the three immense crystal chandeliers that hung from the dome. Her mother was just about to reply when the Regent himself came in the doorway.

The three ladies sank into deep curtseys and the earl and his son bowed. The Regent came across the polished floor to greet his guests, making a genial comment about Lydia's upcoming nuptials.

At this point in his life, the future George IV was almost as fat as Princess Caterina claimed him to be. His stomach protruded before him and his jowls sat in folds around the fashionable high neckcloth he wore under his bright blue coat. His hair was carefully brushed into the flyaway look currently popular among the Corinthian set. Charity looked at his coat and his hair and his brightly colored waistcoat and immediately thought, *Augustus would never let himself look like such a cake.*

After chatting amiably for a few moments, the Regent said, "Prince Augustus, his mother, Princess Caterina, and his cousin Count Adamov have already arrived. I will have you shown to your rooms, as I am certain the ladies will want to rest before the exertions of the evening. If you wish some refreshment you have only to ask."

Everyone bowed and curtseyed again, and the Debritt family followed a servant up the staircase to the elegantly furnished bedrooms that had been assigned to them. Charity immediately went to the window of her room and looked out, hoping to see the sea. But her window opened to the east, onto the lawn and the low wall that separated the palace from the Pavilion Parade. She was still standing there, watching the well-dressed members of the *ton* stroll up and down the aptly named street, when her mother came in.

"I have ordered some tea, Charity. It is to be served in the small anteroom just along the corridor here. You may join us."

Charity stifled a sigh. "Very well, Mama. I will be along in a moment."

"Make certain that your dress for tonight is unpacked and hung to get out the wrinkles."

"Yes, Mama."

Her mother looked at her with the expression of suppressed annoyance that Charity was so familiar with.

What does she want me to say? Charity thought with baffled impatience. For a moment mother and daughter stared at each other. Then Lady Beaufort turned and went out of the room, leaving the scent of her perfume to float in the air.

Charity's dress for the Regent's dinner was a simple gown of white muslin worn over a pale pink satin slip. The high waist was encircled by a pink ribbon, and narrow pink trim decorated the hem. A single strand of pearls and pearl button earrings comprised her jewelry. The scooped neckline of her dress was modest, her satin slippers were pink, and her high kid gloves white. Lady Beaufort had sent her own maid to braid Charity's hair in a coronet on the top of her head, encircled with pale pink roses.

Charity regarded herself in the gilt-framed pier glass that was one of the amenities of her room, and smiled with delight. Her dress might be simple, but it was appropriate to a young lady, not a child, and she thought she looked rather nice. *I wonder what Augustus will think of me,* she thought as she turned from one side to the other, examining herself.

Someone knocked on her door. She called, "Yes," and it opened to reveal her father, dressed in the black coat and knee breeches of formal evening wear. "Everyone is in the anteroom waiting to go down. Are you ready?"

"Yes, I am." Charity stepped forward into the light from the window. "How do I look, Papa?"

"You look lovely, my dear," he said warmly.

She smiled. "You look lovely too, Papa."

He laughed and offered her his arm, escorting her along the corridor to the small salon where the rest of her family awaited her.

The minute Charity stepped into the room and saw Lydia, her pleasure in her own appearance vanished. No one in their right mind would look at her with Lydia in the room, she thought. Her sister wore green silk, the exact shade of her eyes, and the lustrous blackness of her hair contrasted dramatically with the flawless white of her skin.

Lydia has bosoms, Charity thought gloomily as she regarded her sister's deep neckline and the cleavage it revealed.

Princess Mariana said, "How pretty you look, Charity."

"Thank you, Grandmama," she replied. Then, heroically, "You look beautiful, Lydia."

Her sister smiled radiantly. "Thank you, Charity. Are we ready to go downstairs now, Mama?"

"I believe so," the countess replied.

Harry, who was dressed in evening clothes like his father, bent and whispered in Charity's ear, "This is going to be the most colossal bore."

She managed a travesty of a smile, but all the while she was thinking dismally, *Augustus will fall in love with Lydia. I wish I hadn't come.*

* * *

$\mathcal{A}$s Harry predicted, the evening seemed interminable. It began with a long reception line in the Chinese Salon, where the Regent greeted each of his guests and introduced them to the Prince and Lydia. After the principals in the reception line there came, in the following order: Princess Caterina, the Prince's mother; Princess Mariana, the Prince's great-aunt; the Earl and Countess of Beaufort, the bride's parents; Count Adamov, the Prince's cousin; Lord Stepfield, the bride's brother; and finally Charity, the bride's sister.

At her spot at the end of the line, all Charity received from the endless stream of guests was an indifferent greeting before they moved off to find someone more interesting to talk to. For her part, however, she was aware that in some way she represented the Prince, and so she stood as straight and tall as she could and smiled pleasantly at the sea of faces that sailed by her.

After an hour, the reception line broke up and the crowd spilled over into the Pavilion's gallery, a room of immense length and perfectly suited to a party of this size. Its central section was surrounded by a Chinese canopy of trelliswork, hung with bells. The brass and iron chimneypiece was worked in imitation of bamboo, and on either end of the gallery was a Chinese staircase made of cast iron and bamboo, with glass doors beneath. Unlike the salon, this room was amply provided with seating. Sofas in the Chinese and Japanese style were scattered everywhere, and footmen circulated with glasses of champagne.

Charity found an out-of-the-way post next to a gilded Chinese cabinet and watched the Prince as he made his way around the room with Lydia on his arm. It fascinated her just to observe him as he talked to other people—the direct nod he would give, the turn of his head as he listened.

On his arm, Lydia sparkled like a diamond. At last she had her chance to parade her royal bridegroom before her world, and her beauty and charm and confidence proclaimed her a perfect prince's consort.

Never before had Charity been envious of her beautiful sister, but envy her now she did. She hated herself for feeling jealous, but she couldn't seem to help it.

A voice said reproachfully, "I haven't seen you mingling with the guests, Lady Charity. You must hold up your end, you know."

She recognized the voice with its slight accent and turned to smile ruefully at Franz. "No one wants to talk to me, Count. I'm too young."

His brilliant blue eyes flicked over her new dress. "You look quite grown up to me," he said. "And very pretty."

"Thank you," she said a little mournfully. "But Lydia looks beautiful."

For a moment both of them looked at the exquisite figure dressed in green silk standing beside the Prince as he spoke to Lord Castlereagh. Then Franz said, "Your sister is extremely beautiful, that is so, but in your own way, Lady Charity, so are you."

Charity laughed at the compliment. "It is very

kind of you to say so, Count. Have *you* been doing your duty and talking to people?"

Franz was standing underneath a sconce, and the light reflected off his burnished gold hair as he nodded. "Indeed I have, and I am ready for an intermission. I understand there are refreshments in the drawing room. Would you care to accompany me?"

"I would love to," she said sincerely. "It is so hot in here that I am afraid I might faint. And I *never* faint."

"I have been told that the Regent has a habit of overheating his rooms," Franz said as he offered her his elegant black-clad arm. "Perhaps it will be cooler in the drawing room."

Charity rested her hand on his arm and went with him, feeling very grown up. When they reached the drawing room they found that a long table had been set with an immense number of silver dishes filled with food. Smaller tables were scattered about where people could sit and eat their supper.

The drawing room was not as crowded as the gallery, but it was still quite hot. While Franz went to get her some food, Charity sat at one of the tables and contemplated the gilt-bordered white walls decorated with Chinese pictures, lanterns, and flying dragons.

"My, the Regent has certainly fallen in love with things Chinese," she said to Franz as he rejoined her with two plates.

"Chinese decoration is very popular in Europe as well," he said. "There are some lovely Chinese rooms at Schonbrunn." He set a plate in front of her and signaled to the footman who was serving champagne. When the man came over, Franz took a glass of champagne and put it in front of Charity, then got another for himself.

Charity looked uncertainly at the glass before her. She had been drinking punch all evening. "I don't know if Mama would approve of champagne," she said.

Franz's eyes became even more brilliant than usual. "But Mama is not here," he said.

Charity shot him a mischievous glance. "An excellent point." She picked up the glass and sipped tentatively.

Franz said incredulously, "Is this the first time you have tasted champagne?"

Charity nodded and took another sip. "I like it," she said, pleased with her new discovery.

He laughed, and they both began to eat, chatting easily.

They were finishing their food when the Prince and Lydia came into the room. When the other diners saw who had just entered, they all rose and bowed. The Prince smiled and gestured for them to resume their seats, then he escorted Lydia over to his cousin's table. "Do you mind if we join you?"

Franz gestured to the two empty chairs and said, "Of course not." Two lackeys scurried to hold the chairs for the Prince and Lydia, and Franz asked his cousin, "Do you want some food?"

"I don't want anything, thank you," the Prince replied, "but Lady Lydia is a trifle hungry I believe."

"Take a rest, Gus," Franz said easily. "I'll get a

plate for Lady Lydia," and he moved off toward the food table.

"How much longer is this likely to go on, do you think?" Charity asked. From the expression in her voice, it was quite clear that she hoped it would be over soon.

"No one can leave until the Regent does," the Prince replied gloomily.

Lydia's laugh sounded like clear bells. "Nonsense. It is a lovely party and I wish it could go on forever."

The Prince and Charity exchanged a look. Lydia accepted a glass of champagne from the deeply bowing footman and took a sip. She looked so incredibly lovely as she sat there that jealousy twisted inside Charity once more. She looked from Lydia's perfect face to the high, white breasts that were revealed by her low-cut green silk gown, and took another swallow of champagne.

For the first time, Lydia noticed the glass in front of her younger sister. "You aren't drinking champagne?" she said in horror.

"Lady Charity is having her first glass of champagne at my insistence." It was Franz, returning with a plate of food for Lydia.

It was actually Charity's second glass, but she didn't think Lydia had to know that.

Lydia took a dainty bite of her food and waved to someone across the room. Franz said something amusing to her and she turned her head to answer him. The Prince said to Charity, "I saw you valiantly holding up one of the Chinese cabinets, but there was no chance to come and speak to you. I'm sorry."

"That's all right," she replied, instantly cheered by his apology. He had noticed her after all. She saw him surreptitiously stretch his neck, as if his neckcloth was too tight, and said, "Are you as hot as I am?"

"It's simply awful." He looked gravely at her new dress. "At least you don't have to wear a coat and a smothering neckcloth. You actually look cool in that pretty white dress."

Charity smiled radiantly. "Maybe China is hot and the Prince is trying to imitate the climate as well as the decoration."

The Prince laughed. He looked so nice when he laughed, she thought. He looked young. "Oh well," he said. "I expect I can survive it—for the sake of Jura."

Franz said, "Doesn't Lady Charity look lovely?"

"Very," the Prince said.

Charity could feel herself flushing with embarrassment.

"That hairstyle is very good on you, Charity," Lydia said graciously. "It gives you height."

Franz said, "Do you dance, Lady Charity?"

She looked at him in alarm. "A little."

"We shall have to dance together one of these days. You are a perfect height for me."

There was a strangely caressing note in his voice, and his blue eyes were full of admiration.

Franz is flirting with me, she thought in astonishment.

"Gus will have a ball once we get to Jura and you can dance with me then," Franz said.

"Charity is not yet out." There was a sharp note in Lydia's voice that made Charity look at her in surprise.

After Lydia had finished her supper, the four of them returned to the gallery. At midnight the Regent took leave of his guests, and shortly after that, to Lydia's extreme displeasure, the Prince also went upstairs to bed.

7

he engaged couple and their respective families remained one more day in Brighton as guests of the Regent and then returned to London. During the ride home, Princess Caterina discoursed at great length to her son about the Regent's hospitality and the flattering attention he had shown her. Apparently her opinion of the "fat prince" had changed. In truth, she was just the sort of voluptuous older woman whom the Regent had always admired, and he had flirted with her shamelessly.

The Princess also voiced her approval of Lydia. "That one is not only beautiful, she understands the superiority of her position. She will not embarrass you, Augustus."

The Prince, who was profoundly relieved to get away from the overheated stuffiness of the Pavilion, said, "Thank you, Mama."

The princess next looked at Franz. "I understand

you received a letter from Austria while we were in Brighton, Franz. How are your dear mama and papa?"

"Very well, thank you, Princess," Franz replied.

The princess had the whole of the front-facing carriage seat to herself, while the two men sat opposite her. At Franz's words, the Prince turned his head sharply and looked at his cousin. "I didn't know you had received a letter. Did your father say anything about the treaty?"

Franz replied in a mild voice, "You can hardly expect him to view Jura's situation in regard to Austria in the same way you do, Gus. He has lived in Austria for the last ten years. My mother's family has been part of the emperor's court for generations—my mother is one of the empress's ladies-in-waiting. My father does not regard Austria as a threat to Jura's independence and he thinks it is a mistake to introduce England into Jura as you have done."

With a rustle of deep green taffeta, Princess Caterina sat upright and said indignantly, "Those Austrians have taken for themselves the crown of Lombardy and Venice. They will look to take Jura next. I think Augustus is right to make this treaty."

"I agree with you, Aunt," Franz said soothingly. "I am merely telling Gus how my father views the situation."

The princess leaned back against the blue velvet squabs of the coach and said contemptuously, "Marko has been seduced by the von Herzogs."

"That is not true." There was an unusually sharp

edge in Franz's flexible voice. "My mother's family were extraordinarily kind to my father and me when Jura was occupied by the French."

The princess indicated her disagreement by a sniff. "Watch out, Augustus," she said to her son. "Prince von Herzog will be scheming with Marko to find a way to throw you out so that he can put an Austrian puppet in your place."

Franz went rigid.

The Prince glanced at his cousin's profile, then said sternly, "Mama, that is a terrible thing to say. Uncle Marko may not agree with me, but that doesn't make him a traitor."

The princess sniffed again.

The Prince reached out, laid a hand on his cousin's tense forearm, and said quietly, "I am sorry that your father doesn't agree with my strategy, Franz, but be assured that I can understand his disagreement without suspecting him of treason."

Franz turned and looked at him. His blue eyes were brilliant. "Can you? I am glad to hear that, Gus."

The Prince looked at him for a moment in silence, then he removed his hand, leaned his head back against the velvet cushion, and said wearily, "I cannot describe to you how anxious I am to get home."

"We should be there in two more hours," Franz said.

The corner of the Prince's mouth quirked. "I was talking about Jura."

A mail coach passed them going in the opposite

direction and a cloud of dust floated in the open window of the chaise. The princess wielded her fan vigorously and said, "I too received a letter while we were at Brighton and you will be happy to know, Augustus, that my father writes to tell me that all of the Vecchios will be at your wedding."

The Prince thought of the vast array of his mother's incredibly arrogant Venetian family and repressed a shudder.

At his shoulder, he heard Franz murmur, "Won't that be nice?"

"I thought you would be glad," the princess said complacently as she folded up her fan.

The Prince exchanged a glance with his cousin, but neither man was foolish enough to say what he really thought.

Franz turned to Lydia and said with amusement, "You should have seen Gus's face when his mother announced that all of her family would be coming to the wedding."

"Was he upset?" Lydia inquired. "I thought the Vecchios were an extremely noble Venetian family. I should think he would be glad of their attendance."

"They are stupendously noble," Franz replied. "They even number a doge or two among their ancestors. As every one of them will be sure to tell you—again and again and again."

The two of them were walking along one of the paths in Hyde Park. It was five o'clock in the afternoon, the heat of the day had dissipated, and they had decided on the spur of the moment to leave the phaeton with their groom and walk for a while along the pedestrian paths.

During the season, the park at this hour would be filled with members of the *ton,* riding and driving and walking, out to see and be seen. It was July, however, and Franz and Lydia were virtually alone as they strolled along a pretty wooded path near the lake.

As had happened so often before, the Prince was busy and Franz had been left to escort Lydia; a duty, he assured her, that he prized most highly. For her part, Lydia found Franz much easier to talk to than the Prince and would have been perfectly happy to accept him as a substitute if she had not felt slighted by the Prince's seeming lack of interest in her.

She said now, "Mama would be scandalized if she knew we were walking together without my maid to chaperone me."

The sun shining through the trees dappled the shaded walk in front of them with patches of sunlight, picking out in particular a patch of purple-red foxglove that grew on the left side of the path. Franz said with amusement, "Your maid did not come with us in the phaeton."

"Which is precisely why I should not have got out of it," Lydia retorted.

He turned his head to look at her. "Are you afraid of me?" The amusement was still in his voice.

She lifted her chin, which was framed by the green bow of her satin and tulle bonnet, and looked back. "Should I be?"

They passed the patch of foxglove and entered on a section of the path where the trees were thicker and the sunlight more scattered. In the woods to their right, a squirrel scurried up a tree, startling a bird, which took flight screaming its protest.

Franz scanned the face Lydia had lifted to him, from her forehead, to her eyes, to her mouth, and there his eyes stopped. He said in a slightly deeper voice than usual, "My dear, a woman as beautiful as you are should always be afraid when she is alone with a man."

Lydia's long lashes lowered to screen her eyes. "But you are a gentleman," she said.

Franz laughed softly. "Even gentlemen can be tempted, my dear Lydia."

She was silent, her eyes on the path in front of them.

He said to her profile, "We are to be cousins after all. Surely I may call you Lydia."

"The Prince calls me *Lady* Lydia," she said.

"Gus does not know you as well as I do."

They walked side by side in silence, each excruciatingly aware of the other, then Lydia said, "Every time we have an engagement to do something together, he sends you to take his place."

The path before them suddenly opened up to a view of the Serpentine. The still lake water glittered in the late-afternoon sun.

"There has been quite a lot to do in regard to the treaty," Franz said in excuse of his cousin. "Gus has been busy with matters of state."

A small branch lay across the path and as Lydia

stepped over it daintily she said, "Surely he could have found the time for a drive in the park!"

Abruptly Franz stopped walking, and, surprised, Lydia stopped with him. He removed her hand from its correct position on his forearm and turned her to face him. "Listen to me, my dear," he said, and for once there was no amusement whatsoever in his voice. "If you expect Gus to act the role of a lover, you will be disappointed. In his view, your marriage is part of a very important treaty he has negotiated with your government. To him, you are a visible sign of Britain's commitment to Jura's independence. I am sure he is also hoping that you will provide him with a son to succeed him on Jura's throne. But don't look to him for the kind of attention you are accustomed to receiving from your English admirers. Gus is not a man for women."

Lydia looked alarmed. "What do you mean by that? 'He is not a man for women'?"

For a moment Franz looked puzzled, then his face broke into its customary amused smile. "I don't mean to suggest that there is anything aberrant about him." His blue eyes glinted. "I can assure you that Gus is perfectly normal in his appetites. Perhaps I should have said that he is not a man for the *company* of women. And when you think about what his life has been like for the past ten years, surely that is only to be expected."

Lydia's lovely full mouth was looking sulky. "You are not painting a very attractive picture of marriage for me."

"On the contrary," Franz said, "there are many attractive things about this marriage for you. Don't forget, Gus is making you a princess."

The sulky expression did not disappear from Lydia's mouth. "A princess without a prince."

A bunny hopped across the path about six feet away from them. More rustling in the woods indicated the ongoing activity of squirrels. Except for the wildlife, they were completely alone.

"Damn," Franz said mildly. "Now you are worried. I should have had enough sense to hold my tongue."

Lydia was a tall girl and their eyes were almost on a level. She said in a low voice, "I always thought I would marry a man who adored me."

"And rightfully so," he replied agreeably. His eyes were intensely blue. "Since the day you were born, every man who has seen you has probably adored you."

She lowered her gaze to his neckcloth. "But not the Prince."

Franz did not reply.

She raised her eyes to his. "And not you."

Impossibly, his eyes grew even bluer. "What makes you think that?"

Bravely, she sustained his gaze, and a little color flushed into her long white throat. "Isn't it true?"

Slowly he shook his head. Then he reached for her gloved hand, turned it, and lifted it to his mouth. As his lips touched the veins of her exposed wrist, her pulse began to hurry. "Beautiful Lydia," he murmured. "Beautiful, beautiful Lydia. No, it is not true."

* * *

The Prince arrived back in Hanover Square half an hour after Franz and Lydia had left for the park. "Is his lordship at home?" he asked as he relinquished his hat and gloves to the footman who had opened the door for him.

"The only family member who is at home is Lady Charity, Your Highness," the footman replied.

The Prince nodded. "Where is she, Robert?"

The footman's eyes sparkled with delight that a Royal Prince had remembered his name. "I believe she is in the garden, Your Highness," he said.

The Prince walked the length of the house and let himself out the back door, which opened on a patio and small garden. Charity was sitting at a small wrought iron table, a book propped in front of her and a half-filled glass of lemonade beside it. Hero was sleeping in the shade of a pear tree a few feet away.

"Am I disturbing you?" the Prince asked courteously.

She looked up from her book and her small face lit. "Oh, it's you, Prince. No, not at all. How was your meeting? Was the treaty all right?"

He had viewed the final draft of the treaty today in order to approve it before it was formally drawn up for his signature.

As he crossed the stone patio toward her table, she suddenly realized the inadequacy of her greeting and jumped to her feet. As she began to curtsey, he waved his hand in an impatient gesture and said, "For heaven's sake, don't do that. Sit down."

She ignored him, spreading her sprigged muslin skirts and dipping gracefully until her knee almost touched the ground. She then spoiled the effect by shooting back up with more energy than grace and said, "Mama would have heart palpitations if she knew I had forgot to curtsey to you."

He gestured to the empty chair across from hers and said, "May I join you?"

"Of course you may join me," she replied. As they both sat down she said again, "I am dying to know how your meeting went. Was the treaty all right?"

He turned his chair so that he could stretch out his long legs and replied, "There was only one small change. Castlereagh said he would have it ready for my signature tomorrow." A smile he could not quite contain tugged at the corners of his firm mouth. "I told his lordship to alert the Royal Navy that we shall be ready to sail for Jura in two days' time."

The look that came over Charity's attentive, wide-browed face made him suddenly uneasy. "What is the matter?" he demanded.

She sighed gustily. "I hate to have to tell you this, Prince, but while *you* may be ready to sail in two days' time, and while Father and Harry and I may be ready to sail in two days' time, I can assure you that Mother and Lydia will *not* be ready. Not in two days' time."

He was astounded. "Why not? They have known about this trip for weeks. Surely they are prepared."

She raised her shoulders almost to the level of her ears in a giant shrug. "I can't tell you why they won't be ready, but they won't be," she replied. "It always takes Mama forever just to move from the country to London. I can imagine how long it will take for her to change *countries*."

The Prince's frown deepened. "There is a great deal to be done in Jura to prepare for the wedding. My people were cheated out of the spectacle of a coronation and I want this wedding to be as big a show as I can make it. I need to get home as soon as possible." Impatiently, he began to tap his forefinger on the arm of his chair.

Charity watched him, an identical frown on her own clear forehead. Suddenly her eyes opened wide. "I just had an idea," she said.

His finger stopped tapping and he lifted an eyebrow. "What is it?"

She leaned toward him, as if to confide a secret. "Take two ships," she said, her sparkling eyes showing childish delight in her suggestion. "You can leave for Jura in two days' time, and Lydia can follow you in a few weeks. That will give you a chance to do all the things you need to do without having to bother with Lydia, and she will have all the time she needs to get ready."

She sat back, an expectant expression on her face as she awaited his response.

"You don't think your sister would object to not having my escort?" he asked doubtfully.

She looked at him as if he was ten years old and enunciated, "I think she will object far more to being rushed onto a ship in two days' time."

He leaned back in his chair and regarded Hero as the dog drowsed in the sun. The more he thought about this idea, the better he liked it. Charity had hit home when she said it would be far easier to return to Jura without Lydia to worry about.

Charity's voice intruded into these pleasant thoughts. "Besides, we will have Papa's escort. Surely that will suffice."

The Prince's frown returned. "Your father must sail with me. We have trade issues to resolve. He would not be available as an escort."

Charity's lips parted. Then her cheeks flushed and her eyes turned almost golden. She sat bolt upright on her chair and said, "May I come with you and Papa, Prince? I want so much to see Jura, and if Mama is there she will stop me from going to the places I want to. I know she will. Oh, please please please may I come?"

The Prince could not help but smile. "I do not have the authority to decide that," he said gently. "You must speak to your parents."

"Papa will let me go," Charity said. She bounced on her seat. "I know he will."

The smile died away from the Prince's face and he sighed. "I cannot leave your sister and your mother without a male family member to escort them, Lady Charity. If I should decide to sail without them, I'm afraid that your father will have to stay behind as well. And, needless to say, if your father does not come, you cannot come either."

"They will have Harry!" Charity cried passionately. "*He* can escort Mama and Lydia."

Charity's raised voice woke Hero, and he lifted his head to look at her with bemused wonder.

The Prince replied regretfully, "I do not think Lord Stepfield is old enough to understake such a responsibility."

"He is three and twenty," Charity said. "I think that is old enough."

The Prince simply shook his head.

"When you were three and twenty you were old enough to direct a campaign against the French." There was a definite note of accusation in her voice.

"Your brother's life has not been like mine," the Prince replied soberly. "I was much older at twenty-three than he is."

Hero got up, stretched his front and then his back, and ambled over to Charity.

"I know!" Charity's smile was blinding. "Leave Count Adamov to escort them. He and Lydia get along famously."

Hero sat at Charity's feet and looked up at her in silence, waiting to be acknowledged.

The Prince also looked at her in silence.

She leaned toward him, the locket that was her only jewelry swinging against the delicate skin of her throat. "Please, Prince, oh pretty, pretty please," she said. "I want so much to have the chance to see Jura without Mama around. And Lydia will be almost as much of a nuisance as Mama. It will be such fun to be on our own for a while!"

The Prince realized that she was right. He wanted time to meet with his friends, to organize his council of state, to have formal wedding announcements sent out, to prepare the capital for a spectacular show. He could do all of this much more efficiently

if he didn't have to worry about entertaining Lydia
and her relatives.

Once she was his wife, she would have her own
activities to occupy her. He was rather vague about
what those activities might be. His mother had spent
at least half her time in Venice, and when she was in
Jura all he could remember was that she always
seemed to have things to do.

If she had a baby, that would occupy her, the
Prince thought. It would be a good thing for Jura,
too. He had been Jura's only heir for twenty-seven
years and had found the burden a heavy one. If
something should happen to him, the direct line of
succession from father to son that had characterized the Adamov dynasty for centuries would be
broken.

His mother had said that his father was proud of
his remaining in Jura to fight, but Augustus remembered how his father had begged him to accompany
his parents to the safety of England. *Our whole hope
of retaining the Adamov dynasty depends upon you,*
his father had said. *You do not have the right to put
your life in jeopardy.*

In the ensuing years he had jeopardized his life
many times, and he had always felt guilty doing it. It
would be a great relief not to have to shoulder the
whole burden of his dynasty alone.

All of this passed through his mind in about thirty
seconds, then he looked at the eager young face
across from him. At last he said, "I will see what I
can do."

"Hurrah!" Charity cried, snatching the ribbon off

her hair and waving it over her head. She looked at the Prince through the tumble of golden-brown locks and laughed giddily.

He laughed back. It was the only thing one could possibly do in the face of such incandescent joy.

8

harity had predicted correctly that neither Lady Beaufort nor Lydia would be ready to sail in two days' time. When the ladies were offered the choice of leaving immediately with the Prince, or sailing a few weeks later with Franz, they chose the latter option with alacrity. Consequently, the wind-blown group gathered on the dock in front of H.M.S. *Falcon* this chilly, overcast July morning did not include either the Prince's bride or her mother.

The *Falcon* was one of the largest of the navy's ships, carrying a hundred and one eighteen-pounders mounted on three gun decks. If the nation had still been at war, it would have stood at anchor out in the bay, ready to sail at a moment's notice. In these days of peace, however, the *Falcon* was in port, enabling the Prince's party to board the easy way, via a gang-plank.

Besides the Prince, the Jura-bound group included Count Hindenberg and Marshal Rupnik, Princess Caterina, Lord Beaufort, Harry, and Charity. At first Lady Beaufort had refused to allow Charity to travel with just her father to look after her, but when she learned that Princess Caterina was going she changed her mind. Harry had been almost as eager to see Jura as Charity, and so he too was going with the earlier group.

The wet, salty wind blowing off the water was strong enough to flatten Charity's clothes against her body and cause her to hold on to her hat. She was relieved when the young officer who had come ashore with the ship's captain said to her father, "We may go aboard, my lord."

Lord Beaufort offered Charity his arm, and she rested one hand on his sleeve while continuing to hold her hat to her head with the other. They walked forward into the wind and stepped onto the gangplank. Harry came after them, and then Count Hindenberg and Marshal Rupnik.

An honor guard of ten sailors awaited them on deck, forming an aisle next to the boarding gate through which the passengers entered. As Charity and Lord Beaufort moved away from the sailors and stepped under the shadow of one of the gun decks, a whistle split the air with sudden, deafening sound.

Charity jumped and her hat tilted forward over her nose. She shoved it back again, looked toward the gangplank, and saw that the sailors who formed the naval "sideboy" had removed their hats, as had every other officer and sailor on deck.

The Prince was coming aboard, his mother on his

arm, Captain Wilson, the ship's commander, at his side. Charity's eyes sparkled as she regarded the tall, slim figure passing with such natural dignity through the honor guard that had been arranged for him.

He is so perfect, she thought with delight. It filled her with joy to know that the Augustus she had dreamed about for so many years had not been a figment of her grandmother's imagination, that he really did exist in the world. The wind gusted and she jammed her hat more securely on her head, all the while watching as the Prince bent to listen to something the captain was saying to him. The Prince had effectively dealt with the hat-and-wind problem by dispensing with the hat, and the stiff breeze blowing off the water ruffled his long hair as he fixed his clear, direct gaze on the captain.

Captain Wilson was explaining a navigational problem. "The wind is blowing in the wrong direction to enable the *Falcon* to sail away from the dock, Your Highness. If the ship is to leave Portsmouth without delay it will be necessary to tow her out by using the ship's boats—quite an exhausting task for my men, who will have to row for hours. If there is no urgency, I would prefer to wait until the wind changes."

The Prince was usually the most reasonable of men, but now that his feet were actually on the deck of the ship that was going to take him home, he felt he could not wait one more minute to be under way. The voice in which he conveyed this information to the captain was mild and faintly apologetic, but definite. Captain Wilson's lips tightened slightly, but he bowed his head and turned to give the necessary orders.

So it was that by nightfall the *Falcon* was out in the Atlantic, sailing toward Spain and Gibraltar, where it would pass into the Mediterranean and so on to the Adriatic and Jura. The Prince was in high spirits as he sat at table in the captain's quarters to partake of dinner. Rather to his surprise, the only people in his party to join him, Captain Wilson, and Wilson's second-in-command, Commander Nelson (who informed them that he was not related to the late hero), were Lord Beaufort and Charity.

He looked at the empty places that had been set for the princess, Harry, Count Hindenberg, and Marshal Rupnik, and said, "Where is everyone else?"

Captain Wilson said, "I regret to tell you that we have a few absentees due to sickness, Your Highness. The seas have been quite rough today, and I'm afraid it isn't going to get better for a while. We appear to be heading into a storm."

Charity said cheerfully, "I looked in on Princess Caterina and she was in bed. She looked green."

Her own complexion was its usual delicate pink and white and her brown eyes were sparkling. The Prince thought with amusement that clearly his mother's condition had not been serious enough to disturb Charity's enjoyment in what she obviously regarded as an adventure.

Lord Beaufort said, "My son is not feeling well, but fortunately I myself have never been subject to seasickness. We must hope that the seas are calmer tomorrow."

The captain invited his guests to be seated and the soup course was brought in. The Prince listened courteously to Captain Wilson's conversation and watched Charity as she tried to cope with the oscillating liquid in her soup plate. She stared intently at the plate, then as the ship rose to one side and the soup rushed to the opposite end of her plate, she quickly dipped her spoon in and filled it. She glanced up triumphantly and found the Prince's gaze on her. He winked, then turned back to his conversation with the captain.

When dinner was finished, the Prince invited Lord Beaufort to his cabin for a glass of port. The earl accepted, and as the two men moved toward the cabin door, Charity said quickly, "Please, may I come too, Prince?"

He turned in surprise and found himself engulfed in a pair of huge golden-brown eyes. He heard the earl say something in an impatient voice, but when Charity spoke again it was to him. "I won't get in your way, Prince, I promise. It is just that my room is so tiny that it makes me feel as if I can't breathe."

With her wide brow, big eyes, and pointed little chin, he thought that she looked more than ever like a forlorn little kitten begging to be brought in out of the cold.

Lord Beaufort said, "If you get into bed and close your eyes, you won't see the size of the room."

"I am much too excited to sleep, Papa." The big reproachful eyes glanced at Lord Beaufort, then returned to the Prince. "Please, Prince. If you are going to talk about state secrets, I'll swear on the Bible not to tell."

He laughed. "We are not going to discuss state secrets, Lady Charity. If you wish to join us, it is all right with me if it is all right with your father. We are going to discuss trade, and that will probably put you right to sleep."

The remarkable eyes turned to Lord Beaufort. "*Please,* Papa."

"Oh all right," the earl said with a sigh. "But you can't have any port."

The Prince had been given the cabin that normally belonged to Commander Nelson. It was considerably larger than the small closet Charity occupied, but not nearly as large as the captain's cabin. A narrow berth was fitted into a recess along one wall, and on the other wall there were two doors, one of which Charity supposed must be the water closet. The commander's room also boasted two portholes and had a fine Persian rug on the floor.

As the door closed behind them, the Prince looked around and made a discovery. "I am afraid I am short a seat. If you and Lady Charity will take the chairs, my lord, I will sit on the bed."

"I'll sit on the bed, Prince," Charity said blithely, heading in the direction of the low berth. "I'm the smallest and it's awfully close to the ground. You and Papa won't have room for your legs."

She was absolutely right. "Thank you, Lady Charity," the Prince said gratefully.

The earl grumbled, "I have a feeling that your mother would not approve of this at all, Charity."

"She's not here," Charity pointed out with a radiant smile. As she was lowering herself to the bed, the ship suddenly listed in the opposite direction, catapulting her forward. The Prince instinctively opened his arms to catch her as she cannoned into his chest.

A pair of startled brown eyes blinked and looked up at him. "Goodness," Charity said.

He turned her around and marched her back to the berth. He reached out with one hand to anchor himself on the corner of the recess and said with a laugh, "Sit down quickly, before the ship rolls again."

She dropped to the berth with the flexibility of the very young. He remained where he was for a moment, standing over her, his hand braced against the wall. "All right?"

She looked up at him. "All right."

The earl laughed. "I think I shall forgo the port, Prince. I don't fancy having it spill all over me."

The Prince grinned and went to take one of the room's curve-backed wooden chairs, gestured Lord Beaufort to the other, and the two men settled down to talk.

The Prince's main concern for Jura's future was to get its economy, which had been stifled by the occupation and the ensuing British blockade, back into gear. One of the reasons that Jura had successfully resisted an Austrian takeover for so many years was that it had always had a prosperous economy that was independent of the Habsburg empire. The Prince did not think it would be difficult to restore the extensive trade that Jura had always maintained with the German Confederation, but now that northern Italy was under Austrian rule he was concerned about that market.

In the earl he had a sympathetic and knowledgeable listener. Lord Beaufort was half Jurian by birth, and his many years in the English government had made him very aware of the delicacy of the balance of power in the region of the Adriatic.

Both men knew that the problem facing Jura was that Austria wanted Jura's port of Seista. Having both Venice and Seista would give the Austrians a stranglehold on the Adriatic. Needless to say, this was not a situation that the Great Powers viewed with equanimity, which is why Jura had been awarded its independence in the Final Act of the Congress of Vienna. However, the Prince was under no illusion that the emperor had given up on his hopes of acquiring Seista.

The earl understood this as well, and the two men debated the means by which the Prince could restore the vigor of the Jurian economy and at the same time avoid the blocks that Austria was sure to put in his way.

It was after midnight when the Prince finally looked toward his berth, expecting to see a sleeping Charity. Instead she was sitting cross-legged, her dress spread discreetly over her ankles, her back propped against the wall. She looked as alert as she had been two hours ago.

"I thought you would be asleep," he said in surprise.

The brown eyes were affronted. "I was listening to you and Papa. It was much more interesting than going to sleep."

"Interesting?" he said incredulously.

Lord Beaufort laughed. "Charity read *The Wealth of Nations* this year and in consequence has become a great proponent of free trade."

The Prince looked at the youthful face of the earl's daughter, and she told him earnestly, "Austria should not be allowed to impose tariffs on Jurian trade."

He realized with astonishment that she really had been listening. And what was even more amazing, apparently she had understood.

Overnight the *Falcon* sailed into the heart of the storm, and by morning rain was lashing the ship's decks. The Prince borrowed rain gear from an accommodating Commander Nelson and went up on deck to get some air. As he was returning down the narrow staircase that led to the deck of his stateroom, he found Charity sitting on the stairs, just far enough down to shelter her from the rain.

"Good heavens," he said in surprise, stopping a few steps above her. "What are you doing here?"

She stood up and turned to face him. "I was trying to get a little air. My room is so stuffy. It's almost as bad as the Regent's Pavilion."

At that he laughed.

"This rain is so boring," she said disconsolately. "I thought I would be able to be out on the deck where I could watch the sea and the sky and perhaps see Gibraltar as we passed through, but all it does is rain and the captain said I could not go up on deck.

"It is very windy up there," he said briskly. "You might get blown overboard."

She hunched her shoulders. "Huh!"

He thought that it was probably not a good idea for her to be wandering unescorted around a naval ship. "Where is your father?"

"Even Papa did not feel very well this morning. He threw up his breakfast."

"Oh." He was just about to suggest that perhaps she ought to return to the safety of her room, when she peeked up at him hopefully and asked, "What are you going to do, Prince?"

He didn't know. The rain was indeed a nuisance, and he felt it would be unfeeling of him to order her back to her small, stuffy room. "Do you play chess?" he asked doubtfully.

She broke into her blinding smile. "I am a stupendous chess player," she informed him. "Do you think there is a set we might use?"

"There's one in my cabin," he said. "Come along."

They spent the rest of the day playing chess. True to her word, Charity was highly skilled at the game, playing with a single-minded intensity that he found enchanting. She hunched over the board, chewing on her hair and shooting him suspicious looks as she scrutinized his most recent move. He looked at her long, curved lashes as she stared at the pieces, muttering to herself, and thought that one day she would be a beautiful woman.

I hope she doesn't grow up too soon, though, he thought as she raised her hand and made a shrewd move with her knight. *She is delightful just the way she is.*

The following day the sky cleared, the sea smoothed, the seasickness victims arose from their beds, and the Prince's opportunities to be alone with Charity were over. The *Falcon* sailed through the sunny Mediterranean, around the heel of Italy and into the Adriatic. There for the first time the vessel turned north, sailing in the direction of the twin jewels of the Adriatic: Venice and Seista.

It was a brilliantly sunny and hot July day when the *Falcon* sailed into the Gulf of Seista. The Prince stood alone on deck and looked past the long waterfront to the narrow streets behind that sloped upward to San Giovanni Hill, upon which were perched the three great landmarks of Seista's history: the ruins of a Roman basilica; a colossal medieval fortress; and the splendid Renaissance Cathedral of San Giovanni.

The Prince felt the warm sun on his bare head as he looked from the ships tied up in the port—which had a history dating back to ancient Roman times— to the dominating height of San Giovanni Hill, and he felt a weight lift from his chest.

He was home.

Part Two

JURA
1815

9

Julia, the capital city of Jura, was situated on the Mira River some fifty miles inland from Seista. It had been founded and named by Augustus Caesar in 34 B.C., and part of the wall the Romans had built to enclose the city could still be seen. Seista was strongly Italian in its architecture and landscape, but the capital showed the influence of the many races that made up Jura's population. Only the Turkish influence, so obvious in most of the cities of eastern Europe, was absent from Julia. The armies of Suleiman the Magnificent had subdued Hungary, and even reached the gates of Vienna in 1529, but the Ottomans had never been able to cross the Kava, the river that separated Austria from Jura. Jura had held the line against the Turks for almost five hundred years, and so while the buildings of Julia showed the influence of Rome, Italy, Germany, Austria, and the Slavic nations, there was no sign of Ottoman influence.

As the coach carrying Charity to the Prince's palace drove along the west side of the Mira, she stared out its window at the sight of the city spread out upon the opposite bank. Against the clear blue sky the Gothic spires of the Cathedral of Saint Peter rose majestically above the palaces, churches, and homes of the Jurian capital.

"That is the cathedral where Augustus will be married," Princess Caterina, who was sharing the chaise with Charity, informed her.

"It looks very beautiful," Charity murmured without turning around.

She kept her eyes glued to the city as the coach rolled past the substantial stone bridge that connected the west bank with Julia. The Prince's residence, called simply the Pfalz, or Palace, because his grandfather had not been able to decide upon a name he liked, lay several miles to the south of the city limits. As the last houses of Julia disappeared from view, Charity turned her eyes to the waters of the blue-gray Mira as it flowed peacefully under the summer sky.

I'm here, she said to herself in wonder. *I'm actually here. This is Jura. That river is the Mira. Soon we will be at the Pfalz.* Her excitement was so tangible it felt like a bubble inside her chest; she had to breathe carefully to keep it from exploding.

At last they reached the bridge that serviced the palace, and the coach turned onto the stone roadway and crossed the slowly moving water of the river. As they drove eastward, Charity looked at the gently rolling countryside and longed to be able to put her head out the window to get a better view. When finally the coach passed through a beautiful wrought iron gate, she could contain herself no longer, rolled the window all the way down and poked her head out so she could see the palace as they approached.

Princess Caterina said, "Put that window up."

Charity pretended she had not heard.

"My father had the Pfalz built," Princess Mariana had told her granddaughter many times. "He engaged the same two architects who built Schönbrunn for the Empress Maria Theresa. It is not as large as Schönbrunn, of course—our palace has one hundred and twenty-six rooms whereas Schönbrunn has well over a thousand—but the architecture is very similar."

Charity had never seen Schönbrunn, but the view in front of her now was all she had hoped for. A golden-hued Baroque palace fronted by fountains lay at the end of the wide, graveled drive. The Pfalz was indeed built like Schönbrunn, with a central section flanked by two wings that curved away from it to form the shape of a U. In the middle of the front section a splendid double fan-shaped stairway led to a balcony that gave access to the main door of the palace. The balcony was supported on paired columns, which formed a ground-level colonnade along both sides of the main section. The pediment was decorated with statues and trophies, as was the balustrade.

Charity was able to take all this in before a hand grabbed her dress and pulled her back into the carriage. "You act like a servant girl," Princess Caterina scolded. Charity was beginning an apology when the princess suddenly gasped in horror.

"The statues!" she cried. "Where are the statues?" She was staring out the window Charity had vacated, at the fountain they were passing. Charity turned back to the window to look.

The central statue of the fountain, a huge magnificent sculpture of Poseidon, was intact, but it appeared that the smaller statues that should be surrounding the god were missing. All that could be seen was bare piping.

"Barbarians!" the princess cried in outrage. "They robbed the fountain. Augustus must find out who took the statues and get them back."

She continued indignantly in this vein as the carriage rolled to a halt at the front door of the Pfalz, where the Prince and Lord Beaufort, who had traveled in another carriage, awaited them.

A liveried footman hurried to set the carriage steps, and another opened the door. As the princess was helped down she directed a stream of excited Italian at her son concerning the lost statues.

"I didn't tell you about the theft because I hoped I would be able to recover the statues before you saw the fountain, Mama," the Prince replied in the same language. "Napoleon's marshal, who lived in the Pfalz during the occupation, took them—and a number of other things as well. But King Louis is sympathetic and I think we will get them back."

This reassurance calmed the princess a little, although she continued to mutter unflattering epithets about the French under her breath as they mounted the beautiful fan staircase to the second, and main, floor of the Pfalz.

Charity's eyes enlarged noticeably as she passed through the immense glass door into a huge room, whose ceiling was so high that it included the floor above. This immense domed ceiling was decorated by a large painting of Apollo on the Chariot of the Sun. Gilded statues representing the Four Seasons stood in the four corners of the room, and the white walls with their elaborate gilt moldings were hung with tapestries. Three huge windows, which were topped by three more windows set below the ceiling, looked out upon the gardens and the park. This room, the princess informed Charity and her father, was called the Banqueting Room and was used by the royal family for state dinners and receptions.

"This room and the Music Room next door take up the entire central part of the house," she continued. "Your chambers are in the east wing. I will have someone show you to them as I'm sure you must be weary from the journey."

Charity didn't feel at all weary, but politeness dictated that she allow herself to be escorted to her bedroom, where she was to "tidy up and rest." She trudged dutifully along behind a white-wigged servant, who took her down a long passageway to her bedroom. As the door closed behind the servant, Charity looked around the pretty white-paneled room where she had been deposited. The fireplace was green marble and the hangings on the four-poster were of green silk. The pictures on the wall attracted her attention, as they were all mountain views of the Jurian Alps.

The room's single window was very large, taking up almost an entire wall. Charity looked out and was delighted to find she had a view of the garden and the park. The garden was composed of magnificent ornamental flowerbeds crossed by wide avenues laid out in geometrical shapes. Behind the garden, the woods of the park stretched as far as the eye could see.

As Charity stood there gazing out, a figure dressed in riding clothes emerged from the palace and ran lightly down the terrace steps to the pathway parallel to the house. It was the Prince.

Without stopping to think, Charity whirled around and dashed out of her room to follow him.

"Where are the stables and how do I get there?" she demanded of the startled lackey she met at the end of the passageway.

He gave her directions and she raced down an elegant carved staircase to the ground floor, which was taken up by the largest room in the Pfalz. This immense chamber lay below the Banqueting Room and the Music Room and was divided into three sections by pilasters. Green-and-gold plasterwork embellished every wall, the floor was marble, and the ceiling was decorated by frescoes.

Charity did not notice any of this, however. She hurried to an immense glass door on the back wall, opened it, and exited onto the terrace. The south facade of the house facing the park was similar to the main one. The central section featured pilasters that framed eleven large windows, topped by a balustrade.

Charity followed the path the Prince had taken,

which led her along the length of the Pfalz's east wing and down a gently sloping hill, at the bottom of which lay a group of buildings that the lackey had informed Charity were the stables.

She had been horribly disappointed when they had not stopped at Lipizza on the way from Seista to Julia, but the Prince had told her that he had most of the trained Lipizzaners in his own stable at the Pfalz, and she was determined to see them as soon as she could. It was not until she walked into the stable-yard, hatless and gloveless in her wrinkled travel dress, and encountered the amazed stares of a variety of grooms, that she began to think that perhaps she had been a little precipitate.

Charity gave the closest groom a friendly smile and announced herself as Lady Charity Debritt in search of Prince Augustus. Before the groom could reply, the Prince himself walked out of the stable building, which was of the same golden hue as the palace. He was accompanied by a slender, gray-haired man, also dressed in riding clothes, and it was this man who first noticed Charity. He said something to the Prince, whose head swung around sharply in her direction. He stopped walking and continued to look at her.

I shouldn't have come, Charity thought in dismay. Slowly she crossed the yard until she was standing in front of him. "I saw you leave the house in riding clothes and I followed you," she confessed, bravely looking up into his face. "If I am in your way, I'll go back."

The faint frown that had marked his brows lifted,

and his gray eyes glinted with sudden amusement. "Don't tell me. You want to see the Lipizzaners."

His amusement lifted Charity's spirit and she smiled back. "I desperately want to see them. Are you going to ride one of them, Prince?"

"I might."

Charity's eyes sparkled with indignation at this terse reply. She said testily, "Nothing is more annoying than people who won't give one a direct answer."

His amusement deepened and he said, "Lady Charity, may I present my new *écuyer*, Lord Louis Hunersdorf, the esteemed author of *Guidelines to the Training of Horses in the Most Natural and Best Manner.*"

To the obvious astonishment of both men, Charity replied enthusiastically, "I have read your wonderful book, Lord Louis. I thought your instructions on how to achieve lightness of the forehand were particularly illuminating."

"You have read my book, Lady Charity?" the Horse Master repeated in wonder. "But I thought you were English!"

"Apparently not all the English are as unenlightened about horsemanship as we have supposed, Louis," the Prince said with a smile.

"Most of them are," Charity replied frankly. "We have no manège riding in England outside the circus, which is why I have been so anxious to see the Lipizzaners."

"I regret that His Highness's horses are not at the level we would like," the *écuyer* said regretfully. "They spent most of the war years turned out on pasture in Hungary, and it will take more than the six months we have had them back to return them to where they were before the evacuation."

"I am planning to stage a mounted carousel as one of the entertainments for the wedding," the Prince explained. "Lord Louis is going to put together a series of quadrilles that the horses can manage."

Charity clapped her hands. "How marvelous. I can hardly wait to see it."

The Prince said briskly, "Well, we'll start by showing you the stable, then the manège, and perhaps I will have enough time to ride Schani for you."

She clapped her hands again. "Who is Schani?"

"He is my own horse. I got him when I was fifteen and he was five. He's seventeen now and his joints are just as springy as they were when he was young. We have always been the best of friends."

Charity had one of the most wonderful afternoons of her life as she accompanied the Prince and his *écuyer* around the stables. The Lipizzaners were housed in a big airy stable, with large individual stalls deeply bedded with fresh straw and dutch doors that opened into individual paddocks. The manège, or indoor riding arena, was a three-story building that resembled a Greek temple, with an open riding ring inside surrounded by a gallery for viewers. This is where Charity sat watching while the Prince rode his pure white Lipizzaner under the instruction of Lord Louis.

For as long as she could remember, Charity had wanted to ride the way the Prince was riding now. She had not been able to do so for two reasons:

There was no one in England with the knowledge to teach her, and it was impossible to ride in the classical manner in a sidesaddle. When her grandmother had been a girl in Jura, she had been taught to ride astride in the correct fashion, and Charity had always secretly dreamed that one day she would go to Jura and learn to ride that way too.

Watching the elegance of the Prince on his white stallion, how much in harmony they were, more like a single creature than two separate beings, the light airiness of the stallion's *passage* seeming to be performed on his own rather than at the command of his rider, tears stung Charity's eyes. She did not think she had ever been so happy.

The Prince's return home was marked by one distinctly unharmonious note. When he returned to the palace after a delightful afternoon at the stables with Louis and Charity, he was informed that his uncle, Duke Marko, had arrived at the Pfalz and desired to speak with him.

The Prince was in his bedroom about to change out of his riding clothes when his secretary, Lord Stefan Weyr, brought him the news. Lord Stefan was a year younger than the Prince and had been one of his comrades during the war years. He was much more than the Prince's secretary; he was one of his closest friends.

The Prince looked now at the sympathetic expression on the round, cherubic face of Lord Stefan and sighed. "I suppose I shall have to see him."

"You don't have to see him immediately," Lord Stefan pointed out. "I can put him off if you want."

The Prince ran his fingers through his hair, dislodging one wavy blond lock so it fell forward over his forehead. He said gloomily, "It might as well be now. Get it over with."

"That's what I think," Lord Stefan agreed.

"All right. Bring him along to my study."

Lord Stefan nodded and left the room.

The Prince signaled to his valet to hand him his jacket, which he put on without assistance. Before he left the vast elegance of his bedchamber to go next door to his study, his valet made certain that his hair was in order once again.

The Prince's grandfather had cherished display and elegance, and the palace he had built reflected this love. On the other hand, the Prince's father had been a man of simple tastes and abstemious habits, and his study, which the Prince had inherited, was an unpretentious room with dark green walls and dark green velvet draperies at the windows. A portrait of the Prince's Hungarian grandmother hanging on the wall over the fireplace was the only decoration. The room was very much as his father had left it, as it contained very little to tempt the light fingers of Napoleon's marshal.

The study looked like the room of a man who worked at his job, and the Prince's father had certainly worked at his, spending hours each day at his desk laboring at the administration of his country. It was largely due to Prince Ivan's enlightened leadership that Jura had been so prosperous before the war.

By the end of the previous century, the country had established a vigorous economic life based on the exploitation of local mineral and agricultural resources. The nation had boasted a sufficient degree of autonomy to sustain a self-reliant middle class as well as the traditional hereditary nobility.

The French occupation had broken Prince Ivan's heart, and he had lived out the rest of his life in England, a shadow of his former self. No enemy forces had occupied Jura since Attila the Hun in the fifth century, and Prince Ivan was convinced that he had failed in his trust.

The Prince thought of his father as he stood by the green-draped window of his study awaiting the entrance of the late ruler's younger brother. In most ways, Ivan and Marko had been as different as two brothers could possibly be. Whereas Ivan's tastes had been simple, Marko loved ceremony and extravagance; whereas Ivan had been a devoted family man, Marko was a notorious rake; whereas Ivan had been noted for his brain, Marko was famous for his charm.

Augustus had always liked his uncle Marko without quite trusting him. So when the tall, still-slim duke came into the room and held out his arms, the Prince went willingly to receive his embrace.

"Gus!" Duke Marko said. "How wonderful to see you after all these years. You have grown so tall! You must have at least three inches on me."

The Prince stepped back and looked down into his uncle's eyes—eyes that were only slightly less blue than his son Franz's. "You look just the same, Uncle

Marko," he said. "The years have scarcely touched you at all."

"Look closely, my boy," Marko said jovially. "My hair is gray now, not blond."

"A bagatelle," the Prince said with a smile. He gestured to the gold velvet sofa. "Come and sit down. May I offer you something to drink?"

"No thank you, Gus." As the two men seated themselves, Marko said in a more sober tone, "I imagine you know why I am here."

The Prince stretched his long legs in front of him and turned his head toward his uncle. "You don't like the treaty with England."

"I don't like the treaty with England," Marko agreed. "In fact, I think it is folly, Gus, and I am very angry that you did not consult with me before you signed it."

The Prince's mild expression did not change. "I did not know that I had to consult with anyone," he replied. "I was of the understanding that I had the power to make such decisions on my own."

Marko's long, thin nose, an inheritance from his Hungarian mother, quivered. "You have the power, certainly. The question is, do you have the judgment?"

The Prince's right hand had been lying relaxed on his thigh, and now his index finger tapped once against the tight fawn-colored fabric of his riding breeches. "I believe I do," he replied.

"Do you realize how angry you have made the emperor by this treaty?" Marko demanded.

"I believe I do." The Prince's voice was still mild but his finger tapped once again.

"You can't," Marko snapped. "If you did you would never have signed it. Giving England access to Seista is a direct slap in the face to Austria, Gus!"

"I was not aware that part of my duty as Prince of Jura was to please Austria. In case you have forgot, Uncle, Jura is an independent nation and as its ruler I have the right to make whatever alliances I choose."

Marko's handsome face flushed with anger. "Not without consultation!"

The Prince stilled his tapping finger. "I did consult my advisors, and they all agreed that the English treaty was a good idea."

"You did not consult your advisors," the duke rejoined. "Hindenberg and Rupnik are as opposed to this treaty as I am."

A little silence fell as the Prince looked steadily into his uncle's angry face. Then he said slowly, "Perhaps you did not understand me. I consulted *my* advisors, Uncle—not my father's."

Duke Marko's head snapped back as if he had just received a blow. He scowled. "And just who *are* these advisors, Gus?"

"I discussed the treaty with Count Viktor Rozman, Lord Stefan Weyr, and Lord Emil Sauder."

The duke looked thunderstruck. "You can't be serious. There is not a one of them that is any older than you are! What can they possibly know about diplomacy?"

The Prince got to his feet and walked to the window, where he stood looking out for a moment, his back to Duke Marko. Then he turned and answered his uncle's question. "They are men who remained in Jura during the French occupation and fought for the independence of their country," he said. "They know how to value that independence in a way that others perhaps do not. I do not think I could find better advisors anywhere."

Now Marko got to his feet. "You and your compatriots were cut off from the world for ten years, Gus," he said, making a visible effort to control his temper. "I would never belittle your efforts to free Jura, but it is essential that you widen your horizons if you wish to lead our country in the coming years. We can no longer afford to dwell in the past. Austria is not our enemy, Gus, but it will be if you turn Seista over to England."

The Prince's firm mouth set hard. "I am not turning Seista over to England. I am opening up trade with England and giving the English navy the right to use Seista as a port. There is no direct threat to Austria in either of these actions."

"Damn it, Gus!" Marko shouted. "You know that there is! That port is of far more value to Austria than it will ever be to England. It is perfectly placed for a trade route from Vienna."

"Perhaps you have lived in Austria for too long, Uncle Marko," the Prince said. "You appear to have Austrian interests more deeply at heart than you do Jurian interests."

"They are the same! That is what I must make you understand, Gus. It is in Jura's best interest to remain friends with a great empire that lies not only to its north, but across the Adriatic as well, now that Austria has been given northern Italy."

"Jura has maintained its independence for over eight hundred years, Uncle," the Prince said, his voice hardening. "Let me make this clear. As long as I am the prince, I will never allow Jura to become a satellite of the Austrian Empire."

Gray eyes stared into blue.

"All right," Marko said grimly. "You have made yourself very clear, Gus."

"Good." The Prince's voice softened. "I hope you are planning to stay for dinner."

"That is kind of you, Gus, but they are expecting me back at my palace in Julia for dinner."

The Prince nodded.

Duke Marko made a stiff bow. "I am sorry you do not agree with me, Gus. I have had far more experience of the world than you and I believe my advice has some value."

"I will always value your advice, Uncle," the Prince replied. "But upon this particular subject I am afraid we must agree to disagree."

The duke gave one more stiff bow, turned, and walked out of the room.

10

$\mathcal{L}$ ydia arrived in Jura exactly three weeks to the day after Charity and the Prince. The Baroque splendor of the Pfalz was far more impressive than she had expected, and she was standing between her mother and Franz, surveying with approval the lofty magnificence of the Banqueting Room, when the Prince arrived to welcome her. He was followed almost immediately by Lord Beaufort and Charity. Harry, her father explained, was not at the Pfalz at present, having gone on a visit to the countryside.

After the initial greetings, the Prince courteously asked Lydia about her voyage.

"It was very pleasant," she replied truthfully. "The weather was excellent, the sea was calm, and Captain Edwards was most attentive to all our needs." She bestowed a gracious smile upon her fiancé. "I hope your voyage was as enjoyable, Prince."

He did not return her smile but replied gravely, "I

am afraid that we were not as fortunate as you, Lady Lydia. The sea was quite rough for a while, and a number of people were ill."

"Even I was ill," Lord Beaufort said humorously, "and I am accounted a good sailor."

Franz said, "I'll wager that you weren't sick, Gus."

A glint of amusement showed in the Prince's gray eyes. "For a while there, Lady Charity and I were the only two left standing."

Lydia glanced at the small figure of her sister, who was standing between the Prince and Lord Beaufort. Charity's cheeks had a peach-colored glow that could only have come from being out in the sun without a hat. Her hair was tied at the nape of her neck with a ribbon and hung in a single thick braid halfway down her back. She looked about fourteen.

It's a good thing that Mama has come, Lydia thought. *Charity has probably been running wild with only Papa to look after her.*

Franz was speaking to the Prince. "I will never forget the time when we were youngsters and our parents packed us off to Venice to stay with your grandparents." He looked at Lydia and Lady Beaufort. "A sudden storm came up and everyone on board—including the crew—was sick. But not you. Every time I straightened away from the rail after puking up my guts and saw you standing there with not the slightest tinge of green to your complexion, I hated you."

Lady Beaufort frowned in disapproval of the vulgar reference to puking and guts.

The Prince's amusement increased. "You were certainly a pathetic sight," he agreed.

They all stood talking for a few more moments, and then the Prince called for servants to escort the new arrivals to their bedchambers. As Lydia prepared to depart, he touched her arm lightly and said, "If you wouldn't mind, Lady Lydia, perhaps you and I might have a private talk after you have refreshed yourself."

"Certainly, Prince," Lydia replied, her regally calm exterior not quite in tune with the sudden tightening she felt in her stomach.

He nodded gravely. "I will send someone to direct you—in half an hour?"

Lydia, who had every intention of bathing and completely changing her clothing as well as redoing her hair, stared at him as if he were mad. "Let us make it an hour and a half," she said.

He looked completely nonplussed at this reply.

He is accustomed to being obeyed, Lydia thought. *Well, he will have to learn that he can't issue orders to me.* She lifted her chin and gave him a haughty green stare.

"It takes Lydia quite a long time to do her *toilette,* Prince," Charity explained.

There was a pause. Then he said expressionlessly, "I see. Well then, let us say an hour and a half."

Lydia rewarded him with a smile, which once again he did not return. Then she turned away to accompany her mother and Franz out of the Banqueting Room.

"This is only a temporary accommodation for you, Lydia," Lady Beaufort assured her daughter as they followed a bewigged lackey out of the Pfalz's

main section and into the east wing where the guest
rooms were located. "Once you are married, you will
have the Princess's Apartment, of course."

Lydia did not reply, and the lackey opened a bedroom door and informed Lady Beaufort that her
maid would be with her immediately. As the door
closed behind her mother, Lydia and Franz continued down the passageway together.

"Where is the Princess's Apartment?" she asked
him a little breathlessly.

"In the other wing, next to Gus's rooms," he
replied.

"Oh," Lydia said.

They walked a few more steps in silence, then
Franz said in a voice that sounded strangely harsh.
"This is reality, my dear. Gus is not some imaginary
prince out of the *Arabian Nights*. He is a man, and
you are marrying him."

Abruptly Lydia felt as if all of the air was being
squeezed out of her lungs. Then the lackey opened
another door and bowed her inside.

"Will I see you later?" she asked Franz with suppressed urgency.

"We will meet at dinner," he replied, his face
wearing an unusually angry look.

The room Lydia had been assigned was furnished
in the style of Louis XIV and was far more elegant
than her quarters at home. She was standing in front
of the gilt-framed pier glass, looking at her reflection, when her maid came in, followed by several
footmen carrying her baggage.

"I have an appointment with the Prince in an hour

and a half, Agnes," she said to her maid. "Will you send for a bath?"

Precisely an hour and twenty minutes later, Lydia sat in one of the gilt chairs that was placed in front of her bedroom's marble fireplace, hands folded in her lap, awaiting the Prince's summons. Finally a knock sounded on the door and another white-wigged lackey announced that he had been sent to escort her to His Royal Highness.

As she passed through the magnificent Music and Banqueting Rooms that took up the entire central section of the Pfalz, Lydia kept thinking: *I will be a princess. This magnificent palace will be my home. People will address me as Your Royal Highness. I will be the envy of all my friends.*

But these heretofore magic words did not have their usual effect. As she followed the lackey into the west wing of the palace it occurred to her that during the course of their brief engagement, she had never been alone with the Prince for more than a few minutes.

He had never even tried to kiss her.

I'm nervous because I have not had an opportunity to get to know him, she reassured herself. *I'm glad we are going to have this opportunity to talk in private.*

The lackey stopped before an open door and turned to her. "The Walnut Room, my lady," he announced.

"Thank you," Lydia replied and stepped over the threshold with every appearance of calm assurance.

He was standing at the window, looking out, but

when the lackey announced her name he turned and crossed the floor to stand in front of her. "Prince," she said, bestowing upon him her most charming smile. She held out her hand and he lifted it briefly to his lips. His mouth felt cool and impersonal on her bare fingers. Then he gestured to a wood-trimmed tapestry sofa and asked her to be seated.

Lydia looked from the walnut wood walls to the walnut furniture and said gaily as she took the indicated seat, "I can see how this room earned its name, Your Highness."

He nodded and seated himself beside her on the sofa. "I thought it was important that I go over with you the plans I have made for our wedding," he said.

He could at least smile, Lydia thought resentfully. Her face outwardly serene, she folded her hands in her lap and listened as he began to describe to her the extensive festivities that would attend their wedding. Finally he got to the wedding ceremony itself.

"The archbishop will marry us in the cathedral. You will be driven there in a coach, and I expect the streets to be packed. My people are most eager to see you."

She pictured the scene—herself in her gorgeous bridal gown, the adulation of the cheering crowds— and brightened.

He was going on: "Your sister will be one of your bridesmaids, of course, as well as several of my Venetian cousins."

A sudden cloud descended over the delightful picture in Lydia's mind. No one she knew would be there to view her conquest. Strangers were to be her bridesmaids, not the girls from home who would have been green with envy at the sight of her triumph.

He was still talking, and she made an effort to focus her attention. "How aware are you of the political implications of our marriage?" she heard him ask.

Lydia anxiously searched her mind. "Doesn't it have something to do with the English navy being able to use Seista as a port?" His gray eyes were trained on her face, but she was finding it surprisingly difficult to meet them.

"That is part of it," he replied. "But it is Jura's relationship with Austria to which I was referring."

"Oh," Lydia said cautiously, and saw a faint look of impatience cross his face.

He said in a clipped voice, "The reason I chose an English bride was to cement the treaty I made with Great Britain."

"Of course," Lydia said with dignity. However, when he continued to go on speaking about alliances and politics, indignation began to rise in her heart.

We are going to be married, she thought. *I don't know him and I am going to have to sleep with him, and all he can talk about to me is politics!*

Eventually, he finished and looked at her as if waiting for an answer. She decided to assert herself a little. "The wedding plans sound very nice, Prince, but I must confess I would have liked it better if you had consulted me. It is my wedding too, after all."

He continued to regard her for a long silent moment. She noticed that his right index finger had begun to tap slowly on the arm of the sofa. He said, "If you had accompanied me to Jura three weeks ago, as I requested, I certainly would have consulted you, my lady. You were not here, however, and I thought that I had made it quite clear that I wished to be married before the end of the summer."

Lydia looked into her future husband's cold gray eyes and thought defiantly, *I will not let him intimidate me.* She lifted her chin and said in a voice that was every bit as cool as his, "If you had given me more than two days' notice, perhaps I would have accompanied you, Prince. It was unreasonable of you to expect me to drop my own plans and leave for Jura in so short a time."

His finger continued its tapping on the sofa arm. His face was perfectly expressionless. "I expected nothing, my lady," he said. "I merely offered you the opportunity to accompany me. Since you did not avail yourself of it, however, I do not see that you have the right to complain that you were not consulted about the wedding plans."

Spots of color stained the porcelain skin over Lydia's high cheekbones. She was a breathtakingly beautiful woman and not accustomed to being looked at as if she was a soldier who had failed in her duty. *What is the matter with him?* she thought.

Taking a deep breath to calm her nerves, Lydia once more tried her most charming smile. "Since we are to be married, I think it would be proper for you to address me as Lydia."

His finger stopped tapping and his expression turned from cold to mystified. She leaned toward him a little, so he would be sure to catch the scent of her perfume, and looked up through her long dark lashes. It was a trick that had melted the hearts of dozens of men.

The Prince, however, made no motion to draw closer to her or to draw her to him. "Thank you," he said. "And you must call me Augustus."

Lydia's lashes lifted and she stared at him. *He is really very handsome,* she told herself. *That cleft in his chin is extremely attractive.* She said in her most seductive voice, "Franz calls you Gus."

He was regarding her as if she were a puzzle he couldn't quite decipher. "You may call me Gus as well if you like."

Her lashes fluttered and she replied softly, "I think I would like that very much."

He glanced at the clock on the mantel. Lydia couldn't believe her eyes. She was practically sitting in his lap, and he looked at the clock!

How could she possibly marry such a cold-blooded man?

He was getting to his feet and making some comment about an appointment he had to keep. He put his hand out to help her up, then, when she was standing beside him, he bent to kiss her cheek. "I hope you will be happy here in Jura, Lydia," he said.

"Thank you," she replied stiffly.

A lackey came in to escort her back to her room.

At dinner that evening, Lydia saw the Prince's smile for the first time. It came in response to something that Charity had said, and the boyish grin he gave her in response made him look younger and more approachable than Lydia had ever seen him before.

There were six of them seated at the table in the private dining room that was situated in the Prince's wing of the palace: the Prince and Franz and the five Debritts. In the absence of Princess Caterina, who was visiting the same friends in the country as Harry, Lady Beaufort took the chatelaine's seat opposite the Prince. Lydia and Charity were on either side of him, and Franz and Lord Beaufort sat on either side of the countess.

The deep red and gold china on the table was Meissen, the floor of the room a richly decorated parquet. On one of the white walls decorated with rococo molding hung a large, gilt-framed painting of the Jurian Alps.

Conversation was general during the first course, but as the soup was removed and the fish course served, Lord and Lady Beaufort began to speak together about some problem on one of the Beaufort estates. Franz said to the Prince, "I imagine this food is a trifle more palatable than the fare you got in the mountains, Gus."

The Prince looked amused. "You imagine correctly."

"What kind of food did you eat?" Lydia asked. She did not quite dare to call him Gus.

"When we were lucky, goat meat roasted over a fire," he replied.

Lydia shuddered delicately.

"What does goat taste like, Prince?" Charity asked.

"Tough," he replied, turning to look at her.

She made a reply that Lydia could not hear, and that was when the Prince smiled.

Then Franz claimed Lydia's attention, asking if she had had a chance to view the gardens yet, and she turned away from the Prince to answer him. Throughout the time that the fish course was served, eaten, and removed, Lord and Lady Beaufort spoke together, Lydia and Franz spoke together, and Charity and the Prince conversed.

What on earth could her sister be talking to the Prince about in such an animated fashion? Lydia wondered as she half listened to an amusing story Franz was telling her. The stern look she was accustomed to seeing on the Prince's face was quite gone as he spoke to Charity.

Lydia strained to hear and caught the words, ". . . I got quite a good shoulder-in today. Lord Louis said it was very correct."

A faint line dented Lydia's perfect brow. What on earth were they talking about?

The Prince said, "Louis told me today that you are one of the best students he has ever had."

Students? Lydia thought in bewilderment.

He was saying, "If you continue to improve, perhaps I will let you ride Schani."

Good heavens, they were talking about horses!

Well if that is the only topic of conversation that can make him smile, then I suppose he will never smile at me, she thought resentfully. Lydia had never shared Charity's devotion to the equine species.

Conversation became more general as the meat course was served, and it remained that way all through dessert. The Pfalz household had always followed the European tradition of ladies and gentlemen leaving the table at the same time, so after dessert the entire party retired to a salon that was painted in a deep, rich red. Portraits of the Prince's ancestors decorated the walls, a single crystal chandelier hung from the white ceiling, and gilt chairs with red upholstery were gathered around several occasional tables.

"Would anyone like to play a game of hearts?" Lord Beaufort said genially.

"That sounds very pleasant," Lady Beaufort replied.

"Prince?" Lord Beaufort asked.

"I would enjoy a game of hearts," the Prince replied.

Lord Beaufort's eyes fell on his eldest daughter. "Oh," he said. "You don't play, do you, my dear?"

"No, Papa, I do not," she replied.

Lord Beaufort looked to Franz. "The count will take you for a walk in the garden, won't you, Count? You will enjoy that much more than being stuck inside on such a fine night, Lydia."

"I will be delighted to take Lady Lydia for a walk in the gardens," Franz said softly.

For some reason, Lydia found herself flushing.

A brief silence fell as the Prince and Lord Beaufort looked at each other. Then the Prince said pleasantly, "I am certain you will wish to play with your spouse, Lord Beaufort."

A resigned look slowly spread over the earl's face.

"Of course." He gestured his wife toward the square gilt table in the corner of the room. "My dear?"

As the older couple walked away, the four young people remained together for a moment. The Prince said to Charity in a lowered voice, "Is your mother a better player than my mother?"

"No," Charity said.

"Ah," said the Prince. And smiled.

That is two smiles she has got out of him, Lydia thought resentfully.

Franz said with amusement, "Do I deduce from these maneuvers that Lady Charity is a good card player, Gus?"

"She's wicked," the Prince replied.

Lydia said in an arctic tone, "I gather you have played cards together before."

"We've been playing almost every night," Charity said. She grinned. "It was Papa's turn to get me as a partner, Prince. You were unfair."

"I simply did not wish to divide a couple so newly reunited," he returned blandly.

Franz chuckled. "You are very young to be so accomplished at cards, Lady Charity. How did you learn to play?"

"My brother once had a tutor who was a great card player and he taught me," Charity said. "The winter that Harry was laid up with a broken leg, we played all the time."

"What tutor was that?" Lydia said with a frown.

"Mr. O'Neill."

Lydia's frown deepened. "The young man with the limp?"

Charity nodded.

Finally the Prince remembered his fiancée. "I think you will find the Pfalz gardens lovely, La—ah, Lydia. They were modeled after the gardens at Versailles."

He wants to play cards and he's happy to be rid of me, Lydia thought with a mixture of anger and bewilderment.

In all her life, no man had ever been anxious to be rid of her. And this was the man she was going to marry!

She turned to Franz and was comforted by what she saw in his eyes.

At least Franz is not indifferent to me, she thought. *And he is much more handsome than the Prince.*

She smiled into Franz's blue eyes, rested her hand on his arm, and allowed him to lead her out into the moonlit gardens.

11

The wedding of the Prince of Jura was scheduled to take place during the third week in August, and the elaborate preparations for this joyous event occupied the Prince during those times when he was not tending to the business of the country. Charity usually saw him only at dinner and on the occasions when he visited the stables to see how the carousel was progressing.

Even after Lady Beaufort's arrival, Charity managed to spend a great deal of time in the stables. To her great relief, her mother proved to be too occupied with wedding plans to pay much attention to her younger daughter. She knew that Charity was taking riding lessons from the Prince's *écuyer*, but she did not know that "learning to ride in the classical way" meant that Charity was also learning to ride astride. Charity shuddered to think what Lady Beaufort would do if she ever caught her daughter in breeches and high boots, so she was very careful never to allow her mother to see her in such garb.

There is nothing wrong with what I am doing, she told herself every morning as she walked down to the stable correctly clad in a long riding skirt. *If Mama objects I will show her the picture of Marie Antoinette that hangs in the Music Room.* The painting in question portrayed the murdered queen as a young girl riding a horse in the manège in Vienna, dressed in breeches and riding astride.

How can it be indecent when the daughter of the empress of Austria rode in such a fashion? Charity told herself righteously as she changed her skirt for breeches in the small dressing room tucked into a corner of the riding hall.

Several weeks passed in this pleasant manner. Then one morning, exactly a week before the wedding, Charity went for an early ride around the park with Lord Louis and returned to the palace at about ten o'clock. As soon as she walked in the door she knew that something was wrong. The air was almost vibrating with tension.

Mama has found out about the breeches, was her first apprehensive thought. However, this particular fear was alleviated by the fact that all of the servants she encountered as she walked to the indoor staircase were visibly distressed. The Prince's servants, she rationalized, were unlikely to be perturbed by a spat between Lady Beaufort and her daughter.

As Charity reached the main floor, she saw Lord Stefan Weyr, the Prince's secretary, and Lord Emil Sauder, another of the Prince's friends from his wartime days, walking together across the Banqueting Room deep in worried conversation. Without noticing her, they passed into the west wing, which contained the royal family's private apartments.

She had paused when she caught sight of Lord Stefan and Lord Emil, and now she heard someone running up the steps behind her. She spun around and saw Count Viktor Rozman, another of the Prince's friends. He nodded to her as he passed, his usually good-natured face looking extremely grim. He too went directly into the west wing.

What in the world can be happening? Charity wondered in alarm.

She had reached the wide rococo arch that led into the west wing when she literally bumped into her brother. "Charity!" Harry said, grabbing her by the shoulders to keep her from falling. "I was just on my way to the stables to find you."

Oh my God. Mama really has found out, Charity thought.

Before she could say a word, however, Harry rushed on. "The most dreadful thing has happened. Lydia has eloped with Franz!"

Charity felt herself freeze into utter stillness. She stared into Harry's face, hoping to find something there that would tell her he was joking. There was nothing. She said feebly, "Are you joking me, Harry?"

"This is hardly something one would joke about," Harry replied indignantly. "She and Franz left the Pfalz together shortly after midnight to drive to Vienna, where they intend to be married. Lydia's maid found her room unoccupied this morning. Our darling sister was kind enough to leave a note for Mama explaining everything."

"How could Lydia do such a thing?" Charity said in bewilderment. "She was supposed to marry the Prince!"

Harry ran his fingers through his already disordered black hair. "Do you think we don't know that? Lydia wrote to Mama that she was in love with Franz and did not want to marry the Prince. Did you ever hear of anything more outrageous? She jilted a prince one week before their wedding!"

Charity's shock was slowly turning into anger. "This is dreadful," she said. "He will have to call off the wedding—and so many plans have been made!" She glared up at her brother. "How could Lydia do this to him?"

"How could she do it to *us*?" Harry retorted. "Do you know how this makes our family look? I thought Papa was going to have an apoplexy when he heard."

But Charity's sympathy lay with the jilted groom. "Whatever is the Prince going to do? He will be the laughingstock of Europe." Then furiously, "I would like to *kill* Lydia."

"So would we all," Harry replied. His green eyes held a dangerous sparkle.

A servant was coming toward them carrying a silver tray with a covered dish upon it. They watched him pass in silence, then Charity said, "When first you stopped me, I was afraid it was because Mama had found out about my riding astride. Now I wish that was all it was. This . . . this is just too terrible."

Harry nodded in grim agreement. "Papa wants to see you," he said. "That is why I was looking for you."

Charity's eyes widened in surprise. "See me? What does he want to see me about?"

Harry shrugged. "He didn't confide in me, Char. He just sent me to fetch you."

"All right. Where is he?"

"He's waiting in his sitting room."

Charity took a step, then stopped and turned back to her brother. "Is Mama with him?"

"She wasn't when I left him. I think she went to bed with a headache."

"She must be devastated," Charity said somberly.

"She looked awful when I saw her earlier," Harry replied. "She looked old."

As Charity approached the door that led into the sitting room that was attached to Lord Beaufort's bedchamber, two thoughts alternated in her mind: *I can't believe that this has happened,* and *What is the Prince going to do?*

She knocked on the polished wood door and her father called for her to come in.

"Sit down, Charity," he said. The sun shining in the window bathed the pink, blue, and cream Persian rug in a warm glow as Charity crossed it to take a seat upon the pink silk sofa.

She clasped her hands tensely in her lap and said, "Harry told me what happened, Papa. I can't believe that Lydia of all people would do such a thing! She is always so proper."

"Well, she has done it," Lord Beaufort replied

grimly. "And she has left us to deal with the conse-
quences." He sat down beside her on the sofa.

Charity repeated the words she had said to Harry.
"The Prince will be the laughingstock of Europe."
Her fingers tightened their grip on each other. "Is
there any chance of our getting her back, Papa?"

Lord Beaufort shook his head wearily. "I am
afraid not. Too many people know what happened,
and there would be a dreadful scandal."

Charity opened her hands in a gesture of disagreement. "It couldn't be worse than this!"

Once again Lord Beaufort shook his head. "Lydia
was alone with Franz all night, Charity. She is com-
promised. The Prince cannot marry her now."

Charity flopped backward, rested her head against
a sofa cushion, and stared up at the ceiling. "I
thought Franz was supposed to be the Prince's
friend!"

"Lydia wrote to your mother that they were in
love."

Charity's skeptical snort showed clearly enough
what she thought of that excuse.

Picking his words with care, Lord Beaufort said,
"We have been discussing this matter since seven
o'clock, when Lydia's letter was found, and the only
solution we have been able to arrive at is to find the
Prince another bride."

Charity scooted back to an upright position.
"Good heavens, Papa. What woman would marry a
man on a week's notice?"

"Augustus is not just any man," Lord Beaufort
pointed out. "He is a prince."

"True." Charity's face brightened as a thought struck her. "Are there any German princesses available? Such an alliance would help strengthen trade between Jura and the German Confederation, which would be desirable to all parties involved."

Lord Beaufort shook his head. "You see," he said, still speaking carefully, "the Prince is set upon marrying an English girl."

It was Charity's turn to shake her head. "He'll never get an English girl to Jura in time. The wedding is in a week."

Her father's voice became very gentle. "There is an English girl already in Jura, Charity."

Her brow puckered. "There is?"

Then, as he sat there, looking at her in silence, she finally understood.

"Me?" The word came out as a squawk. "Do you mean me, Papa?"

"Yes, my dear. I mean you."

Charity's eyes were so large they seemed to take up half of her small face. "You want *me* to marry the Prince instead of Lydia?"

His head moved slowly up and down in an affirmative gesture. Then he said gravely, "I believe it is the only way possible to salvage this situation. You are Lydia's sister. You have the same blood and the same connections as she did. If you will marry the Prince in Lydia's stead, Charity, I believe we may get out of this horrendous situation your sister has precipitated."

"But Papa," Charity said breathlessly, "I'm too young to be married."

Lord Beaufort shaded his eyes with his hand, as if he found it painful to look at her. "Charity," he said, "believe me, I feel dreadful asking you to do this. If Augustus was not such a splendid young man, I would *not* ask it of you. But the situation is dire. We simply cannot let him face this kind of humiliation." He lowered his hand and looked into his daughter's face. "It is true that you are very young, my dear. But you are far more intelligent than Lydia. I think you would make a wonderful princess for Jura."

Charity pressed her hands against her hot cheeks. "Have you talked to the Prince about this, Papa?"

"Actually, it was the Prince's idea," Lord Beaufort replied.

Charity's lips opened as if to reply, then slowly closed. She stared down at her hands, which were once more clasped tensely in her lap, and for a long moment there was silence in the room. Finally she said in a small voice, "I have always wanted to visit Jura, but I never thought that I would live anywhere but England."

"I know, Charity," Lord Beaufort said. He looked as if he had aged ten years. "And if you feel you cannot do this, I will respect your decision."

She moved her gaze from her hands to the tips of her boots and said nothing. After the silence had gone on for quite a while, Lord Beaufort said encouragingly, "I would expect you to pay frequent visits to England."

At the sound of his voice, Charity drew in a long, shuddering breath. Then, without lifting her eyes from her boot tips, she said gruffly, "All right. I'll do it."

Lord Beaufort's face sagged with relief. He closed his eyes briefly and murmured, "Thank God."

Charity said nothing.

He looked at her bowed brown head and said, "I am proud of you, my dear. You are a credit to your name." He added bitterly, "I am sorry that I cannot say the same of your sister."

Charity nodded, her eyes still on the tips of her boots.

Lord Beaufort frowned. Her demeanor was making him feel acutely uncomfortable. He did not like thinking of himself as the kind of father who would bully his daughter into an unwanted marriage. Without stopping to think, he said, "You don't have to do this if you don't want to."

At last she lifted her head. The large brown eyes that regarded him held an expression he had never seen in them before. "Yes, I do, Papa. We both know that I do."

Lord Beaufort searched his mind for words that would take that look away from her eyes. "Augustus is a fine man, Charity. I feel confident that you will be happy with him."

"Do you, Papa?"

"He admires you. He told me so."

She said with sad wisdom, "I am too young for him."

Lord Beaufort started to say something, then stopped. For a long moment he searched his daughter's face with narrowed eyes. At last he said, "Then

you will have to grow up, my dear. Augustus needs a
woman for a wife, not a child. Age is not a matter of
years, Charity. It is a matter of attitude."

She folded her arms around herself, as if trying to
shield her body. "Yes, Papa."

He could not think of any other encouraging remarks, so he said, "Do you feel that you could see
the Prince, my dear? As you can imagine, he is anxious to speak to you."

"I can see him," she said tonelessly.

"Then I will send him word and he will come to
you."

"All right," Charity said in the same flat voice as
before.

As soon as she heard the door close behind her father, she jumped up and went to stare out the window. This particular window looked out on the front
side of the palace, and Charity's eyes remained fixed
on the water playing in the fountain while her
thoughts flew hundreds of miles and a decade away.

I am going to marry Augustus when I grow up.

She had been seven years old when first she declared that intention to her grandmother. It was a
statement she had repeated many times as she had
listened to her grandmother's exciting stories about
the young prince who had chosen to remain behind
to fight for his country. As she grew out of childhood, she had ceased to talk about marrying Augustus, but she had not stopped dreaming about him. He
represented to her all that was fine and true and honorable, and, when she had met him at last, a tall, slim
young man with steady gray eyes and a cleft in his

chin, she had known all the delight of someone whose dream has come true.

Now she was to marry him, and the thought terrified her.

Even though the warm sun was pouring in the window, she shivered. *I don't know anything about being a princess.* Lydia, with her arrogance and her beauty, could have carried it off, but not Charity. *I am not even officially* out *yet,* she thought in panic. *How can I be expected to fill the role of Augustus's wife?*

It had been fun to dream of a perfect prince, fun to fantasize that he would understand her as her family did not; fun to imagine herself, staunch and brave at his side as he battled the evil empire that threatened his country.

But Charity was old enough to understand the difference between fantasy and reality. She understood that her dream of marrying Augustus had been a child's game. She understood that once she made this marriage, her life would be changed utterly and forever. The responsibility of being Princess of Jura would rein her in more tightly than her mother's strictures ever could. Most profoundly, she understood that all the freedom was about to disappear from her life.

She was dwelling on this dismal thought when she heard the door open behind her. She turned around and watched as the Prince came in. He closed the door and stood there for a moment, making no attempt to come closer.

Charity looked at him, her perfect prince, and the

muscles in her stomach tightened and she could hear the beat of her own heart. *How handsome he is,* she thought. *How could Lydia have preferred the glitter of Franz to the solid gold of Augustus?*

He said quietly, from his position the full width of the room away from her. "Are you quite sure you want to do this?"

She wet her lips with her tongue and replied gruffly, "Yes."

She could see the muscles in his face relax. He crossed the pink, blue, and cream carpet and came to a stop a few feet in front of her. The sun from the window made his blond hair look lighter than usual and illuminated the grave expression in his gray eyes. He said somberly, "Your sister has put me in a damnable position, Charity. If I do not get married one week from today, my people will be deeply disappointed. What is worse, their feelings toward England will not be friendly. And if, after all these elaborate preparations, the wedding is canceled, I will look like a fool. This last situation I could live with, but I cannot live with the other two."

"I understand that," she said in the same tone as before. "Lydia's behavior is unforgivable, and if my marrying you will help to rectify it, then I am willing to do it."

A faint smile flickered across his mouth. "Come and sit down. We need to talk."

She followed him to the pink silk Louis XIV sofa, sat down beside him, folded her hands in her lap, and regarded them intently. She was acutely conscious of the size of him sitting right next to her on the adjacent sofa cushion. She tightened the grip of her fingers, frowned, and told herself to stop being such an idiot.

He said, "Some of the blame for Lydia's action rests with me. Don't lay it all on your sister."

Charity's head turned toward him in surprise. "You? How could you possibly be to blame, Prince?"

He was staring into the empty fireplace and his profile looked as clear-cut and stern as that on a Roman coin. "I scarcely spent any time at all with Lydia. I kept relying on Franz to entertain her. I suppose I can hardly blame them if they fell in love." His voice took on a bitter note. "I certainly did all I could to facilitate it."

"Well," Charity said, knowing that what he had said was true and trying to find a way to excuse him, "you have been very busy."

His profile did not soften. "Yes, I have been busy, but I have not been too busy to find some time to spend with my fiancée. I just did not bother to do it."

"Why didn't you?" Charity asked curiously.

"Because I'm afraid I didn't like your sister very much," he replied, turning his head to look at her. "I knew our marriage was the politically correct thing to do, but I was not looking forward to spending the rest of my life with her."

Charity was utterly astonished. "But she is so beautiful!"

"Yes, she is very beautiful. But—" He looked as if he didn't know if he should go on.

"Yes?" she prompted.

He returned his gaze to the fireplace. "Well . . . it just seemed to me that she was rather stupid," he said in a rush.

Charity blinked.

"Perhaps it was presumptuous of me to think that, perhaps she was very clever about the things that interested her, but she had absolutely no interest in the things that interest me." He shot her a sideways look to gauge her reaction.

Charity was delighted by the Prince's words, although she tried very hard not to show it. She answered honestly, "Lydia is an imbecile about politics, but she would have made a good Princess of Jura. She understands society and social etiquette and protocol and things like that. And she would have *looked* magnificent." Her brow wrinkled with worry. "I will not be able to represent you half as well as she could, Prince."

"You can always learn protocol," he replied in a practical voice. "I think you will make a splendid Princess of Jura."

She turned a little on the sofa, so she was facing him, and said doubtfully, "Do you really think so?"

He too moved so that he was facing her. "I do. And I can tell you one other thing, Charity. I would far rather be married to you than to your sister."

Her heart gave a great *thump*. She stared at him out of huge eyes. "You would?"

He nodded emphatically. "I can talk to you." A smile tugged at the corners of his mouth. "And you play a wicked game of cards."

It was a perfectly sensible answer. Why then did

she feel so disappointed? Gamely she smiled back at him, hiding her feelings.

He picked up her small hands and held them in his.

Her pulse sped up and she flushed.

"There is one other thing I want to make clear to you," he said. "I realize that you are being rushed into this marriage, and I have no intention of asking you to consummate it until you are ready."

At these words, Charity could feel her flush deepening. She wanted desperately to pull her hands away before he could feel the racing of her pulse, but felt she could not. He was going on: "I am older than you by far more than the ten years that separate us. Eventually I will have to have an heir, but there is no rush. I am perfectly willing to wait until you are a little older."

His hands were so large that they almost completely engulfed hers, but his clasp imparted a sense of warmth and strength and protection. Suddenly all of Charity's doubts melted away. Augustus would take care of her.

"And you will tell me when I am doing something wrong? I don't want to disgrace you, Prince."

He gave her fingers a gentle squeeze and then released them. "I think," he said, "it is time for you to call me Augustus."

12

Fortunately, the sky on the day of the Prince's wedding was slightly overcast. If the sun had been beating steadily upon the huge crowds that were massed along the bridal carriage route and outside the great Gothic Cathedral of Saint Peter, large numbers of people would have been overcome by the heat. The welcome cloud cover allowed the citizens of Jura to rejoice in relative comfort.

The Prince had changed the traditional ceremony that called for two processions into the church, first the bridal procession and then the royal procession of the groom. Instead he chose to await the arrival of his bride inside the comparative coolness of the cathedral. His strongest emotion, as he stood in the sacristy with his best man, Lord Stefan Weyr, looking at the discolored spot on the wall where a Madonna by Giovanni Bellini had once hung, was relief.

There had been an uproar, of course, when the news had got out about Lydia's elopement. Julia's two main newspapers had waxed hysterical about the insult to their prince and, had the Jurian diet been in session, there would certainly have been an even greater commotion. However, most Jurian outraged feelings had been soothed by the quick release of the news that the wedding was to go forward, with Lady Charity Debritt assuming her sister's place. Jura was not going to be deprived of its wedding after all, and gradually the grumbling quieted down.

The Prince himself was actually happy with the way things had turned out. He thought Charity would prove a much more satisfactory wife than Lydia. She spoke German—with a Jurian accent!—and she understood the reasons behind his decision to negotiate a treaty with Great Britain. She was also young enough for him to be able to mold her character into the kind of wife and princess that he would find most useful. Lydia's personality had already been formed, and the Prince had seen that her narrow interests and essential selfishness would make her an irritating and unsatisfactory partner.

His reflections were interrupted when Lord Emil Sauder popped his head into the sacristy to announce, "The bridal coach has just arrived. Better get into position, Gus."

The Prince, who was wearing the uniform of the commander-in-chief of the Jurian army, turned to his best man, who was also dressed in military garb. Stefan grinned at him. "Nervous, Gus?"

"Terrified," the Prince replied humorously.

Stefan gave an incredulous snort, and the two men left the sacristy to enter the main part of the church.

Every pew in the cathedral was filled to capacity. The Prince saw his mother in the first row and nodded to her. The princess, who was wearing a white silk hat with an enormous rose on its brim, smiled back brilliantly. The cathedral smelled of incense and burning candles and the mingled perfumes of the women in the pews. The magnificent stained-glass windows did not show to their best advantage because of the lack of sunshine, but even so, the amazing blue that was their primary color glowed with subdued brilliance.

The Adamovs of Jura had always been Roman Catholic, and the ceremony today would be a nuptial mass performed by the ranking prelate in Jura, Archbishop Rudolf Vasi. Charity was not a Catholic, but the Debritts had made no objection to either of their daughters being married in a Catholic ceremony. In religion, as in so many other areas of life, rank prevailed.

As the Prince waited for the music that would announce the entrance of the bridal party, he offered up a brief prayer of thanksgiving that everything had gone so well for him. The transfer of power from his father's rule to himself had been smooth, largely because he had been sensible enough to retain his father's men in their old positions. In actual fact, the positions were merely nominal, as the Prince rarely sought, and even more rarely listened, to any advice men like Hindenberg and Rupnik were likely to offer. His own men, who held positions less important in title, were the ones who had his ear.

As the organ's magnificent tones rolled through the cathedral, the Prince's thoughts turned to his cousin. He had not been half as surprised by Lydia's defection as he had been by Franz's.

What could he have been thinking?

It was a question the Prince had asked himself many times before. What on earth had motivated Franz to run away with Lydia? It would have been far more advantageous for him to marry a girl from the Austrian or the German nobility. To have chosen a scandalous elopement with an English girl did not seem at all like Franz, who, in the Prince's experience, always had an eye on what would most benefit himself.

Perhaps he really is in love, the Prince thought skeptically. It was hard to believe, but no other reason presented itself to account for his cousin's strange behavior.

The Prince himself did not think highly of love as a factor in marriage. His father had fallen in love with his mother, and the resulting marriage had not been a notable success. As Prince of Jura, Augustus wanted a wife who would carry out the duties of his consort with graciousness and with honor. As a man, he wanted a wife who would do as she was told. He had sensed that Lydia would not fit this mold, but he had every confidence that the youthful Charity would. The Prince was extremely pleased with the way things had turned out.

* * *

*I*n later years, Charity would always say that the
only reason she had not jumped up into the driver's
seat of the coach taking her to her wedding, grabbed
the reins, and galloped madly away was the calming
presence of her grandmother sitting beside her.
Princess Mariana, at her granddaughter's special request, had been the person to accompany Charity in
the state carriage as it passed through wildly cheering crowds on its way from the Pfalz to the cathedral
in Julia. Fortunately, the soon-to-be Princess of Jura
was not expected to show her face to the crowds before the wedding ceremony, so Charity could sit
back, clutch her grandmother's hand, and listen to
the older woman's soothing comments as the splendidly plumed Lipizzaners carried her ever closer to
her wedding with the Prince.

Princess Mariana had been delighted when she
learned that Charity was to marry Augustus, and the
faith she had displayed in Charity's ability to per-
form the duties of the Princess had been a sorely
needed boost to Charity's confidence. Lady Beaufort
had been so bitterly hurt and disappointed by Lydia's
action that she had been no help to Charity at all. It
had been Princess Mariana who had taken it upon
herself to broach the delicate subject of the wedding
night to her granddaughter in order to explain just
what Charity should expect to encounter in the initial act of sex. When Charity had repeated Augustus's words about waiting to consummate their
marriage, her grandmother had been astounded.

"But he must have an heir, Charity! That is the first duty of a prince, to give the country an heir."

Charity saw immediately that her grandmother was not pleased with what she had just heard. The two women were in Charity's bedroom in the Pfalz, and Charity, who was sitting on a blue velvet hassock close to Princess Mariana's chair, replied a little defensively, "I know that, Grandmama. Augustus told me that he would have to have an heir. But he also said that there was no hurry."

The princess's eyes, which were so like her own, looked stern. "He is trying to spare your sensibilities." She frowned. "This is the first time I have ever seen Augustus do something stupid."

"I don't think it's so stupid," Charity said even more defensively. "After all, I am only seventeen, Grandmama. That's awfully young to have a baby."

"Bah," said Princess Mariana. She leaned forward, took Charity's chin in her thin, arthritic hand, and held her granddaughter's face captive. "Are you afraid of the sexual act, Charity?" she asked with all the bluntness of a woman of the last century.

Charity could feel the hot color flood into her face and neck. She kept her eyes steady on her grandmother's, however, and replied firmly, "Certainly not. I can throw my heart over any fence, Grandmama. You know that."

Princess Mariana smiled at the equine metaphor. "Yes." She patted Charity's cheek. "I do know that. I shall speak to Augustus and clear up this idiocy once and for all."

"No!" Charity was surprised by the explosiveness

of her own response. She jumped to her feet and walked to the window in order to gain time to collect herself. Once there she turned, faced her grandmother, and managed to say with composure, "I think you can leave such a delicate matter up to Augustus's good judgment, Grandmama. And I would really rather he not know that I have discussed this with you."

After a long look at Charity's flushed face, Princess Mariana had reluctantly acquiesced.

Charity thought back on this conversation now as her carriage stopped in front of the cathedral. The steps were lined with the Household Guard, their ceremonial swords and the gold braid of their uniforms glittering in the morning sun. A splendidly uniformed young man helped her alight from the coach, and her grandmother arranged her train. Then she was going up the stairs, the sun hot on her head, her heart beating so hard and so fast that she was afraid she might faint.

All of her bridesmaids were gathered in the vestibule, along with her father, who came to her immediately and said something nice about how she looked. She heard herself make a reply, and then the great cathedral organ, which had been playing softly, gave forth its full voice. Her father held out his arm, she took it, and they started down the aisle, followed at a discreet distance by her fifteen bridesmaids, none of whom she knew.

The air in the cathedral smelled of incense, and every pew was filled with unfamiliar faces, all of them staring at her. The marble altar was ablaze with golden candlesticks framing the golden tabernacle. Above the altar hung an Annunciation by Titian that was famed throughout Europe. The Prince had managed to recover it from the treasure trove of Napoleon's larcenous marshal only three months before. In front of the altar were two stools, to be used by the royal pair during the ceremony, and behind those two state chairs where they would sit during the remainder of the nuptial mass.

Charity was halfway down the aisle when she saw the Prince standing before the altar rail. He was wearing a dark green uniform, with gold lapels, gold-embroidered loops, and gold-embroidered epaulettes with gold bullion fringes. He looked so intimidatingly tall, so sternly handsome, that her pounding heart leaped into her throat and her hands went clammy.

Who is that strange man? I must be insane. How can I possibly marry a man like that?

She felt herself begin to shake and concentrated all of her willpower on stopping such a shameful display of nerves. She had almost reached the altar when she allowed herself one more glance at the man who was waiting for her. His gray eyes met and held hers and he gave her a faint smile.

It's Augustus, she thought, feeling suddenly limp and stupid with relief. *I will be all right now. It's Augustus.*

When they exited from the cathedral, the area directly in front of the stairs had been cordoned off by a row of Household Guards, and the crowd behind the uniformed line was so thick and deep that Charity could see no end to it. As the bride and groom stepped into the sunlight and became visible to the crowd, there was a blare of trumpets and the noise that roared through the cathedral square was overwhelming.

They stood for a moment on the top of the stairs while the crowd's adulation resounded all around them. Then Augustus put his arm around her and rested a light hand upon her waist. Startled, Charity looked up at him. He bent his blond head and dropped a tender kiss on her lips.

The crowd went wild. Augustus smiled and his hand urged her forward. Together they went down the stairs to the carriage waiting for them at the bottom of the steps. He handed Charity in, then got in after her. The Lipizzaners nodded the gorgeous gold plumes on their heads and moved off into the space created for them by the military line of the Household Guard.

Charity sat in the bridal coach, her hands clasped tensely in her lap, feeling upset and confused. Why had Augustus kissed her?

He was sitting opposite her in the carriage, looking out the window, acknowledging the cheers of his people. He was smiling.

Stupid, Charity scolded herself. *He kissed you because he knew it would please his people. That's what this whole wedding is about—pleasing his people. You have to be very careful, Charity, not to think that he has any special feelings for you.*

For there was no denying that his light, tender

kiss, the first touch of a man's lips upon hers, had shaken her.

All along their drive through the city streets the coach was bombarded by flowers. "The devil!" Augustus said with a laugh, as he ducked back against the cushions. "That last one almost got me right in the face."

Charity managed a laugh. From the street outside all that could be heard was one word, resounding over and over and over again, *Augustus! Augustus! Augustus!*

How on earth will I ever live up to him? Charity thought in miserable despair.

The Prince had been determined to make his wedding a day of celebration for the entire country, and so citizens from all the social classes of Jura had been invited to the wedding breakfast at the Pfalz. The great Marble Room on the ground floor of the palace was thronged with beaming burghers and their wives, as well as the more usual members of the nobility and military. The grandness of the room was echoed by the magnificent wedding cake, which was quite nine feet in circumference and sixteen inches in height.

When Charity and the Prince entered the room the band struck up the Jurian national anthem. All the men bowed and the women sank into deep curtseys, and Charity's feeling of unworthiness deepened. Never had she felt so young, so ignorant, so utterly out of place.

They remained at the reception for an hour and a half, during which time Charity struggled mightily

to be both friendly and dignified, as she thought a
Princess of Jura should be. She felt a bit better when
her grandmother patted her hand and told her she
was doing "very well, little one, very well." However, if someone had asked her the following day to
describe what had happened at the reception and
whom she had spoken to, she would not have been
able to give a coherent answer. She was intensely relieved when her mother came to take her upstairs to
change out of her wedding dress. Her baggage had
already been sent on to the Alpine lake where she
and the Prince were to spend a week's honeymoon.

She met her new husband at a side door and they
got into a carriage bearing no crest and pulled by ordinary horses and drove off without anyone noticing
that they had gone. As soon as they passed beyond
the gates, Augustus heaved a satisfied sigh and
stretched out his legs as best he could. One booted
foot brushed against Charity's fawn-colored traveling dress. She looked at it, but made no attempt to
draw her dress away.

"It went perfectly," Augustus said with palpable
satisfaction. He gave her a warm smile. "You were
wonderful, Charity. You have my undying thanks for
everything you have done. My people were cheated
out of a coronation, but they had a splendid wedding
to celebrate—thanks to you."

"It certainly was splendid," she said. "I felt as if I
were acting in a play."

"You were." He gave her an anxious look. "Would
you mind terribly if I loosened my neckcloth?"

The question and the look were so boyish that all

of a sudden she felt comfortable with him. She laughed. "Go right ahead. As a matter of fact, I think I will take off my hat."

Both of them suited actions to words. Charity laid her bonnet on the seat next to her. Her hair was still braided into the high coronet that she had worn for her wedding veil, and she would have liked to take out all the pins and let it spill loose, but she didn't quite have the nerve to do that. She looked over at Augustus and was surprised to see a tremendous yawn on his face. He covered his mouth with his hands and his eyes watered. "I am so sorry," he said as soon as he could talk again. "I don't mean to be a bore."

Charity grinned and felt even more comfortable. It was hard to feel unworthy of a man who yawned in your face. "Don't bother about me. I had two glasses of champagne at the reception and I feel that if I closed my eyes I could fall right asleep."

"Would you care to take a nap?" he asked, not quite able to disguise his hopefulness.

Charity smiled again. "Why don't we both try to get a little sleep?" she suggested. "It has been rather a harrowing week."

"It certainly has," he agreed fervently, and without further ado he tilted his head back against the cushion and closed his eyes. Charity watched him, watched the long lashes as they lay quietly on the hard cheek-bones, watched as he slid into the profound sleep of the truly exhausted. She remained thus for perhaps half an hour before she put her hat on the floor, curled up on the seat, and fell fast asleep herself.

The rest of the journey and the arrival at their destination would always remain a blur to Charity. She was half asleep when she got out of the coach and accompanied the Prince up a flight of stone stairs. Afterward she would remember a maid helping her to undress and that the wooden floor of the bedroom felt very cold under her bare feet. Then she was in a nice soft bed, one that didn't jolt and jostle her, and she went back to sleep.

When she awoke the following morning she didn't remember where she was. She blinked and looked in bewilderment at a wall covered in a Flemish tapestry she didn't recognize. She turned her head the other way.

A man with sunlit blond hair was standing in front of an open window watching her, and all of a sudden she remembered. Her heart gave the single thud that was becoming almost familiar. "Good heavens," she croaked. "Augustus! What time is it?"

"It is after ten," he replied.

Charity was truly horrified. She sat bolt upright in bed. "It can't be. I never sleep that late."

He smiled at her. "You were exhausted, so I let you sleep. But you can't stay in bed for the entire day."

Charity knew that she couldn't stay in bed for the entire day, but she was feeling extremely awkward about getting out of bed while he was in the room. She stayed where she was, hoping that he would go away.

He held out a hand. "Come over here and let me show you something."

Reluctantly, she pushed her blankets away and slid to the floor. Dressed in her high-necked, pristine white nightgown, she crossed the carpeted floor to join him. Once she looked out the window, however, all thoughts of modesty fled.

"Oh Augustus. How absolutely beautiful."

They were standing at the window of a great stone castle, which was situated on an island in the middle of a lake, surrounded by the Jurian Alps. Charity's eyes moved slowly from the lake's clear, still waters to the snowcapped peaks and she hugged herself in a mixture of awe and excitement.

The Prince said with concern. "Are you cold? You should not be standing here barefoot and in your nightdress."

"I'm not cold at all," she replied. "I'm just thrilled." She tore her eyes away from the landscape to look up into his face, and all of her awkwardness magically disappeared. Instead she felt bubbly and elated, as if she was poised on the threshold of a great adventure. "What can we do today? Can we go exploring? Can we climb one of the mountains?" She put her hand on his sleeve. "Oh please, Augustus, wouldn't that be marvelous? What a view one would have of the lake and the castle!"

He laughed down at her. "We can do a little exploring if you like."

"Hurrah!" She stepped back. "I'll get dressed in a trice." She looked at him expectantly, waiting for him to go.

"Wouldn't you like me to show you around the castle first?"

"I should love to see the castle, but later. Right now, I want to take advantage of this magnificent weather." She looked out the window once again and then back at him. He was making no motion to leave, and she said tentatively, "This is the princess's bedroom, isn't it?"

He leaned his shoulders against the wall next to the window and crossed his arms. "This room actually belongs to both the prince *and* the princess."

Charity was a little uncertain about how to take this news. "You didn't sleep here last night," she said cautiously.

He gestured to one of the bedroom's three doors. "There is a camp bed in the prince's dressing room. I slept there."

"A camp bed?" She felt a pang of guilt as she looked at his long frame leaning against the wall. "Oh no, Augustus, you are much bigger than I am! You should be the one to sleep in this enormous bed. I can easily sleep in the dressing room."

His gray eyes glinted with amusement. "That is very generous of you, Charity, but I can assure you that, compared to some of the places where I have slept, the camp bed is paradise. These arrangements will suffice for the time that we are here at Lake Leive. When we return to the Pfalz we will have separate bedrooms and I shall get my own big bed back."

A thought darted like a bird in flight across Charity's mind: *We could both sleep here in this bed.* Before she could say anything, however, he was asking, "Do you wish to have breakfast brought to you here?"

The moment when she might have spoken had passed.

With some relief, she answered, "I never have breakfast in my bedroom." Her small nose quivered in disgust. "I think it is decadent."

He grinned at her choice of adjective. "Then I will have a fresh breakfast set out for you in the sitting room." He moved away from the window, crossing to the dressing room door he had just pointed out. He put a hand on the latch, then turned to ask, "How long will it take you to get dressed?"

"Fifteen minutes," Charity said.

He stared. "It took your sister an hour and a half."

Charity put her hand up to touch her disordered hair, which was still in the coronet of braids she had worn at her wedding. "Actually, it might take me half an hour," she said apologetically. "My hair has to be redone."

He gave her a brisk nod of approval, the kind a commanding officer might bestow upon a promising subordinate. "I'll tell them to have breakfast in half an hour." And he closed the door behind him.

*M*uch to his surprise, the Prince found his honeymoon to be an utterly delightful and relaxing experience. He and Charity rowed on the lake, fished, and explored the mountain trails on foot and on horseback. As he did these things, the tension of the last weeks that had strung him as tightly as a bowstring slowly began to relax.

Charity was an enchanting companion. Outdoors

she was as game and athletic as any boy, and on the single day that it rained, he spent the morning showing her around the castle, where they vied with each other in making up hilarious stories about their ancestors, whose portraits lined the walls. In the afternoon they played a fierce game of cards, using for money a pile of medieval coins the Prince unearthed from an old chest in the castle's Great Hall.

What surprised the Prince most, when he stopped to think about it, was the ease of their companionship. He had wondered what on earth he would ever find to say to Lydia, but Charity shared so many of his interests that talking to her was like conversing with one of his friends.

It was the conversation they had on the last day of their stay at Lake Leive that made the deepest impression on him, however. They had spread a blanket in a meadow of Alpine flowers to partake of the luncheon that the castle cook had packed for them. The Prince had finished eating and was stretched out on his back, his head propped on his folded jacket, his eyes closed. The scent of the flowers filled his nostrils, the sun was warm on his face, the faint buzzing of bees was gentle on his ears, and he felt amazingly at peace.

He had almost dozed off when he heard Charity say, "Augustus, why do you think Franz ran away with Lydia?"

"He was in love with her," the Prince replied without opening his eyes.

"I don't think Franz is the kind of person who falls in love," Charity said reflectively.

At that he opened his eyes and turned his head slightly so he could see her. "Why do you say that?"

She was chewing on a crust of bread, and she waited until she had swallowed until she replied. "I think he is too conceited to fall in love."

He laughed. "It's hard not to be conceited when one is as good-looking as Franz."

"He wants always to be the center of attention. I noticed that at the Regent's reception when he wanted Lydia and me to notice him and not you, and I have seen it happen a number of times since."

The Prince closed his eyes again. "So Franz thinks well of himself. I am not going to argue that with you, Charity."

She threw the last piece of her crust to some small brown birds, who immediately began to squabble over it. "I don't think he likes you, Augustus."

At that, the Prince pushed himself up on his elbow. He stared at her through a lock of hair that was hanging over his left eye. "Are you serious?"

She nodded slowly. "Yes, I am. I have been thinking about this, and I bet that Franz never dreamed that I would step in to take Lydia's place. He thought that by running away with her he would undo your wedding."

A bee buzzed in front of the Prince's nose, and he sat all the way up, waved it away, pushed his hair off his face, and demanded, "Why on earth should Franz wish to do such a thing?"

The birds had finished with the bread, and Charity linked her arms around her updrawn knees and regarded him thoughtfully. "I don't know. But I don't

like the feeling I have about him. I think he deliberately set out to make Lydia fall in love with him."

He stared at her for a moment in silence, more perturbed by her comments than he wanted to be. Finally
he said, "I have known Franz far longer than you, and
I can assure you that he may be a little selfish and a
little spoiled, but he has always been my friend."

Charity shot him a skeptical look, propped her
chin on her knees, and did not reply.

*Why on earth am I allowing a child of seventeen
to upset me?* the Prince thought impatiently. Out
loud he said, "You must admit that your experience
of people is somewhat limited, given your age."

She rolled her eyes. "Now you sound like Mama."

The Prince found this remark profoundly annoying. "Well, even if Franz did have some deep dark
plan in mind by eloping with Lydia, it has been
negated by our marriage."

The bright sunlight glinted on the gold strands
mixed in with the brown of her hair, and a week of
being outdoors had turned her skin from ivory rose
to the palest gold. He looked into her large brown
eyes and thought that she was a very pretty girl. At
last she said, "That is true."

He lowered himself back on the blanket and
closed his eyes. He was just drifting off when once
more her voice interrupted his descent into sleep.
"Augustus, I have a few things I would like to discuss with you."

The tentative note in her voice was so unusual that
he realized he had to pay attention. He yawned and
opened his eyes. "All right."

"It's about my role as Princess of Jura."

He sat up. She no longer was clasping her knees but had curled her legs sideways under her. Her tan skirt had twisted a little to reveal two small, bare, perfectly arched feet. Charity had stepped in a stream and wet her shoes, so she had taken them off and set them out to dry in the sun while they ate. He found himself staring at those dainty feet and made himself look away.

"You should probably talk to my mother about that," he got out. "I don't know if I can be of much help to you."

To his complete surprise, she asked, "Have you ever read Plato's *Republic,* Augustus?"

He reached out, plucked a bluebell, and slowly began to pull it apart. "Many years ago."

"Well, perhaps you will remember that in it Plato describes his idea of the perfect state. He says such a state should be ruled by a philosopher-king, whose role is to be the guardian of his people. The happiness of this philosopher-king lies in doing his duty to all of his people. For the purpose of this ideal state, according to Plato, should not be the happiness of one class but of the entire community."

He tossed away the denuded bluebell and looked at his wife. "I remember that."

She gazed back at him with touching gravity, and a delicate pink color slowly stained the golden skin over her cheekbones. She said, "I know I am very young, and that I have no experience, but I would like to be a philosopher-princess."

I must handle this very carefully, he thought. When

he spoke his voice was gentle. "And how do you pro-
pose to go about achieving this lofty goal?"

Her great brown eyes continued to cling to his.
"That night on the ship, when you and my father
were talking, you said that the British blockade during the war had caused great economic hardship in
Jura. Remember?"

She had his complete attention. "I remember. Our
economy before the war was strong, and it will be
strong again, but until we can restore the normal balance of trade, many people are hurting."

She said, "I know I can't do anything about the
economy, I don't know enough about it, but I would
like to try to help the people who are suffering because of it." A spark of indignation made her eyes
sparkle with gold. "What seemed so awful to me in
London was that none of the hungry and homeless
people there had anywhere to go for assistance.
Women had to sell themselves into prostitution, Augustus, in order to feed their children!"

He remembered the men who had held up his carriage on the way to London and their bitterness at
being ignored by the very government that they had
helped to save. "We don't have quite the same problem in Jura that you have in England," he said. "We
are a much smaller country, remember."

The delicate pink color had brightened and flew
like a flag in her cheeks. "Can you tell me that there
are no hungry people in Jura?" she demanded. "No
women with sick children who have no place to take
them for medical care? No men who are out of work

and desperate to find a means to feed and house their families?"

He looked at her for a long moment in silence. Then he said somberly, "No, I cannot tell you that."

"I would like to set up offices throughout the country where people could go if they needed help. I don't know how we would find them, but I would like the people of Jura never to feel that their country has abandoned them."

He looked at the grave face of his young wife and felt deeply touched. "I think that is a wonderful idea," he said, "and I will do everything I can to support you."

Her smile was radiant. "Thank you, Augustus. We will both be philosopher-kings!"

"That is certainly not a goal I can quarrel with," he replied.

As they packed up their picnic and prepared to return to the castle, he reflected that in some ways perhaps Charity wasn't as young as he had thought.

13

Charity returned to Julia feeling more comfortable about her marriage than she had thought possible. She and Augustus had always been friends, and on their honeymoon she felt that they had become partners. She knew that someday they would become husband and wife, and even that future consummation no longer held any worries for her.

"Augustus will know when the time is right." She spoke these words with sublime confidence to her grandmother two days after her return from Lake Leive. "Don't worry, Grandmama. It will be perfectly safe leaving this matter up to him."

"Charity . . ." The two women were having tea together in the privacy of the sitting room of Charity's new apartment. "A man has certain needs, my dear," the elder princess explained carefully. "If those needs are not filled by his wife, he may look elsewhere. You would not like that to happen, would you?"

Charity put her delicate Meissen cup back into its saucer and stared at her grandmother in a mixture of amazement and outrage. "We are talking about *Augustus,* Grandmama. He would never do something like that. He is the most honorable man alive. And I am perfectly willing to fulfill his needs. He just has to ask me."

Princess Mariana opened her mouth to say something else, then sighed and shook her head as if accepting defeat. "If you don't mind, Charity," she murmured, "I will have a little more tea."

A week after Charity's return from her honeymoon, her family left Jura to return to England. Princess Caterina had gone back to Venice while the royal couple were still on their honeymoon, but her absence meant nothing to Charity compared to the loss of her own beloved family, and she dreaded the moment of their departure.

On the actual day that the Debritts left, however, Charity performed splendidly. She and Augustus walked out to the coach with them, and as her mother, father, brother, and grandmother got into the carriage, she gave each one a farewell kiss.

Her mother returned the kiss, but Charity could see from the dark circles under her eyes that she was still grieving over Lydia.

Harry gave her a brotherly hug and recommended that she learn to behave herself.

Her grandmother looked into her face and said, "Perhaps I should stay. If you feel you need me, Charity, I will."

In return, Charity enveloped the older princess in

a warm embrace. "I want you, Grandmama, but I don't need you. We have been through this before and it's too late to change your mind. England is your home now and that is where you want to be and where you should be."

Lord Beaufort said impatiently, "For heaven's sake, Mama, get into the carriage. You are coming home with me and that is that." Then, as Princess Mariana obeyed her son, he turned to his daughter. "Don't worry, chicken," he whispered in her ear as he held her tight. "You'll be a wonderful princess. And you'll be coming home for a visit in no time."

Charity breathed in the familiar smell of her father and felt as if her heart would burst in her chest. In a shaky voice, she replied, "I know, Papa. I'll miss you."

She stood next to her husband and watched the Lipizzaners trot past the fountains and through the gate, taking her family away and leaving her behind. She felt Augustus take her arm and say, "We should go back inside."

She gave him a glittering smile. "Certainly."

She walked beside him, letting him be her guide because she couldn't see clearly through the glaze of unshed tears in her eyes. They went up the double fan staircase and into the palace and all she kept thinking was, *I mustn't let anyone see me cry, I mustn't let anyone see me cry.*

Augustus walked and she walked with him, until at last he closed a door behind them and she heard him say in an unusually gentle voice, "It's all right now, Charity. We're alone."

She kept her eyes looking downward so he wouldn't see the tears. "Thank you. I am fine, Augustus."

"You were splendid," he said in that same gentle voice. "I am proud of you."

Despite her effort, two tears spilled over. She dashed at them with her fingers. "I'm s-sorry. I don't mean to be a watering pot."

"I think you are very brave."

She looked up at him out of tragic brown eyes and he stepped forward and gathered her close. She leaned against him, and let the storm break in the safety of his arms.

He held her and thought that she was so small that it was almost like embracing a child. He bent his head and murmured, "I know you are feeling abandoned, Charity, but you still have me. I'm a poor substitute for your family, but I promise I will do my best never to fail you." Her face was buried in his coat just over his heart and she was crying with deep and racking sobs. He smoothed her silky hair and her head felt small and round and vulnerable under his hand.

I have done this to her, he thought. *I have torn her away from her family and her country and forced her to marry a stranger and to live in a strange land. All that concerned me was my own needs; I never once thought that Charity might have needs of her own.*

"I'm sorry, little one," he murmured. "I am so sorry. I will try to make it up to you. I promise I will try."

* * *

Charity was grateful to her husband for his comfort, and when she went to sleep that night she
found that her mind was dwelling less on the sorrow
of her family's absence than on the pleasure of being held in Augustus's arms. The following morning
she rose, determined to start her new life as a
philosopher-princess. In order to accomplish this
goal she called in Lord Stefan Weyr, the Prince's
secretary, and asked him to help her establish an
office.

In fact, the next month saw Charity begin such a
whirlwind of activity that Lord Stefan was moved to
complain. "The Princess is giving me as much work
as the Prince," he groaned to Lord Emil Sauder one
afternoon as the two young men happened to arrive
at the stables at the same time. As they walked up to
the Pfalz together, Lord Stefan told his friend about
Charity's projects.

"Good for the Princess," Lord Emil said admir-
ingly.

"What she is attempting is too ambitious for the
few people she has on her staff," Lord Stefan said.
"She is talking about setting up health centers, temporary shelters . . . These are things we have never
done before. It is a huge undertaking."

"Then tell her to get more people," Lord Emil
said. "Gus won't mind. Tell her she needs her own
secretary, that you don't have the time to do the job
the way it should be done."

"I think I will," Lord Stefan said. "I'd better make
certain it's all right with Gus first, though."

Lord Emil curled his lip. "I can just see Gus telling you that under no circumstances does he want health centers and shelters set up for his people."

Both men laughed.

"You know, Stefan, I think it was a lucky thing that the first sister ran out on Gus," Lord Emil said. "This second one is much better."

This was a judgment with which the Prince heartily concurred. Directly after the Debritt family's departure, the Prince had begun to breakfast privately each morning with his wife. They would meet at six-thirty in the small salon adjacent to Charity's bedroom, both of them in their dressing gowns, and talk over coffee, fruit, and bread. This breakfast quickly became a sacrosanct tradition, honored by all the staff. Nothing short of a declaration of war would induce anyone to interrupt the Prince when he was breakfasting with his wife.

Augustus had begun this ritual in order to give Charity time to speak with him about any problems that she might have, but it was not long before the discussion became mutual and he was telling her about his problems and projects as freely as she told him about hers.

One morning, as they were sitting at the small breakfast table covered with an immaculate white cloth and set with blue-and-white breakfast dishes, he told her about an interview he had had with Chief Minister Hindenberg the previous day.

"The man is impossible!" he exploded as he drank his second cup of coffee. "He is so afraid of Austria that he doesn't want me to make a single independent move. He wants me to consult the emperor before I use the chamber pot, for God's sake."

"Get rid of him then," Charity advised. "He was your father's chief minister and you kept him on and gave him a chance, but if he cannot adapt himself to your policies, then he must go."

A few strands of hair had fallen over Augustus's forehead and he pushed them back with an impatient motion of his hand. "It isn't that simple," he said. "Hindenberg has friends in the diet I don't want to alienate."

Charity chose a peach from the attractively arranged basket of fruit in the middle of the table. "The country adores you, Augustus, and I doubt if there will be a peep of protest in the diet if you let Hindenberg go."

The Prince held out his cup for a refill of coffee, and Charity put down her peach and poured it for him. Then she refilled her own cup. In the last month she had become almost as addicted to coffee as her husband.

"I'll think about it," he said as he frowned into the dark liquid in his cup. "I must admit it would be a relief not to have to listen to him anymore. He puts me in a temper every time he opens his mouth."

Charity picked up her peach once again and the Prince drank half of his coffee. Then he said, "I heard yesterday from Viktor in Vienna. He thinks the emperor is going to impose tariffs on the goods Jura exports to the empire."

Charity lowered the peach from her mouth. "Oh dear. That is exactly what you feared would happen."

"Viktor is going to talk to the ambassadors from Russia, Prussia, and France to see how they would react to such a breach of the free trade agreement arrived at at the Congress."

"You have a treaty with Britain," Charity pointed out.

"I know. But it would be best if we could stop this tax before it is enacted."

Charity nodded agreement and finally took a bite from her peach. She closed her eyes for a moment to savor the sweetness of the fruit, and, looking at her, the Prince noticed how flawless her skin was in the unforgiving brilliance of the morning light. She still had the skin of a child, he thought, close-textured like fine porcelain, with a flush of natural color in the cheeks and on the lips.

He said, "How is the temporary shelter in Julia coming along?"

"Very well indeed." She took another bite of the peach, her healthy white teeth cutting neatly through the juicy flesh of the fruit. She finished eating, wiped her chin with a napkin, and flashed him her wonderful smile. "It is so funny, Augustus. Ever since I had the idea to make it fashionable to show concern for the poor, every baroness and countess in the country is rushing to be a Good Samaritan."

He smiled with amusement. "So I have heard."

Her eyes sparkled. "It is amazing how much power I have just because I am the princess. Yesterday I talked two of Julia's most prestigious doctors into giving one afternoon a week of free examinations to the needy."

He laughed. "Did you really?"

She nodded her head. "I told them that neither you nor I would feel comfortable consulting a doctor who was not compassionate toward those less fortunate than we." Her smile was angelic. "Both of them leaped at the chance to impress us with their charitable solicitude."

"You are diabolical," he said, with genuine admiration.

She inclined her head modestly. "Thank you."

"And ruthless as well."

"Mama used to call it stubbornness," she said. "I must say, I like diabolical and ruthless better." She pushed back her chair, walked to the window, and looked out at the sunlit garden. "How wonderful it is to see the sun again!"

Augustus stared at his wife. The light from the window shone through the thin cotton of her nightdress and dressing gown, outlining her naked body beneath. Her long hair, which was brushed simply behind her ears, streamed down her back, brown and gold in the sun. She suddenly whirled around to face him, and he had a glimpse of high young breasts beneath her nightclothes before she came back to her seat at the table.

"Guess what?" she said.

His heart was pounding and he struggled for composure. "What?" he managed to get out.

"Next week, on the twenty-first, I shall turn eighteen."

He said, not very intelligently, "You have a birthday next week?"

"Yes."

He struggled to pull himself together. "Why didn't you tell me sooner? Of course we must arrange a celebration. Eighteen!"

The word rang in his ears. Eighteen. It sounded a lifetime older than seventeen.

She shook her head in a firm negative. "No festivities, please. We are going to have a big celebration for Ozbald Day, Jura's national holiday, and one celebration a month is quite enough, I think."

He looked into her eyes. They were so intelligent, her eyes. Much too intelligent to be the eyes of a child. "I cannot allow your birthday to pass unnoticed."

She looked down and with her forefinger began to trace an invisible pattern on the white tablecloth. "Well . . . if you would like to give me a present, I might be able to suggest something."

The talk of birthday presents made him feel more comfortable. "Yes? And what could that be?"

She flicked him a glance then went back to creating her pattern. "Favory Dubovina," she said.

She had surprised him. He leaned back in his chair, a small frown between his brows. Louis had told him that the young stallion was one of the most talented he had seen in a long time. He was also very high-spirited. "Have you been riding Favory Dubovina?"

Her finger stilled and she looked at him, her white teeth set into the flesh of her lower lip. "Yes," she said.

"Under Louis's tutelage?"

She nodded. Strangely, that nod did not look

childlike to him anymore. Perhaps it was because he had never before noticed the long, graceful line of her neck. It was like the stem of a flower.

"Lord Louis has been letting me ride him," she explained. "And he said that if I continued to work with him, he would ride him also, so that his training will be perfect."

His frown smoothed out. If Louis thought she could do it, then it must be all right. He stood up. "Very well. Happy Birthday, Charity."

Her lips parted. "Do you mean I can have him?"

"He is yours."

She jumped up from her seat, ran around the table, and threw herself at him. "Oh Augustus, thank you! thank you! thank you!" Her arms were tight around his neck and her body was pressed full length against his. The scent of lavender drifted to his nostrils from her loose hair. His heart began to hammer.

Very gently, he placed his hands on her shoulders and moved her away. She looked up at him, her skin flushed, her face radiant. "You are the best husband in the world," she said.

He tried to smile back but his face felt stiff. "That is nice to know."

She clapped her hands. "I am going to go directly to the stables and tell Lord Louis."

He stood like a statue and watched as she flew out of the room; then he turned and resumed his seat at the breakfast table. He sat for a long time staring sightlessly at some crumbs on the white cloth, scarcely moving until a servant came in to see if he wanted anything else. Then he just shook his head, stood up, and returned to his own apartment to begin his day.

 Life went on as usual, but for the Prince something had changed irrevocably in the way he regarded his wife. The body he had glimpsed through her thin nightrobe, that he had held so briefly in his arms, was not the body of a child, and it had awakened a fire in him that, try as he might, he could not extinguish.

There had not been many women in the Prince's life. The first was the wife of a Jurian baron, who had seduced him when he was sixteen. She had been fifteen years older than he, and experienced in the arts of love. He had acquired a great deal of knowledge that was not academic during that particular holiday from school.

Then Jura had fallen to Napoleon, and the Prince had taken to the mountains. He was twenty-two when he met the widow of Baron Zais, a man who had earned his title by his contributions to the economy of Jura. The baron had owned extensive iron works on the shores of Lake Behinj in the Jurian Alps, and one bitter winter, after the Prince had been wounded in a skirmish, he had convalesced at his widow's lakeside home.

Lady Zais had been forty years of age that winter, intelligent, independent, and sensual. For the previous five years she had been the Prince's occasional mistress.

In addition to these two, there had been several

other high-born ladies at the Congress of Vienna who had been more than happy to sleep with a prince, but he had not been with a woman since Waterloo. This was the reason, he told himself, why he was suddenly looking at his innocent young wife with such inappropriately carnal thoughts.

The Prince's problem was that he had promised Charity she would not have to take up her wifely duties until she was ready. At the time he made the offer, the Prince had not foreseen the quandary this promise would place him in. For the fact was, he was ready to begin a normal married life, but Charity was not.

She had the body of a grown woman. She had the intelligence and compassion of a grown woman. But emotionally she was still a child. He found himself remembering words she had once said to him. *I don't want my life cluttered up by another person. A husband would only get in my way.*

He had gotten in her way more than enough already. He had wrenched her from her home and family and put her into a position she had never expected—or wanted—to fill. And she was doing a splendid job of being Princess of Jura. He was very proud of her.

She didn't need him importuning sexual favors from her. He was quite certain of that.

He was also quite certain of something else. He was miserable.

One morning, after a particularly restless night, he wrote a letter to Eva Zais.

14

"Augustus, may I speak to you for a moment?"

The Prince looked up to see his wife peeking in the door of his office. He put down the pen he was holding and said courteously, "Of course, Charity. Come in."

She crossed to his desk and he watched the way she walked, watched the easy grace of her movements as she took the chair that would place her opposite him. He used to think that lithe fluidity of hers was childlike. He must have been blind.

She gave him a tentative smile. "I am sorry if I am interrupting you."

He felt a pang of remorse. He had been finding excuses to avoid their breakfasts of late; Charity in her dressing gown was just a bit too much for him to bear.

He was tempted to say: *Charity, I want you. Let's make this marriage a real one. Let's go to bed together.*

Let's do it tonight. But the brown eyes gazing at him were troubled. She really had no idea what was bothering him.

For the first time in his life, the Prince actually wished that his mother was present. Charity needed a woman to talk to her, but all of the women of her family had returned to England, and his own mother was in Venice.

It's so typical of Mama, he thought with exasperation. *The one time I need her, she's not here.*

While these thoughts were going through his head, Charity gazed at him with that heartbreaking, tentative smile. He forced himself to smile back and reply, "Of course you are not interrupting me. How may I help you?"

She asked him about some problem with her shelter in Julia. It was not of any major importance, and the Prince was quick to realize that she had used it as an excuse to see him. He made some recommendations, which he was quite certain she had already thought of, and waited for the real reason she had sought him out.

She looked down at her hands, which were folded in the lap of her pretty jonquil yellow afternoon dress, and for a moment her lashes lay upon the delicate skin above her cheekbones.

Desire stirred and he cursed, silently and fluently, and his mouth set into a hard line. She looked at him and said, "Have I offended you in some way, Augustus?"

Wonderful, he thought. *This is just wonderful. Now she thinks she has offended me.*

"Of course not," he said. "Whatever makes you think such a thing?"

"Well . . . we don't have breakfast together anymore."

"Oh. That." He waved a hand. "I'm sorry, Charity. I have been busy."

She swallowed. He watched the motion in her slender neck. "I see."

He cast desperately around for something to change the subject. "Ah . . . are you enjoying your new horse?"

She had a smile that could light up an entire room. "Oh yes. You must come one morning and see him, Augustus. Lord Louis is so pleased with our progress."

"I shall try to do that," he promised, picking up the pen he had been writing with when she came in. Her radiant smile died away, and, taking the hint, she rose to her feet. He said pleasantly, "Don't hesitate to come to see me if you have any more problems."

"I won't." She looked so forlorn that he wanted to leap up, tear around the desk, and grab her into his arms. Instead he sat like a statue and let her leave.

As October passed into November, everything in Charity's life was going smoothly except the most important thing of all: her relationship with her husband. Instead of drawing closer together, as she had expected, they were growing farther and farther apart.

He doesn't find me attractive. It was the only reason Charity could imagine to explain Augustus's withdrawal from her. He liked her as a person. They had become good friends on their honeymoon. But clearly the thought of having a physical relationship with her disgusted him.

I suppose I can't blame him, she thought miserably as she lay awake at night in her lonely bed. *Any man who thought he was going to have Lydia in his arms and then got stuck with me would be disappointed.*

What made this development even more disconcerting was that Charity was finding herself physically very attracted to Augustus. The blinkers of childhood had finally fallen from her eyes, and she was seeing Augustus with the eyes of a woman, for a sexual male.

Everything about him fascinated her and made her want to touch him: his hair, which was long enough to brush the collar of his coat; his gray eyes; the cleft in his chin where she longed to put her finger; his hands, with their strong, finely shaped fingers; the golden gleam of chest hair that she had caught a glimpse of once or twice when they were at breakfast together. She wanted desperately for Augustus to kiss her, but she didn't know how to tell him that, and she was beginning to be horribly afraid that he didn't feel the same way about her.

So stood matters between the Prince and the Princess of Jura when the Prince's uncle, Duke Marko, returned to Julia for the first time since his son had eloped with the Prince's original fiancée. He arrived during a driving rainstorm the first week in

November, spent the night at his own palace in Julia, and the next morning, in a burst of cold sunshine, he went to the Pfalz to see Augustus.

When the Prince entered the salon in the royal apartment where Marko awaited him, the duke did not make his usual attempt to embrace his nephew. He said only, "It is good of you to see me, my boy."

Augustus walked forward, holding out his hand. "It is foolish for us to be estranged."

"That is most generous of you, Gus." Marko put his hand into the large, strong grasp of his nephew. "I am not going to defend what Franz did. He was very wrong. But he is my son, and I feel I must stand by him."

"I understand perfectly," the Prince replied. "Won't you be seated, Uncle Marko?"

In the Prince's father's time, the main purpose of this salon had been to show off the extensive art collection that covered its walls. The art had disappeared with Napoleon's marshal, leaving the room with bare walls and a single blue silk sofa, upon which the men now sat.

Marko looked around the room, his forehead scored with three deep lines. "This is a disgrace," he said. "The paintings in this room were priceless. Do we have any chance of getting them back?"

"I am doing my best, Uncle," the Prince replied mildly.

Marko scanned his nephew's face and said, "I must say, Gus, I did not expect you to be so calm."

The Prince understood that his uncle was not talking about the stolen artwork. "If Franz's elopement had resulted in the cancellation of my wedding, I would not be so calm," he replied. "As things stand now, however, he is welcome to Lydia. I am very pleased with the wife I have got."

"I am glad to hear that," Marko said. "It was clever of you to think of wedding the younger sister."

The Prince did not reply.

Abruptly, Marko got to his feet and paced to the green marble fireplace, which had a large discolored spot on the wall above it where a painting by Tintoretto had once hung. When he reached the fireplace he turned to face his nephew, straightening his shoulders as if preparing for a conflict.

The Prince remained where he was on the sofa. He was dressed in riding clothes and high boots, and it occurred to Marko that instead of seeming lost in the vast emptiness of the room, Augustus actually dominated it. There was a quality about the man that had been absent in the young boy the duke had known. This Augustus was a man accustomed to being in command. It was there in the hardness of his eyes and the firm set of his mouth. It was there in his figure, lounging on the sofa as a lion might bask in the sun. He looked perfectly relaxed, but one sensed the potential for danger in that slim, long-limbed body.

"The last time we spoke," Marko said, "I became angry with you. That was foolish of me, and I beg your pardon for it."

The Prince inclined his head and waited.

"I wish you would just listen to me, Gus," Marko

pleaded. "I don't believe you have any idea of the danger that your treaty with Britain poses to Austria."

Augustus looked surprised. "Danger? Uncle Marko, please don't tell me that the emperor is afraid that Great Britain is going to attack Austria."

"No, I am not going to tell you that," Marko replied. He took a deep breath as if gathering his strength. "Gus, I know that your father brought you up to believe that it was your sacred mission to keep Jura independent, but an independent Jura did not pose the threat to Austria in your father's time that it does today."

The level gray stare never changed. "How is that, Uncle?"

"The French occupation of so much of Europe has helped to disseminate dangerous and revolutionary ideas of liberalism and nationalism. Why should countries that have long been part of the Austrian Empire, countries such as Hungary and Poland, not decide to emulate Jura and declare themselves independent as well?"

The Prince unfolded his long length from the sofa and went to stand at the window, his hands clasped behind his back. The sunlight behind him made his ordinary blond hair look almost as golden as Franz's. "Well, Uncle, perhaps they *could* be as successful as we. Perhaps they *should* be." He made these outrageous remarks in a perfectly normal tone of voice. "After all," he continued in the same manner, "what does Austria have to offer its subject peoples other than a moribund administration that stifles their economies as well as their political vitality?"

Marko shut his eyes and told himself that he must not lose his temper over Gus's wild pronouncements. "I have not come here to argue with you about the value of the Austrian Empire, Gus." He gave his nephew a stern look. "I have come to ask you to think like a prince and take into consideration the welfare of your people."

Something flickered behind the Prince's gray eyes. He replied evenly, "That is something I always try to do, Uncle Marko."

"Then listen to me, please! I am here to bring you a proposal, and I am putting this proposal before you because I am a Jurian and a patriot and I believe that this is in the best interest of my country."

The hidden spark in the Prince's eyes became more noticeable. "What is this proposal?"

Marko finally recognized the flash in Gus's eyes as anger and strove to moderate his own voice. "Austria is prepared to negotiate an alliance with you that would give Austria access to Seista. In return, Austria is prepared to recognize you and your heirs as the legitimate rulers of Jura."

The Prince stared at his uncle as if he couldn't believe what he had just heard. "The emperor already did that, Uncle, when Austria signed the Final Act of the Congress of Vienna." His voice sounded very clipped. "You want me to give away Seista and in return get something that I already have?"

The duke said forcefully, "What you will get, Gus, is peace! I cannot represent too forcefully the emperor's anger about this treaty with England."

Augustus's eyes suddenly narrowed. "Tell me,

Uncle, just what does the emperor plan to do if I do not agree to this so-called alliance?"

Marko allowed an ominous pause to fall. Then he said somberly, "Tell me, Gus, if Austria should move against Jura, who would come to your aid?"

The Prince's face was grim. He did not reply.

Marko took two steps toward the window where his nephew stood. "I have read the Treaty of London, and it does not promise that Britain will commit ground troops to protect the independence of Jura. Oh, Britain will protest to the other Great Powers, but you must know that Castlereagh does not want Britain to be drawn into a continental war." Marko moved another step closer to his nephew. "Gus! Please take what I am saying seriously. It is more important for Jura to be friends with the empire next door than it is to be friends with one that is far away."

The pause that the Prince allowed to fall was far more ominous than the one that had gone before. When he finally spoke his voice was very soft. "You may tell the emperor for me that it is not wise policy to threaten actions that you cannot carry out. I have every intention of standing by my treaty with Great Britain."

After a visibly upset Marko had left, the Prince felt a sudden, violent need to get out of the palace, and so, without a word to anyone, he headed down the path to the stables. When he was halfway there he met Charity dressed in her riding clothes. She had obviously finished her lesson and was on her way back to the Pfalz.

She stopped when she saw him. "Augustus! What is wrong?"

He halted also and rubbed his hand up and down across his face, as if to scrub away his expression. "Is it that easy to see?"

She shook her head. "Of course not. It's just that I know you rather well."

He dropped his hand and sighed. "I just had a talk with Marko and, as usual, he succeeded in making me angry."

"Good heavens." Her fine brows puckered. "I didn't know that Marko was in Jura."

"I received a letter from him a week ago, asking if he could come. I wrote back and said that he could. I suppose I forgot to tell you."

This was the kind of information that would once have been discussed at their breakfasts, but which, since the breakfasts had stopped, there had been little opportunity to exchange. Charity kindly refrained from pointing this out, however, and simply said, "How did he make you angry this time?"

Augustus found that he would very much like to discuss his interview with Marko with his wife. A little farther down the path there was a small garden with a fountain and a stone bench, and the Prince put his hand under his wife's elbow and steered her in that direction. Once they were seated side by side, he began to recount his meeting with Marko. He had gotten as far as telling her about Marko's threat that Austria would launch a military attack against Jura when Charity suddenly leaped to her feet.

"I don't believe it! Austria would never risk an attack on a British ally." She paced up and down in front of him once, then whirled to face him. "Did the emperor really say that, or is that just Marko talking?"

"I don't know." The Prince watched his wife as once more she walked up and down the smoothly cut grass in front of him. "He said he was speaking for the emperor, but I have my doubts. The emperor must know that as soon as Austrian troops march into Jura, Russian troops would invade Poland, and the whole territorial settlement of the Congress of Vienna would go up in smoke. No one wants that."

Once more Charity swung around to face him. "Exactly." Her cheeks were rosy with emotion, her eyes were sparkling. "When I think of the nerve of that man . . ."

"Which man?" he inquired, "Marko or the emperor?"

She shot him an indignant look. "Marko, of course. He is supposed to be *your* ambassador, but it seems to me that he is more concerned with representing the interests of the Austrian emperor than he is with representing you."

For some reason, he was feeling much less upset about Marko than when he left the palace. Charity looked so pretty when she was angry, and there was something supremely satisfying about seeing her angry on his behalf.

"Oh well," he said soothingly, "Marko's wife is Austrian and he has spent so many years there that I suppose his bias is only natural."

She put her hands on her hips and glared at him.

"If that is the case, Augustus, then he is hardly the man to act as your ambassador!"

"I know that." His voice was patient. "That is why I have posted Viktor in Vienna to be my eyes and ears."

She curled her lip. "As far as the Imperial Court is concerned, Marko is your ambassador. You need to get rid of him, Augustus, and officially appoint Viktor."

The Prince frowned. It had been a long time since anyone had told him what to do.

She returned to her seat on the bench beside him. "Huh! The nerve of the man, thinking he could frighten you by threatening an Austrian invasion."

His frown smoothed out and his mouth curved into a smile. She looked up at him and smiled back, and for a brief golden moment they were in perfect harmony. Then she said, "Oh-oh, Augustus, don't move. A bug has just gone under your neckcloth." He remained perfectly still as she knelt beside him on the bench and inserted her finger under the starched white linen. He felt her finger touch the bare skin of his neck as she searched for the insect, and he gritted his teeth and shut his eyes.

As soon as she had discovered and ejected the invading bug, he rose to his feet, thanked her, and said that he must be on his way to the stable. He left her still kneeling there on the bench in the garden.

15

After his meeting with the Prince, Duke Marko returned to his palace in Julia in a very grim frame of mind. Waiting to speak to him were Count Georg Hindenberg and Marshal Jan Rupnik.

Both men stood when the duke walked in. When Marko did not immediately speak, Hindenberg demanded, "Well? Did you talk to him, Marko?"

"I talked to him." Marko came all the way into the library and poured himself a glass of brandy from a decanter set out upon a side table. "Christ, but he is a stubborn bastard! One could reason with my brother, but talking to Gus is like talking to a rock."

"He didn't listen to you?" Rupnik said.

Marko took a swallow of brandy and shook his head.

"He is a fool," Hindenberg said contemptuously. "This country suffered for ten years under a foreign occupation. What we need now is peace in order to rebuild our economy. We do not need another war."

Marko approached the other two, his glass in his hand. "Augustus informed me that he does not think Austria will dare to invade Jura."

Hindenberg got to his feet and began to pace up and down the polished library floor. "What does he know of the world? Nothing! He was seventeen when he went into the mountains, and he was there for ten years. Then, as soon as he emerged from his cave, he went to England and made this insane treaty that has so infuriated the emperor." He halted his pacing and turned to face the duke. "Such a man should not be on the throne of Jura."

Marko met and held his gaze. "Well, he is on the throne of Jura, and there isn't anything we can do about it." The duke finished the brandy in his glass. "All we can do is pray that he is right and that the emperor will not have the nerve to follow through with his threats."

A very grim Hindenberg and Rupnik left the duke's palace a few minutes later and walked halfway down the tree-lined street to the house belonging to Count Hindenberg, a substantial brick residence that had been built by the count's grandfather fifty years earlier. Directly across from it was a small jewel of a Baroque church.

The two men entered the house and went immediately to the count's study, a room that featured several fine paintings that the count had hidden successfully in a subcellar before he left Jura a day ahead of the French army's arrival.

The chief minister and the Marshal of Jura sat down in a pair of heavy carved wooden chairs and regarded each other. Hindenberg's square powerful face looked ruthless. "We must get rid of him," he said, his words matching his look. "He is dangerous. He listens to all the wrong people."

Rupnik nodded. "He cannot be allowed to continue leading Jura along this treacherous path."

Hindenberg slammed his hand down upon the arm of his carved wooden chair. "It is not as if we did not try to warn him. Marko brought him a direct proposal from the emperor, for God's sake. He could have secured his dynasty if he had agreed to an alliance with Austria." He stared at Rupnik and said deliberately, "It is Augustus himself who is forcing us to take this action."

"He has too high an opinion of himself," Rupnik said. "He led our troops into battle at Waterloo and he thinks he is a military man." He snorted contemptuously. "Jurian troops would be squashed like bugs under the foot of a giant if the emperor should decide to send an army against us."

Silence fell in the room as the two men contemplated what they were about to do. Then Hindenberg said, "We must keep this from Marko."

"Do you think he would object?" Rupnik asked.

"Marko is the type who will be more than happy to benefit from a crime so long as he can tell himself that he was not responsible for it," Hindenberg said with derision. He let his eyes rest on his favorite Dutch landscape. "Fortunately, his son is made of sterner stuff."

Rupnik agreed. "Franz has given me the name of a man in the Household Guard who owes him a favor. He recommends we use him for the job."

Hindenberg removed his gaze from the painting and returned it to Rupnik. "What favor?"

"This man fought with the Jurian army at Austerlitz, was wounded and left behind in an Austrian field hospital. Franz personally saw to it that all of the Jurian wounded were evacuated to Vienna, where they received proper care, and then he made certain that the men were repatriated back to Jura. It was through his recommendation that this man got his job in the Guard."

"Good," Hindenberg said. "This is a task for more than one man, though."

Rupnik nodded. "I'm sure this fellow will be able to pick a trustworthy companion."

"You will schedule both men for nighttime guard duty at the Pfalz?"

"Yes. I will have them put on duty outside the royal apartment. They can do it when everyone is asleep."

"We don't even have to worry about Augustus not being in his own bed," Hindenberg said contemptuously. "He does not sleep with his child bride, nor apparently does he sleep with any other woman. What kind of a man is that to lead Jura?"

"He is not the right man, certainly," Rupnik said. He smiled. "But we will rectify that."

The following morning a member of the Household Guard, by the name of Kark, asked a friend to accompany him into Julia so that he could buy a birthday gift for his mother. Once the two young men were away from the barracks and walking through the narrow streets of the city, Kark dragged his friend Artane into a small coffee shop and huddled with him over a scarred wooden table in the corner.

After the fat proprietor had brought them a pot of coffee and two cups, Artane said, "All right, Kark. What is it? You obviously have something on your mind other than your mother's birthday."

Kark leaned forward and said in a shaking voice, "Marshal Rupnik came to see me yesterday. He wants me to kill the Prince while I am on guard at the royal apartments—to smother him with a pillow while he is sleeping!"

At first Artane wouldn't believe that Kark was telling the truth. "It's a joke," he said. "I am not that gullible, Kark. You won't catch me out with this one."

But Kark's bony face was grim, his deep-set dark eyes burning. "It is no joke, Artane. This is not something I would joke about."

Artane finally realized that his friend was telling the truth, and his own lighter eyes widened in horror. "Jesus Christ," he said. "Jesus Christ."

"I didn't know what to do," Kark said tensely. "If I had refused to do as he asked, he would have had me killed to keep me quiet. So I pretended to go along with him."

Artane, who was a big burly man with sandy hair and a scar on his left cheek, turned to look around the coffee shop to make certain that no one could overhear them. He lowered his voice even more and said, "What are you going to do?"

"Well, I am certainly not going to kill the Prince," Kark hissed back.

"Sshhh." Once more Artane gave a quick, hunted look over his shoulder. "Of course you are not going to kill the Prince." He rubbed his nose. "What did Rupnik say exactly?"

"That the Prince's treaty with England was going to cause Austria to attack us and he said that is why it is my patriotic duty to eliminate Augustus."

Artane rubbed his nose again. "Do you think Rupnik is right about Austria?"

Kark's voice rose slightly. "I don't know if he is right or not. All I know is that for ten years Augustus fought for Jura while Rupnik sat on his arse in England."

"Shhh!" Artane said frantically.

Kark looked over his companion's shoulder at the others in the coffee house. "No one is paying the slightest bit of attention to us."

"How did Rupnik come to choose you?" Artane asked.

"He knew that I was one of the men Count Adamov helped after Austerlitz, and he apparently believes that I would like to see Franz become prince one day."

Artane fingered the scar on his cheek. "Do you think the count is involved in this plot?"

"Of course not," Kark said contemptuously. "Franz and Augustus are good friends. I don't think Duke Marko is involved either. It is just Rupnik. I think he is afraid of actually having to lead the army into battle. He certainly did a wretched job of it at Austerlitz." At last he drank some of the coffee that had been sitting untouched in his cup. "He promised me a lieutenancy, Artane. He thinks he can buy me."

Both guardsmen drank their coffee.

"You realize that if we don't do the job, the marshal will find someone who will," Kark said at last.

"We?"

"You have to help me," Kark said tersely. "I can't deal with this on my own."

Artane sighed. "I suppose not." Once again his hand touched his scarred cheek. "I fought with Augustus at Waterloo. He even spoke to me individually before the battle. I like him."

"We must warn him," Kark said. "Who knows what other plans Rupnik may have made? For all we know, we are not the only assassins he has employed."

Artane blew out his breath. "How do we warn him? What chance do you and I have to approach the Prince? We can hardly present ourselves at the front door of the Pfalz and ask to speak to him."

Kark stared in silence at the coffee cup in his thin, bony hand. At last he said, "If we don't have access to the Prince we must talk to someone who has."

"Who?"

"I think Baron Hindenberg is our best choice," Kark replied. "He is Augustus's chief minister and his house is right here in Julia."

"Some more coffee?" the shopkeeper called from behind his counter.

"No, thank you."

The two young men looked at each other.

"We should go to see Hindenberg now," Kark said.

Artane nodded somberly.

Very slowly both guardsmen got to their feet and made their way to the door.

Count Hindenberg was preparing to leave his palace to make a call upon the Austrian ambassador when he was approached by his secretary with the news that two men from the Household Guard were at the door asking to speak to him.

"I would not bother you with this request, my lord," his secretary apologized, "but these men appear to be in great distress. They said it was a matter of life and death."

Hindenberg felt a chill go down his spine. "Did you get the names of these guards?"

"Yes, my lord. Kark and Artane."

God in heaven, Hindenberg thought in horror as he recognized the first name. Abruptly he pulled off the gloves he had just finished putting on and said, "You may bring them to the anteroom, Grasse."

"Yes, my lord."

An hour after his interview with Kark and Artane, Hindenberg was sitting in the marshal's elegant office recounting what had happened. "Apparently Franz was wrong about the loyalty of his friend Kark," he concluded sarcastically.

Rupnik's face looked even gaunter than usual.

Hindenberg went on: "The friend he has dragged into this is a veteran of Waterloo who admires Augustus greatly."

Rupnik swore.

The marshal's office was in one of the more extravagant rococo palaces in Jura, which for the last fifty years had been used as an office building for the Jurian military establishment. The two men were standing close together near the wall farthest from the door, and their voices were pitched very low. Rupnik asked the crucial question, "Have they told anyone else?"

"No."

"You are certain?"

"I made certain." Hindenberg's hard eyes held an ironic expression. "They came to me because they knew I could get the Prince's ear in a hurry. I told them that I would take care of it, that they should tell no one else."

"Then . . . it's a problem, of course, but we can rectify it," Rupnik said.

Hindenberg agreed. "We will have to kill them, of course."

Someone knocked upon the marshal's closed door and both men jumped.

"What is it?" Rupnik called in a voice that was too loud.

"I have that report you wanted, Marshal." The voice of Rupnik's secretary came clearly through the shut door.

"Later," Rupnik said.

Both men strained their ears to hear the sound of

footsteps going away from the door. When all was quiet once more, Hindenberg said doubtfully, "Can you arrange to have them killed?"

"Certainly." Rupnik's voice was almost casual. "One can always hire an assassin for a small job such as that. It is finding someone who is willing to assassinate a prince that is more difficult."

"I don't think I would try using the Household Guard again," Hindenberg snapped.

Rupnik's hooded eyes fixed themselves on the chief minister's face. He said slowly, "This might be a job we will have to do ourselves."

Hindenberg shook his head. "It's too dangerous. Always make sure there is at least one dupe between you and the crime."

Later that same afternoon, Kark and Artane huddled together in a secluded corner of the stables that were attached to the Household Guard barracks. Their hiding place was concealed from the rest of the stable by a wall of baled hay, but they kept their voices to a low murmur so that they would not be heard.

"I don't think Hindenberg has done anything to warn the Prince," Kark said. His face was white and tense-looking in the dim stable light. "He's had the whole day and no one has sent for us to testify."

From the other side of the barrier of hay came the *thud, thud, thud* of a hoof kicking at a wooden stall door. "Stop that, Cesar!" a groom yelled.

"What if he *isn't* going to say anything?" Kark asked.

The two men looked at each other and found in the other's apprehensive eyes a confirmation of his own deepest fears.

Artane wet his lips. "What if Hindenberg is in the plot with Rupnik?"

The strain on Kark's face deepened. "I am beginning to think that he must be. What other reason would account for his delay in warning the Prince? This is not something one takes one's time about."

Thud, thud, thud came the hoof again.

"If that stallion comes up lame tomorrow, the marshall will have our heads," a groom grumbled.

"He wants his supper," another voice said.

"It's too early. Better take him out into the stable-yard and walk him around for a bit."

There came the sound of a stall door opening. "Look at that! The brute tried to bite me!"

"The horse is as miserable as his master," the first voice agreed.

Kark and Artane listened to the sound of the animal's hooves going up the aisle.

Artane said, "If the two of them are in it together, then our lives aren't worth a single mark."

"I know."

Artane smashed his fist into the baled hay. "The only way we can save ourselves now is to warn the Prince."

"But how?" A nerve twitched in Kark's lean cheek. "We don't have access to him, and you can bet your pay that Hindenberg will make certain that we don't get access."

"There must be *someone* who can help us!"

Kark's eyes widened abruptly and his head lifted. Artane saw the change. "What is it?"

"If we can't see the Prince, perhaps we can see the Princess," Kark said.

Both men had done escort duty for the Princess when she left the Pfalz to go into Jura or to pay visits to local villages. "If we can get her attention, she will listen to us," Kark said hopefully.

"How do we go about getting her attention?"

"I know that she rides every morning with Lord Louis," Kark said. "If we get into the Pfalz stable area tomorrow morning, perhaps we can find a way to talk to her."

"All right," Artane said. "Now for the most important question of all: How do we manage to stay alive from now until tomorrow morning?"

"We hide," Kark said.

"Where?"

"In the woods near the Pfalz. Then, in the morning, we put on our uniforms and tell the guard at the gate that we are on escort duty. Once we get into the palace grounds, we'll go straight to the stables and wait for the Princess."

Artane drew in a long breath, then slowly let it out. "All right," he said. "But let's get out of here as soon as possible. I don't feel safe."

At eight o'clock the following morning, Kark and Artane presented themselves at the side gate the Household Guard customarily used when reporting for duty and told the sentry in the guardbox that they were there to do escort duty for the Princess. The man in the box happened to be a temporary substitute for the original guard, who had gone to relieve himself, and he did not know that the original sentry had received orders from the marshal that two guards by the names of Kark and Artane were not to be admitted to the palace grounds.

Unaware of how lucky they had been, Kark and Artane proceeded along the pathway that went to the stables. One of the grooms in the stableyard told them that the Princess was already in the manège taking a lesson from Lord Louis Hunersdorf.

"Let's go," Kark said to Artane, and the two men turned and began to walk toward the building that looked like a Greek temple but was in reality the riding hall. They heard Lord Louis's voice as soon as they entered the vestibule.

"Very nice, Princess. A little more from behind, perhaps. There! That is it! Now try to hold that while you go around the ring."

Kark, with Artane following, moved to the doorway of the ring and looked in. The second- and third-floor galleries on either side of the rectangular sand ring were empty; the only onlooker to the lesson was an immense portrait of the Prince's grandfather riding a splendid Lipizzaner that hung high over the horses' entry door. In the manège itself a single horse and rider were trotting around the perimeter of the ring.

Kark thought that the Princess looked very small on the muscular gray stallion. She was dressed in a full-skirted velvet coat, breeches, high black boots, and a gold-encrusted tricorn hat. The only thing about her that proclaimed her sex was the long braid that rippled along her back in rhythm with the horse's swinging tail. She trotted right in front of the two guardsmen and never noticed them, so intensely was she concentrating on the horse.

"Keep the forward," Lord Louis called as she continued down the long side of the ring. "Don't let him get behind your leg."

The rider did not appear to do anything in response to this instruction, but the gray stallion's neck suddenly lowered and lengthened and Lord Louis called, "Good."

Kark and his companion waited fifteen long minutes for the Princess to finish. Kark was so afraid that someone would come in and find them that he felt sick to his stomach, but neither he nor Artane dared to interrupt the lesson.

Finally it was over and the Princess was smiling and swinging down from the saddle with all the athleticism of the slim boy she resembled. She had halted not far from where the two guardsmen stood, and Kark jerked his head toward Artane and stepped resolutely into the ring.

"Your Highness." The radiant face under the tricorn hat was utterly feminine, and the look she turned on the approaching strangers was completely without fear. "Yes?"

Kark thought in sudden panic, *What if she doesn't believe us? What will we do then?*

Lord Louis, who had been standing in the center of the ring, began to walk toward them. "Who are you men?" he said, far more suspicious than the Princess of the unusual presence of two Household Guards in the manège. "What are you doing here?"

Kark said to the Princess, "Please, Your Highness, you must listen to us. There is a plot against the Prince's life. If you wish to save him, you must listen to us."

At his words, all of the lovely color drained from her face. "A plot? Against his life?"

"Yes, Your Highness."

Lord Louis stopped beside the Princess and glared at the guardsmen. "What is going on here?"

To Kark's immense relief, the Princess said, "These men have something to tell me, Louis. May we borrow your office?"

The slender, gray-haired *écuyer,* who was dressed in a more tailored coat than his pupil's, looked at Kark and Artane with hard eyes. Then he said, "All right, as long as I can accompany you."

"Thank you, my lord," Kark said with heartfelt gratitude.

Lord Louis signaled to a groom to come and take the stallion, and the four of them crossed the ring, went out into the hallway, up a flight of stairs, and into Lord Louis's office.

It was the Princess who took charge of the interview. As soon as the door had closed behind them, she turned to Kark. "All right. Tell me about this plot."

"Two days ago Marshal Rupnik came to see me," Kark began, and he proceeded to recount the entire story of his interviews with both Rupnik and Hindenberg. As he was talking, all of the girlish softness left the Princess's face; it seemed to become thinner, its delicate bones more prominent, and her large brown eyes turned almost purely gold.

When he had finished his story she asked no questions but said immediately, "Both of you come with me to the Pfalz. I want the Prince to hear this for himself."

Even her voice was different, Kark thought. He saw the golden eyes move to Lord Louis. "You come too, Louis," she said. "We may have need of you."

Kark and Artane followed the Princess and Lord Louis up the path to the palace, in through the ground-level door, up the stairs, and through the same arched doorway that they had been assigned to guard that very evening. They went halfway along a wainscoted passageway before the Princess stopped in front of a closed door and commanded Lord Louis, "Take them in there. I will find the Prince."

Lord Louis opened the door and gestured for the two guardsmen to enter. Kark went first into a very pretty salon, with plasterwork designs on the painted walls. The large mirror on the wall between the windows reflected back the tense figures of the three men as they stood in silence waiting for the Princess to return.

At last the door opened and the tall figure of the Prince filled the doorway. He came into the room, the Princess after him.

Kark stiffened to attention and saluted, and Artane did the same.

The Princess shut the door.

"Which of you is Kark?" the Prince said. He was in his shirtsleeves with the cuffs rolled up, and his hair was damp. Evidently he had been in the middle of washing up, and his wife's tale had disturbed him enough that he hadn't bothered to wait to put on a coat.

"I am, Your Highness." Kark took a half step forward to identify himself.

The Prince's gray eyes narrowed as they moved to Kark's face. "Tell me," he commanded, "exactly what Rupnik said to you."

Kark drew a deep steadying breath and proceeded to recount the entire conversation once more.

Augustus listened with not a muscle moving in his face. When Kark had finished he said, "Now tell me about your conversation with Hindenberg." Once again Kark complied.

The Prince was silent when Kark concluded his tale, his face as calm and expressionless as a mask.

"Hindenberg has made no attempt to speak to you?" the Princess asked her husband.

"None," the Prince replied in a voice as calm and expressionless as his face. But one look into his diamond-hard eyes revealed the fact that he was very angry indeed.

Lord Louis said, "Hindenberg must be part of the plot, Your Highness. There can be no other reason for his failure to warn you."

"That is certainly how it looks." The Prince turned to his *écuyer.* "Louis, will you bring Emil to me?"

Lord Louis went to fetch the Prince's friend, and the four people left in the room listened to the door close behind him. The Prince went to the window and stood gazing out. The Princess stood in front of a delicate plaster cherub on the wall and looked at her husband's taut shoulders and rigid back.

They waited in silence. At last the door opened again to admit the broad-shouldered young noble whom Kark knew to be one of the Prince's closest friends. Augustus turned to face Lord Emil Sauder and briefly, in that deceptively calm voice, he related the plot. He ended by saying, "I want you to take a contingent of guards, go to Rupnik's office in the city, arrest him, and bring him back here to me."

Lord Emil's dark eyes were blazing. "I will go immediately, Gus."

Lord Emil left and once again the room was silent. For the first time since he had come in, Kark saw the Prince look at his wife, who was now sitting on the sofa.

"This is not going to be pretty, Charity," he said. "Do you want to stay?"

"Yes," she said.

He nodded. "All right."

"These guards must be hungry, Augustus," she said. "They hid in the woods all night and then came directly to see me. Perhaps Louis could take them into the morning room and order them some food."

The Prince looked at his *écuyer*. "Do you mind, Louis? The fewer who know about this at the moment, the better."

"Of course I don't mind," Lord Louis said.

Kark was extremely happy to follow the *écuyer* out of the room. He would feel much more comfortable being at a safe distance from the dangerously angry Augustus.

$\mathcal{L}$eft alone with her husband, Charity also recognized the clamped-down anger in Augustus. He had gone back to staring out the window, and she looked at his uncombed hair curling on his bare neck and something inside her clenched hard. Never before had she thought of him as vulnerable, yet now, as she stared at those tender blond ringlets, she felt how exposed he was in his royal position.

Who knows where else his enemies might be? If Rupnik had not approached this particular man . . . if Kark had not thought of trying to see me . . . if . . . if . . . if . . . If not for all of these ifs, Augustus would be dead.

She shivered and hugged her arms around her as if she were physically cold. "Rupnik is the commander of your Household Guard, Augustus," she said abruptly. "He is sworn to protect you! If you cannot trust him, then whom can you trust?"

He turned to face her. "I know whom I can trust, Charity." His face was grim. "My mistake was in keeping my father's ministers and not replacing them with my own men. You were right, I should have got rid of the old guard. It is a mistake I will not repeat."

She looked into his cold gray eyes. She desperately wanted his comfort and, throwing pride to the winds, said in a small voice, "I am so afraid, Augustus."

He responded as she had hoped he would, coming over to the sofa, sitting beside her and taking her hand. "There is nothing to be afraid of. I am perfectly safe and we will get rid of these villains before they can make any more mischief."

She took the initiative and moved closer to him, snuggling into his arms, closing her eyes and resting her cheek against his chest. For a moment his arms tightened, gripping her hard against him. His cheek came down on her head, and she felt sheer bliss. Then his head lifted, his arms loosened, and he said, "There is no need to upset yourself, my dear. All will be well."

His voice sounded stiff. His body was rigid. His loose arms rejected her. She drew away and moved to the farthest corner of the sofa. "I'm sorry," she said in a subdued voice. "I didn't mean to be a baby."

Because she wasn't looking at him she didn't see the involuntary way his hand reached toward her. After a moment he got up and resumed his post by the window. They remained together in silence until Lord Emil returned. He was alone. "Where is Rupnik?" the Prince demanded. "Were you too late to catch him?"

Lord Emil said grimly, "Yes, Gus, we were too late. When he saw me coming with the guard, he killed himself."

16

$\mathcal{L}$ord Emil had better luck catching Hindenberg, who, when brought to the palace, swore to Augustus that he was not a party to Rupnik's plan. When the Prince confronted him with Kark and Artane, however, he collapsed and fell to his knees, begging for mercy.

Augustus turned him over to the Chief Justice of Jura for a trial whose outcome was in little doubt. Charity voiced the general opinion of all of those who cared for Augustus when she pronounced, "I hope they hang him. A man like that, a man who would betray his own sworn prince, does not deserve to live."

"I could not agree with you more, Your Highness," Lord Emil said heartily. He, the Prince, Charity, Lord Louis, and Lord Stefan had gathered in the Princess's sitting room after Count Hindenberg had been led away. Everyone was drinking coffee.

The Prince looked at his wife and shook his head in sorrow. "Can this bloodthirsty woman be the same sweet and charitable girl who has worked so hard to open shelters and health clinics for Jura's poor?"

"I most certainly am the same person," Charity replied vigorously. "And this same person also wants to know if Duke Marko was involved in this heinous plot."

Her question was greeted by a significant silence. Everyone looked at the Prince.

He was frowning into his coffee cup. "I don't know," he replied. "I would like to think that he was not, but I don't know."

"Arrest him," Lord Stefan recommended. "It is the only way to insure your safety, Gus."

The Prince shook his head. "I have absolutely no evidence against him."

"Lord Stefan is right. You must do something to insure your safety, Your Highness," Lord Louis urged.

"I am doing something, Louis," the Prince replied. "I am appointing Lord Stefan to be my chief minister, Lord Emil to be my new marshal, and Count Viktor Rozman to replace Marko as my official ambassador to Austria." He moved his gray gaze to Charity. "I have learned my lesson. From now on I will have only my own people around me."

"So Marko will go free?" Lord Stefan said in a flat voice.

The Prince leaned back in his chair. "Franz will hold him in check, Stefan. Believe me, he will not want his father involved in any nefarious schemes to overthrow me. He will keep a close eye on Marko."

"I don't trust Franz," Charity said. "How can you consider him your friend, Augustus? Look what he did to you. He ran away with your intended bride a week before your wedding."

The Prince was still holding his coffee cup and now he lifted it in a flourish to her. "And in doing so, he did me the greatest of favors."

Lord Stefan raised his cup as well. "He did all Jura a favor, Your Highness."

"He most certainly did," and Lord Emil's cup was also lifted into the air.

"To Princess Charity," Lord Louis said with a smile as he raised his own cup to his favorite pupil.

Charity blushed and laughed as the men toasted her with their delicate Sevres coffee cups, and the subject of Franz was dropped.

The dark mood cast over the Pfalz by the conspiracy of Rupnik and Hindenberg quickly dissipated under the excitement of getting ready for Jura's national holiday, Ozbald Day. This anniversary was celebrated annually to honor the Battle of Ozbald, the country's great sixteenth-century victory over the Turks. It would be the first official celebration of the holiday since the war, and Augustus was anxious to restore all of the traditional functions that had been in abeyance for over a decade.

A week before the anniversary date, Julia's palaces began to fill with the country's nobles, who were pouring into the city in order to attend the festivities that Augustus had planned. On Saturday morning, exactly four days after the Rupnik-Hindenberg plot had been discovered, the Prince received a note from Eva Zais stating that she was in Julia and asking him to come see her.

He stood in front of the pier glass in his dressing room and held out his arms so that his valet could put on his blue coat. He had been given the note when he returned from his morning ride, and his mind had been completely preoccupied ever since he had read it.

I have to see her, he thought. *It would be unforgivably discourteous not to see her.*

"Is there anything else I can do for you, Your Highness?"

"What?" For a moment he looked blankly at his valet. Then he said hastily, "Oh, no, that will be all, Hans. Thank you." Once he was alone he walked to the window and stood staring out at the gardens, thinking of Eva.

After a moment, he brought himself up short and told himself that he was married, that he could not expect to resume his comfortable affair with Eva with Charity living right here in the palace with him. It would not be right. It would be a sin.

Augustus certainly knew enough history to be aware that most princes were scarcely paragons of morality. A sovereign's duty was to produce a legitimate heir; what he did after that was not judged too harshly. But Augustus was a young man who held himself accountable for all of his promises, and he knew that to betray his promise to Charity was wrong.

He leaned his forehead against the window glass, closed his eyes, and tried to ignore the clamoring demands of his celibate body.

I will pay a visit to Eva. I am certain that is all she is expecting. She knows that I am married. She will understand that anything that was once between us must be over.

He drove a pair of Lipizzaners, with only a groom to accompany him. The Zais Palace in Julia was one of the newer edifices, built in the last century in the neoclassical style. The Prince alighted quickly and told his groom to drive the horses around to the stables in the back. The last thing he wanted to do was to advertise to the world that he was here.

It never once crossed his mind that Eva would not be at home.

A servant opened the front door of the palace before he reached it, and, as he stepped into the marble-floored hallway, she was standing there waiting for him. She had cut her hair, and the sun shining in through the fan window over the door lit its pale gold like a halo. Her face was in shadow, so he could not see the color of her eyes, but he knew that they were green.

"Your Highness," she said, and sank into a graceful curtsey. "How kind of you to call. Will you be pleased to come in and partake of some refreshment?"

"Thank you," he said. His mouth was dry and his heart was thudding. "It is good to see you again, Lady Zais." He followed her into a salon that he had never seen before and that appeared to be decorated with Empire style furniture and many busts of Roman emperors. He scarcely noticed his surroundings; his senses were too filled with the scent of her familiar perfume.

 $\mathcal{E}$va sat beside the Prince on a backless Roman couch and served him coffee. She had been deeply surprised by the letter she received from him a month ago. She had been the recipient of a number of letters from Augustus during the course of their rather long relationship, so she knew very well what they were usually like—short, informative, and very much to the point. What had made this one so extraordinary was that it had been about absolutely nothing at all.

Augustus did not write letters about nothing, and she had known immediately that something was wrong. She looked now at the tensely strung man sitting beside her and realized that her instinct had been correct. Something was very wrong indeed.

What is it, Augustus? She opened her lips to say the words, but then held back. She knew him well enough to understand that it was impossible to breach his reserve with questions; one had to wait until he was ready to confide. In dealing with Augustus, patience was the supreme virtue.

That was how it had been when they first met. Young as he was, she had wanted him from the start. And it had not been just because he was a prince. There was something about Augustus that made a woman feel . . . made her feel . . . Eva sipped her coffee and lowered her suddenly heavy eyelids. Made her feel like going to bed with him. She shot him a swift sideways look. *It's that damn dimple in his chin that does it.*

She had waited for him that first time, waited until he had looked at her with an expression she recognized, and then she had let him know that she desired him too. So this time also she would wait.

She thought that the problem had to be his marriage. Trouble with a woman would be the one thing that would have made him turn to her. Triumph flickered through her at the thought. Eva had never fooled herself into thinking that Augustus would wed her, but when she learned of his marriage to a young and lovely English girl, it had hurt. It had hurt far more than she thought it would. It was petty of her, perhaps, but she was glad the marriage wasn't a success.

All the while these thoughts had been going through her mind, they had been chatting about the upcoming festivities for Ozbald Day.

"You have given us back our national pride," she told him now.

He laughed a little harshly. "I have given Jura a few national celebrations, that is all I have done so far."

"No." She shook her head and fell silent for a moment, trying to find the words to explain to him what he meant to the people of his country. "I remember how I felt when first I saw you. Your men brought you to my villa because you had been injured and I remember looking at you as you sat there in front of

my fire: young, haggard, feverish, wounded. I remember how I thought, 'That is my prince. He has
not run away like so many of the other nobles. He is
staying and he is fighting for us.' And I felt such
pride in you, Augustus. I felt, 'If he can fight for
Jura, then so can I.'"

He looked at her with darkening eyes. "Did you
really think that, Eva?"

She smiled at him. She was a lovely woman and
looked at least ten years younger than her age. "I
did."

He was very pale and a muscle jumped in his
cheek. He said hoarsely, "Eva, I should get out of
here."

By now his eyes were so dark they were nearly
black, and she had no trouble at all recognizing the
emotion that they held. "My dear," she said softly,
"what is between you and me is between you and
me. It cannot hurt anyone else."

He shook his head, like a man trying to shake off
a slowly overpowering narcotic. She reached out,
picked up his hand, and laid it on her breast.

His fingers closed, instantly. He groaned. Then his
mouth was coming down on hers and she surrendered to the intense pleasure of his kiss.

Two days before the anniversary of Ozbald Day,
the Prince imported a traveling circus. The residents
of Julia and the farmers from the surrounding area
and their children were entertained by dancers who
performed on tightropes and acrobats who leaped on

and off of horses, by a pony that could count, and a man who could swallow fire.

"There was even a man who rode four horses at once, Augustus," Charity said as they ate a small supper with their respective staffs before going into Julia for the evening's entertainment.

The Prince looked at his wife's sparkling eyes and laughed. "Now how could he do that?"

She paused with a forkful of chicken held halfway to her mouth. "The horses were lined up four abreast and he stood with one foot on each of the outside horses. He galloped them, Augustus! It was so exciting. I wish you had seen it."

"Did you attend the circus as well, my lady?" Lord Stefan asked Lady Stefanie Havek, the young woman who had become Charity's chief lady-in-waiting.

"Indeed I did, my lord," Stefanie replied with as much enthusiasm as Charity. "I liked the tightrope dancers the best."

Charity nodded, her mouth full of chicken. When she had swallowed she added her recommendation. "They were excellent also. Indeed, if we did not have to attend this masquerade tonight, I would have gone to see the circus again."

"I realize it is outrageous of me to expect you to give up a circus for a mere masquerade ball, my dear," the Prince said teasingly. "What an ogre you must think me."

Everyone at the table laughed.

Charity felt a frisson of alarm run up and down her back at the sound of that gently teasing tone.

Something was different about Augustus. She had thought so yesterday, and today the change seemed even more evident.

For some reason, the Prince had transformed back into the man he was on their honeymoon. For these last two days he had been relaxed and comfortable with her, as he had been at Lake Leive and during those few wonderful weeks after they had returned to the Pfalz. He was as he had been before he stopped having breakfast with her, stopped confiding in her, stopped being alone with her.

Charity, who had suffered greatly from his aloofness, realized that she should be jumping with joy to have her husband back. But some deep feminine instinct was making her feel profoundly uneasy about this too-sudden about-face. If someone had asked her to explain her uneasiness, she would have been unable to articulate a reason, but it was definitely there.

Husband and wife rode together in the royal coach and chatted pleasantly the whole way into Julia. The masquerade was being held in one of the loveliest of the city's Renaissance palaces, and as a footman handed Charity out of the coach, she gazed with appreciation at the brilliantly lit scene before her.

The palace steps were lined with footmen holding torches, and as she and the Prince waited, a red velvet carpet was spread for them to walk upon. Lady Stefanie, who had arrived in the carriage ahead of the royal one, stepped forward to straighten Charity's pink satin train and make a quick adjustment to her diamond tiara. Then she and Augustus were slowly ascending the stairs, where they moved through the palace to stand in the doorway of a large salon that had been arranged as a ballroom for the evening. Charity listened to their names being intoned by the majordomo: "His Royal Highness Prince Augustus and Her Royal Highness Princess Charity."

Is that really me? she thought. *Will I ever grow accustomed to hearing myself called by that name?* Then, as they progressed down the center aisle of the room, where the crowd parted for them like the Red Sea for Moses, the men bowed and the women sank into deep curtseys and she wanted to laugh and say, *It's only me, Charity Debritt. You really don't have to do that.*

But she felt the weight of the satin train behind her and the pinch of the beautiful diamond tiara digging into her scalp and knew that she wasn't Charity Debritt anymore, she was the Princess of Jura. Her life was irrevocably changed, and she had better get used to it.

Everyone in the room wore dominoes and masks except Charity and the Prince. For the first few dances they sat in gilt chairs upon a low dais that had been erected for them in the front of the room, but then the orchestra struck up a waltz and Augustus turned to her and said with a grin, "May I have this dance, Madam Wife?"

As they stood together on the floor, Charity with her train swept over her arm and her head not even reaching to his shoulder, she looked up into his eyes and said, "Please don't take big steps, Augustus, or I shall never keep up with you."

"Don't worry," he promised, and moved off into the dance.

Dancing with Augustus was the most blissful experience of Charity's life. She loved the feeling of being so close to him, their bodies in such harmony that they moved as one. She felt she could go on dancing with him forever, and when the music stopped she swayed a little, not wanting to be parted from him.

They finished next to a lavender domino that Charity recognized as belonging to Lady Stefanie, and the Prince evidently recognized Lord Emil as her partner because he made a comment to him about the music. The four of them began to move off the floor together when the music for the next dance began. The Prince asked Stefanie to dance and Lord Emil asked Charity.

Charity danced once more with her husband during the course of the evening, and he spent some time sitting beside her on the royal dais and chatting with visiting friends, but Charity noticed that he danced twice with a blonde woman in a dark green domino and mask. He danced with several other women also, but only once. And his head did not bend to theirs with that air of intimacy that was like a dagger to her heart.

Charity was never one to shirk an unpleasant task, so when she and the Prince were on their way home in the carriage, she asked him, "Who was that woman you danced with, Augustus? The woman in the green domino?"

He showed no surprise at her question, but answered with perfect readiness. "Baroness Zais. She was very good to me during the war. She nursed me back to health once when I was wounded."

It was too dark to see his face, but his voice sounded perfectly normal. *She nursed him when he was injured.* It was not until she felt relief flood through her that Charity realized how afraid she had been.

She inhaled deeply and turned to look at his shadowy profile. "I didn't know that you had been injured."

"I took a bullet in the shoulder. It wasn't that bad a wound, but it wasn't healing. Stefan and Emil brought me to Eva's villa, and she took care of me."

Eva. At his use of the baroness's Christian name, a little of Charity's relief dried up.

They entered the Pfalz together, and when Charity said that she was tired and was going directly to bed, the Prince seconded her. "It's been a long day."

The two of them walked in the direction of the west wing, where their respective apartments lay. From his position behind them in the Banqueting Room, Lord Emil called, "Don't forget you have an early appointment tomorrow, Gus."

"I will remember," the Prince called back over his shoulder.

There had been an oddly urgent note in Emil's voice, and Charity gave her husband a curious glance. They passed the two Household Guards stationed at the entrance to the west wing and Charity asked, "Is the meeting about the conspiracy, Augustus?"

"What?" He looked at her in confusion. Then his brow smoothed out. "No, no, nothing like that. It is just the French ambassador—nothing unusual."

They had reached the door to her apartment, and he looked down at her. "You looked lovely tonight, my dear."

"Thank you, Augustus," she replied gravely.

He bent from his much greater height and kissed her cheek. "Sleep well."

Impulsively, Charity reached up to fling her arms around his neck and kiss him on the mouth, but her arms had scarcely moved before he stepped away. She blinked in surprise. He had moved so quickly he almost jumped.

A muscle twitched in his jaw. He wasn't quite meeting her eyes. "Good night, my dear."

"Good night, Augustus," she replied quietly, and turned away to allow him to continue along the passage to his own rooms.

Her maid was waiting to undress her, but once she was in her nightgown with her hair brushed out, she did not get immediately into bed. Instead she dismissed her maid, put on her dressing gown, and paced restlessly around her bedroom for a good half hour, her mind in turmoil. For some reason, it bothered her terribly that she had not been able to kiss her husband good night. At last she realized that she was far too agitated to sleep.

I must speak to Augustus. We have to make things right between us. We have to make this marriage a real one. I won't sleep a wink if I don't see him and tell him how I am feeling.

Abruptly, before she could change her mind or lose her courage, she acted. The Prince's apartment was right next to hers in the palace's west wing; the door on the west wall of her bedroom led into her dressing room, and the door in her dressing room led into his dressing room. Charity picked up the candle from her bedside table and, for the first time in her life, walked through all of those doors. She didn't stop until she was standing at the very last one, which led from the Prince's dressing room into his bedroom. There she hesitated, but the urgency of the impulse that had driven her to make this move was still strong, and she drew a deep, uneven breath and knocked.

The only reply was silence.

She knocked again.

Still there was silence.

This time, along with knocking, she called his name.

Nothing.

An image of Augustus lying smothered in his bed flashed into Charity's mind, and she pushed the door open and burst inside.

The room was empty. The bedcovers had been turned back, but the pristine smoothness of the sheets and pillows indicated clearly that no one had slept there. There was no sign of Augustus anywhere.

At first, Charity was stunned. Where was he? He had gone to bed when she did, a little more than an hour before.

Perhaps he had not gone directly to bed, she

thought. Perhaps he was sitting up in one of the other rooms of his apartment, deep in conversation with . . . with whom? He had left Lord Stefan and Lord Emil behind in the Banqueting Room. She remembered the words Lord Emil had called after him: *Don't forget you have an early appointment tomorrow, Gus.*

She had thought the appointment must be very important for Emil to have reminded him. But Augustus had told her it was only the French ambassador. So . . . so perhaps Emil had said that because he knew that Augustus would be out very late tonight and he didn't want him to oversleep.

Charity began to shiver uncontrollably. "No," she said out loud. "No. I won't believe it."

But the image of Augustus dancing with a blonde woman in a dark green domino kept rising in front of her tightly shut eyes. *Eva,* an insistent voice kept whispering in her ears. *Eva. Eva. Eva* . . .

Abruptly, Charity fled, running blindly back to her own bedroom, where she threw herself onto her solitary bed and began to sob as if she would never be able to stop.

17

oward dawn Charity was so exhausted that she
fell into a fitful sleep, and the following day
her schedule was so busy she simply didn't have
time to brood about what had happened the previous
night. She attended Ozbald Day parties at three different venues in Julia and then drove to an orphanage in a nearby town for a party there.

She shared her carriage with Lady Stefanie on the
way back to the Pfalz after the orphanage party, and
she was grateful for her lady-in-waiting's cheerful
company. Stefanie's chatter helped keep her mind
off her upcoming meeting with Augustus.

Charity was profoundly nervous about meeting
her husband after what she had discovered the night
before. She didn't know how she should behave,
what she should say, what she should do. She had
never felt so young, so stupid, so utterly unsophisti-
cated.

She knew well enough what she wanted to say. *I trusted you and you betrayed me.* Those were the words she wanted to hurl at him, like stones to break the glass wall of his indifference. But she was sophisticated enough to realize that he would not see the situation as she saw it, nor would the world see it her way either. Her grandmother had warned her. *If a man cannot find satisfaction at home, then he will look for it elsewhere.*

She had refused to believe that Augustus was like that, but apparently he was.

Charity was still listening to Lady Stefanie as they mounted the Pfalz's double fan staircase and entered the Banqueting Room. There they were met by Helmut, the palace chief of staff, who gave Charity a long-suffering look as he informed her that Princess Caterina had arrived an hour ago with an entourage of Vecchios in tow. Charity would find her mother-in-law in the sitting room of the Princess's Apartment, taking tea.

"Good heavens," Charity said.

Helmut nodded in gloomy sympathy.

"Does His Highness know his mother is here?" she inquired.

"Not yet, Your Highness. He has not yet returned from the hunt."

Lady Stefanie said, "She never wrote to let you know she was coming, Your Highness?"

Charity shook her head and straightened her shoulders. "Well, I suppose I had better go and see her."

"Would you like me to come along?" Stefanie inquired.

Charity flashed her a quick smile. "No, but thank you for offering, Steffi." She looked back at Helmut. "You said that she was in my sitting room?"

"Yes, Your Highness. I am very sorry, but she insisted, and it is very difficult to refuse Princess Caterina when she insists on something."

"Yes," Charity said. "I know." Thinking to herself that this was a most inopportune moment for Augustus's mama to appear, she crossed the Banqueting Room and entered the west wing.

Princess Caterina looked perfectly at home in Charity's private sitting room. She was dressed in a rich green velvet afternoon gown, which matched her eyes, and her posture on the sofa was designed to display her magnificent figure in the most attractive manner. She looked up as Charity entered and announced in ringing Italian, "I have come." She then held out her hand and inclined her face so that Charity, the reigning princess, could come over to kiss her cheek. After Charity had performed this office, Caterina informed her, "It was my duty. I know how much my presence will mean to my good people of Jura."

Charity, who had thought she would never laugh again, felt the familiar bubble of amusement that the princess always induced in her. She said, "How lovely to see you, Princess. What a nice surprise this is."

The princess beamed. "Sit down, my child. Sit down." She graciously gestured for Charity to sit in one of her own chairs. Once Charity was seated, Caterina looked her up and down. "I am glad to see that you are dressing better," she pronounced. "You have taste. Those clothes that your mother chose for you . . ." Here she gave a dramatic shudder.

Charity, who had no impulse to leap to her mother's defense, merely murmured, "I am happy that you like my dress, Princess."

Next her mother-in-law gestured to the three other people in the room with them. "Allow me to make you known to my companions. You will have met them at the wedding, but that was a time of such confusion, no? Perhaps you will not remember them."

Charity turned attentively to the two men, who had stood when she came in, and the single woman, a cronelike figure dressed all in black, who had remained sitting in the most comfortable chair in the room. Princess Caterina said, "Allow me to present my nephew, Gian Carlo Vecchio." Gian Carlo was a very good-looking young man, with the princess's red-gold hair and green eyes. He bowed to her. "And this is my cousin, Antonio Vecchio." Antonio was another good-looking young man, only he had dark hair and eyes, and as he made his bow he flashed a smile that showed beautiful white teeth. "And this is my aunt, Madonna Maria Vecchio. I hope you will excuse her if she does not rise to curtsey; she is very arthritic."

"How do you do, signores, Madonna," Charity replied in the excellent Italian she had learned from Caterina. "Welcome once more to Jura."

"Your tea tastes like water," Madonna Vecchio said in a deep, gruff voice that matched her mustache.

There was a moment of startled silence, then Charity replied, "I am so sorry. Shall I send for more?"

"No." The princess's aunt waved a dismissive hand. "That would probably taste like water as well."

"Aunt Maria." The beautiful young man, who looked more like Caterina's son than Augustus, spoke in a reproachful tone. "You are rude."

"No Germans know how to make decent food," Aunt Maria informed Gian Carlo. "Poor Caterina, such a penance it must have been to live in this country for so many years."

"Jura is not like most German states, Aunt," Princess Caterina said. "It has the advantage of lying directly across the Adriatic from Venice and so has benefited from exposure to our culture and our cuisine." As if to prove this point, the princess picked up a small pastry from the almost empty plate in front of her and ate it.

A skeptical snort was the Madonna's only reply to this defense of Jura, but she too ate a pastry.

One of the young men began to comment on the Italian look of some of the churches he had seen in Julia, and the other agreed, mentioning a particular palace that had caught his eye.

As Charity sat listening to this conversation, she began to wonder if perhaps the Vecchios had taken over her entire apartment. When at last a small silence fell in the rush of Italian voices, she asked, "Have you been given comfortable rooms, Princess Caterina?"

Her mother-in-law sighed. "As comfortable as possible under the circumstances." As she spoke, Madonna Maria's clawlike fingers reached out and snatched the last pastry from the plate. Charity thought that for someone who complained about the cooking, it seemed as if the Madonna had sampled quite a bit of it.

Princess Caterina was looking sadly at Charity. "It is an odd feeling to be in the east wing, which is why I chose to take my tea in here. I was certain you would not mind, Charity. After all, this apartment was mine for far longer than it has been yours."

"Of course I don't mind," Charity replied. "I am very happy that you decided to return for Ozbald Day. It will make the first celebration of the anniversary since the war a truly special day indeed."

The princess bowed her head modestly. "That is what I thought. That is why I took such heroic measures to be here."

As she was finishing her last sentence, the door opened and Augustus stepped into the room. He was still dressed in his hunting clothes: high black boots, light tan breeches, and a brown riding coat. His face was more highly colored than usual from his day outdoors, and his hair looked as if he had run his fingers through it to try to restore it to some semblance of order.

Charity's heart lurched into her throat the moment she saw him.

He was not looking at her, however—he was looking at his mother and he did not seem overjoyed.

"Mama! What are you doing here? Why didn't you write to let me know you were coming?"

From her seat upon the sofa, the princess opened her arms. "Augustus," she said dramatically. "My son." Clearly she had already determined in her mind how she was going to play this scene. "Come and kiss your mama."

A muscle twitched in the Prince's jaw, but he crossed the floor, bent, and dutifully surrendered himself to the soft perfumed embrace of Princess Caterina. As he straightened up his eyes met Charity's and he lifted an eyebrow, managing to convey in that single gesture a partnership between them against the gathered Vecchio clan.

Charity quickly looked away from him. By now her heart was thundering and the blood was pounding in her head.

I have to pretend that I don't know, she thought, as she listened to Augustus greeting his cousins and his aunt. *I must hope that the baroness is only in the city for the Ozbald celebration and that she will leave afterward. Perhaps then I can get him to notice me. Perhaps then he will consummate the marriage and he will not feel any further need to turn to the baroness.*

The pounding of her blood finally began to quiet and Princess Caterina's words reached her ears. "I have been telling Charity how much I miss this apartment. After all, I lived here for many more years than she has."

The Prince turned around on the sofa and gave his mother a long, hard look. "If you are trying to get

Charity to give the Princess's apartment up to you for the duration of your visit, Mama, forget it."

Princess Caterina looked deeply hurt.

It suddenly occurred to Charity that it might be easier for her to reside at a distance from Augustus until Baroness Zais had left Julia. She opened her mouth to offer her rooms to the Prince's mother, but Augustus had been watching her. "No, Charity," he said firmly. "You have the biggest heart of anyone I know, but I will not let Mama take advantage of you. It would not be right. It would not be *proper.* You are the princess, you are my wife, you should be the person residing in the royal apartments." He turned his eyes back to his mother. "And that is the end of the discussion."

Princess Caterina said haughtily, "I never once asked to use this apartment, Augustus. You overreach yourself."

"I beg your pardon, Mama," the Prince said.

"I believe I will retire to my room and take a nap," the princess said with dignity. She rose from the sofa and the three Vecchios stood with her. The Prince and Charity followed suit.

"There is to be a performance tonight, Princess, at the opera house in Julia," Charity said. "I very much hope that you, your nephew, your cousin, and your aunt will accompany us."

"An opera? How lovely," the princess replied.

"What is being sung?" Madonna Vecchio demanded.

"The Magic Flute," Charity said.

Madonna Vecchio sniffed. "Mozart is well

enough, I suppose. But it is the Italians who truly understand how to compose music for the human voice." Her upper lip quivered in a way that made her mustache dance. Charity bit her lip. "At least the opera is to be sung by an Italian company," the Madonna stated rather than asked.

The Prince replied evenly, "I was fortunate enough to procure a company from Munich which is renowned for its rendering of Mozart."

Antonio Vecchio said loudly, "How wonderful, Augustus. I am very much looking forward to hearing them."

While Antonio was speaking, Gian Carlo had put his hand under Madonna Maria's arm and was firmly leading her from the room. Antonio offered his arm to Princess Caterina and winked at Augustus. "Don't worry," he said. "Aunt Maria won't come. I'll make sure she has a glass of sherry, and that will put her right to sleep."

"Thank you, Tonio," Augustus said with heartfelt gratitude.

Antonio grinned and escorted the princess out of the room.

Charity had been right when she deduced that the Prince was not overjoyed to see his mother. A month ago, he would have welcomed her, but now, when he was embroiled again in an affair with Eva, she was a complication he didn't need.

Augustus's conscience had begun to bother him. He tried to hold on to Eva's words: *Whatever is be-*

tween you and me is between you and me. It cannot hurt anyone else. But deep in his heart, he knew that was untrue. It had been true once, before he was married. It was not true now. Now it was hurting someone. It was hurting Charity.

She doesn't know. How can it hurt her if she doesn't know?

He answered his own question: Other people knew. Stefan knew. Emil knew. And soon more people would know. It would get around the court—these things always did. And Charity would continue to walk in her beautiful innocence, the loveliest, kindest girl in all the world, and people would pity her.

The ugly reality of what he was doing had hit him on the night of the masquerade when he had left her at the door of her apartment, fully intending to go back to Julia to meet Eva. He had bent his head to kiss her cheek, and it had struck him like a blow how he was deceiving her. Even more than that, he had realized that he didn't want to leave, that he didn't want to go to Eva, that he wanted to stay right there, with Charity.

He had had to pull away from her quickly, to stop himself from reaching for her and kissing her and taking her to bed and making her his wife in deed as well as name.

He had gone to Eva, but for the first time he had fully recognized that it wasn't Eva, that it wasn't just physical satisfaction, that he wanted. He wanted his wife. But his wife was still a child. And he was betraying her.

As a succession of carriages carrying the royal family and their friends left the Pfalz that evening to travel into Julia for the opera, Augustus felt that he had enough women to contend with already without having his mother thrown into the mix.

The Prince got out of his coach in front of the mid-sized Baroque building that was Julia's opera house and waited while his party assembled so they could all go in together. He took Charity's arm while Gian Carlo took Caterina's and Antonio followed as they made their way to the royal box, which was placed in a prominent position to the left of the proscenium stage.

Princess Caterina proceeded directly to the front of the box, where she stood like a figurehead at the front of a ship for ten minutes, acknowledging greetings. There were three galleries of boxes in the opera house, and tonight, for this special performance, they were filled to capacity with men in black cutaway tail coats with white waistcoats and breeches and silk stockings, and women wearing glittering jewels on their deeply cut evening gowns and tiaras in their elegantly dressed hair. These were the people who were bowing and curtseying to Princess Caterina and making little clapping gestures to indicate their delight in her presence.

Charity was sitting quietly in one of the gilt chairs, looking through her program and talking to Gian Carlo. Augustus watched the delicate line of her jaw as she turned her head in his cousin's direction and replied to something he had said.

Finally Princess Caterina decided that she would

sit down, and as Augustus watched, she evicted Gian Carlo from his seat next to Charity and took it herself.

The Prince felt a stab of approval at this sensible action on his mother's part. He turned his eyes back to the opera house, running them over the candlelit expanse of gallery boxes, then down to the seats on the floor where sat the townspeople in their churchgoing best. It was an eminently civilized sight, and it brought a faint smile to the Prince's lips.

"It is a good feeling to know that the monster is locked up and that civilized life can begin again." Put out of his seat, Gian Carlo had come to join the Prince.

"Yes," Augustus said. "It is a good thought."

His cousin's green eyes, which were so uncannily like his mother's, rested on Charity. "Your wife, she is very lovely. So delicate and dainty—like a little deer."

Augustus scowled. He didn't like Gian Carlo looking at Charity. He didn't like him calling her a little deer. He grunted in reply.

His cousin shot him an amused look. "I only look and admire, Augustus. I do not touch."

At that moment the first notes of the orchestra sounded, and the Prince was able to turn away from Gian Carlo as the men took the two empty seats.

*M*ozart's music was divine and the opera company from Munich sang like angels. In all of her life, Charity had never heard such beautiful music, and for the length of the evening she was transported out of the world in which she lived into some other place entirely. The Vecchios proved to be perfect companions for her first opera experience. They were Italian, and they revered music and listened with the same raptness as Charity. Discussing the performance with enthusiasm in the carriage on the way home, she found in Gian Carlo a particularly sympathetic listener. As the two of them talked together, Charity's cheeks became flushed with the excitement of finding someone who shared her feelings and her passion.

In fact, she was feeling so exalted by the experience of her first opera that she sailed off to bed without noticing that Augustus had spoken scarcely a word the whole way home in the carriage.

18

The long-awaited national holiday finally dawned, and all Charity could think about was that she was going to have to spend almost the entire day in the company of her husband and his mistress. The euphoria induced by Mozart had disappeared overnight, replaced by a morning fog of dull depression.

The first activity on Ozbald Day was a Mass of Thanksgiving in the cathedral in Julia. Charity arose reluctantly from her lonely bed and stood like a doll while her maid arrayed her in a new dress and new red velvet pelisse lined and trimmed with chinchilla. The matching red velvet bonnet was topped with ostrich plumes, which gave her an illusion of height. When a lackey arrived to announce that the carriage was waiting, she walked steadily down the Pfalz's fan-shaped outdoor staircase to the shining black coach that was harnessed to four perfectly-matched gray Lipizzaners.

The Prince was waiting for her.

She cast one fleeting glance at him as she reached his side, then looked quickly away. He was very elegant in a double-breasted dark blue coat, a white waistcoat, fawn-colored pantaloons, and the polished Hessian boots that he had bought from Hoby's when he was in London.

"Mama is coming with us," he informed her.

To her astonishment, she found she had to suppress a giggle. She looked back up at him, her eyes dancing with amusement. "You couldn't sound more dismal if you were announcing the arrival of the plague."

At that moment, Princess Caterina appeared at the top of the staircase and began to make her descent. Her red-gold hair, worn under a small, stylish hat, shone in the sun, and her green velvet pelisse called attention to her splendid coloring.

"She looks beautiful," Charity said sincerely.

The Prince's eyes flicked over her own small, red velvet person. "I think you must be the sweetest girl that God ever created," he said fervently.

Charity flushed. What a nice thing for him to say! "You should tell your mother that she looks beautiful, Augustus," she said in an undertone. "You never compliment her, and she adores compliments."

Princess Caterina swept up to join them. "Augustus. The little Charity. How nice you both look."

"You look beautiful, Mama," Augustus said.

The princess became radiant. "Thank you, Augustus. Thank you."

"We should get into the carriage," the Prince said. "We don't want to be late for mass."

Charity, who was profoundly grateful not to be alone with her husband, encouraged her mother-in-law to talk. The princess, who never needed much encouragement, monopolized the conversation the entire way into Julia. In front of the cathedral they met up with Gian Carlo and Antonio, who escorted Caterina into the church. Then Charity rested her hand on Augustus's arm and walked proudly beside him down the center aisle. The altar was aflame with candles whose light glittered off the golden candlesticks and tabernacle. The pews were packed with the nobles and burghers of Julia, all of whom had turned to watch their prince and princess make their way down the aisle to the front pew.

Charity knew, without turning her head, without flicking her eyes, when they passed Baroness Zais. Then they had reached their places and she and Augustus stood as the choir sang the national anthem. The archbishop intoned some words in Latin, Augustus crossed himself, and the Mass of Thanksgiving began.

After the mass had concluded, Charity and Augustus processed back up the aisle, back down the cathedral steps and into the royal coach, where they were joined by Princess Caterina. They were then driven a short distance to the twelfth-century city hall for a breakfast reception given by the mayor and other city representatives. After the reception, they returned to the palace to prepare for the grand reception that Augustus was holding at the Pfalz that afternoon.

* * *

The Prince was thinking that all of the events he had planned for Ozbald Day had turned out beautifully. He looked around the elegant company crowded into the Banqueting Room and realized that this reception was as successful as all of the other events had been.

Less than two years ago, Napoleon's marshal was living in this palace, and French troops were quartered in the city and around the countryside, he told himself. *These Ozbald Day celebrations have surely proved to my people that life in Jura is back to normal.*

Why then, he wondered, did he not feel happier?

One reason was, he answered himself, his narrowed eyes on the red-gold hair of his Venetian cousin, he did not like the way Gian Carlo was hanging around Charity. It seemed to him that every time he looked her way, there was Gian Carlo, fanning her face, making her laugh, bringing her a glass of punch. Augustus scowled as his cousin bent his head close to Charity's to say something in her ear.

"Why are you frowning?"

He jumped. Then he recognized the voice as belonging to Eva Zais, and he forced a smile as he turned to greet her. She was dressed in her favorite shade of green, which matched her eyes, and the candlelight in the room was kind to her. He said lightly, "I was having evil thoughts about Napoleon's marshal, who took the marvelous Tintoretto that used to hang on that wall."

She laughed and said something in return, and he made an effort to give her his attention. He was still speaking with Eva a few minutes later when he had the distinct sensation that someone was looking at him. He turned his head and met a pair of golden-brown eyes that immediately jerked away. Brilliant color flared into Charity's cheeks and she looked up at Gian Carlo and said something to him.

Sweat broke out on the Prince's brow and on the back of his neck. God. The look in Charity's eyes . . .

She knows, he thought. *Dear God in heaven, she knows.*

"Augustus?" It was Eva. "Are you all right?"

"Yes, yes, of course I'm all right."

He wasn't all right. He felt sick. He felt as if someone had just punched him in the stomach.

"You went rather pale."

He was saved from having to reply by the announcement that the musical part of the reception was about to begin. He gave Eva a strained smile and said, "I must escort my wife."

"Of course," Eva replied.

As Augustus crossed the floor toward Charity, his heart was hammering and two words kept repeating themselves over and over in his mind. *Charity knows. Charity knows. She was looking at Eva and me. She knows, she knows, she knows . . .*

At last he was standing before her. "My dear," he said. "I believe it is time for us to go into the Music Room."

She didn't look at him. Charity, who had the most honest eyes in all the world, was afraid to look at him. Instead she looked at his neckcloth, nodded her head, and replied in a small voice, "Very well."

He held out his arm and, in a tentative gesture that just about broke his heart, she rested her fingers lightly upon it. Then, together, they led their guests into the Music Room for the performance of Beethoven's *Eroica* that the Prince had arranged to be played by the court orchestra.

There was another pair of eyes observing this by-play between Augustus and his wife and Augustus and his mistress, and the fireworks that ended the Ozbald Day reception were as nothing compared to those Princess Caterina put on for her only son when she asked to meet with him privately as the last explosion died away from the sky and the guests prepared to return to their homes.

"I am rather tired, Mama," the Prince said when he was confronted by his mother as they returned from the garden where they had observed the fireworks. "Couldn't this wait until tomorrow?"

"No, Augustus." Princess Caterina had draped a magnificent sable-lined cloak over her gown when she went outside to view the fireworks, and as they stepped back indoors she beckoned to a servant to take it from her. "What I have to say to you cannot wait."

The Prince's lips tightened. He said with controlled impatience, "Very well, Mama. We can go into the Music Room if you like."

The princess looked around the crowded room. "No one can leave until you do, and I do not think you will wish to have what I say to you overheard by anyone else, Augustus. I recommend that we go to your apartment, where we can be in privacy."

The Prince repressed a sigh. He was in no mood for his mother's dramatics, but there was no courteous way to avoid her. "Very well, Mama," he said, and offered her his arm.

He took her to the sitting room where he had found her taking tea with Charity the other day and sat beside her on the sofa. "Now," he said, his clipped voice indicating that she should be as brief as possible. "What is the problem?"

She lifted her forefinger, with its long, perfectly tapered nail, and pointed it at him like a weapon. "You, Augustus. You are the problem. What can you be thinking, to take up with a mistress so soon after you are married?"

He was thunderstruck. This was the last thing he had expected her to say. He opened his mouth to reply, but nothing came out.

Princess Caterina had not finished, however. She lifted her chin, which was still remarkably firm for a woman of her years, and threw another thunderbolt. "I am a woman of the world, Augustus. I understand perfectly that men have wives and men have mistresses. But at least have the decency to wait until your first child is born!"

The Prince could feel the blood drain from his face. He looked away from his mother, unable to meet her eyes. There was a long moment of silence, then she said, "Never did I think that I would have to say this to you, my perfect son, but I am ashamed of you, Augustus."

The Prince gave up trying to defend himself and buried his head in his heads. "Oh God, Mama," he groaned. "You are right. I have behaved like a perfect ass. And the worst part is that Charity knows. I saw her looking at Eva and me tonight. *Jesus.* I have been such an idiot!"

The princess stared at the long cramped fingers of her son buried in his blond hair. "But why, Augustus? Charity may not be a beauty like her sister, but she is a pretty girl and, believe me, she is much much nicer than that other one. Are you in love with this Baroness Zais?"

He shook his head. "No, Mama, it is nothing like that." Slowly the Prince raised his head, and then, looking straight ahead and not at her, he explained to his mother the promise he had made to his bride to delay the consummation of their marriage and the effect this had had on him.

The princess was aghast. "Never did I think a son of mine could be so stupid," she informed him. "So, once you found yourself in such difficulty, instead of turning to your wife, you took up with your old mistress?"

Put like that, it did sound stupid. "Yes," the Prince said, staring at the carpet.

Princess Caterina arose from the sofa and walked to the fireplace, where she turned and faced her son. The Prince was forced to look up from the carpet to her face, and she announced with deliberate drama,

"Well, Augustus, it must stop. If your father was here he would tell you that your duty to Jura is to produce an heir, and you cannot get an heir from your mistress! You must go to Charity, apologize to her for what you have done, and beg her to forgive you and to take you into her bed."

The Prince tried to imagine such a scene and winced. "Oh God, Mama, I have made such a botch of things. I doubt if Charity will ever want to speak to me again, let alone take me into her bed." He looked with a mixture of apprehension and hopefulness at his mother, who had maintained her posture before the fireplace. "Do you think you might be able to speak to her first? You know, explain things a little bit? I mean about Eva and such?"

It was the first time in both their memories that he had ever asked her to do anything for him, and the princess looked immensely gratified. She made a sweeping gesture which was supposed to indicate maternal warmth. "I will be happy to do that for you, my son. Then, when you go to see her, the explanations will be over with and all that will be left is the apology." She gave him an angelic smile. "I am sure you will manage that charmingly."

"I would be so grateful to you, Mama," he said thankfully.

She was radiant. "You know I would do anything for you, Augustus, my beloved son."

Charity sat in front of her dressing table and stared into the mirror while her maid brushed her hair. She looked exactly the same as she always did, she thought gloomily. The misery of the day hadn't aged her one bit. Her skin was still fresh and clear, her hair was shining, and she didn't have circles under her eyes.

It's terrible to be young, Charity thought. *No matter how much you suffer, you still look the same.*

Her maid finished brushing her hair and began to divide the whole mass into three strands to braid it for the night. "Did you get a chance to watch the fireworks, Anna?" she asked.

The two young women discussed the fireworks while Charity's hair was arranged into a single long braid and secured with a pink velvet ribbon. Charity had just risen when a knock on the door surprised them both. Anna came back with a note from Princess Caterina requesting an interview immediately.

Charity was heartsore and tired and Augustus's mother was one of the last people she wished to see, but courtesy and curiosity won out. "Of course I will see Princess Caterina. She can come along here to my dressing room, if that will be convenient."

"I will say so."

The Italian servant went to inform his mistress of Charity's answer, and Charity dismissed Anna and began to walk up and down in front of her dressing table in her pink velvet dressing gown and small pink slippers. Much more quickly than she had expected, the door opened and Princess Caterina, still dressed in the golden gown she had worn to the reception, came in.

"Good heavens," the princess said, stopping dead just inside the dressing room door and staring at Charity, who stood in front of her dressing table. "No wonder poor Augustus thinks he is married to a little girl. You are encased from toe to chin in pink velvet. And the braid!" Shaking her head, the princess commenced to advance upon Charity. "No, no, no, no. My dear, if you want a man to think of you as a woman and not a child, you must try to look like a woman and not a child."

Charity tried to back away, but was trapped by the chair of her dressing table. "Unbutton that dressing gown," the princess ordered.

Hastily Charity unbuttoned her warm pink velvet outer garment to reveal the chaste, high-necked white cotton nightgown underneath.

The princess cast her eyes upward and declared, "I have wronged my son."

At those words, a healthy spark of anger flashed through Charity. Before she had time to consider the wisdom of her words, she shot back, "No, Princess, it is your son who has wronged me!"

Princess Caterina heaved a long sigh. "I know all about it, my child. That is what I have come to speak to you about. It cannot be allowed to go on. Augustus knows this—"

"He does?" Charity's voice soared dangerously high. "Then why hasn't *he* come to see me? Why has he sent you?"

The princess frowned. "I am about to tell you this, if you will give me the chance. Now, let us both sit down." She arranged herself on the comfortable chaise longue and gestured Charity to the far less comfortable dressing table chair. "Augustus has not come because he is embarrassed," she began. "He knows he has wronged you, and he does not know how to explain to you why he has acted as he did. So he has asked me to do that for him."

Charity sat, her back ramrod straight, and waited.

Princess Caterina made an airy gesture. "It is quite simple, really. Augustus is a man, men have certain needs, and if they cannot have those needs—"

Charity leaped to her feet. "I don't want to hear another word about men and their needs," she shouted. "Augustus has a wife. That is one reason why men have wives, so they can satisfy their needs. But instead of turning to his wife, he chose to go back to his old mistress. And I mean *old*," she added nastily. "Good heavens, Baroness Zais has to be as old as you are, Princess."

Had Charity been thinking clearly, she would never, ever have said such a thing. She most certainly did not mean to imply that the princess was old. The words she used were unfortunate, however, and they struck Princess Caterina in a most vulnerable place.

When the princess spoke her voice had cooled considerably. "Augustus felt he had made a promise to you not to consummate the marriage until you were ready. He felt that you had given him no sign that you were ready, and so, rather than disturb your innocence, he sought out Eva Zais. I have reminded him that his primary duty to his country is to produce an heir, and for that he must have congress with his wife. I am here tonight to determine whether or not you are willing to fulfill your marital duties."

Something had gone wrong. Charity was too upset to perceive what had happened, but she was not too upset to feel that *something* had happened. The princess was angry with her. She bit her lip and said, "I am sorry if I have offended you, Princess Caterina. I didn't mean—"

"Stop." The princess held up a commanding hand. "I asked you a question and I demand an answer. Are you ready to assume the physical responsibilities of marriage?"

Charity closed her hands into tight fists, stuck her chin in the air, and said grimly, "Yes. As long as Augustus gets rid of *her.*"

The princess rose majestically to her feet. "You will never have to worry about the baroness again."

"Good."

"I will go now and tell Augustus of our conversation."

Charity felt the bottom drop out of her stomach. *Will he be coming here tonight?* She could have asked that of the Princess Caterina who had entered her dressing room, but she couldn't ask it of the cold-faced woman who was now staring at her so icily. "V-very well," she managed to stutter, and stood twisting her hands together as her mother-in-law left the room, closing the door emphatically behind her.

Slowly Charity moved into her bedroom. The bed had been turned back and warmed with heated coals, and Charity took off her pink velvet dressing gown and stepped on a footstool to climb into the billowy depths of the large gilt four-poster. She left the bed-side lamp burning and sat up against her pillows, thinking over her conversation with Princess Cate-rina. Then she climbed back out of the bed, returned to her dressing room, and proceeded to unbraid her hair and brush it out until it spilled in a shining golden-brown mantle around her shoulders and down her back.

She returned to the bedroom, climbed back into bed, and thought some more. Next she unbuttoned the top three tiny pearl buttons that secured the neck-line of her nightdress. She regarded the skin she had bared, then undid the next three buttons as well. She was wondering if it would be too daring to undo one more when she heard the latch on her dressing room door lift. Augustus stepped into the open doorway.

He was still dressed in his evening clothes and was holding a candle in his right hand. He looked across the room into her widened eyes and said, "May I come in?"

Her heart was pounding. "Yes," she said. "Come in, Augustus."

He came across the floor and placed his candle on her bedside table, beside the lamp. Her heart was pounding so hard she was sure he could hear it. "Charity, I have come to tell you that I am sorry. Af-ter all that you have done for me, I hurt you. I am more sorry than I can ever say."

To her absolute horror, she felt her lips begin to tremble and her eyes to fill with tears. *Not now,* she thought in panic. *Not now, when I am trying to get him to see me as a woman and not a child.* She swallowed hard, trying to stifle her emotions.

"I hate her," she heard her voice saying gruffly. "I would like to boil her in oil and . . . and stake her in the desert to die of ant bites . . . and . . ."

"Charity!" But he was laughing and he sat on the edge of the bed and reached out and pulled her against him. "Poor Eva. Believe me, she does not deserve such a horrible end. It was my fault, for thinking you were still a child."

"I'm *not* a child!" she said it fiercely, angrily, as a challenge and a promise as well.

"I am very glad to hear that," he replied, and the arms around her tightened and she felt his lips come to rest on her hair.

I love you, Augustus, she thought, as she pressed her cheek against his shoulder and inhaled the wonderful scent of him. *I love you, I love you, I love you . . .*

19

Her hair under his lips felt like fine silk, just as he had always imagined it would. He lifted his hand and slid it under the silken fall to rest on the fragile nape of her neck. "I don't want to hurt you," he whispered. "I never wanted to hurt you, Charity."

The brown head that was buried in the shoulder of his evening coat moved in a negative gesture. She said, her voice a little muffled, "You can only hurt me if you turn away from me, Augustus."

He moved his fingers along the fine line of her jaw, caught her chin, and lifted her face away from his shoulder. Then he bent his head and kissed her. Her arms came up around his neck and her head fell back, her lips sweetly yielding to the pressure of his mouth.

She was so sweet. She tasted so sweet. With her arms around his neck and her head tilted back, her body was pressed against his and he could feel every line of her through the thin cotton of her nightdress.

"Charity." His voice came out sounding like a croak. He moved his mouth over her face, kissing her eyelids, her cheeks, then coming back once again to her mouth. His kiss deepened and he held her closer. The blood began to pound in his veins. It took all of his willpower to lift his head, to make certain he wasn't frightening her. "Are you all right?"

She blinked, and then her face broke into its wonderful smile. "Oh my, Augustus," she said breathlessly. "Oh my."

Relief and desire flooded through him in equal measure, and he smiled back. "Does that mean you want to go on?"

She nodded twice. "It certainly does."

"Just a moment." Wasting no time, he stripped off his evening coat and white neckcloth and threw them on the floor. Then he began to kiss her again, leaning her back until she was lying on the pillows and he was bending over her. He felt her hand touch the back of his bare neck in a tentative caress, and the sensation was exquisite. Her high young breasts were pressed against him and he increased the pressure of his lips, asking her for more.

Her mouth opened for him and, hesitantly, her tongue answered to his. She was arched up against him, her lovely body taut and trembling. He slid a hand inside her nightdress and caressed her breast. It was as silky and smooth as the rest of her. He felt her nipple stand up against the palm of his hand, and he groaned.

He pulled away and looked down into her face once again. Her eyes were half closed and her mouth was swollen from his kisses. Under their heavy lids, her golden eyes watched him with wonder. He said softly, "Would you be very upset if I removed my clothing?"

She shook her head, her lovely hair swinging with the movement of her head. Her siren's mouth quirked mischievously. "Go right ahead."

He ripped his shirt over his head and stripped off his shoes, stockings, knee breeches, and drawers in record time, consigning them to the floor along with his shirt and neckcloth. Then he turned back to her, determined to woo her until she was dizzy with passion, until she actually wanted him to do what he wanted to do right now but would delay doing for as long as he humanly could.

As he turned toward her, the light from the bedside candle reflected off his naked flesh and concentrated face and for a moment he saw fear flash in her eyes. "It's all right, Charity," he said, trying to speak quietly, soothingly, trying to keep his mounting passion from coarsening his voice. "Trust me. Everything is going to be all right." He stretched out beside her and began to kiss her and kiss and kiss her, trying to drug her with kisses so she would forget to be afraid and let him do what he had to do and not struggle against him.

After a while he moved his kisses to her throat. Then he finished unbuttoning her nightdress and, laying bare her breasts, he closed his mouth on first one pink nipple and then the other. He felt her breath suck in hard and then her body arched up toward his, seeking him. He reached down and pushed up her nightdress, his hand running caressingly along her leg until it reached the place that would bring ecstasy to them both.

Charity stiffened, and he kissed her some more and murmured to her and gently began to caress her soft, secret flesh, until her legs began to part voluntarily. When finally her hips began to lift toward his, he swung himself over her and, slowly and carefully, exerting such superhuman control that he was shaking with it, he slid into her.

The feeling of her tightness closing around him almost sent him over the edge. Struggling for gentleness, he pushed and then set his teeth and pushed harder, until he heard her cry out and he felt himself pierce through the barrier of her virginity.

"It's all right," he panted. "It's all right, Charity."

Sweat was pouring off him and he shut his eyes.

"Put your legs around my waist," he said.

She did, and that was what finished him.

When at last he came back to earth, his heart was hammering so hard he thought his ribs might break, and he was clutching Charity so tightly he thought he might break her too. He groaned, rolled off her, sat up, and looked apprehensively into her face. There were tears on her cheeks.

"Charity!" He was horrified. "Did I hurt you that much?"

She said in a small voice, "It wasn't that bad." Her still-damp cheeks gleamed in the candlelight and her long lashes were stuck together from her tears.

Looking at her, he felt as if his heart would break. In the same small voice as before, she said, "Would you mind just holding me for a while?"

"Of course I'll hold you." He lay back next to her and gathered her carefully into his arms, resting his cheek against her hair. "I am so sorry it was painful, my dear. I understand that the first time is always hard for a woman. It will get better, I promise you. It won't hurt like that again."

She nestled closer. "The first part was very nice."

He kissed her temple. "I'm glad about that."

She felt so small, so slight as she cuddled against him. He thought with some degree of awe of the courage it must have taken for her to trust herself to him, who was so much larger and stronger than she. And she had been a virgin. He was the first man she had ever known.

At that thought, feelings he had never felt for a woman before, feelings of protection and possessiveness blazed in his heart. As he felt her stir in his arms, he vowed that the next time, he would show her the joy that a woman could find in a man's embrace. He would call upon all the skill he had learned from sophisticated women of the world to bring joy and rapture to his young wife.

Charity said, "I like to be close to you like this. Are you going to go back to your own bed?"

"Do you want me to?"

"No. I want you to stay here with me."

He smiled. "Then that's what I will do."

* * *

Augustus proved true to his promise to himself, and in the following weeks his sexual awakening of Charity proved so successful that her whole idea of herself, of who and what she was, changed profoundly. For the first time in her life she became conscious of herself as a sexual being. She walked differently, held her head differently; she even had a different expression on her face.

She had loved Augustus before, but in some ways it had been the love of a young girl for a man whom she placed upon a pedestal. Now that she was sleeping with him, now that she knew what it was like to feel him inside her, the quality of her love had deepened and become the love of a fully awakened woman.

Sex is a powerful narcotic, and for the halcyon period of time that was her true honeymoon, Charity's satisfied body blotted out any doubts that Augustus' feelings for her might not be as strong as hers for him. Both her grandmother and his mother had emphasized his need for an heir. For the moment this practical consideration was buried. But it was not forgotten. Like the snake lurking in the garden of paradise, it awaited only the strategic moment to strike at Charity's heart.

Late one evening in early December, Charity returned unexpectedly from a trip to Seista and the Prince came into her dressing room while her maid was helping her undress. He sat on the side of the chaise longue and watched in silence as Charity tied her velvet dressing gown and told Anna she could go to bed. Once the maid had left, he said, "I didn't think you were coming back tonight."

She sat in a small upholstered chair. "I finished sooner than I thought I would and I decided to come home instead of waiting until tomorrow."

He smiled, but made no attempt to approach her. "A wise decision."

She scanned his face. "Has something happened, Augustus?"

He gave her a quizzical look. "Am I as transparent as all that?"

"Of course not," she replied soothingly. "I just thought you looked a little worried."

He sighed. "Yes, well, something has happened today while you were gone. The emperor has appointed Franz to be his ambassador to Jura."

Charity stared at him in amazement. "Franz? He can't have appointed Franz, Augustus. That would be the most dreadful insult to you."

He ran his fingers through his hair. "Well, he has appointed Franz. I received official notification from the Imperial Court today."

"Franz isn't even an Austrian!" Charity said indignantly. "How can he be the Austrian ambassador if he isn't an Austrian citizen?"

"Apparently he holds dual citizenship in Austria and Jura," Augustus replied.

"This is outrageous," Charity stated. "You must protest this appointment to the emperor, Augustus. Good God, if Franz comes to Julia, he will probably bring Lydia with him. Can you imagine the gossip that will cause?"

Augustus said soberly, "There will be more gossip if I protest this appointment than if I accept it as if it were a matter of no consequence. Obviously, I am not pleased with the emperor's choice, but Franz will be as anxious to avoid scandal as we are. I will welcome him to Jura, accept his ambassadorial credentials, and you will welcome Lydia. We will behave in exactly the same way we would if Count Esterhazy had been appointed the Austrian ambassador. It is the only dignified way to handle this matter."

There was a long silence, then Charity sighed. "I suppose you're right."

"There's no 'suppose' about it. I am right."

She stuck out her lower lip. "The difference between us is that you've forgiven Franz and I haven't."

He stretched his arms over his head. "I have more than forgiven Franz. I am grateful to him." He stood up, crossed to her chair, and sat on his heels in front of her. "Just think, I might have been stuck for life with Lydia."

He cupped his hands around her face and kissed her. She rested her own hands on his shoulders, closed her eyes, and kissed his back. After a few moments, he moved her hands behind his neck and began to rise, until he was standing fully upright and her feet were swinging off the ground. Holding her there, close to his chest, he looked into her eyes and said, "I'm glad you decided to come home."

Her eyes sparkled mischievously. "My escort was very put out."

"The hell with your escort."

"That's what I thought."

He began to walk toward the door that led into her bedroom, carrying her as if she weighed nothing. Charity felt her body moving along with his and her insides began to melt. The first time she had known this kind of desire, she had been frightened by the intensity of her own feelings. But she was no longer the girl who had first lain with Augustus all those weeks ago. All of her fear and shyness had been burned away by the blaze of passion that had ignited between them. Now when Augustus pulled off her robe and looked at her naked body, she reveled in the expression she saw in his eyes. He thought she was beautiful, and so she felt beautiful. She loved to look at him as well, to see his body, lean-muscled and golden in the light of the lamp that they always left on.

Most of all, she loved to yield to him. To feel him filling her emptiness, his hardness softening her, opening her, until she was overwhelmed by such a flood of sensation that she actually cried out, so intense was the pleasure.

The only thing missing was the words. *I love you, Charity. I love you, Augustus.* They were never said, but as soon as that thought surfaced, Charity pushed it away. She told herself that she didn't need words when she had this.

They slept together in Charity's bed and made love again in the morning before they went off to attend to their separate duties.

The days before Franz arrived in Jura went by with clocklike regularity. In almost every area of her life, Charity was having success. Her lessons with Louis were going better than ever; her plans to create an organized social assistance system for Jura's poor were beginning to coalesce; and, to her delight, she even had her beloved dog returned to her, when Harry arrived unexpectedly one day with Hero in tow.

Charity was in the stableyard, having finished her lesson, when the huge brown Newfoundland came galloping down the path and threw himself at her, barking hysterically.

"Hero!" she cried with almost identical rapture. "How did you get here?"

She tried to hug the dog, or even to pat him, but he was so excited that he couldn't stand still. He raced around her and then jumped on her, almost knocking her to the ground.

Two grooms came running to her assistance, but she waved them away. "It's my dog," she said. "I can't believe it! Oh, Hero, I missed you so much."

At last Hero was able to stand quietly enough for her to scratch behind his ears in his favorite spot. She was sitting on her heels next to the dog when she looked up and saw her brother coming into the courtyard.

"Harry!" she shrieked, jumping up and running to him. Hero barked excitedly and followed, frisking around Harry too.

He hugged her hard. "It's great to see you, Char." He held her away so he could look at her. "I see you're still wearing breeches."

She was indeed wearing breeches, but her double-breasted green velvet coat flared out at her waist into a full skirt that reached to her knees, leaving visible only her polished black high boots. Her hair hung in a single braid from beneath her green-and-gold tricorn hat.

She laughed. "But what are you doing here?"

He shrugged. "Papa said he had promised you he would send Hero to Jura, and I volunteered to be the one to bring him."

Charity looked up into her brother's wide green eyes and knew instantly that there was more behind his visit than merely transporting Hero. She decided diplomatically that she would not ask just yet. "I am so glad to see you, Harry. Come back to the palace with me and we'll see if Augustus is free."

"I have a letter to the Prince from Papa," Harry said. "He wanted me to deliver it personally."

Charity, her brother, and her dog went up to the Pfalz, only to discover that Augustus had gone into Julia. Charity took Harry to her sitting room for a chat and sent for refreshments. Hero curled up next to her feet, so close that his fur spilled over onto her boots.

They chatted about his journey until a servant had delivered a tray with biscuits and coffee. When they were alone again, Charity asked, "Do you know what Papa's letter is about?"

"Well . . . I think part of it has to do with me." Harry was regarding his boot tips with great interest.

"Oh?" Charity said mildly.

Harry lifted his eyes from his boots. "The truth is,

I got into a bit of trouble, Char, and Papa went into a rage. He said that I could spend the next six months in the country or I could keep you company in Jura." He gave her an engaging smile. "I decided it would be more fun here with you."

Charity handed him a cup of steaming liquid. "What kind of trouble?"

Harry's expression became so lugubrious it was almost comical. "You won't believe this, Char, but I let myself be taken in by a hardened gamester. Can you believe it? I never thought I could be such a gull."

Charity, who did not find Harry's gullibility as astonishing as he appeared to, made noises of sympathy.

He took a sip from his cup and looked at her in surprise. "Since when did you start to drink coffee in the afternoon?"

"Augustus converted me. He drinks it all the time."

"Oh." Harry took another sip and continued with his tale. "I thought Layton was a first-rate cove. He was an army officer, Char! He fought at Waterloo!"

Charity widened her eyes in a semblance of horrified disbelief. "Did he cheat you, Harry?"

Harry was evidently soothed by her response, for his gloom lifted slightly. He nodded. "He took me to this gambling hell and I lost a huge amount of money. He kept telling me that the luck was bound to change . . . Well, you know how it is, Char. It didn't."

She nodded wisely. "Was Layton in partnership with the gambling hell?"

He stared. "How did you know that?"

"He wouldn't have bothered to set you up if he wasn't going to get a cut, Harry," she said practically.

He was looking gloomy again. "Papa was enraged. You know how he is about gambling—I doubt if he's lost a hundred guineas in his entire life."

Charity, who had heard her father lecture her mother many times about the evils of gambling, did know. "It is not a vice for which Papa has any sympathy."

"He came down on me like a ton of bricks. Said I would have to go into the country, but then he changed his mind and said I could take Hero to Jura and deliver a letter to the Prince at the same time."

At this point, as if responding to his name, Hero arose from his supine position to sit in front of Charity, his eyes fixed on her face, his tail wagging, his whole posture a mixture of adoration and hopefulness.

"By any chance, do you want to be petted?" she asked him.

His tail wagged faster.

She laughed and began to scratch his chest. Hero's eyes glazed over in bliss. Over the dog's enormous head she said to Harry, "Lydia will be here in a few days as well. We shall be quite a family party."

Harry, who had been drinking his coffee, looked thunderstruck. "Lydia? Are you serious? How can she have the nerve to come to Jura after what she did to Augustus?"

"Franz has been appointed ambassador to Jura from Austria," Charity said. "Of course Lydia will come with him."

Harry almost choked on his coffee. "Good God. The emperor appointed *Franz*?"

"He did it to insult Augustus, of course," Charity replied. "But Augustus is perfectly willing to be friends with Franz, and now that you are here we can make it seem as if we are having a happy family reunion. The emperor won't like that at all."

She stopped scratching Hero's chest, sat back in her chair, and met her brother's disbelieving stare. "Augustus is willing to be friends with Franz?" he repeated. "I should think he would want his head on a plate."

Charity said demurely, "You see, Augustus thinks Franz actually did him a favor by saving him from Lydia. He is not angry with Franz at all."

Harry looked at his sister's face, and for the first time appeared to register the change in her. "You look different, Char," he said. "More . . . grown up."

Her lashes dipped in acknowledgment. Harry was still staring at her in wonder when the Prince walked in the door.

20

"Augustus!" Charity said. "I thought you had gone into Julia."

"I just got back." The Prince looked at Harry, who had leaped to his feet and was beginning to bow. Augustus held out his hand and crossed the room to greet him. "How are you, Harry? This is a pleasant surprise."

"Thank you, Your Highness," Harry said.

The Prince gave him a friendly smile. "I believe we can drop the titles now that we are brothers, Harry. Call me Gus."

Harry felt immensely flattered and glanced at his sister to see her reaction. She was looking at her husband, and the expression on her face made Harry blink.

Augustus turned to his wife. "I see you have been reunited with your faithful friend." He snapped his fingers and Hero came over to greet him. With a tone of sobriety that contrasted with the warm radiance of her face, Charity said, "Harry has a letter for you from Papa, Augustus."

The Prince straightened up. "So you are more than just the dog-deliverer, Harry."

"Yes," Harry said. "The letter is in my bag. Shall I go and get it?"

"If you wouldn't mind," Augustus said quietly.

Harry moved as fast as he could without running and was back in Charity's sitting room in under five minutes. The Prince had joined his wife on the sofa and they were speaking together in low voices when he returned.

Augustus held out his hand for the letter and then waved Harry to his original seat. Silence fell. Charity leaned toward the coffee table in front of the sofa and poured herself a cup while he read. The letter covered several pages and Augustus took his time.

Harry, who knew that some of the letter was devoted to his own sins, shifted uncomfortably on his seat. Charity put the coffee cup she had just filled on the table and didn't drink a drop of it.

At last Augustus looked up. "Apparently your father is unhappy with your behavior, Harry," he said mildly.

Harry suddenly realized that he very badly did not want to look like a fool in front of Augustus. As he flushed, he thought that he should have gone into the country and let someone else deliver Hero. "I was a gullible idiot," he said bitterly. "Papa had a right to be angry."

Charity said, "Harry thought the man was honest because he was an army officer who had fought at Waterloo."

Augustus said, "Those are impressive credentials."

Harry said, the bitterness still evident in his voice, "That is what he said, at any rate. I never did anything to check on him."

The Prince looked rueful. "I have always thought that one of the more inefficient characteristics of human beings is that wisdom can't be passed from one generation to the next. It seems that as a species we are doomed always to learn the hard way." He smiled at Harry. "The important thing, however, is the learning, and I am sure you have done that, Harry."

"I certainly have," Harry replied fervently.

"You are welcome to remain here in Jura for as long as you wish, and I will write your father accordingly," Augustus said.

Suddenly Harry felt better than he remembered feeling since he left that wretched gaming hell. "Thank you . . ."

As he hesitated, Charity said firmly, "Gus."

"I have to get used to it," Harry said, his cheeks flushing bashfully. "But thank you, Gus."

The Prince nodded and glanced at his wife.

Charity immediately said, "Luncheon will be in an hour, Harry. I will see you again then."

Harry jumped to his feet. "Of course. I will go to my room and er . . . rest."

The Prince said humorously, "You needn't do

anything that drastic, Harry. But I would like to be in private with your sister for a few moments."

Harry strode to the door. "Certainly, certainly." He turned and glanced at the couple on the sofa. Charity's eyes were sparkling with amusement and suddenly he felt comfortable again. "I'll see you later, Char," he said, and went out.

Charity turned to face her husband. "What did Papa say?"

Augustus began to fold the letter. "He is in agreement with me that the emperor will not take military action against Jura. In fact, he is astonished that such a possibility was even mentioned."

She said slowly, "I suppose the emperor thought he had nothing to lose."

"Perhaps," he replied grimly.

"What did Papa say about the possibility of Austria imposing tariffs on us?"

"He said that Britain will honor its treaty with us, and if Austria imposes tariffs on Jurian goods, then England will place a tariff on Austrian goods."

Charity raised her arms over her head. "Hurrah!"

Augustus laughed and said, "I could use a cup of coffee."

After she had poured his coffee, he drank half the cup, then said, "Now, on to more serious matters. What the devil am I going to do with your brother?"

Charity smoothed a fold of her riding coat's full skirt and said thoughtfully, "Do you think it might be possible for him to act as a sort of assistant to Emil? It was a terrible blow to Harry that Napoleon was defeated before he was old enough to join the army. He wanted my father to purchase a commission for him when he finished Eton, but Papa insisted that he go to Oxford first." She clasped her hands loosely in her green velvet lap. "Harry has always wanted to be a soldier. I'm sure that is one of the reasons why he was so easily duped by that dreadful man. He would be thrilled to work with the Marshal of Jura."

There was a sharp line between the Prince's brows. "I can't just appoint Harry to Emil's staff, Charity," he said impatiently. "Those positions are filled by men who earned them."

"I know that, Augustus, and I didn't mean that Harry should be part of the military staff. Perhaps he could act as Emil's secretary."

Silence. Then the Prince said reluctantly, "Well, I'll speak to Emil about it."

She gave him a warm smile. "Thank you, Augustus. Tell Emil that he doesn't have to keep Harry if the arrangement doesn't work out."

"All right." He sighed. "I confess, I had much rather have your brother here at court than your sister."

"I couldn't agree more. When are Franz and Lydia arriving, anyway?"

He put his empty cup on the table. "Within the week, I believe."

Charity said with rising enthusiasm, "Do you know, Augustus, having Harry here might work to our advantage. I can pretend to be so happy to have my brother and sister with me here in Jura, and you can be kindly and say how nice it is for Charity to have her family around her, and it will actually look as if the emperor did us a favor by appointing Franz."

He was looking at her attentively. "Do you think so?"

As they both knew, appearance counted for everything in the embattled world of diplomacy. The emperor's appointment of Franz had been perceived by that world as a deliberate insult to Jura's Prince. If Augustus could turn that insult around and make it appear to his advantage, then the emperor would be the one to look foolish.

Charity said, "Why don't we have a big reception to welcome Lydia and Franz? We can invite all the other ambassadors and their wives and all of your government ministers. And Harry of course."

A slow smile was spreading across Augustus's lips. "Charity, you are wicked. That is a brilliant idea."

Her own smile exploded. "Do you think so?"

"I do. Talk to Stefan about it." He glanced at the clock that was on the mantel and got to his feet. "I'm late for a meeting. I'll talk to Emil and let you know what he thinks about taking on Harry."

"All right."

She remained on the sofa, the velvet skirts of her coat spread around her, and watched him go out.

Two days later, Lydia and Franz arrived in Julia, and Franz immediately called on the Prince to present his ambassador's credentials.

Augustus received his cousin in the small audience room that was part of his private apartment. A large Chinese vase, which Napoleon's marshal had missed, stood in front of the window, and a crystal chandelier in the style of Louis XIV hung over a large gilt-trimmed table that had two chairs set on one of its long sides. Franz was standing behind one of the chairs, facing the door, when Augustus came in.

For a moment the two men looked at each other in silence. Then Franz said, "Do you want to murder me?"

"Not at all," the Prince replied. He came into the room and regarded his cousin gravely. He did not hold out his hand.

"What can I say to you, Gus?" Franz said. "What I did was abominable. I know that. My only excuse was that Lydia had me in such a state that I would have done anything to get her into bed with me."

"You put me in a damnable spot," the Prince said mildly. "If I had had to cancel the wedding, the country would have been in an uproar."

"I wasn't thinking, Gus," Franz said ruefully. "At that point, I'm afraid that another part of my anatomy was in control."

The Prince, who vividly remembered his own torment when he had not been able to approach Charity, finally relented and held out his hand. Franz came swiftly around the table to take it and the two cousins stood for a moment, hands clasped, looking into each other's eyes.

Then the Prince loosened his fingers and Franz

stepped back. "I'm sorry, Gus," he said with apparent sincerity. "Thank God you were able to save yourself from my folly. Marrying Charity was a brilliant stroke."

The Prince nodded.

"She may yet prove to be a better consort for you than Lydia," Franz went on. "She is so young that it should be easy to train her to be the sort of wife that you want."

The Prince, who had once had the same idea himself, laughed.

Franz said soberly, "If you will find it too uncomfortable to have me attached to your court, I will go back to Vienna. I confess that I accepted the emperor's appointment because I wanted to return to Jura, but I will go away again if that is what you wish, Gus."

The Prince knew very well that Franz was trying to disarm him. If Augustus had been unwilling to accept Franz, he would have protested to the emperor when the appointment was made. Franz knew that his seemingly generous offer was perfectly safe.

"Nonsense," the Prince said. "Of course I will not be uncomfortable having you attached to my court." His gray eyes narrowed. "Unless you have come bearing more threats from the emperor?" he added.

Franz laughed and shook his golden head. "I know you well enough to know that threats will never sway you, Gus. I told that to the emperor as well."

"I am glad to hear that."

Franz reached out to touch the Prince's arm in a gesture of affection. "You never change, Gus. Even when we were boys, once you set yourself a course of action, nothing on earth could prevent you from following it."

The Prince did not reply.

Franz's eyes became very blue. "Lydia is with me, you know."

The expression on the Prince's face did not change. "Charity assures me that she will be happy to receive her sister."

There was a pause, and then Franz smiled. "I know we can't be to each other what we once were, Gus. But I hope we can still be friends."

The full force of Franz's charismatic charm was trained on the Prince, who recognized the deliberation with which it was done but could not help responding to it. "Of course we can, Franz," he said. "Of course we can."

That night Augustus told Charity about his meeting with Franz. She had been sitting up in bed reading a book when he came into the room wearing his dressing gown and slippers. He had not spent a night in his own bed since he and Charity had become lovers.

"Stefan told me that you saw Franz today," she said, closing her book and putting it on the table beside her bed. She had not seen Augustus since they had breakfasted together, and she was anxious to hear how the meeting had gone.

"I did." She watched as Augustus went around to his side of the bed, took off his dressing gown, and got in under the covers next to her. He usually wore only his drawers to bed, having got out of the habit of wearing a nightshirt during his years in the mountains, and his upper torso was naked. He stretched his long body out comfortably, folded his arms behind his head, and looked up into her expectant face.

A fire was burning in the fireplace but still the room was cold, and he had only pulled the blankets up to his waist. Charity, who had her warm velvet robe on over her nightgown, said, "Aren't you freezing?"

"No. I'm comfortable."

She looked at the lean, powerful, recumbent body next to her in the bed and felt a sense of amazement that he was actually there. She wondered if she would ever stop feeling this way. *Perhaps, after we've been married for twenty years,* she thought with wry humor.

"Well, what happened between you and Franz?" she asked.

His blond hair was tousled from when he had pulled his shirt over his head, and it hung over his forehead like the forelock of a little boy. She thought it looked sweet, a sentiment she would never confide to him in a million years.

He said, "It was very civilized. Franz presented his credentials to me and I accepted them."

All thoughts of his forelock vanished. "That was all?" she said incredulously. "You must have had some sort of a conversation!"

His face took on a distinctly sardonic look. "We spoke for perhaps five minutes, during which time Franz did me the honor of saying that he knew I would not be intimidated by threats."

"Anyone who knows you knows that," Charity said scornfully. "Didn't he say anything at all about eloping with Lydia?"

He shrugged his bare shoulders, which were much stronger-looking than one would expect from one of his slender build. "He told me that he was in such a fever of love that his judgment was overcome by his passion."

He sounded amused, which for some reason annoyed Charity. "It wasn't funny when it happened," she snapped.

He raised an eyebrow at her tone of voice. "I realize that, Charity," he replied. "It is just that Franz is usually so self-possessed that it was strange to hear him admitting to such an emotional excess."

This comment made her feel even more annoyed than before. "I don't know that I would call love an emotional excess, Augustus."

"It is if it causes one to do harm to one's country." She was finding his reasonable tone more and more irritating. "I have forgiven Franz—I even think that his actions worked to my own benefit—but I simply cannot understand how he came to do what he did."

"He was passionately in love with Lydia," Charity said with annoyance. "Like Paris with Helen of Troy."

"Yes, and we all know how that affair turned out, don't we?" he said ironically. "Fortunately, I had enough sense not to plunge Jura into war in order to retrieve Lydia."

Frustration added fuel to Charity's growing hostility. How could she argue with him? Everything he was saying was perfectly sensible. He spoke as a prince, whose love life was governed by his duty to his country. She wanted to throw something at him.

He reached up a hand and captured a strand of her hair, pulling her head down to his. "Mmm," he said. "You smell so good."

Out of nowhere, Princess Caterina's words dripped like poison into Charity's mind: *Augustus's primary duty to his country is to produce an heir.*

One had to admit that he was certainly trying his best, Charity thought resentfully, and for the first time ever, she felt resistance to him stiffen her body. She wanted him to say that he loved her, that she was the most important thing in the world to him, that he would have run away with her just as Franz had run away with Lydia.

I would run away with you, Augustus, she thought. *I would do anything for you.*

"Kiss me," he commanded.

After a brief hesitation, she rested her lips lightly on top of his. He let go his hold on her hair and pulled her down so she was lying on top of him. The familiar sweet dizziness of desire began to seep into Charity's blood. Their kiss deepened.

She lifted her head and whispered, "Would you kiss Lydia like this?"

"Never," he replied, rolled her over so that he was on top, and began to kiss her again. Charity closed her eyes and surrendered to the passion that was swelling in her loins.

But after he had fallen asleep, instead of snuggling up next to him as she usually did, she moved to the far side of the bed and curled up into a ball, feeling cold and forlorn and quite thoroughly miserable.

21

Two days before he was to leave for Lake Leive to spend Christmas, the Prince held a reception to welcome Count Franz Adamov to Jura. It was a glittering affair attended by the entire ambassadorial corps as well as a number of members of both houses of Jura's diet. Franz and Lydia arrived a little late, and as they alighted from their coach, Franz stood for a moment in silence, regarding the lighted double-fan staircase before him.

As Lydia took his arm, he turned to her and said, "I have always thought this to be the most beautiful palace in Europe."

Lydia lifted her face, framed by the sable of her velvet hood, and smiled. "It is much smaller than Schönnbrun."

"Smaller, perhaps, but more perfect."

The new ambassador and his wife climbed the well-lit staircase and entered into the two-story-high

Banqueting Room, which was already filled with guests. One lackey took their coats and another announced their arrival. As their names were pronounced, a hush fell upon the assembled company and everyone turned to look at the door.

Franz had expected this first meeting with his countrymen to begin awkwardly, but he was perfectly confident that he could carry it off. He felt Lydia's fingers tighten on his arm and he walked her forward, allowing everyone to see what a stunning couple they made. In his first, lightning-quick survey of the room he had located the man that he most wanted to speak to, and now he guided Lydia in the direction of Count Boris Heusse and his wife.

"Count," he said with his most charming smile as he stopped beside the small, thin, bespectacled man who was one of Duke Marko's best friends. "How nice to see you again. My father asked me to bring you his greetings."

The count's voice was a little stiff as he made a small bow and replied, "That was kind of him, Franz. How is Marko doing?"

"Very well, thank you, sir." Franz turned to the short, plump pigeon of a woman who was the count's wife and bathed her in the radiance of his smile. "It is wonderful to be back in Jura."

No woman had ever been able to resist that smile, and the little countess was no exception. "It is nice to have you back, Franz." She looked at Lydia and the warmth faded from her face. "Countess," she said.

Franz took his wife's hand into his. "Please don't blame poor Lydia for our escapade, ma'am," he said with an engagingly rueful look. "I was the one at fault. I simply swept the poor girl off her feet."

The plump little countess tried and failed to look severe. "You were very wrong, Franz. You behaved very badly. You could have had the entire country in an uproar."

Franz looked contrite. "I know. I could have broken Gus's precious treaty with Great Britain. But he managed to retrieve the situation and, in truth, I cannot say that I am sorry that I stole his bride." He raised Lydia's hand to his lips and kissed it.

She turned her angel's face to him and smiled.

The countess sighed and said wistfully, "Ah, love. It has its own imperatives, does it not?"

Franz's voice deepened. "I knew you would understand, Countess."

Count Heusse said in a gruff voice, "Let me take you around the room, boy. It might make things a bit more comfortable for you."

Franz gave his father's friend his most boyish smile. "Thank you so much, sir."

"Nonsense," the count grumbled. "It is the least I can do for Marko's son."

Count Heusse's sponsorship did indeed break the ice, and as Franz and Lydia moved from group to group they were almost universally welcomed. Marko had always been popular with the diplomatic community, being a part of it himself for so many years as Jura's ambassador to Austria, and most of those present actually knew Franz better than they knew the Prince.

Franz was talking to Viktor Becker, the president

of the lower house of the diet, when a stalwart older man in livery announced from the doorway, "His Royal Highness Prince Augustus and Her Royal Highness Princess Charity."

Everyone in the room turned to the door. The men bowed and the women curtseyed as Augustus and his wife appeared at the doorway. Augustus made a small gesture indicating that they could rise, and advanced into the room, Charity at his side. She gestured and someone stepped up to join her. To his surprise, Franz recognized Harry Debritt, his brother-in-law.

Beside him, Franz heard Lydia make a small sound, and he glanced at her. Her face was frozen and her dilated eyes were fixed on the small figure of her sister as she stood beside the Prince, her head not quite reaching the height of his shoulder.

Franz perfectly understood his wife's feelings. He turned his head until his lips were close to her ear and warned in a low voice, "Careful."

She shot him a startled look. He held her eyes for a moment, and then she bit her lip and looked away.

Franz's eyes returned to the royal couple. *It's just bad luck that Gus is so damn tall,* he thought. *He wouldn't be half as impressive if he were my height.*

The Prince was impressive, however. There could be no doubt about that. He was perfectly friendly as he went around the room speaking to different people, but he had an aura of authority about him that was unmistakable. He had not had that air when he was a boy, Franz thought. It was something he had acquired in the mountains.

When we were boys, Gus was always the quiet one, Franz thought. *I was the one who was the leader.*

It had been a distinct shock for him to meet his royal cousin again after a separation of almost ten years. Franz had not been overjoyed by the Prince's transformation. Gus was still quiet, but there was a power in his quietness that had not been there before.

Franz had always thought he would make a better prince than his cousin, but it wasn't until he actually saw Gus in his royal role that the corrosive poison of jealousy had started its work. He had stolen Gus's bride in an effort to humiliate him. He had set out to do it the moment he first saw Lydia, and he had been successful. He was always successful.

But Gus's humiliation had never happened. He had, with his usual damn coolness, simply married Lydia's younger sister.

In their circle of the room, the royal couple, accompanied by Harry, were coming closer to Franz, and for the first time he fixed his gaze on the diminutive figure at the Prince's side. What he saw caused his brows to draw together.

When Franz had last seen Charity she had been a charming child, but the girl he was looking at now was not a child any longer. The brown eyes were still huge, but the soft girlish roundness of her face had given way to a more defined look. Her high cheekbones were more prominent, more like Lydia's, and her mouth had changed its expression.

She looks like a woman, Franz thought. And his

eyes went speculatively to his cousin, who had always professed that he knew nothing about women. *I wouldn't have thought Gus had it in him,* he thought sardonically.

"Ah, there you are, Franz," the Prince said. His voice was perfectly affable.

Franz bowed. The Prince held out his hand with demonstrable friendliness, and the cousins shook. Then Augustus turned to the woman at Franz's side and said, in an equally friendly manner, "How are you, Lydia? You are looking beautiful as ever."

Lydia curtseyed and said breathlessly, "Your Highness. I am happy to see you again."

"Are you?" The Prince sounded amused.

Sudden fury shot through Franz at that note in Gus's voice. He repressed it, however, and said, his own voice soft and caressing, "You look wonderful, Princess. Marriage must agree with you."

The large doelike brown eyes looked straight at him but their expression wasn't doelike at all. Charity said, "It does." Then she turned to Lydia and held out her arms. "How lovely to see you, Lydia. Isn't it wonderful that Harry is here as well?"

Lydia hugged her sister with a noticeable lack of enthusiasm. "Lovely to see you too, Charity," she murmured.

There was a fractional pause, during which time Franz saw Charity deliberately step on Harry's toe. Harry then said heartily, "Great to see you, Lydia!" and enveloped her in a bear hug that displaced her shawl and made her beautiful eyes flash.

The Prince looked at Franz and murmured, "It is

so nice for my wife to see her family again. She has been looking forward to Lydia's arrival."

Charity slipped her arm through Lydia's. "Why don't we three sit down and have a nice chat together? I have a letter from Papa I'm sure you'll like to hear. Come along, Harry."

Lydia cast an anguished glance at Franz as Charity bore her inexorably off toward a corner of the room. Franz looked at the Prince and said with amusement, "I wondered why you arranged this reception for me, Gus. It was very clever of you."

His cousin's eyes were cool. "The credit goes to Charity."

"Then it was very clever of her."

Suddenly Augustus smiled. "It is good to have you back in Jura, Franz," he said. He touched his cousin briefly on the shoulder, then turned away.

While the Prince and Princess went to Lake Leive to spend Christmas, Franz remained behind in Julia, wooing many of the nobles who were his father's friends. Count Adamov was possessed of a silver tongue and enormous personal charm, and he used both to denigrate his cousin in the most reluctant, regretful, sorrowful fashion imaginable. The upshot of this campaign was that he succeeded in convincing eight malcontent noblemen that it was their duty, as Jurian patriots, to remove Augustus from the throne of Jura and replace him with Marko.

On a bitterly cold morning in January, the eight met in the library of the Julia palace of Count Boris

Heusse in order to concoct a plot that would bring about this end. The men sat around a large library table drinking coffee, Franz at one end of the table and Count Heusse at the other.

"We have to come up with something better than Rupnik and Hindenberg did," Baron Ladislaus Zapolya said sarcastically. "None of us wants to end up with a noose around our neck."

A shudder ran around the room at the thought of the fates of the previous plotters against Augustus.

"There is no need to kill Augustus," Baron Heusse said fussily.

Count Sigismund Corvinus motioned impatiently with his hand. "And just how the hell are we to remove him from the throne without killing him?"

Franz spoke in a voice that was perfectly calm and reasonable. "Arrest him and get him out of the country before word gets out to the people what has happened."

All eyes turned to the composed face of the Prince's cousin. "Easily said, Franz, but not easily done," Baron Hertling remarked irritably.

"How on earth are we to arrest him?" Lord Nikola Appel said. "We aren't military men. Augustus would walk right through us, and then where would we be?"

"We certainly don't want to involve the Household Guard again," Count Heusse said.

"God no," Lord Nikola said fervently.

Franz's blue gaze turned on Baron Zapolya, who responded promptly, "My brother-in-law commands one of our cavalry regiments. If I tell him that we must replace Augustus in order to avoid an Austrian invasion, I believe he will listen."

Baron Hertling downed his coffee as if it were a shot of brandy and said nervously, "What if he doesn't? What guarantee would we have that he won't go straight to Augustus?"

Baron Zapolya lifted one of his thick black eyebrows. "Marc has always thought that he would make a wonderful Marshal of Jura, but as long as Augustus is prince, Emil Sauder has that position sewn up."

A thoughtful silence reigned as the men digested this piece of information. Then Count Heusse said warningly, "We can't risk any of your brother-in-law's men running to Augustus, Ladislaus. Look what happened to Rupnik and Hindenberg."

"I will instruct Marc not to inform his men about their mission until they are actually on the way to arrest Augustus," Baron Zapolya said reassuringly.

"This is all very well," Baron Hertling said in his testy voice, "but what the devil are we to do with him after he is arrested?"

All eyes in the room turned to Franz.

"Put him on a ship and send him to England," Franz replied coolly.

A rumble of nervous laughter greeted this comment.

Franz did not smile. "I believe that will be the best solution for everyone. Gus has relatives in England who will take him in. He can live a perfectly comfortable life in exile." He quirked one golden eyebrow. "As we all know ourselves from personal experience."

"What if Great Britain demands that Augustus be restored?" Baron Hertling asked nervously.

Once more Franz flicked a glance at Baron Zapolya, who responded by saying firmly, "The British government does not wish to become involved in the internal affairs of Jura. Their ambassador may make a formal protest, but Britain will not lift a finger to restore Augustus to his throne."

The clink of a coffee cup being returned to its saucer was the only sound. Then Lord Nikola Appel said, "I think you are right."

Murmurs of assent came from the others at the table.

"Are we all in agreement, then?" Count Heusse asked crisply. "Ladislaus?"

"Aye."

Nikola?"

"Aye."

Methodically, Count Heusse went around the table until he came to the last man. "Leopold?"

Baron Hertling looked somberly at Franz. "There will be no bloodshed?"

"None," Franz replied, his blue eyes steady.

"Then—aye," Baron Hertling said.

The tension that had been building in the room suddenly relaxed. More coffee was poured as the men talked to each other in low voices.

Count Heusse gave them a few more minutes, then called them to attention once more. "Augustus will be back in Julia at the beginning of February for the opening of the diet," he said. "We must do it before then, while he is relatively isolated in the country."

"Where is he now?" Baron Hertling asked.

"He and the Princess are presently at Zosi," Franz said. "They are expected to remain there for a week, and then they will return to Julia for the opening of the diet."

"Zosi is perfect for us," Baron Zapolya said. "We can put Augustus and his English wife into a carriage and get them to Seista within hours. They will be well on their way to England before word leaks out about the coup."

"We must act quickly," Baron Hertling said nervously. "The quicker we act, the less chance there is of our plans coming to the wrong ears."

Sober nods from each man around the table greeted this comment as the fates of Rupnik and Hindenberg flashed once more through everyone's mind.

Baron Heusse asked, "Where is your brother-in-law's regiment stationed, Ladislaus?"

"Lipizza. I will go down there immediately and speak to him. Let's meet again tomorrow morning and I'll give you his reply."

With murmurs of agreement, the somber-faced group of conspirators broke up.

22

Something changed in Charity during the long night she spent lying awake at the far end of the bed from Augustus. The sensual magic that had carried her through the last few months suddenly wasn't enough anymore.

Her feelings were complicated by the fact that she suspected that she was with child. Part of her was thrilled by this thought, but another part wondered if this would signal the end of her intense relationship with Augustus. It was not that she imagined he would once again take up with his mistress; rather she feared that he'd been paying attention to her because of his desire to beget an heir and not because he felt an inassuageable need for her.

These doubts, sown weeks before by Princess Caterina's words, blossomed on the night of the diplomatic reception and caused Charity to change toward her husband. No longer could she respond to him in the same generous, wholehearted way she once had. He had never told her that he loved her, and now the absence of those three words began to spread like poison through her heart. For the first time in their marriage, Charity actually began to pretend that she was asleep when Augustus came to bed.

This transformation in their relationship took place during the Christmas holiday, which they spent at Lake Leive, and then continued during their vacation at the Prince's villa of Zosi, where they moved so that Augustus and his friends could do some hunting. To the great relief of both Augustus and Charity, Princess Caterina had decided to return to Venice for the holidays, so they were spared her less than soothing presence. Harry accompanied the royal couple, but Charity's main distraction during this period was a new friend who had joined their party. He was the younger son of one of Jura's nobles, whom Charity had met when he came to Julia to study with Lord Louis. Lord Maximilien Broder was only twenty and totally mad about horses, and Charity had invited him to accompany the court on its Christmas journey several weeks before her falling-out with Augustus.

As things had turned out, she was very glad to have Max's company. With Harry following Augustus like a puppy and Lady Stefanie spending all of her time with Emil, Charity turned to Max for companionship during the day. They spent hours discussing the different horses in the stable, their training, the work Lord Louis was doing with them, and the rides both of them had had on them. It was a topic of conversation neither of them ever tired of.

The court had been at Zosi for almost three weeks when one night Charity came into the bedroom she shared with Augustus to find him standing, arms folded, in front of the window.

"No cards tonight?" she asked lightly, stopping at the foot of the bed and turning in his direction. She didn't quite raise her eyes to his face.

"I rather thought I might like to see my wife tonight," he replied evenly. "I haven't seen much of her lately."

She raised her eyebrows. "I have been right here, Augustus. You are the one who is out hunting all day and up late all night, playing cards with your friends."

The fingers that were resting on his folded arms tightened so that the knuckles noticeably whitened. "You don't appear to have missed my company very much. You seem to have been very well entertained by Broder." There was a dangerous note in his voice that she had never heard before, and she darted a quick glance at him.

At the sight of Augustus, his ruffled blond hair, his gray eyes, the cleft in his chin, her heart turned over. Suddenly she wanted desperately to touch him, to smooth back his hair, to kiss his chin . . .

The set of his mouth was grim, and she tried to remember what he had just said. Something about Max.

"Max is a friend of mine," she said reasonably. "If you can spend time with your friends, surely I may spend time with mine."

"My friends are of my own sex," he retorted. "You don't see me closeted half the day with some pretty young girl, do you?"

Charity stared at her husband's grim, angry face and realized with shock that he was jealous. Abruptly she turned away so that he couldn't see her face.

Augustus is jealous of Max, she thought in thrilled wonder and amazement. *He's jealous of me.*

She turned back to her husband, a look of wounded innocence in her widened eyes. "Augustus, what are you saying? Surely you don't suspect that my relationship with Lord Maximilien is anything more than friendship?"

It was his turn to look away from her. "Of course I don't," he said gruffly. "It's just . . . It's just . . . Oh, I don't know, it just seems to me that you have been different of late."

Yes, Charity thought grimly, *I haven't been falling into your arms every time you lift your eyebrow.*

"You have been busy with your friends," she repeated.

He went back to scowling.

Charity felt a twinge of satisfaction that she could upset him the way he could upset her. She walked to the bed, unbuttoned her robe, put her foot on the footstool, and climbed in. "Are you coming?"

He came.

The Prince was thoroughly upset. In the way of men, he had thought that his marriage was just perfect. His wife was passionate, generous, and right there in his bed, night after night after night. Not only that, she was exactly the sort of person with whom he felt comfortable in every other way. He could talk to her and she would understand, he could confide in her and she would be discreet. Perhaps best of all, she shared his vision for his country. She was going to be a great Princess of Jura.

He loved her. He adored her. He thought he was the luckiest man in the world to have got her. It simply never once occurred to him to tell her any of those things. After all, she never said any of those things to him and it didn't bother him one jot.

Had she said them, had she said, *I love you, Augustus,* he would have returned the sentiment immediately. But she didn't, and so he didn't either. Why should he? Everything was going perfectly.

And then things started to go wrong. He wasn't quite sure when it happened, but he first noticed it when they were at Lake Leive for Christmas. He came into their bedroom one night, and Charity was asleep. Charity was never asleep. She always waited up for him, to discuss his day and, of course, to make love.

He wasn't upset the first time. After all, the poor girl had a right to be tired once in a while. But when it began to happen on a regular basis, he began to worry. He missed the sex, certainly, but it was more than that. He worried that something had come between them. If he should lose Charity . . .

Very little in life had ever scared the Prince, but the thought of losing Charity did.

Then he began to notice all the time she was spending with the slim, dark-haired, dark-eyed boy, Lord Maximilien Broder. The Prince discovered from Louis that Charity and Lord Maximilien were both his students and that Charity had invited the boy to accompany the court to Lake Leive and to Zosi.

Augustus had a very difficult time refraining from sending Lord Maximilien home. Only the knowledge that doing so would precipitate a huge scandal stopped him. Even confronting Charity with his suspicions did not restore his serenity. She had asked him if he suspected her of having an affair with Lord Maximilien and, when he looked into her eyes, he had realized that he did not suspect her of that, that he had never suspected her of that.

He was jealous because she had found a male friend whom she liked more than him. He didn't want her to like anyone more than him.

He took her to bed, and did everything in his power to show her how he felt about her, and for one wonderful night things between them were the way they had been before. As he lay awake, watching her sleep, rejoicing that she had not turned away, that she had nestled against him in the way she used to, he prayed fervently that whatever it was that had gone wrong between them had been made right.

Charity was still asleep when the Prince arose the following morning to go hunting. It was snowing when he and the men returned to the villa later in the morning, and they were divesting themselves of their warm coats in the hall, which was decorated with a variety of glassy-eyed hunting trophies, when a servant approached him carrying a folded letter on a silver salver. Augustus instantly recognized the seal.

"Go ahead," he said to the others. "I will join you in a moment." As the rest of the company moved toward the big room that served as the villa's main gathering space, he opened the letter and read it through. Then he read it through again. Slowly he folded it and tucked it inside his breast pocket. At last he followed the others into the room.

Charity and her ladies were inside, comfortably ensconced in front of a big fire. Lady Stefanie Havek had a book in her hands, which she evidently had been reading aloud for the entertainment of the women.

Charity looked up from her seat on the sofa in front of the coffeepot and smiled when she saw him.

The Prince's heart leaped and he moved directly toward Charity's sofa. The lady who had been sitting next to her quietly moved to another seat and the Prince took her place and asked his wife, "Is there any coffee?"

"I'll send for a fresh pot." She leaned forward and rang the bell on the table in front of her.

A servant came in with a fresh pot of coffee and the Prince had just taken his first swallow when the door opened once again, this time to admit his personal bodyguard, Kark, who was accompanied by a stranger.

"Your Highness," Kark said, and the note in his voice caught the attention of the entire room. "I am sorry to interrupt you, but this man says he has a message of extreme urgency."

The Prince stared at the burly middle-aged man who was standing beside Kark and thought he looked vaguely familiar. He felt Charity move infinitesimally closer. "What is your message?" he said.

The man took a few steps forward, then fell on his knees. "I bear a letter for you from Baroness Zais, Your Highness." And he brought forth from beneath his coat a much-folded piece of paper.

Charity stiffened.

"Bring it here." As Augustus reached for the letter, he recognized the man walking toward him as one of Eva's most trusted servants. He accepted the letter, opened it, and read:

They are going to arrest you, Augustus. I heard it from Marc Luska last night. He told me he was going to be the new marshal. There is a cabal of noblemen and they are sending Colonel Luska with his cavalry regiment to arrest you. Franz is behind this. Augustus, you must get away before they catch you. God knows what Franz plans to do.

Augustus stared at the familiar handwriting of his old mistress in shock. *Franz,* he thought numbly. *I can't believe it.*

His eyes went over Eva's note one more time, struggling to comprehend. *Arrest you . . . regiment of cavalry . . . Franz.*

As if from a great distance he heard Charity's voice. "What is it, Augustus? Is something wrong?"

He froze. *Charity,* he thought. *Dear God in heaven, Charity is here.* His heart began to pound. He had never been so frightened in his life. *He will kill her too. She may be with child. He can't take the chance. He will have to kill her too.*

Stefan's urgent voice cut through his paralysis. "For God's sake, Gus, what is it?"

He focused his eyes on the man who was now kneeling before him. "Do you know what is in this letter?"

"I do, Your Highness. I left Lipizza as soon as I could. I would estimate that I am about an hour ahead of them."

He heard the fear in Charity's voice. "Ahead of whom? What is happening, Augustus?"

At last he turned to look at her. "This is information that a regiment of cavalry is on its way to Zosi to arrest me."

She went white to the lips.

Stefan said sharply, "Who is the letter from?"

He looked away from Charity. "It is from Eva Zais. Colonel Luska confided the plot to her last night. Apparently he was trying to impress her—he told her he was going to be the next marshal."

Stefan's round, cherubic face looked as grim as it was possible for it to look. "Does she say who is behind this?"

"Franz." Even as he said the name he couldn't believe it. He could feel the shock run through the room.

Kark, who had been standing at the door, spoke up.

"Your Highness, if you remember, Marshal Rupnik chose me to carry out his assassination plot because he knew I had been helped by Franz and he thought I would be loyal to him."

Emil let out his breath in a long hiss.

Charity's hand clutched his arm. "Augustus, he must have been behind Rupnik's plot." Her voice wavered, then steadied. "He will kill you, Augustus. He wants to be the prince himself."

At last his brain began to function. "I don't plan to wait around to find out what Franz intends to do." He looked from Stefan to Emil. "We'll ride to Namek."

The two men leaped to their feet, as if they would be away that very minute.

Augustus put a reassuring hand over Charity's clutching fingers and said to Kark, "Have horses saddled for me, Lord Emil, Lord Stefan, Mr. Debritt, and the Princess. Immediately!"

"Yes, Your Highness." Kark turned and ran out of the room.

Charity's hand had tightened convulsively when he said her name, and Stefan took a step toward him. "Gus! You can't mean to take the Princess! Namek is deep in the mountains. It will take us at least five hours to get there and the weather is getting bad."

"She is coming with us," he said.

Emil said, "She will be perfectly safe here. Franz is married to her sister, for God's sake!"

Then Charity spoke. "He is right, Augustus." The calmness of her voice belied the tense grip of her fingers on his arm. "I would slow you down. You must save yourself."

He turned to look into the large brown eyes that were regarding him so steadily. "I am not leaving you here to the mercy of my enemies."

"Christ, Gus, it's snowing!" Emil was almost shouting. "Believe me, she will be better off here."

"I will only get in your way," Charity said. "You must save yourself."

He tightened his hand over hers, glanced at the other people in the room, and said tersely, "Leave us."

Stefan and Emil looked furious, Harry looked worried, and the women looked petrified, but no one dared to protest. As the door closed behind Stefan, Augustus turned to his wife. "Charity," he said, "I have a very important question to ask you. Do you think you might be with child?"

Gold flared in the warm brown of her eyes. "I . . . I might be," she said. "I'm not sure."

The fear that had so paralyzed him before knifed through him again at her words. He shut his own eyes briefly so she would not see it. Then he said as calmly as he could, "I cannot leave you here if there is a chance that you are with child. Franz must know that the only way he will be able to replace me as prince is to kill me. Do you think he will let you live if he knows you are carrying my child? My heir?"

He heard her breath catch as he looked intently into her face. "Do you understand?"

Her chin came up. "I understand perfectly, Augustus. I know my duty to Jura as well as you. I will come."

"Thank God." He bent his head, kissed her hard. "Dress in your breeches and your warmest coat and take a change of clothes in a pillowcase."

She nodded soberly, jumped up, and ran out of the room.

Fifteen minutes later, the Prince, his wife, her brother, and his two closest friends galloped out of Zosi in the gently falling snow and headed north, toward the safety of the Jurian Alps.

Half an hour after their departure, Franz, accompanied by Colonel Luska and his cavalry regiment, rode into Zosi to find that the birds had flown.

Charity had never been so cold in her entire life. It had not been so bad at first; they had galloped along the main road north, passing small peasant villages of twenty or so houses each, and the exertion of the swift pace had kept her relatively warm. Then they had slowed down, turning eastward to smaller tracks as they began their climb into the mountains.

The snow kept falling, making their progress more and more difficult. Augustus assured her that the snow was a good thing, that it would hinder any pursuit, and that anytime she wanted to stop, they would.

But Charity was determined not to slow the men down, so she tied her woolen muffler across her nose and around the lower part of her face, and rode on.

The snow continued to fall. It covered her muffler, then melted with the warmth from her breath and the muffler became wet. The higher they ascended into the mountains, the colder Charity became. Her feet were the worst; they were so cold that they hurt. After a while the pain was so great that tears ran down her face. She told herself that as long as she felt them she was all right; it was when she couldn't that she was in trouble. Despite the pain, she tried to flex her toes to keep the blood moving. She put her hands under her horse's mane to try to warm them up, but his mane was wet and the trick didn't work.

Augustus rode next to her until the track became too narrow for their horses to go side by side. By then they were high in the mountains, close to Mount Eisen, the highest peak in the Jurian Alps. There would be no place to stop until they reached Namek, the tiny village that had been Augustus's headquarters for a good part of the war.

Surely they must almost be there, Charity thought, as the track became steeper and steeper. The horses were laboring, up to their knees in snow, and the world was nothing but a blur of white.

Augustus, who was riding right in front of her, was just a blur in the snow, but she heard him call encouragingly, "Just another ten minutes, Charity, and we'll be there."

She could hear the worry in his voice and opened her mouth to assure him that she was all right, but her teeth were chattering so badly she couldn't form any words.

Then, at last, the track leveled off and they reached what in the summer would probably be a mountain meadow. "We're here!" Augustus shouted back to her, and Charity blinked the snow away from her eyes and looked at the collection of five or six snow-covered huts that evidently formed the village of Namek. She heard Augustus's voice but couldn't

understand what he was saying. Then he was beside
her horse, reaching up to lift her down. Instead of
setting her on her feet, he held her in his arms and
began to walk toward one of the huts.

"Emil rode ahead and warned them we were coming," he said in her frozen ear. "Natalya has built you
a big fire. We'll get you warm in a trice."

He pushed open the door and carried her inside
the single-room hut where a fire was indeed blazing
in a large stone fireplace. A woman was already
there, making up the bed that, along with a rough-
hewn table and chairs, comprised the hut's furniture.

"You had better get your wife into some dry
clothes right away, lad," the woman said to her sovereign prince in a voice that was distinctly disapproving.

"I know, Natalya," Augustus replied. "Do you
think you could bring her saddlebag and something
hot to eat as well?"

"Surely," the woman said, and the flames briefly
shot higher in the draft of air as she opened the door
and closed it again.

When they were alone, Augustus put Charity on
her feet in front of the fireplace. "You look like a
mummy," he said as he briskly began to unwind her
muffler. Charity's teeth chattered as the wet wool
was peeled away from her face.

He kissed her cold wet nose. "You'll feel better
once we get you out of these clothes." He tossed the
muffler away from the fire and plucked off her hat.
Her hair, which had started off the day in an elegant
knot, cascaded down over the wet fur of her coat.

The hat followed the muffler to the floor, then he stripped her wet leather gloves from her frozen fingers and tossed them aside as well.

"Can you hold out your arms?" he asked gently. She did as he asked and he eased off her fur coat, which was matted and wet with melted snow. Then he dragged a chair from the table to the fire and told her to sit down so he could take off her boots.

"I t-think my f-feet w-will c-come off w-with them," she said through chattering teeth.

"No they won't." He guided her to the roughly carved wooden chair. Then, matter-of-factly, he turned around, gripped her boot by the ankle, and said, "Push."

Without argument she set her other foot on his rear and pushed. Tears ran down her face as the boot came off her frozen foot. They repeated the same procedure with the other boot, then he pulled off her socks and inspected her toes.

"They're red, not white," he informed her as he began to rub them. "No frostbite. You'll be fine."

His rubbing was bringing the blood back into her toes, and the feeling was both exquisite and painful. "I'm s-so g-g-glad," she chattered.

He was still rubbing when a knock came on the door. "Come," Augustus called.

"I have Charity's saddlebag," she heard Harry say. "And yours too, Gus."

He left off rubbing her feet and went to the door to receive the saddlebags from Harry. Harry went out again and Augustus came back to the fire. "I have your extra clothing here," he said. "You'll feel much better once we get you into your nightgown. Then I'll wrap you up in a blanket."

"A-all r-right." She stood up and he helped her to strip down to the flannel chemise and drawers she had put on for warmth. Then he pulled her full white nightgown over her head, wrapped her in a blanket, and sat her once again on the chair. From his own saddlebag he extracted a pair of enormous woolen socks, which he proceeded to put on her feet.

Still kneeling in front of her, he said, "Natalya will be coming soon with something hot for you to eat. That will make you feel better."

"H-how about you? You are s-still wearing your wet clothes. You should change t-too."

"I will," he said, "but I must see to a few things first. Will you be all right if I leave you for a while?"

"I am f-fine, Augustus," she said, pulling the deliciously warm blanket more closely around her and holding her feet in their enormous socks out to the fire. "Go d-do what you have to do."

By the time Natalya returned, Charity's teeth had stopped chattering. She looked up into the beautiful clear pale blue eyes of her elderly hostess as she took the soup she was offered and said gratefully, "Thank you so much."

"I am glad to be of help," the woman returned. Her eyes looked fierce. "But it is a terrible thing that our prince must once more be in fear for his life."

"That is so," Charity replied. "But it is good that he has friends he can trust."

The woman's expression softened, then she left Charity alone with the wonderful hot soup.

She had finished it all and was feeling distinctly drowsy when Augustus came back into the room and joined her in front of the fire. "Warmer?" he asked as he shed his coat. Under it he was wearing a thick wool shirt with a collar. His hunting trousers were wool as well.

"Much warmer," she said sleepily.

"Good. The snow is stopping, but it has done its work. I don't think there will be any pursuit in this kind of weather."

She made an effort to come awake. "Are the horses all right?"

"The horses are fine. They have been put in a barn, toweled dry, and are now greedily eating hay."

He pulled a chair up next to hers by the fire, and bent to remove his boots. This was an easier operation than Charity's had been, since he was still wearing his hunting boots and not high riding boots like hers.

His damp hair had begun to dry at the edges and looked almost gold in the light of the fire. "How about you?" she asked. "Have you had some soup?"

"Yes." He stretched his feet in their thick woolen socks, which she noticed were dry, toward the fire.

"Where are Harry and the others?"

He wiggled his toes and sighed with pleasure. "They are staying with Natalya and Karl."

Charity looked around the one-room hut that was sheltering them. "Whose house is this, then?"

"It used to belong to Natalya and Karl, but after the war they built a larger house. They use this now as their guest house."

Charity's eyes moved slowly from his feet to her own, which peeked out from under her nightdress encased in an identical pair of wool socks. "Are these your extra socks, Augustus?"

"Yes." He smiled. "They're a little big on you."

"I brought an extra pair of my own socks. I don't like to steal yours."

"Charity, those thin cotton things are useless. No wonder your feet were so cold."

"These are much warmer," she admitted.

"Tomorrow I'll see if Natalya can find you a wool pair. Mine will never fit under your boots."

Her toes had ached when they first began to thaw, but now they felt blissfully warm. She sat straighter in her chair so she would feel less sleepy and asked, "Is this the house where you stayed during the war?"

"Yes."

Charity looked around the shadowy room, from the rough-hewn bed to the wooden table and chairs, to the single rag rug that adorned the unpolished wooden floor. There was one window, the ceiling was low, and the only light was generated by the fire.

"It is heavenly," she said.

He laughed.

They sat for a few moments, gazing at the fire in companionable silence. Then Charity said, "What are you going to do now?"

He turned his head to look at her. "Go to bed."

He knew perfectly well what she had meant, but she let him evade the question. "Amen," she said. "I am exhausted." She stood up and, still clutching her blanket, padded over to the bed, shuffling a little in her over-large socks. She slid her hand under the quilt to feel the sheets. "They're cold," she announced tragically.

He yawned and stretched and stood up. "We'll keep each other warm."

She watched in silence as he stripped down to his drawers and the linen shirt he wore under the wool one. "I would advise you to keep on your socks," he said as he approached the bed, still wearing his.

"Nothing on this earth would persuade me to give them up," she declared.

He reached the bed, pulled back the quilt, and lifted her in. Then he went around to the other side and got in himself, turning to her immediately and gathering her close. She cuddled close to him, nestling her head into the warmth of his shoulder.

He pressed his lips against her hair. "I'm so sorry, Charity," he said huskily. "I'm so sorry I had to put you through such an ordeal."

His voice was so tender. He had taken such exquisite care of her. She would have been so happy if his concern had been for her. She shut her eyes. *What a terrible person I must be, to be jealous of my own child.*

"Go to sleep," he said. "Everything will look better in the morning."

23

$\mathcal{F}$ranz was incandescent with fury when he arrived at Zosi with Colonel Luska's cavalry regiment and found only Charity's ladies in residence. It took all of Stefanie's courage to meet his blazing eyes and tell him that the Prince had received a letter early in the morning and had left immediately, taking his wife, her brother, and Lords Stefan and Emil with him.

"Who delivered this letter?" Franz demanded, the softness of his voice in contrast to the violence of his eyes.

"I did not know the man, Count," Stefanie said steadily.

"Well, then," Franz said, with a pleasantry that somehow managed to be absolutely petrifying, "Perhaps you can tell me where I might find this messenger now."

"I believe he left, Count." Stefanie's face never changed, even though she knew perfectly well that Baroness Zais's servant was hiding in one of the villa's attics. She also professed not to know the Prince's destination, but this was one question to which Franz already had guessed the answer.

"He has headed for the mountains and his old network of supporters," he told Colonel Luska, "Look at the weather. We won't catch him now."

After a private conversation with Luska, which left the colonel pale as a corpse, the cavalry regiment returned to its headquarters in Lipizza while Franz rode by himself back to Julia in the snow. During the hours he spent on the road he forced himself to push his anger aside and focus on the problem posed by Augustus's escape.

The Prince now would know who was his enemy. It was essential that Franz act before Augustus did.

Dark had fallen when his tired horse crossed the bridge over the Kava and trotted wearily into Julia. Franz rode directly to the stable of Count Boris Heusse and ordered the count's grooms to see to his horse. Then he walked across the stableyard to the palace, where a servant let him in.

"Franz!" Count Heusse smiled at the wet figure who was standing in his Chinese anteroom. "Have you accomplished it then?"

Franz did not return the smile. "Someone warned him," he said. "He got away to the mountains."

The count staggered and reached out to steady himself on the edge of a fragile Chinese-style table. "Oh no," he said. He looked absolutely aghast. "What are we going to do?"

Briefly, Franz told the count the plan he had decided upon during his ride back to Julia. Next he told him to send for the rest of the conspirators.

"But it's dinnertime, dear boy," the count protested, having been interrupted in the midst of his own meal.

Franz merely looked at him, and the count left the room to send servants to all the appropriate homes. Within half an hour, the treasonous allies were gathered around the big table in the count's library listening in appalled silence as Franz told them what had occurred at Zosi earlier in the day.

"Oh my God, oh my God," Baron Hertling moaned. He had wrapped his arms around himself and was rocking back and forth in his chair, like a woman who has just learned of the death of a beloved child. "He will have us executed. We must flee the country right away."

Lord Nikola Appel slammed his hand down on the table, causing the baron to jump and almost knock over the inkstand that had been placed in front of him. Lord Nikola ignored the trembling baron and said loudly, "How the devil did Augustus find out? Someone must have warned him. I want to know who did it!" He glared around the table, his eyes touching the face of each of his fellow conspirators. "Who betrayed us?"

The rest of the men darted fearful glances around

the table as well. Then Franz said, in the same cold voice with which he had informed them of his mission's failure, "I believe Colonel Luska is the culprit. Apparently, in an effort to impress Baroness Zais, whom he wishes to wed, he told her that he had expectations of becoming Marshal of Jura. This occurred yesterday evening—and Augustus was warned early this morning."

"He told Eva Zais?" Baron Zapolya, the colonel's brother-in-law, said incredulously.

Franz's eyes glittered like blue glass. "That is what he confessed to me."

"Jesus!" Lord Nikola exploded, causing Baron Hertling to jump once again. "Eva Zais and Augustus have been lovers for years. Everyone knows that!"

Franz said, "Apparently they are lovers no more, but also apparently the lady still feels a certain loyalty to him. She must have sent to warn him. There is no other way he could possibly have discovered our intentions."

It was Baron Hertling who voiced the question that had been on every man's mind since he had heard of the Prince's escape. "Did Luska tell her our names?"

Franz looked at the apprehensive faces that were turned to him and replied evenly, "He says he did not, but can we believe him?"

Baron Hertling wrung his hands. "What are we going to do? What are we going to do? He will kill us. I know he will kill us."

"He will certainly kill us if we do nothing but sit

around and moan," Franz said contemptuously. "Obviously we must proceed with our original plan. The only real change in our strategy is that, instead of being on a ship to England, Augustus is now hiding in the mountains."

"That is a big difference," Hertling bleated in reply.

Murmurs of fervent agreement came from the other men.

"It is not so different as you may think," Franz returned. "We have the power base of Julia and he does not. We have the resources of the newspapers and the printing presses. We have the wherewithal to get our message out to the people. Augustus has none of these things available to him in the mountains."

"That is so," Lord Nikola said. "If we move fast, we can have this coup accomplished before he is able to retaliate."

"Exactly," Franz said. "Once they are made aware of the situation, I believe the nobles of Jura will stand with us."

"Franz is right," Count Heusse said firmly. "The first thing we must do is issue a proclamation declaring Marko to be our new prince. As Franz has said, I am quite certain that we will have the nobles behind us."

"The commons worship Augustus," Baron Hertling moaned.

"They will not worship him if they think he is leading them into another war," Franz said coldly.

"Franz is right," Baron Zapolya said.

"What about the Household Guard?" Lord Nikola said. "Will they rally to Augustus?"

Franz shook his head impatiently. "Not if we act swiftly. First we must issue this proclamation." He gestured to the scroll that lay on the table before him. "This will explain our actions, and legitimize them. Once the population has digested what is in this proclamation, support for Augustus will waver."

"What is in this proclamation?" Baron Hertling demanded.

"Exactly what we all decided should be in it," Franz replied. "I will read it to you and I believe you will find it both succinct and compelling." Slowly he unrolled the scroll, held it spread open on the table before him. Then he read:

To the Nobles and Commons of Jura: In the name of God and of that Peace which all men of good will both Desire and Deserve, Jura, through us, has cast out her most contentious prince, Augustus, and summoned to the throne in his stead, Marko, the Brother of our late beloved prince, Ivan.

We take this momentous step because the said Augustus has shown himself a Tyrant who is indifferent to the best Welfare of his People. To prove this charge, we submit these Facts to the people of Jura and to the World.

He has betrayed his Country by willfully, and without proper Advice, making a Treaty with a Foreign Power and that gives that Power's navy the Freedom of one of our most Precious Treasures, the seaport of Seista.

He has willfully Antagonized the Emperor of Austria, to the degree where Austria is considering the taking up of Arms against us, thus destroying the Peace won so dearly with Jurian lives.

He has endangered Jura's lifeblood, her Trade, by causing the Emperor of Austria to threaten to place Tariffs on Jurian goods, thus Rendering them Non-Competitive in the empire's vast markets.

Because the said Augustus has acted Dangerously and Arbitrarily, without counsel of either chamber of the Diet, and in Defiance of his country's Welfare, we declare him Unfit to be our Prince and call upon all right-minded Jurians to stand with us and welcome Prince Marko to serve in his Stead.

Franz's voice died away, and for a moment the popping noise coming from the logs upon the fire was the only sound in the room. Then Baron Zapolya said, "That's good."

"Yes, it is," several other men agreed.

"We will publish this proclamation tomorrow," Franz said. "Julia will get it immediately and we will send it off to the rest of the country. The diet convenes in four days and I will read this proclamation to the assembled chambers on opening day and ask for their support. Once we have the support of the diet, we will have succeeded in our mission. The military will not act in defiance of the legislative body."

"What if the diet does not give its approval?" Baron Hertling said.

"It will," Franz replied. "I will make the speech myself. The representatives will listen to me."

The assembled men looked at his supremely confident face and believed him. The sense of relief in the room was palpable.

Franz picked up a pen and said, "Now all that we must do is sign this proclamation." And he dipped the pen into its adjacent inkstand and wrote in a clear, elegant script: *Count Franz Adamov.*

There was perfect silence while he waited for the ink to dry. Then he passed the paper to Lord Nikola, who was sitting next to him, and Lord Nikola signed his name as well.

In this way, the paper went around the room until it came to the last man, Baron Leopold Hertling. "I don't know," the baron said nervously.

"If you are not with us, Baron, you are against us," Franz said coldly. "You joined us because you agreed with our complaints against Augustus, but if you are too fearful to sign your name, you may go. Just do not expect to be included in any of our future plans."

After a moment, Baron Hertling, hand shaking, signed the paper.

24

January 28, 1816

hen Charity opened heavy eyes the morning after their arrival in Namek, the Prince's side of the bed was empty. A fire blazed in the large stone fireplace and she realized that Augustus must have built it when he got up. A knock sounded on the hut door, it opened, and Natalya came in. She was carrying a tray of food, and Charity's stomach heaved as the smell of bacon reached her.

"Please, Natalya," she said faintly. "Not now. I will eat later."

"The Prince said for me to bring you breakfast," the woman said as she continued to advance toward the bed, the smell of bacon becoming ever stronger.

"I—I haven't been feeling very well in the mornings lately," Charity said. "Please—take it away before I become sick."

Without another word, Natalya turned and went out again, carrying the vile-smelling food with her. Charity breathed deeply and slowly to settle her stomach, and was just thinking that she should try to get up so she could find Augustus, when the door opened once more and Natalya came back in, this time without the tray. Charity struggled to sit up and the woman said quickly, "Please, stay where you are, Princess."

Charity's stomach protested the change in equilibrium, but she fought the sick feeling down and pushed herself up against her pillows, meeting Natalya's eyes, which were bright with curiosity. "Are you often ill in the mornings, Princess?"

"Sometimes I am," Charity replied cautiously.

Natalya removed her gray wool cloak and folded it across one of the chairs that was set around the table. Then she came over to the bed, stopping a few feet away from Charity and regarding her out of piercing blue eyes. "Do you feel better later in the day?"

Slowly, so as not to overset her stomach, Charity nodded.

The blue stare became brighter. "Are you with child, Princess?"

Charity's eyes fell away from that razor-sharp look. She bit her lip and did not reply.

Natalya asked in a calm, practical voice, "How long has it been since last you bled?"

In truth, it was a relief to talk about this to someone at last, and Natalya's age made Charity feel a little as if she were speaking to her grandmother. She looked up and met the woman's eyes. "About eight weeks," she confided.

"And this is unusual for you?"

"Yes. I am usually very regular, once a month."

The old woman smiled at her warmly, came over to stand next to the bed, and patted Charity's shoulder. "Then, Princess, I think it is probably safe to conclude that you are with child."

Charity gave her a trembling smile in return and was about to ask her a question when the cabin door opened and the Prince came in. He closed the door behind him and was halfway across the room when Natalya, hands on hips, confronted him. "Augustus, what were you thinking of, to drag this child on such a horrendous ride when she is carrying your heir. She might have miscarried!"

The Prince stopped dead and looked anxiously at his wife. "Are you all right, Charity?"

"I am perfectly fine, Augustus," she replied calmly. "Do not worry, your heir is safe."

"No thanks to you," Natalya snapped at him. "I repeat, what were you thinking of, to drag a pregnant girl from the comfortable safety of Zosi out into a snowstorm?"

Augustus looked at the old woman as if she were insane. For the first time, Charity noticed that he was dressed as if he were going to be riding out somewhere; his coat was fully buttoned and his wool scarf was draped around his neck. Only his head was bare; he was holding his hat in his hand. " 'The comfortable safety of Zosi'?" he repeated incredulously, still staring at Natalya. "Perhaps you have not noticed,

old woman, but I rode here in fear for my life. Did
you expect me to leave Charity behind in a place
where I was not safe myself?"

"Franz would not have harmed her, and she might
have lost the child," Natalya said. "It was foolish in
the extreme to have brought her with you."

August was now walking toward the bed. His
anxious gaze was still on Charity, but his words were
directed to Natalya. "Charity is the most precious
thing in the world to me," he said. "Nothing on this
earth would induce me to leave her to the mercy of
Franz." He reached the bed and looked down into his
wife's suddenly flushed face. "Are you sure you are
all right?"

"Y-yes," she stammered.

He bent down and kissed her forehead. When he
straightened up again the gray eyes that looked into
hers were deadly serious. "I hope you do not lose
this child, my dear, but it is your health that is my
main concern." His lips curved in a wry smile, but
his eyes remained grave. "I can always get another
child, but I cannot get another Charity."

Charity felt her eyes fill with tears. "Oh, Augustus . . ."

He picked up her hand. "I have to leave," he said.
"Emil and I are riding into Sostri, which is the near-
est town where we can get a newspaper."

All Charity wanted to do was to ask him if it was
true, if he had meant what he had said to Natalya,
that she really was the most precious thing in the
world to him, but she looked up into his face and realized that there was no time for a personal discus-

sion. He was leaving . . . and then the realization of what he had just said registered in her brain. She pushed herself up straighter and glared at him.

"Are you mad, Augustus? You can't just walk into a town and buy a newspaper! Who knows where Franz may have his spies!"

He shook his head impatiently. "I will be perfectly safe in Sostri, Charity. The mountain people are loyal. But it is twenty miles away and the roads are clogged with snow. The papers from Julia are usually a day late, and they may be even later because of the weather. Don't look for me to return today."

He was leaving. He had just said that she was the most precious thing in the world to him, that he could not get another Charity, and now he was leaving. He might be captured. She might never see him again.

Charity gazed up at her husband, her heart in her eyes, and said, "I love you, Augustus. Please be careful."

He bent down from his great height and kissed her mouth. "I love you too. Take care of yourself. Listen to Natalya."

He straightened up and turned away, his mind already on what he was going to be doing next. Charity sat in silence and watched as the door closed behind him, her mind focused on the words that had changed everything for her.

Charity is the most precious thing in the world to me.

And he said it so matter-of-factly, as if it were

nothing out of the ordinary, as if it were something that everyone in the world must know!

And then, when she had told him that she loved him, he had replied *I love you too* in the same perfectly matter-of-fact manner.

She didn't know whether to laugh or to cry. *Have I been making myself miserable all this time for no reason at all? Did I simply have to speak first to get this magnificent reassurance of his feelings for me?*

"You have had no cramping or stomach pains since you arrived?"

It took Charity a moment to realize that Natalya was still in the room and was speaking to her. She finally managed to reply, "No, no. I have felt fine, Natalya, really."

"That is good," the older woman said. "I think it would be a good idea for you to remain in bed for the day, Princess. Just to make certain. You don't want to do anything that might risk the life of your child."

"No," Charity agreed, "I don't want to do that."

Natalya gave her a brisk nod and an approving smile. "You are good for Augustus. I am happy that he has married you. And you, Princess, are a very lucky girl to have married a man as wonderful as our prince."

"Yes," Charity replied honestly. "I am."

January 30, 1816

Augustus was away from Namek for two days, and when he returned he was in possession of a newspaper dated January 28. He and Emil rode into the tiny mountain village late in the afternoon, put their horses in the big barn that housed an assortment of animals, and went toward Natalya's house, which had smoke pouring out of its chimney.

Their entrance sent a blast of cold air across the room, and the two women seated by the fire turned to see who had come in. Charity was holding wool for Natalya while the older woman spun it, and in the firelight, with her grave young face and her plain blue dress and her long hair in a simple braid, Augustus thought she looked like a Giorgione Madonna. *I wish I could have a painting of her as she looks just now,* he thought.

Then she saw him and her face lit with joy, and he thought that he would like to have a painting of her looking like that also.

"Augustus!" She dropped the wool, jumped to her feet, and ran to him. He laughed and lifted her against his cold wool chest in a giant hug.

"What a nice greeting," he said, returning her to her feet.

"Gus! You're back!" It was Stefan coming in the door, and behind him Harry Debritt, Charity's brother.

"Did you learn anything?" Stefan demanded.

"Yes, we did." He sniffed the air and looked at Natalya. "Is that mutton stew I smell?"

Her blue eyes glowed. "It is indeed, Augustus. If you will take off your coats and come to the table, I will serve it."

Augustus looked around the room. "Where is Karl?"

"He will be here," Natalya said about her husband. "He was bringing in the goats."

As the Prince and the other men divested themselves of their warm outerwear, he looked around the room with pleasure. It was only the second time he had seen Karl and Natalya's new house, which he had paid for, and he was pleased with what he saw. This room was twice as large as the single room in the hut where they had lived before, and it also had two separate bedrooms as well as a loft.

The Prince went toward the table and the others followed, Charity sitting on one side of him and Emil on the other. Karl came in as his wife was bringing bowls of stew to the table and took his place as well.

The stew was delicious. The Prince ate with relish and checked out of the side of his eye to see if his wife was eating. He was relieved to see that she was.

"Have some bread, Augustus," Natalya said.

He took a slice of the crusty white bread that Charity passed to him. "Delicious," he pronounced. "No one makes bread as good as yours, Natalya."

"Your wife made that bread," Natalya said.

"Charity made this bread?" He turned to her in astonishment.

She raised one delicate eyebrow. "You don't have to look so incredulous, Augustus."

"It's just . . . I didn't know you could bake bread."

"I couldn't," she returned serenely. "Natalya showed me."

He shook his head in wonder. "Well, it is nice to know that if we are thrown out of Jura and become vagabonds, at least we won't starve."

Now she looked fierce. "That isn't funny. No one is going to throw you out of Jura."

From the other side of the table, Stefan said, "You said you had learned something in Sostri, Gus. What was it?"

He took another bite of Charity's bread. It really was delicious. "If you look in my coat pocket you will find a newspaper with Franz's proclamation on the front page."

Stefan jumped up, went over to where the coats were hung on nails hammered into the wall, and extracted a newspaper from the Prince's pocket. He stood for a moment by the door, reading the paper. He muttered something under his breath and Charity commanded, "Read it out loud, Stefan. We all want to know what it says."

Slowly, Stefan returned to the table, still reading as he walked. When he reached his chair he did not sit down, but stood behind it and began to read the proclamation out loud.

Augustus listened to Stefan read the words that Franz had written about him and still found it hard to believe that it was his cousin, the boy he had grown up with, who had said these terrible things. *Betrayed his Country,* Franz had written. *Willfully Antagonized the Emperor of Austria . . . acted dangerously and Arbitrarily . . . Unfit to be our Prince . . .*

As soon as Stefan stopped speaking, a chorus of indignation arose from around the table. Charity's voice was the clearest. "That is outrageous!" She turned to look at him. "No one could possibly believe that any of that is true."

Augustus, who had thought deeply about the things that Franz had written, answered, "But I did act arbitrarily, Charity. I knew very well what my father's old counselors would say about a treaty with Great Britain, and so I did not ask them for their advice. I went ahead and did what I thought would be in the best interests of Jura, and I acted on my own."

"It was your legal right as Prince of Jura to do that," Stefan said as he quietly resumed his seat.

"I know that," he agreed. "I would not have done it otherwise. But Franz is being very clever. He is not just attacking my judgment; what he is saying here is that I should not have acted without the consent of the diet. He is talking about changing the prince's prerogatives, about making Jura more of a constitutional state, and this may very well find favor in the diet."

Harry looked puzzled. "I don't understand, Gus. This proclamation doesn't say anything about a constitutional change."

The Prince rested his fork on the table and explained, "Franz has gone beyond even what he put in the proclamation. I have information that he is going to address the diet on its opening day and ask both chambers to vote to replace me with Marko. As I said, Franz is very clever. If Jura's legislative body rejects me and calls upon Marko to be its new prince, that will leave me in a very awkward situation indeed."

"Where did you hear this?" Stefan asked sharply.

"Emil and I met John Vardo as we were leaving Sostri this morning," Augustus said. He gave Charity a quick glance and explained, "Vardo is Sostri's representative to the diet." He looked back across the table at Stefan. "John was already in Julia for the opening of the diet, and he learned that Franz had told the mayor that he would ask for a vote on the issue of who is to be the prince. John hired a horse and rode like hell to get back to Sostri so he could tell me what was happening."

"How did he know you would be in Sostri?" Charity demanded.

"He knew I would be somewhere in the area," Augustus explained. "John often helped us during the war."

"Damn Franz," Stefan said violently. "Do you think he has a chance of getting a favorable vote, Gus?"

The Prince answered soberly, "He has a very good chance if his side is the only side the diet hears."

He could hear Charity's breath catch in a little sob.

"What are you going to do?" Harry asked. He sounded curious, not concerned. He seemed perfectly confident that Augustus would know exactly what to do about this situation. The Prince looked at the rest of the faces at the table and saw the same confidence in every gaze.

I hope their faith is rewarded, he thought a little wryly. Out loud he said, "It's simple. In order to counter Franz's charges, I must address the diet my-self."

The wind blew noisily in the chimney and the fire hissed. Otherwise the room was silent. Finally Stefan said, "Franz won't let you near the building."

"He won't know I'm there until it's too late," Augustus said calmly.

"How will you do it?" Stefan asked.

"Emil's father's estate is just outside of Julia. I'll ride there tomorrow and then, on the following day, go into Julia in Count Sauder's coach. As a noble, he is a member of the upper chamber, and he will be expected to attend the opening-day ceremonies. The coach will deposit us right in front of the Diet House and there I will be. Franz will have no choice but to allow me to speak for myself."

Emil said, "Gus is right. Once he is on the premises, Franz will have to let him speak. It will look as if he's afraid of him if he doesn't."

Stefan said slowly, "It does sound like a good plan."

Natalya got up and began to clear away the dishes. Charity rose to help her.

"No, no, Princess," the older woman said. "It is not right that you should help me."

"I want to," Charity replied serenely, and she plucked her husband's bowl from in front of him.

Augustus smothered a grin. That serenity of Charity's was a powerful weapon. He had seen her get her way countless times by using that same sweet, implacable composure.

The men continued to discuss the situation as the

women cleared the table. Then Augustus heard Charity say, "I believe I will go to bed, Natalya. I am feeling a little tired."

"Go right along, Princess," Natalya said, and Augustus watched as his wife put on her coat and went quietly out the door.

He remained at the table for another half hour discussing his plan, then he excused himself, put on his coat, and went out into the night. The inky sky was filled with a dazzling array of brilliant stars. Only in the mountains did the stars look like this, he thought, as he inhaled the cold frosty air deeply into his lungs.

The fire was burning brightly when he stepped into the guest hut, and Charity was sitting up in bed, propped against her pillows. Their eyes met as he came in the door.

"A cold night," he said.

"Yes."

He divested himself of his heavy coat at the door and hung it on the nail provided for such a purpose. Next he pulled off his boots and placed them neatly along the wall under his coat. Wearing his hunting shirt and trousers and warm wool socks, he padded silently across the room to the foot of the bed, where he stopped and looked at his wife.

Her long-sleeved white nightgown was immaculate in the firelight. Her hair looked clean and shining and her skin looked rose-petal soft. He was suddenly acutely conscious that he had been wearing the same clothes for the last four days and that he had slept for the last two nights in a smoky, smelly inn.

"I haven't had a bath since we left Zosi," he said. "I'm not clean enough to get into bed with you."

"Don't be ridiculous," she said. "You look tired. Take off your clothes and get in here under this nice warm quilt."

He wanted to get in with her so much that he didn't have the strength to protest any further. "I am tired," he admitted, and, walking to his side of the bed, he began to pull his heavy, smoke-smelling shirt over his head. He said, his voice a little muffled by the folds of his shirt, "I never thought about being dirty when I was hiding in the mountains before, but that was because everyone else was just as dirty as I was. You look so dainty and clean in your white nightdress. Your hair is shining just like it always does." He tossed his shirt on the floor and began to unbuckle his belt.

"I haven't had a bath either," Charity said. "I've just sponged here and there. We can be dirty together."

He finished stripping off his trousers and cast one rueful glance down at his slim, long-muscled body. "I probably smell," he said apologetically.

"I like your smell."

He got into bed, reached for her, and pulled her close. "You are wonderful," he said fervently. He lowered his mouth toward hers. "God, I have missed you."

Now that the corrosive doubt that had stood for weeks as a barrier between them had finally fallen,

Charity's body flamed up at his very first touch. His mouth on hers was hard and hungry, and she met him eagerly, lifting herself to press against him, running her hands over the muscles of his shoulders and back, rejoicing in the feel of him under her fingers, under her lips, against her skin, so strong, so alive, so *hers.*

"Charity." He was kissing her throat, moving his head lower, to her breasts, which were made easily available by the nightgown buttons she had so conveniently left open for him. She felt the roughness of his beard on her tender skin and the erotic feel of his mouth on her nipples. Her whole body began to quiver, like the strings of an instrument that has been struck. He continued to kiss her and stroke her and she trembled as if she were being splintered into a million pieces.

The muscles of his back felt rock-hard under her tense fingers and a sweet, hot liquid surge of sensation answered to the touch of his own fingers in her softest, most secret flesh. And then he buried himself within her and she opened to him, opened to his urgency, his maleness, everything inside her quivering and softening beneath his powerful thrusts until a mighty orgasm rolled up from deep inside, so that her whole body shuddered violently again and again, the pleasure intensifying with each roll of sensation until her mouth opened in a silent scream of finality and fulfillment.

Afterward, he lay quietly, his body bathed in sweat, his heart hammering, his head driven into the hollow of her shoulder. She felt the heat of him, the weight of him, and thought her heart would break with love. She turned her head and rested her lips on his damp blond hair. "I love you," she said.

"I love you too," he replied. He still sounded out of breath.

She smiled. Unbelievable to think that it had been as easy as this.

A little time passed. "Augustus? You're not going to sleep, are you?"

"Mmm?"

"Wake up," Charity said. "We have to talk."

He yawned hugely. "I'm sorry, Charity. I didn't mean to fall asleep on you like that." He removed his head from her shoulder, sat up, rubbed his head, and gave her a charming, boyish grin. "You tired me out."

"Do you want me to apologize?"

"No!" He rubbed his head again, making a thorough job of ruffling his hair. "I need to talk to you as well." Another quick grin. "I might even be able to pay attention to a conversation, which I certainly could not have done when I first came into this room."

He looked so pleased with himself. Charity smiled warmly back at him, and as they settled against their pillows for the promised talk, he picked up her hand.

Charity began. "You are set on this? You will challenge Franz in front of the diet and ask them to vote for which of you they want to lead Jura?"

"I have to do it," he replied. "There is no other way out of this fix that does not involve bloodshed."

"I know that you are right, Augustus, but I am afraid."

"It will be very democratic," he assured her. "Quite like the Americans. There is nothing to be afraid of."

"Augustus . . ." She bit her lip. "I do not think this will happen, but . . . what if the diet chooses Franz? What will happen then?"

"Then I will have lost and you will be the wife of an ex-prince of Jura." She could hear the smile in his voice as he said, "Perhaps we can take up horse training for a living. Or you can sell bread."

Charity didn't respond to the joke. "Will Franz let you go, Augustus? If the vote goes against you, will Franz let you go?"

"He will have to, Charity. It is very undemocratic to kill the person you have beaten in an election. The Americans would be horrified."

She did not smile.

"I am not going to lose the vote, Charity." He spoke with calm assurance. "It is Franz who will be discredited, not me."

"I know." She squeezed his hand. "No one in their right mind would choose Franz over you."

He didn't answer.

"Lydia was not in her right mind," she added.

He laughed.

"I suppose we must leave for Julia tomorrow if you are to be there in time for the opening of the diet," she said.

"Charity." She could feel his own hand tense. "I want you to remain here. I will send for you as soon as the diet meeting is over, I promise. But I will be much more comfortable if I know you are safe here in Namek."

She pulled her hand away from his and turned to look at him. "You just told me it would be safe for you to go to Julia. If it is safe for you, why wouldn't it be safe for me?"

"I think there is a ninety-nine percent chance that you will be safe in Julia," he said reasonably. "I am just not willing to risk that last one percent chance that something could go wrong."

She looked into his reasonable eyes and said with great calm, "I want to be there if something should go wrong even more than if everything goes right."

He frowned. "Listen to me, my dear—"

But she shook her head. "No, Augustus. I am very sorry not to oblige you, but I am going with you to the opening of the diet."

His mouth took on the look that meant his mind was made up, but before he could speak she said hastily, "I didn't think you loved me, you know."

He blinked at the change of subject. "I beg your pardon?"

"I didn't think you loved me. That is why I was so distant over Christmas."

He was still looking bemused. "Why on earth wouldn't you think I loved you?"

"You never said so."

He began to look more alert. "Is that why you were always asleep when I came to bed and why you were always talking with that Broder fellow?"

"Yes."

"Good God." He stared at her. "Well, why didn't you say something to me, for God's sake? How could you think I didn't love you? I hung around you like a bee around honey!"

Her loose hair streamed forward, hiding her face, and she pushed it back behind her ear. "Your mother told me that you only wanted an heir."

"My mother?" He almost shouted the words. "I can't believe what I am hearing. Are you saying that you were foolish enough to actually listen to my mother?"

She sighed. "I am afraid that I was."

He thrust his fingers through his hair, which needed a cut quite badly, and said disgustedly, "I might have known that Mama would manage to screw things up."

She tilted her head to look at him and at the sight of him in the lamplight her heart turned over. Getting a firm grip on herself, she said steadily, "You do love me, don't you Augustus?"

"Yes," he replied. "I can't imagine my life without you. And I am sorry I was so stupid and never told you how I felt." He frowned. "I'm . . . I'm not very good at that, Charity. I've spent most of my life with men, and men don't talk very much about their feelings." He gave her an apologetic look. "I'm sorry."

Her smile was radiant. "I love you so much, and I am so happy, Augustus. And you can make me even happier by letting me come into Julia to the diet with you."

His face changed, becoming still and quiet. His

gray eyes narrowed. "Have you been trying to manipulate me?"

Charity's heart began to thump. All of a sudden he looked so cold. "No, Augustus. I am trying to explain how happy I am to discover that you love me the way I love you. I am so happy to be here at Namek with you, and I want to go to Julia with you as well. If I thought my presence would be a danger to you, or to our child, I would not ask to come. But if you turn into the kind of husband whose idea of 'keeping Charity safe' is not allowing me to take *any* reasonable risk at all, I must warn you that I am going to rebel."

Silence fell as the two of them looked at each other.

At last he said, "I am a man, I am accustomed to taking risks. You are a woman. It is different."

She said, "I want to go with you."

A muscle twitched in the corner of his jaw. At last he said, "All right, you may come with me. I am going to spend the night at Count Sauder's villa outside the city, and you will remain there until after the diet session. If all goes well, I will return to you there. If something should go wrong, you will still have time to get away."

She looked at his face and knew there was no way in this world that he would ever allow her to attend the diet session. She said softly, "Thank you, Augustus," and leaned over to kiss his cheek.

"Don't worry," he said sternly. "Everything is going to be just fine."

"I know it is. Let's go to sleep, love."

He leaned over to blow out the candle, and when he turned back to pull the quilt over his bare shoulder he reached out, caught her around the waist, kissed her between her neck and her shoulder, and mumbled, "Remember, I love you."

The easy tears of pregnancy once more flooded Charity's eyes as she sniffed and assured him that she returned his sentiment.

25

$\mathcal{F}$ebruary 1 dawned mild and clear, the kind of day that could trick the hibernating flowers into thinking that spring had finally arrived. As Count Josef Sauder's new chaise pulled up before the handsome Renaissance-style building that housed Jura's diet, the old-fashioned coach directly in front of his deposited a slim elderly man and then pulled away. The passenger began to walk toward the building, leaning noticeably on an ebony cane.

"Good," said Augustus. "Count Cherny is here."

Count Sauder watched as Jura's chief justice made his way into the building, then he said, "If you wish it, Your Highness, we can wait here in the chaise until Count Adamov has gone in."

"Make a grand entrance, do you mean?" the Prince said ironically. He shook his head. "I rather think I will leave that to Franz. We'll go in now."

"Very well," Count Sauder replied and rapped on the window to signal that they were going to alight.

The two men descended from the chaise and crossed the brick walkway to the shallow steps that led to the main entrance of the diet building. The count's heart accelerated as they reached the massive front door. He took a deep breath and glanced at Augustus, whose face looked perfectly calm.

The diet porter opened the door and they stepped into a beautifully paneled vestibule. Two members of the commons were talking together in low-voiced conversation, and when they saw who had come in, their eyes widened and their mouths dropped open.

"Good morning," the Prince said pleasantly.

The two men bowed hastily. "G-good morning, Your Highness," they chorused in reply.

Augustus walked to the carved oak door that led into the Chamber of Nobles. Another porter opened it with a reverent bow, and the Prince stepped inside. Count Sauder followed.

The count could feel the tension in his stomach as he looked around the large horseshoe-shaped room that was the Chamber of Nobles. The formal opening of the diet was the only time that the commons joined with the nobles, and in order to accommodate the people's representatives rows of benches had been set up in the open area inside the horseshoe. These benches, as well as the cushioned seats that belonged to the nobles, were almost entirely filled. The hum of men's voices gradually died away, and in less than half a minute the attention of the entire room had fixed on the man standing in front of the door.

Augustus.

The name was breathed in shock, in disbelief, in dismay, and in relief as the assembled diet recognized the tall slim figure standing beneath the archway engraved with the solemn words: Justice and Truth. Augustus was dressed in the attire that distinguished the majority of the men in the room: black morning coat, light beige breeches, and polished black boots. He wore no crown, no velvet cloak, and carried no staff of state. Yet, as he walked across the open floor with his long, flowing stride, he somehow managed to look every inch a prince.

The entire room watched in breathless silence as Augustus reached the dais and stood for a moment, thoughtfully contemplating the Royal Throne of Jura. This was the throne upon which he had sat two years before, when he had been crowned by the archbishop, and where he had sat to open the diet for the first time since Napoleon's defeat. For a moment they confronted each other, throne and prince, then, with the lithe grace that characterized all of his movements, Augustus stepped up onto the dais.

A sigh, as if a hundred breaths had been released at the same time, went through the room.

The Prince did not sit down. Instead he stood beside the high velvet chair, symbol of the Princes of Jura, and rested his hand on its back. In this position he faced the chamber, and for the first time the watching men got a clear look at the face beneath the brushed blond hair.

He looked grave. The steady gray eyes swept once around the chamber, coming to rest on Count Boris Heusse and the rest of the signers of the proclamation, who were sitting next to each other in the first row of nobles. Augustus said, in a voice that was quiet but perfectly audible to those in the last row of seats, "We'll wait for Count Adamov, shall we?"

The room was so silent that when someone sneezed, Count Sauder actually jumped. Three more diet members filed in, shot startled glances toward Augustus, then scurried to find seats. Then the door opened once again and Franz stood there, framed in the archway.

A good entrance, Count Sauder thought as he watched Franz make certain he had everyone's attention. Then he walked in, his bright hair shining like spun gold in the reflected sunlight of the large crystal chandelier. He had not yet seen Augustus.

Franz stopped in the center of the empty space that lay between the throne and the commons, turned and faced the assembled diet, a preoccupied look on his face. In his right hand he carried a rolled-up scroll of paper; his left hand was empty. His brilliant blue gaze went around the assembly. Then, at last, he realized that something was wrong.

He spun around and saw the Prince.

Augustus, whose hand was still resting casually on the back of the throne, said chidingly, "It was very rude of you not to invite me to my own overthrow, Franz, but I decided to come anyway."

Franz's shoulders went rigid. He said something,

which Count Sauder, strain as he could, could not decipher.

Augustus replied, "I'm afraid it will not be as easy to get rid of me as you thought it would be."

At that, Franz swung around to face the chamber once again. His eyes were glittering. "How nice that Prince Augustus is here to try to defend his actions before the diet."

"I will be happy to *explain* my actions." Augustus stepped down from the dais and came to stand beside Franz. He looked down at his cousin from his superior height and said in a hard voice, "And I would like to hear you explain yours."

"That is precisely what I came here to do," Franz replied crisply, seemingly not at all intimidated by the Prince's taller presence.

There was no humor in Augustus's smile. "Excellent. We'll make it a debate, shall we? The diet can decide the winner."

Franz's return smile was brilliant. "And the winner will be the Prince of Jura."

The Prince lifted an inquiring eyebrow. "Are you seeking to be prince yourself? I thought you were acting for your father."

For the first time, Franz showed a trace of anger. "I am," he snapped. "That is what I meant."

Augustus did not look as if he believed that. He did not pursue the subject, however, but instead said to the assembled members of the diet, "A debate needs a moderator." His eyes came to rest on a single face. "Count Cherny, as Chief Justice of Jura I know we can count upon you to be fair. Will you act as moderator in this disputation between me and Count Adamov?"

"Certainly," the chief justice replied. Slowly he began to make his way from his seat to the front of the room.

Augustus signaled to a clerk, who ran to bring a chair for the chief justice to sit in.

The room was so silent that the sound of Count Cherny's cane as it clicked against the marble floor was perfectly audible. At last he reached the heavy oak chair that had been set for him and slowly he lowered himself into it, using its carved arms for support. He rested his cane against the chair's arm, looked at Augustus, and said, "How would you like to proceed, Your Highness?"

Augustus said, "Count Adamov is the one who arranged for this historic vote to overthrow an hereditary prince. Let him speak first."

The two opponents had taken up stances on either side of the chief justice. He turned now from Augustus to Franz and asked, "Count Adamov, do you feel that you have just cause for removing Prince Augustus from his hereditary position as Prince of Jura and replacing him with your father, Duke Marko?"

"Regretfully, I do," Franz replied.

The justice turned to Augustus. "Are you prepared to answer these charges, Your Highness?"

"I am," Augustus replied.

Franz said, "Are you willing to abide by the vote of the diet?"

For a brief moment the two men locked eyes. Then Augustus said once again, "I am."

Jesus, Count Sauder thought, and the word was a prayer not a blasphemy.

Baron Anton Krek, who was seated next to him, muttered, "This is unbelievable."

The chief justice said, "And you, Count Adamov? Are you willing to abide by the decision of the diet?"

"I am," Franz returned. His eyes were intensely blue in his white face.

Somewhere in the rows of commons a man blew his nose.

"Very well," the chief justice said. "As Prince Augustus indicated, you are the one who initiated this discussion, Count, so you may state your case first."

Franz has to be furious, Count Sauder thought. *This is not what he intended at all.*

But Franz's face was perfectly calm as he faced the assembled members of Jura's diet. He had always had charisma, Count Sauder thought, and now he trained the full force of that intense personal power upon the men who were to act as his judges.

"This is not a happy experience for me," he began in a sober voice. "I searched my conscience for a long hard time before I made the decision to bring this matter before the diet." He turned to his cousin and his voice took on a distinctly sorrowful note. "I am very fond of you, Gus, and I appreciate the patriotism and heroism you demonstrated during the long years of the French occupation. But I cannot let you continue on this course that is so dangerous to the country we both love. I finally decided that I must speak out."

Augustus lifted an ironic eyebrow. "Go ahead and speak, then."

Franz turned back to his audience, the sorrow still sounding in his voice. "I believe that everyone present is aware of the proclamation issued to the country by myself and some of the leading nobles of Jura. I believe that our charges against Prince Augustus are set forth quite clearly in that document. I will just take a few moments to elaborate on these charges."

Franz's voice hardened. "The Treaty of London. That, my lords and gentlemen, is the crux of my concern. As soon as Napoleon was defeated at Waterloo, Prince Augustus, through his English relatives, approached the British government about making an alliance with Jura. He did this entirely of his own accord and against the advice of his chief minister and the marshal of Jura's armed forces."

Here the chief justice interrupted. "Do I understand you to be saying, Count, that Count Hindenberg and Marshal Rupnik knew of this treaty before it was signed and disapproved of it?"

"That is what I am saying," Franz replied.

The chief justice turned to the Prince. "Is this true, Your Highness?"

"Yes," Augustus said. "It is true."

Next to Count Sauder, Baron Krek blew noisily out through his nose.

Franz continued: "Prince Augustus was so committed to allying Jura with Britain that he contracted a marriage to an English girl. Once again, he did this without the advice of his ministers, whom he knew would prefer him to marry a German princess."

Franz lifted the roll of paper he held in his hand. "As our proclamation stated, the Treaty of London has so thoroughly antagonized the Austrian emperor that the very independence of Jura is in danger. Emperor Francis regards the presence of the British navy in Seista as a direct threat to the empire's holdings in northern Italy. By making this treaty, Prince Augustus has upset the balance of power that was so carefully constructed at the Congress of Vienna."

Franz paused, and Count Sauder could feel the attention of the men around him as concentrated as if it were a physical thing. The chief justice spoke into the silence. "Count Adamov, did the emperor tell you directly that he is opposed to the Treaty of London?"

"He spoke to me about it when he named me ambassador to Jura," Franz said. "One of the tasks he assigned me was to try to talk some sense into Prince Augustus. Unfortunately, I was unable to accomplish this. No matter what I said, the Prince remained set on maintaining the treaty with Britain."

A little whisper of sound went around the room as men shifted in their seats and looked at each other.

Franz turned back to address the assembly. "The question we must ask ourselves, my lords and gentlemen, is this. Why did Prince Augustus make such a dangerous treaty? By signing it, he has given up one of our most precious assets, the seaport of Seista, and has received nothing in return."

Count Sauder looked from Franz to Augustus. The Prince was standing with his hands clasped loosely behind his back and the gray eyes that were watching his cousin were remote and unreadable.

Franz turned to look at Augustus also. "My father warned you also," he said. "Twice he brought you messages from the emperor that Austria would be forced to take severe measures if you would not repudiate the British treaty. Twice you ignored those warnings."

The Prince looked back at his cousin and the expression on his face did not change.

Franz lifted a hand. "Even now, Gus, even now, if you would change your mind and promise to reject this treaty, I would drop these charges and support you."

Everyone in the chamber stopped breathing.

Augustus said calmly, "I have no intention of reneging on the Treaty of London."

Franz closed his eyes.

"Jesus," Baron Anton Krek breathed.

Slowly Franz opened his eyes and for a moment he looked positively shattered. He gathered himself, but his blue eyes glittered as if he were holding back tears as he said, "I cannot tell you how sorry I am to hear that."

Augustus's mouth set in a hard line as he looked back, and the cleft in his chin became more pronounced. Then the chief justice spoke. "Count Adamov, were Count Hindenberg and Marshal Rupnik aware of these threats, and is that the reason for their actions against Prince Augustus?"

"Yes." Franz looked directly at the justice. "Let me make it perfectly clear, my lord Chief Justice, that I do not approve of what they did. Violence can never be the answer for a civilized society. That is why I have brought this problem before the diet."

Franz turned away from the chief justice and once again faced the assembled diet. His voice when he spoke was clear and firm. "My lords and gentlemen, that is why we are here today. Prince Augustus is well aware of the dangers to which he is subjecting the country by holding to this pernicious treaty. If Austria decides to retaliate by imposing tariffs on our goods, then our trade will receive a heavy blow. Half of our exports are sold into the empire. And, if the emperor goes even further and decides to take Seista—and Jura—by force of arms, we will find ourselves at the mercy of the military might of the largest empire in the world. We cannot withstand that kind of a challenge, my lords and gentlemen. If that should happen, I am afraid that our seven-hundred-year history as an independent nation—the very thing that Prince Augustus, with his misguided policy is trying to protect—will be lost."

He raised his hands. "It is for you, the members of the diet, to decide. I leave it in your hands."

There was profound silence in the room. The chief justice's face was somber as he turned to Augustus. "Your Highness, do you care to answer these charges?"

The Prince never looked at his cousin as he replied to Count Cherny in a courteous voice, "I will be happy to explain to the diet why I signed the Treaty of London and why I think it is in the best interest of Jura to keep that treaty in place."

Count Cherny said, "Thank you, Your Highness."

Count Sauder noticed that there was a subtle but definite note of deference in the chief justice's voice when he addressed the Prince. *After all,* the count thought, *one does not easily forget that Augustus spent ten years enduring hardship and danger in the service of his country while Franz was living comfortably in a palace in Vienna.*

It was the Prince's turn to move a little closer to the first row of seats. He looked slowly around the room as he spoke, his eyes occasionally stopping on a particular face. "Why, you ask, did I make a treaty with Great Britain?"

A number of the members of the commons actually bobbed their heads at him.

Augustus slowly began to pace up and down the floor. "I did it for this reason: We are a very small country. We have always had the Austrian Empire to our east and to our north, but in the past we shared a border, as well as the Adriatic, with Italy. At the Congress of Vienna, Venice and the lands of northern Italy which border ours were given to Austria. The result of that distribution of land? We are surrounded *on every side* by Austria and its satellite nations."

A low murmur went up among the rows of the commons. The Prince waited until it had died down before continuing. "Did I think that the Austrian emperor would like to add Jura to that list of satellite nations? Yes, I did. Did I think that he would send troops into Jura in order to subdue us?" And here Augustus turned to look at Franz. His voice was very deliberate as he said, "No. I did not think it then and I do not think it now."

"Oh, Gus," Franz said in a voice that sounded ineffably sad.

The Prince turned back to the diet. "I was not concerned with the military power of Austria; I was concerned with its economic power. Should the emperor seek to pressure us by imposing tariffs on our exports to the empire, our economy would be crippled. We depend upon being able to export our products to Austria, Hungary, the Slavic nations, and northern Italy. If Austria taxed those products, we could not be competitive in the marketplace. And, while the principle of free trade was one that was paid lip service at Vienna, I did not think that the economic woes of a small nation such as Jura would be of much concern to anyone. In short, I thought we needed an economic ally, and that is why I made the treaty with Great Britain."

Count Sauder looked at Franz, who was looking skeptical.

All of a sudden the Prince swung around and looked at Franz as well. "You accuse me of acting without advice, of making this treaty solely on my own authority. That is not true. I did not consult with my father's advisors, I consulted with *my* advisors. And they were all in agreement that a treaty with Britain would benefit Jura."

The chief justice spoke. "Would you mind giving us the names of these men, Your Highness?"

"They are my present chief minister, Lord Stefan Weyr, Marshal Lord Emil Sauder, and Ambassador Count Viktor Rozman."

The chief justice's shrewd dark eyes went from the Prince to Franz, then back again to the Prince. He said, "These are all very young men, Your Highness. Did you not think it would be wise to consult with men who had more years of diplomatic experience?"

"I consulted with the men whom I trusted," the Prince said flatly. "For ten long years I lived and fought with these men. I owe my life to them. They are patriots whose sole interest is the safety and the independence of Jura."

For the first time it seemed as if the Prince had struck a nerve in Franz, for he interrupted in a sharp voice, "Are you implying that your father's ministers did *not* have Jura's best interests at heart?"

In order to speak to Franz, Augustus had turned away from the assembly of delegates. Now, in silence, he walked back to his original place on the chief justice's right, faced his cousin, and said softly, "If you remember, I consulted with one other person whom I trusted, Franz. I consulted with *you*."

"The devil!" someone behind Count Sauder said out loud.

The chief justice frowned in the direction of the offending noble, then he asked, "Is this true, Count Adamov?"

"Yes, it is true." Franz sounded infinitely weary. "Prince Augustus can be most persuasive, and when he asked me what I thought of his idea, I went along with it." He was speaking directly to the chief justice now, not looking at the Prince at all. "It was not until I received a letter from my father that I realized how dangerous such a treaty could be."

"And when precisely did you hear from Duke Marko, Count?" the chief justice inquired.

"Before I left London."

"And did you tell His Highness that you had changed your mind about the treaty?"

"I told him of my father's letter, yes," Franz replied. "And my father also came to Jura in person to warn Prince Augustus of the dangers of this treaty. Unfortunately, the Prince would not listen." His remarkable blue-eyed gaze moved from the chief justice to the Prince. "I am able to admit that I made a mistake and take the steps to rectify it. Unfortunately, that is not true of you, Gus. You have always been like that. Once you make up your mind, nothing can change it."

The Prince looked back at him and did not reply.

Franz turned to the chamber and said quietly, "This is a dangerous trait in a man who has the welfare of an entire country in his hands."

There was a rustle of sound in the chamber as men exchanged glances. *Damn,* Count Sauder thought in frustration. *The man is slippery as an eel. He has an answer for everything.*

Then Augustus spoke. "My lord Chief Justice, I would like to ask you a question if I may?"

"Certainly, Your Highness."

"What do you think Russia would do if Austria broke the European peace and marched into Jura?"

Count Cherny didn't reply immediately as he contemplated the question. Then he said slowly, as if he had just figured out the answer to a riddle, "Russia would march into the territory it wants in Poland that is held by Austria."

The murmur of voices in the chamber was the loudest it had been since the debate had begun. The chief justice held up his hand for quiet and gradually the voices subsided.

"Precisely," Augustus said crisply. "And I cannot believe that the Austrian emperor would be foolish enough to leave the gates open for Russia just because he would like access to Seista. Austria already has a port on the Adriatic; she has Venice. Jura may be a thorn in the emperor's side, but he is not going to disrupt the balance of power so precariously achieved at Vienna in order to acquire it."

Baron Krek turned to Count Sauder. "Very true, very true. Why the devil has Marko been raising such a fuss? Let the emperor stew in his own juices. He can't touch Jura!"

Color had flushed into Franz's fair-skinned face, and he snapped, "If Prince Augustus is so certain of Jura's safety, why then did he feel it was necessary to make a treaty with Great Britain?"

"I believe I have already answered that question," the Prince said mildly. "I made the treaty with Great Britain in order to safeguard Jura's trade. I have received assurances from Great Britain that if Austria places a tax upon Jura's exports, Great Britain will retaliate by ceasing to buy or sell to the Austrian market. That is not a threat the emperor will dare to challenge."

The noise in the room was so loud that it took the chief justice a full minute before his demands for order could be heard. When finally a semblance of quiet had been restored, he said, "I believe that you have answered most of Count Adamov's charges, Your Highness. Is there anything more before we proceed to a vote?"

"Yes," said Augustus. He turned to look at his cousin, his mouth set in a line that looked distinctly grim. "I have answered Count Adamov's charges. Now I would like him to answer mine."

26

Throughout the debate, Count Sauder kept glancing at the men who had signed the treasonable proclamation along with Franz. They had remained immobile, upright and silent in their first-row seats, seemingly aloof from all that surrounded them. But when Augustus issued his challenge to Franz, Baron Leopold Hertling bowed his head and covered his eyes with a hand.

How the devil did Franz get Hertling to go along with this? Count Sauder thought. *He is such a mouse of a man.*

The count's eyes, which had been attracted by Hertling's sudden movement, now returned to the space in front of the throne where Augustus and Franz confronted each other. Franz's flexible voice vibrated with a mixture of pain and incredulity as he said, "Charges? What charges, Gus?"

There was no discernable emotion on Augustus's

face as he answered his cousin. "It took me a long time to figure it out. As you mentioned earlier, once I make up my mind I don't change it easily. I made up my mind about you when we were boys, Franz. I decided then that you were my friend, and that is how I have regarded you ever since. *That* is the dangerous mistake I am guilty of, not the signing of the Treaty of London."

"Oh Gus," Franz said, his voice plangent with sorrow. "I have always been your friend. I am still your friend. Believe me, the decision I made to challenge you today was exceedingly painful to me. But I believed—and do still believe—that you have put Jura in grave jeopardy by this treaty. I felt that my first duty was to my country." He looked steadily at the Prince and his voice deepened with sincerity. "I think that you, of all people, will understand that."

The Prince nodded thoughtfully. "Is that why you tried to have me assassinated, then? Because of your sense of duty toward Jura?"

At the word "assassinated," a murmur crossed the audience.

Franz looked horrified that the Prince could even suspect him of such a hideous thing. "I sent men to Zosi to *arrest* you, not assassinate you, Gus," he corrected.

The Prince lifted an eyebrow. "Then you did not instigate the assassination attempt by Hindenberg and Rupnik?"

An uproar rose from the ranks of the diet representatives. The chief justice, who did not have his gavel, finally restored the chamber to order by banging his cane against the arm of his chair. When finally all was quiet again, Franz spoke, and this time he did not sound sorrowful. He sounded angry. "I cannot conceive how you ever came by such an idea. I had nothing to do with that plot. I know you won't believe this now, but I *am* your friend. I have never wished you harm."

"But you have done me harm," the Prince replied evenly. "You have done everything in your power to humiliate and discredit me. It amazes me that it took me so long to see it."

Franz's golden head lifted suddenly, as if he had received a blow to the chin. "Humiliate you?" he said in an incredulous tone. "What are you talking—" Then, as if he had received a sudden illumination from heaven, "Oh. You mean my elopement with Lady Lydia."

"That certainly was not the act of a friend, was it?" the Prince said. "If it were not for Princess Charity, I would have been humiliated indeed." His tone became conversational. "You would have liked that, Franz, would you not? You must have been furious when I managed to avert being a jilted bridegroom."

Franz took two steps toward the Prince and held out his hand, all of his movements graceful as a dancer's. His motion brought him to a place where the large chandelier would reflect the sunlight from the window directly onto his golden hair. "You can't believe that, Gus! I explained to you how Lydia and I fell in love, how we struggled against it. Neither of us wished to hurt you. You told me that you understood. Don't you remember?"

Augustus did not move. "What I have finally understood is that you are incapable of loving anyone but yourself."

For a moment more, Franz held his graceful posture of supplication, then he dropped his hand and looked from the Prince to Count Cherny. "My lord Chief Justice," he said. "Is it possible to call a halt to this undignified discussion? We came here to allow the diet to vote for whom they wished to be Prince of Jura. I have said all I have to say on the subject, and it appears that Prince Augustus has nothing to add to the debate but personal insults. I suggest that it is time to move to a vote."

The chief justice turned to the Prince. "Have you anything else to say, Your Highness?"

"I do indeed," the Prince replied cordially. "In fact, I have not yet begun to make my case."

Baron Krek groaned. "I have to pee and the best part is just coming up."

"Hold it," Count Sauder advised. He looked at Franz, who was regarding Augustus with a mixture of sorrow and pity, and added, "I don't think you'll want to miss this."

Augustus resumed his slow pacing back and forth in front of the commons. "Since I have returned to Jura there have been three attempts to undermine my authority," he began. "The first and the least important was, as I have just mentioned, the seduction of my intended bride. I will not go into this matter; you are all well aware of what happened just one week before the date set for my wedding."

The nobility sat motionless, but several members of the commons nodded in silent agreement.

The Prince stopped his pacing in the center of the floor and turned his somber face to the chamber. "The second attempt against me was a bit more dramatic—an assassination attempt, ostensibly led by my chief minister and my marshal."

From his place behind Augustus, Franz snapped, "I had nothing to do with Rupnik and Hindenberg's plot."

The Prince continued to speak as if he had not heard his cousin. "The third attack was this attempted coup d'état."

The diet stirred restlessly.

Augustus's voice hardened. "What else can I call it? Count Adamov sought to justify the disposal of a legitimate and hereditary ruler by persuading the diet to vote in favor of such an action. And let me assure you that he had no intention of allowing me to speak for myself. If I had not been warned in advance, the Princess and I would have been captured at Zosi by a regiment of cavalry directed by Count Adamov. I very much doubt that his plans included escorting me to Julia to speak in front of the diet."

Baron Krek shifted on his seat in an effort to relieve the pressure on his bladder. "Augustus is right," he muttered. "Franz wanted to get him out of the way."

Behind the Prince, Count Sauder saw Franz shake his golden head in vehement denial of the charge.

Baron Krek groaned, gave up, and went in search of the water closet.

Once more the Prince began to walk back and forth in front of the commons. "Upon reflection, I have come to the conclusion that the count's elopement with my intended bride was more a matter of personal pique than anything else. In the words of my wife, he wanted to see me made the laughing-stock of Europe." He paused, a thoughtful frown on his face. "I think he also wanted to show me that he could have what I could not."

Once again Augustus halted, this time on the east side of the room close to a marble bust of Augustus Caesar. From this position he looked across the floor at Franz. "If this was the worst of his sins, I could forgive him. But I cannot forgive him for what has brought us all together this morning."

Franz answered his cousin, scorn in his voice. "What about Rupnik and Hindenberg, Gus? I thought you were going to make me the villain of that plot as well."

"I will get to that," the Prince replied imperturbably. "For now I wish to discuss this business with Austria." He turned to face his audience, his hands clasped loosely behind his back. "Several months before Christmas, Duke Marko made me an offer from the Austrian emperor—a verbal offer, nothing was in writing. The terms of the offer were thus: If I would renounce the Treaty of London and allow Austria the use of Seista, the emperor would engage to extend the protection of his empire to Jura. The emperor—according to Duke Marko—also engaged formally to recognize my family as the ruling dynasty of Jura."

Stunned silence reigned in the chamber. Finally the chief justice said, "But these things were recognized by all of the nations at the Congress of Vienna."

The Prince half turned so that he could see Count Cherny. "I thought the same thing, my lord Chief Justice. In fact, I found the offer insulting. I am sure that the members of the diet must find it insulting as well."

A chorus of agreement came from the benches. One man was actually heard to say, "Marko has lived in Austria for too long. He's forgotten which country he owes allegiance to!"

The Prince lifted a hand and quiet was restored. He continued: "When I rejected this offer, as naturally I did, Duke Marko then informed me that if I would not throw the British out of Seista, the emperor was prepared to invade Jura and take Seista for himself."

Heavy silence blanketed the chamber.

"I asked Duke Marko if he had heard this directly from the emperor and Duke Marko said that he had."

The silence remained thick and somber as the Prince reached inside his coat and extracted a piece of paper, which he held up so that all in the chamber could see it. "Now comes the interesting part," he said.

Count Sauder glanced at Franz to see how he was reacting to this ploy and surprised a look of blazing violence in the gaze that he had turned on Augustus. The count blinked, and when he opened his eyes again the expression was gone and Franz was looking calm.

The Prince continued to speak as he slowly unfolded the paper. "Immediately after this meeting with Duke Marko, I wrote to my father-in-law, who is the treasury secretary for Great Britain, telling him of the Austrian threat and warning him that if the emperor should retaliate by taxing Jura's products, I would expect Great Britain to hold to its side of the treaty and support us."

Count Sauder glanced at the row of conspirators, who were still sitting upright, with the single exception of Baron Hertling, who was slumped in his place.

The Prince continued: "In his reply, Lord Beaufort assured me that Britain would indeed honor its agreement, and in the same letter he expressed amazement that the emperor would make such a reckless threat." He looked bleak. "For the first time I began to wonder if perhaps the emperor's intentions had been misrepresented to me."

Baron Hertling's moan was audible throughout the chamber.

Augustus continued, each word falling like a missile into the quiet room, "At last I did what I should have done immediately after Duke Marko left. I wrote to the emperor and I instructed Count Viktor Rozman, Jura's ambassador, to deliver the letter in person. Count Rozman did this, and I have here the reply, signed by Emperor Francis himself and sealed with the Imperial Seal." The Prince glanced at the paper in his hand. "In this letter the emperor assures me that he never threatened an Austrian invasion of Jura. He states that he cannot imagine who might have said such a thing to me, but it is completely untrue. Austria has every intention of honoring the Final Act of the Congress of Vienna, which guarantees the independence of Jura."

The silence in the room exploded into a roar of voices. Count Sauder watched as, amid the noise, Augustus turned his head in the direction of his cousin. Count Sauder was the only one besides the Prince to see the mocking smile that briefly lit Franz's face.

Gradually the uproar subsided of its own accord. The chief justice, who had not even attempted to call for order, waited until the room fell silent before he said sternly to Franz, "Do you know anything about this, Count Adamov?"

Franz's expression was one of almost boyish bewilderment. "No, my lord Chief Justice," he said.

"Then we must assume that Duke Marko lied to the Prince," the chief justice said.

"I cannot believe such a thing of my father," Franz said firmly.

"Then can you suggest how Duke Marko came to convey this extraordinary threat to Prince Augustus?"

"I am certain that my father believed he was speaking the truth," Franz said. "How this confusion arose I do not know."

The chief justice looked toward the Prince. "Do you have any thoughts on this matter, Your Highness?"

"Yes I have thoughts," Augustus returned. "I think that Duke Marko was assured by his son that the emperor had made these threats against Jura. I think that the duke acted in good conscience and was truly motivated by his concern for Jura."

Franz looked at Augustus with a strange smile. "Do you have any proof of this extraordinary accusation?" he asked softly.

"No," the Prince replied. "But it all fits together, like one of the puzzles we used to do when we were children. First you elope with my intended bride. Then Rupnik chooses as his assassin a man who is beholden to you."

The chief justice said sharply, "How is that, Your Highness?"

"When Guardsman Kark asked Marshal Rupnik how he had chosen him for the job, Rupnik informed him that he was chosen because Kark was helped to his place in the Household Guard by Count Adamov and Rupnik was certain that Kark would be loyal to the count."

"The devil!" said the newly returned Baron Krek.

"Did Rupnik implicate Count Adamov in any other way?" the chief justice demanded.

"No, he did not, and to be truthful, at the time it never occurred to me that Count Adamov might be involved. But when I learned he was coming to Zosi to arrest me, and when I read this proclamation, it finally became clear to me that in Count Adamov I had a devious and deadly enemy."

"Really, Gus," Franz drawled. "Aren't you being a little dramatic?"

"Am I?" the Prince returned, his face grim.

In the ensuing silence, every eye in the room slowly turned to focus on the figure of the chief justice. Count Cherny's chair was placed just below the dais, and the high-backed red velvet throne, with its gilded lions, loomed behind him as a potent reminder of what was at stake here today.

Count Cherny said, "There are eight other names on this proclamation besides Count Adamov's. Would any of those men care to make a statement?"

Someone moved, and then Count Boris Heusse rose to his feet. "My lord Chief Justice," he said in a calm, clear voice, "my colleagues and I have been deeply surprised by what we have heard here today. We signed that proclamation because we believed Count Adamov when he informed us of the emperor's threats against our beloved country. If this is not true, then we have no quarrel with Prince Augustus. Indeed, I rejoice that our country can continue to be led by such a proven patriot as Prince Augustus has always shown himself to be."

In the silence that followed Baron Heusse's comments, Baron Krek said to Count Sauder sotto voce, "Heusse is dumping Franz and trying to save his own skin."

The chief justice said, "Count Heusse, what were your plans for Prince Augustus if you had been successful in arresting him at Zosi?"

The count replied promptly, "My lord, our plans were as Count Adamov told you. We planned to issue our proclamation and then escort Prince Augustus to Julia to face a vote of the diet."

The chief justice did not look as if he believed this statement. However, he turned to the Prince and asked, "Prince Augustus, are you willing to accept Count Heusse's account of this attempted coup?"

"I am," Augustus replied steadily.

"Augustus can't possibly believe him," Baron Krek said cynically.

"Neither do I," Count Sauder replied. "But this is the best way. No one wants to put these men on trial for treason."

"God, no," the other replied fervently.

Augustus was saying much the same thing. "I am willing to believe that the Jurian nobles who signed that infamous proclamation were misled by Count Adamov and acted in what they thought were the best interests of their country. However"—and his voice hardened—"in the future, I would prefer that these nobles kept to their own estates and refrained from meeting as a group."

"I believe that is a very fair request, Your Highness," the chief justice said. "Are you gentlemen in agreement?"

Yeses and ayes issued from the mouths of the frightened conspirators.

"And what of Count Adamov?" the chief justice asked Augustus next.

"You have no proof against me," Franz said calmly. "All you have is speculation."

Augustus suddenly looked very weary. "I don't want him in Jura," he said to the chief justice. "I never want to see him again."

"I can revoke his passport," Count Cherny said. "Will that do, Your Highness?"

The two men, Prince and Chief Justice of Jura,

looked at each other, both thinking the same thing. *We do not want an international incident over this.*

Slowly Augustus nodded his head. "Revoke his passport," he agreed. Then, without another word, he walked to the door. The room watched in silence until he had disappeared into the vestibule, then Count Cherny said, "I do not believe that any vote of the diet is necessary."

There was a murmur of agreement. Count Cherny paused, to see if there might be any objections, but no one spoke. Finally he said, "We will meet back here tomorrow at ten o'clock so that Prince Augustus may formally open the February 1816 session of the diet."

Franz stood alone as the members of the diet began to get to their feet and talk among themselves. Count Sauder watched as the chief justice approached him and said something. Franz's face was pinched and white and the eyes he turned to the chief justice glittered with sudden naked hatred.

Count Cherny took a step back. Then Franz's normal expression returned and he shrugged and replied to the chief justice. The two men left the chamber together.

27

While Charity was waiting for Augustus to return to Count Sauder's villa, she drank four cups of coffee and almost wore out a portion of the count's Chinese rug with her pacing. The coffee did nothing to calm her nerves, which were already overwrought by early pregnancy, and when Augustus finally walked into the count's elegant Chinese salon, she collapsed on the sofa and burst into tears.

Harry, who had been standing against the fireplace for the last hour trying to calm her down, quietly moved to the door and went out.

"Charity!" The Prince strode across the room, sat beside his wife, and gathered her into his arms. "There's nothing to cry about, my dear. Everything went just as I told you it would. Franz is disgraced and I am still the Prince of Jura."

All of the fear and tension that Charity had been bottling up inside for so many days exploded into a storm of weeping. She pressed her face into his coat and sobbed uncontrollably.

"Don't," he kept saying as he patted the back of the blue wool dress she had been wearing for days. "Charity, love, don't. It can't be good for you to upset yourself like this. There is no need." He increased the tempo of his patting. "You're ruining my coat."

The Prince had been more lucky than Charity in that he had left a change of clothes at Count Sauder's the last time he had visited. This had been fortunate indeed, as neither the count nor Emil were close enough in size for him to borrow anything of theirs and no one had deemed it prudent to return to the Pfalz.

Charity felt the sogginess under her cheek and struggled to control herself.

"Here." He put a large white handkerchief in her hand and she lifted her face out of his coat and scrubbed it dry with the square of linen. Then she blew her nose.

"It is amazing how such a little appendage can make so much noise," he said humorously, and she managed to produce a watery smile.

"I'm sorry, Augustus. I don't know what came over me. I'm not usually such a watering pot."

"No, you're not," he agreed. He was looking at her anxiously. "Are you all right now?"

She blew her nose again and took a deep, steadying breath. "Yes."

"Would you like to hear what happened at the diet this morning?"

"Yes." She sniffed and straightened up and her eyes fell on the empty coffee pot and cups that were scattered on Count Sauder's elegant bamboo-style table. "Would you like some coffee, Augustus?"

"I would love some coffee," he said fervently.

She picked up the bell that was reposing on the table along with the empty cups, and while they waited for the fresh coffee to be brought he started to tell her what had taken place that morning at the diet. The coffee came in, she poured him a cup, prudently refrained from having any more herself, and listened intently as he continued his recitation. She said nothing, only nodding her approval a number of times, but when he told her what he had decided to do about Franz, she exploded.

"You just let him go?" She couldn't believe what she had just heard. "He deserves to be hung, drawn, and quartered." She glared at her husband in outraged indignation. "I can't believe that all you did was revoke his passport!"

He was looking at her in bemused amazement. "I used to think you were such a sweet little thing," he said wonderingly. "I never suspected you were so bloodthirsty."

"I am exceedingly bloodthirsty when it comes to your safety," she assured him. "Just because Franz isn't allowed to enter Jura doesn't mean he will stop plotting against you, Augustus! He managed to influence Rupnik and Hindenberg from Vienna without any trouble."

He replied in a soothing voice that only succeeded in irritating her further, "He has been discredited here in Jura, and he has been discredited with the emperor as well. I think we have disabled him, Charity. There is nothing for you to worry about."

"I am not a child, Augustus," she flared. "The man is dangerous. You have every reason to arrest him. He lied to you!"

At this last comment a thoughtful look came over the Prince's face. "You know, Charity, I am not so certain that he did lie."

Silence fell as she digested this comment. Finally she said, "Are you saying you think it is the *emperor* who is lying and not Franz?"

He finished his coffee and returned the delicate Sevres cup and saucer to the table. "Not necessarily."

She frowned. "I don't understand."

He swung around on the sofa to face her, which caused some difficulty as his long legs got tangled up in the legs of the table. He muttered a curse under his breath and she smiled. Finally he got himself sorted out and began to explain his thinking to her. "I doubt that Franz would have gone as far as he did if he had not first cleared his actions with someone in Vienna. His little coup attempt did not involve just Jura; it involved Austria as well. If Franz had been successful in putting Marko on the throne of Jura, you can be certain the deal was that Austria would recognize the new prince as legitimate and in return Jura would defer her national interests to the interests of the empire."

Charity was thinking furiously. "But you don't think the person involved in Franz's plot was the emperor?"

"There is a good possibility that Francis wasn't involved."

"Who do you think this other person was?"

He looked at her in silence and did not reply.

"Metternich," she said at last.

He nodded briefly; his face was very somber.

"Oh Augustus." Her hands began to twist his handkerchief into a knot.

He said, "My suspicion is that Metternich agreed to this plan because he felt he couldn't lose. He would win if I gave in and agreed to renounce the Treaty of London. He would win if I didn't give in and Franz was able to discredit me and replace me with the more compliant Marko. The worst that could happen is what did happen—which leaves Austria in the same position it was in before. Metternich has gained nothing, but he has lost nothing either."

Charity had been growing more and more indignant as he spoke. "If that is so, then Metternich is worse than . . . than Machiavelli. Why on earth are you trying to keep this quiet, Augustus? Don't you think the emperor should know what kind of devious plot his chief minister was involved in?"

He said patiently, "I have no proof, Charity. And even if I did, that is a Pandora's box I do not want to open. It wouldn't be smart for me to antagonize the emperor any more than I already have. It is better for both countries to pretend that only Franz was involved in this plot."

"What about Marko then?" she demanded next. Her hands had stopped twisting the handkerchief and held it now balled within her fist. "How much do you think he knew? Remember, he told you that he had spoken directly to the emperor, and that most certainly was a lie."

He shrugged. "What do I think? I think that Marko was a pawn. I think that Franz told him the message he was to deliver came directly from the emperor, and when I asked Marko if he had spoken to the emperor himself, he wanted to show me how important he was and so he said that he had."

She scanned his face. "Then you don't think Marko was involved in the coup attempt?"

"I don't know, Charity. I don't think so, but I don't know."

Her fine brows were knitted in thought. "The men who signed that outrageous proclamation were all Marko's friends."

"I realize that," he replied calmly. "They were all men who felt that they had been shut out of power in my administration and that they would count for something under Marko. I am sure Franz played on that ambition."

She closed her other hand around the fist that was holding his handkerchief. "Well, I think you should take away Marko's passport as well as Franz's."

"I will," he promised. "He has lived comfortably in Vienna for many years; it will not be a hardship for him to continue to do so."

She scowled. Her sense of justice was still outraged by this too-easy solution. She said stubbornly, "I still think you should execute Franz."

"He is your sister's husband."

"He is a snake. Lydia would be well rid of him."

"I cannot just execute him, Charity," Augustus pointed out reasonably. "He has to have a trial first. And I just finished telling you that I don't want to risk alienating Austria any further. It is best if I simply exile him and let things be."

"Huh." Charity narrowed her eyes. "I never trusted him."

"Unfortunately, I did." He looked somber. "It is still hard for me to believe that the cousin I grew up with is the man that Franz has turned out to be."

She loosened her grip on his handkerchief and the temper died away from her eyes. When she spoke again her voice was soft. "He is like a sun-filled mountain meadow that you feel perfectly safe running across, only to discover too late that the beautiful wildflowers are hiding a series of treacherous sinkholes."

"A good metaphor," he said wryly.

They sat in silence for a while, both lost in their own thoughts. Charity was the one to speak first. "What do we do now?"

He looked at her and said, "Go home."

They began to smile at the exact same moment, and he put down his coffee cup and reached out to gather her into his arms. "I'm glad you're here," he said. "I'm glad you made me bring you."

Her head was resting against his chest and she was listening to the steady beats of his heart: *thump, thump, thump, thump, thump.* So even, so steadfast, so strong, so calm.

Thank you, God. Thank you for keeping him safe. Thank you for bringing him back to me.

"It seems like an age since we've been at the Pfalz," she murmured.

"Mmm. It will feel good to get back to my own bed."

Against her cheek, his heartbeat went reassuringly on.

"Your bed or mine?" she said.

She could feel the rumble of laughter deep in his chest. "Is there a difference?"

She moved her head in a slow negative. "No."

Outside the snow began to fall, and inside the door opened three times as various people looked in, but Charity and Augustus sat on, wrapped in the peace of each other's arms.

The formal opening of the Jurian diet occurred a day later than scheduled, but it was certainly one of the most memorable opening days in the legislature's long history. To Charity's delight, Augustus had asked her to attend. She had had every intention of going, but it was sweet to know that he wanted her to come.

They rode into the city together, and the shining black royal coach drawn by four perfectly matched gray Lipizzaners stopped first at the Diet House's main door to let Charity and Harry out. Then it moved off to take Augustus around the block to the door from which he would be making his entrance.

Inside the vestibule, Emil and two of Charity's ladies were waiting for her. Stefanie came over to straighten her green velvet hat, which matched the green velvet pelisse she wore. "You look wonderful, Your Highness," she said.

Charity took a deep breath and hoped her face did not show the flutters she was feeling in her stomach. "Thank you, Steffi. Shall we go in?"

The porter, who was dressed in knee breeches, white stockings, and a long-tailed coat, opened the door for her. As she stepped through he announced to the chamber in ringing tones: "Her Royal Highness, Princess Charity."

The assembled men rose to their feet. As Charity came into the chamber proper, escorted by Harry and followed by the rest of her party, the initial sound of men standing and chairs scraping died away and total silence reigned in the large room.

I wonder if I will ever grow accustomed to this kind of attention, she thought as she began to walk down the aisle in the direction of the stairs that led to the spectator's gallery. She glanced quickly at the crowd of bowing men, nodded a brief acknowledgment, then focused on the path in front of her, anxious to reach the shelter of the gallery.

It isn't so bad when I am with Augustus, she thought. *Then I know that everyone is looking at him, not at me.*

She was halfway past the rows of chairs occupied by the commons when the two men who represented Julia began to clap. They were followed immediately by the representatives from the other parts of Jura where Charity had begun to set up her relief centers. In a heartbeat the entire chamber, nobles included, joined in a sustained ovation that lasted until she and her party had disappeared into the enclosed staircase.

Charity's face was flushed and her eyes were bright as she turned to Emil at the top of the stairs. "Was that for me?" she asked, not quite believing that it could have been.

He smiled. "It certainly was, Your Highness."

Harry, who was grinning like a maniac, said, "I doubt very much if Lydia would have received such a welcome. I'm proud of you, Char."

"It was because I represent Augustus," she said breathlessly.

"No," Emil said definitely. "It was for you, and it was well deserved. It was in recognition of all the good that you have done for the people of Jura, Your Highness."

"Wait till I tell Papa," Harry said. "He will be pleased as punch."

"Here, Your Highness," Lady Stefanie said. "This is your chair."

Charity moved to the high-backed state chair Stefanie had indicated and took her place in the center of the gallery. Her heart was still pounding and her face was still flushed. She had never expected such a thing to happen!

Gradually the buzz of talk in the chamber died down and an air of expectation took its place. Finally the moment they were all waiting for happened; the doors in the rear of the chamber, doors which had been reserved for the reigning prince since the Diet House had first been built, opened. A deep voice, which Charity later learned belonged to the Lord

High Steward, boomed, "His Royal Highness, Prince Augustus."

The spectators' gallery jutted out over the door, so Charity couldn't see the royal procession until it was on its way up the aisle. The first person to come into her view was the Lord High Steward, Count Mark Helmer, who wore his state robes and carried the staff of state on a crimson velvet cushion trimmed with gold braid. He was followed by the Lord High Constable, who was carrying the sword of state. After these two noble members of the Prince's ceremonial household came the President of the Chamber of Commons, Viktor Becker, and the Chief Minister of State, Lord Stefan Weyr.

At long last Augustus came into her view. He was plainly dressed in a black frock coat, white breeches, and Hessian boots. He wore the gold sash of his army rank under his coat, along with a white waistcoat and a white tie. Around his shoulders hung the royal robe of state, and upon his head he wore the ruby-encrusted crown of Jura.

There was no ovation for Augustus. The occasion was too solemn for such an unbridled outburst of feeling. Everyone present was aware of how narrowly Jura had averted a disastrous constitutional crisis. Even the older men, who regretted seeing their powers pass to another generation, were relieved that their rightful prince still sat on his throne.

The procession reached the front of the chamber and Augustus stepped up on the dais and took his seat upon the throne. The folds of his red velvet cloak fell neatly around him and the diamond badge of the Order of St. Michael, Jura's highest honor, glittered on his shoulder. The president of the commons stood at the right of the throne and the chief minister stood at its left. After putting the staff of state into the Prince's hand, the Lord High Steward took his place behind Augustus, as did the Lord High Constable.

"His Royal Highness asks that you be seated," the Lord High Steward intoned, and the men representing the nobles and commons of Jura did as requested. Then everyone stared at Augustus.

He looks so natural sitting there, Charity thought. *It never ceases to amaze me how comfortable he can look under such intense scrutiny.*

It was tradition for the Prince to make a speech to the diet before declaring it officially open, and this is what the chamber was waiting for. Charity, who knew what Augustus was going to say, was anxious to see how his words would be received.

When he began to speak, the Prince's voice was quiet yet perfectly audible even to those in the spectator's gallery. "My lords and gentlemen," he began. "Today is a momentous occasion in the history of our country. Thanks to your faith in me, we have together averted a crisis that would certainly have disrupted our nation's political and economic well-being and which may have ended in the ultimate loss of seven hundred years of independence."

The Prince was not speaking from a prepared text but instead was looking directly at his audience in such a way that later each man would feel that Augustus had been speaking personally to him.

"I was born and reared to be the Prince of Jura," he said quietly. "All of my schooling and my military training was directed toward this end. Pride in the independence and the economic strength of my country has been instilled in me since my earliest years." Here the Prince paused and let his gaze move slowly around the chamber. "When Jura was overcome by Napoleon, I did my best to thwart the ongoing occupation by the French. And when the French were finally defeated, I did my best in Vienna to convince the other countries that Jura deserved to keep its seven-hundred-year-old independence." He paused and looked for a moment at the staff of state he held in his right hand. "I was successful in accomplishing this, and Jura's independence was recognized by all of the Great Powers of Europe in the Final Act of the Congress of Vienna."

Once more his gray gaze flicked from face to face in the audience. "My lords and gentlemen," he said quietly, "I pledge to you today that I will uphold that independence for as long as there is breath in my body."

For the first time the absolute silence in the chamber was broken by a stir of movement.

Augustus waited for silence before he went on. "Our history is a proud one, but I am well aware that a nation that looks only to the past is a nation that has lost its energy. I do not wish that to happen to Jura. The late great struggle with France has caused to be spread around Europe revolutionary ideas of nationalism and constitutionalism. For seven hundred years, Jura has had the luxury of its own nationhood—something for which other European peoples have long yearned.

"For five hundred years my family has ruled Jura in relative peace and prosperity. But the role of a ruling prince is changing in today's world. Today we have a better-educated population than ever before. Today we have a thriving middle class, who are well able to make informed decisions about national policy."

The room was so quiet that it didn't seem as if anyone could be breathing.

The Prince went on. "For all the time that the Adamov family has ruled Jura, the diet's chief responsibility has been the levying and distribution of internal taxes. This is a great and solemn power, but I think that the time has come for the educated representatives of Jura's population to take a more active role in the governing of our country."

A great sigh ran around the room, as if a collective breath had been let out.

Augustus said quietly, "In my judgment, it is time for Jura to become a constitutional as well as a princely state, and I am willing to work with the members of the diet to achieve that end."

Charity's heart was swelling with pride and tears were running down her face.

"I was reared to believe that my sacred duty was always to do my best for my country. I have done that in the past and I hope to continue to do that in the future."

Slowly Augustus rose to his feet. He lifted the staff of state until it was upright in front of him and said, "I declare this session of the National Diet of Jura to be open, and I will leave you gentlemen to your deliberations."

The silence in the room was electric as the Prince returned down the aisle and exited through the doors from which he had entered. The sound of the door closing echoed through the chamber. Then pandemonium broke out.

Charity wiped the tears from her face as she watched the assembled diet react to Augustus's speech. The response of the nobles was mixed; the younger ones were excited while the older ones looked dour. The commons, on the other hand, were ecstatic.

Emil's voice sounded in her ear. "Do you wish to leave now, Your Highness?"

She plied her handkerchief one more time, annoyed with herself for her emotional display. "Yes, I am ready," she said to Emil, and she and her party went down the stairs. The chamber was still in an uproar. Stefan Weyr and Viktor Becker, the president of the commons, were standing together talking, neither of them making the slightest attempt to bring order to the assembly. Charity turned to Emil and said, "I do not want to walk down that aisle again. Let's go out the back door."

Emil's eyes flew to Stefanie, who said immediately, "Your Highness, that door is reserved for the Prince's use only."

"Augustus won't mind if I use his door," Charity said. "I really do not want to parade past those men again."

Harry said practically, "If we leave now, no one will even notice us."

"Then let us go." Charity put her hand on Harry's arm and walked determinedly toward the wide double door that was set under the spectator's gallery. Reluctantly, the rest of her party followed.

The street outside was empty. "Gus probably has the coach waiting for you at the other door, Your Highness," Emil said. "If you will wait here, I'll go and fetch him."

"Thank you, Emil," Charity said.

Five minutes later the matched Lipizzaners turned the corner, followed by the shining black royal coach. It pulled up in front of the curb and Emil jumped out.

The liveried footman who was riding next to the coachman set the steps for Charity and she entered the coach and took her seat next to Augustus. Harry looked in and said with a display of rare tactfulness, "I'll go back to the Pfalz with Emil."

"Thank you, Harry," the Prince said gravely.

The footman closed the door and climbed back to his seat next to the coachman. The coachman made a kissing sound and the Lipizzaners moved forward. Charity turned to her husband. "You were wonderful!"

His smile was wry. "The *idea* of shared responsibility is easy to suggest; the implementation is going to be much more complicated."

"That is true, but you will do it."

"I hope so. Your country offers us an excellent model of how ruler and legislature can work together."

"Oh, you are not going to copy the Americans, then?" she said with mock innocence.

"Please. I don't want to put myself completely out of a job," he replied with rueful irony.

She laughed and reached out to take his hand.

"That is why I made the proposal that I did," he went on. "In my heart, I know I am perfectly capable of running Jura in an effective and enlightened manner, but if rulers don't bend with the times sooner or later, they are going to find themselves pushed out of their jobs whether they want to go or not."

Silence fell, then Charity said, "I hope you don't mind my using your special door, Augustus, but I did not want to walk by all those hysterical men."

He raised their clasped hands to his mouth and kissed her fingers. "You can have anything of mine that you want."

She sighed. "I am so happy that it's almost frightening."

His hand tightened. "Don't be frightened. I am going to make very certain that you remain happy for the rest of your life."

Charity felt the tears prickling behind her eyes. "Oh no," she wailed, "I'm going to cry again. I can't seem to stop myself."

"That's all right," he said tenderly. He regarded her magnificent headwear. "I would like to hug you, but that bonnet is in my way."

That made her laugh. "I'll take it off."

"That would be a help."

She untied the emerald green ribbon under her chin and removed her velvet bonnet. Then she moved closer and rested her head on his shoulder. He slipped his arm around her waist.

There was silence for a while as the well-sprung coach rolled over the paved road that led from Julia to the Pfalz. Then all of a sudden Charity's stomach growled. The Prince laughed, and she removed herself from her place in his arms and looked up at him. "Do you know, I didn't feel sick this morning." Her brown eyes were amazed. "And I'm starving! I haven't been this hungry in months."

He grinned. "That is good news."

She frowned thoughtfully. "What do I want to eat?"

"I have no idea," he replied.

Her face lit up. "I know. Strawberries! I must have some strawberries!"

The Prince refrained from pointing out that it was February and hardly strawberry season. The staff would find strawberries somewhere, he thought with confidence. He looked into his wife's glowing face and said firmly, "Then strawberries you shall have."